Waylon University Series

I Dare You
I Bet You
I Hate You
I Promise You

Stand-Alones

Dear Ava
Fake Fiancée
The Revenge Pact
The Last Guy (with Tia Louise)
The Right Stud (with Tia Louise)

MY Darling BRIDE

ILSA MADDEN-MILLS

Montlake

Published by Montlake, Seattle

www.apub.com

Amazon, the Amazon logo, and Montlake are trademarks of Amazon.com, Inc., or its affiliates.

ISBN-13: 9781662514005 (paperback)
ISBN-13: 9781662514012 (digital)

Cover design by Letitia Hasser
Cover photography by Michelle Lancaster
Cover image: © VectorShow / Shutterstock

Printed in the United States of America

MY
Darling
BRIDE

Chapter 1

GRAHAM

A February wind blows across the field. Narrowing my eyes, I embrace the cold like it's armor.

There's palpable tension in the air as we line up. Even the stadium is silent. With five seconds left on the clock, we need a touchdown to win. Jasper, our quarterback, barks out instructions, and we tighten up, poised, hands in the turf, eyes focused on the defense.

I shift my weight, ready to run.

Football is in my veins, the rhythm and cadence of the players, the smell of sweat, the feel of grass beneath my feet, the sky above me.

This is where I belong. On the field. Winning games.

So when the ball is snapped and Jasper tosses it to me, my hands make the perfect catch.

Tucking it under my arm, I run for the goal line. The thrill of the chase is on, the greatest high there is, and my body vibrates with excitement.

Their defense plows toward me, and I pass through them like a ghost.

Almost there.

One. More. Yard.

The crowd jumps up, cheers deafening as they chant, *Graham, Graham, Graham!*

I never see the tackle coming. The defensive lineman appears in a blind spot, and the hit sends me flying back, but I steady myself, digging my feet into the turf. Crying out in frustration, the defender yanks my face mask down.

Pain radiates to my head as I collide with the ground.

Air whooshes from my lungs.

Too many players are on top of me. I can't breathe.

Fear paralyzes me as darkness overtakes my vision.

My hands twitch to move, to grab my chest, my head.

The world around me slowly disappears as the fans' cries fade to white noise.

Something. Is. Wrong.

I feel my heart slowing, not all at once, but with long ponderous beats—then it doesn't beat at all.

◆ ◆ ◆

What is this?

Am I dead?

The question echoes in my head, a whisper that comes from every-where and nowhere all at once.

No way.

I'm in the prime of my health. I woke up this morning with the world at my fingertips.

Terror digs its claws in.

God, someone, hello? Are you out there?

I haven't been perfect, but please, I need more time, I need to help my brother, I need to . . .

Just as that thought is formed, colors flash in my head, smearing together like oil on a canvas, bleeding into one another. I did acid once in college and tripped. I sat back on the fraternity couch as the world unfolded in unbelievable pictures. It feels like that.

I see a kaleidoscope of vibrant images slipping and sliding together, filling me with powerful emotions.

I see my brother as a kid, chasing me, right on my heels as we look for adventures.

I see my father, walking away from us, his suitcase bumping over the ground.

I see my mother playing the piano.

Divina appears, the woman who shattered my heart.

I see my teammates.

It's a mess of pictures, blending and meshing together into incomplete memories.

They fade as new visions appear.

An endless highway in the desert.

I smell sunshine and vanilla.

I taste sparkling wine.

A woman's face appears, slipping in and out of my vision.

She smiles and beckons to me.

Who is she?

A waterfall of pale-blonde hair.

Emerald eyes.

Fragile yet strong.

Is she an angel?

I want to know because . . .

I adore her.

All I feel is perfect tranquility.

Peace.

Happiness.

Amazement ripples over me.

It's as if I'm on the cusp of great knowledge.

On the meaning of life.

On the meaning of *my* life.

She disappears like sand in my fingertips, and I cry out, yearning to cling to the memory, to figure out the significance.

All that's left is the blackest black and endless cold.

Death creeps in like a shadow.

I get it now.

You don't just see your life flashing before you when you die; you see the life you *could* have had.

Unbearable grief washes over me.

I'll never know who she is.

◆ ◆ ◆

Electricity fires over my body as my heart pushes out a beat. Then another. And another.

My eyes squint open to paramedics. The wind hits me and I gasp, dragging in air.

I'm alive.

Was it all a dream?

Medics push Jasper out of the way, but he juts back between them with his elbows, then kneels on the ground next to me, his face ashen.

He's taken his helmet off and rakes a hand down his face. His wild hair hangs around his shoulders. "Jesus Christ, man, you nearly got your head pulled off. We thought you were fucking dead!"

I was.

I was.

I swallow, wincing at the pain in my head. At least I can feel my arms and legs. I'm not paralyzed. Football isn't an easy sport. It's brutal, and if rules aren't followed, then shit goes wrong. Shit has gone wrong.

He gives me a grimace, which is weird because when we lose, he's our cheerleader.

"W-we lost?" I twitch, anxious to get off the gurney.

He pushes me back down. "You scored, G. We're champions. I'm not even worried about football. Hey, stop moving. They're taking you to an ambulance."

The medics finally get him to move as I rethink the lost look on his face. He was thinking this was *it* for me. I'll never play again.

Black and gold confetti, the Pythons' colors, rains down from the sky as I remember catching the pass, the run, the hit, but the rest is hazy.

I saw something.

Someone.

A hissing sound comes from me as pain ripples in my head; then everything goes black.

Chapter 2

EMMY

A few months later

The hot Arizona sun, a pool, and a beverage. Sounds delightful, but the sun is a volcano, the pool belongs to a shithole place called the Golden Iguana, and my beverage is a tepid bottle of Fiji water. Not to mention, there's a sketchy scorpion poking its head out at me from the rock garden. I saw one in my bathroom earlier, scurrying over the tile. Screaming bloody murder, I smashed my sneaker on it, then promptly vomited in the toilet. Goodbye, shoes. I can never wear them again, and I may not be able to go back in my bathroom. And if I see one more prancing around like they own this motel, I'm packing my shit and leaving.

There's one thing that makes me smile: the motel sign has a faded green-and-gold iguana on it, standing upright and grinning as he welcomes you with open arms. He reminds me of that insurance lizard. I've named him Darcy.

Welcome to Old Town, a small place outside Tucson in the middle of the Sonoran Desert. A six-hour drive from Vegas, it seemed the last place Kian would look. Sure, I could have caught a plane back to New York, but I wasn't thinking straight when I left the Bellagio.

The Vegas Incident unfolded so fast. As soon as Kian let me go and stormed out of the room, I ran from the hotel, hopped in a taxi, and told the driver to hit the highway. I didn't have a plan, and I couldn't think of what to do or where to go, so I just told him to head east.

This is where I ended up, and I just wanted to sleep.

Pushing Kian out of my head, I swim the length of the pool several times, trying to wear out my body, hoping that will stop my brain from mulling over the past few days.

I cling to the edge of the pool as a Lamborghini with blacked-out windows roars into the parking lot, the engine growling like a beast. Low slung and shiny, the car is lemon yellow, the golden bull emblem sparkling in the sunlight. It parks next to a rusted pickup truck.

"I guess the Four Seasons was booked," I snark to myself, then wince at my raspy voice. My throat is swollen and aches horribly.

When no one gets out of the car right away, hair rises on the back of my neck.

Wait a minute . . . did Kian rent a different car and follow me?

Nah. He had a bachelor party last night, which means he's sleeping it off today; plus, I only grabbed a small bag of essentials when I left. My suitcase is still in the room at the Bellagio, along with most of my clothes. For all he knows, I'm wandering around the casinos, pissed at him.

Whatever. It doesn't matter. I'm overthinking it.

I'll never let you go, Emmy.

I push Kian's last words away as I sink underwater, swim to the ladder, and scramble up the steps. I gather my book and sunscreen, then adjust my hair around my shoulder, hiding the purple bruises on my neck. Sliding on my flip-flops, I'm dripping water as I make my way to the gate that leads to the rooms, keeping a wary eye on the car.

The driver's side door opens, and a dark-haired man gets out.

I'm not even aware of how relieved I am until my shoulders sag. Not Kian.

Stretching his arms up and rolling his neck, the man squints at the sun, swears under his breath, then reaches inside the car. His back is broad. Like, fucking big. He must be at least six and a half feet tall. He thrusts on a pair of aviators and glares at the iguana on the sign as if he's got a personal vendetta. I don't know what he has against Darcy.

Muttering a curse, he slams the car door, then shoves a ball cap over his hair. The hat casts his face in shadow, giving him a dark aura.

Lambo looks about as cuddly as a steak knife.

Dressed in designer jeans that cling to his thighs and an expensive-looking button-down with the cuffs rolled up, he has a blade for a nose, sculpted cheekbones, and sensuous lips. Tall. Broad. Muscled. Sex on a stick. Swipe right, ladies.

He takes long strides yet somehow manages to appear graceful—no, scratch that, athletic.

My guess? He's felt the crack of bone under his hands.

He exudes broodiness. My favorite.

I allow myself to picture just what kind of sexual damage he might cause, wondering at the thrill of being caught up in his arms when he unleashes.

Oh yeah. I'd ride that stallion like a cowgirl gone wild.

I mentally slap myself.

No. More. Men.

My next date will be with a rom-com and a kitten. A cat would be a superb boyfriend—hair balls but no drama.

As I'm picturing kittens dancing around a ball of yarn, Lambo slings a duffel over his shoulder and heads to the front office.

Goodbye, sexy beast. Enjoy your stay at the crappiest motel in Arizona.

Hustling, I head in the opposite direction and take the rusted metal stairwell up to the third-floor-balcony breezeway that leads to my room.

The motel is a squat, crumbling hulk of faded teal stucco with the rooms on the outside. My room is sparse and ugly with ceramic tile instead of carpet and a bed frame that used to vibrate but doesn't work anymore. As soon as I walked in last night, I stripped off the bedding, checked the mattress for stains, then settled for sleeping on the top sheet with towels as my covers.

Around the motel, tumbleweeds blow and grass pokes through the asphalt. It's like something out of an old western movie. Last night I heard wolves howling, the lonely sound echoing in the silence. Perhaps I wouldn't feel so solitary if my headspace were clearer.

There's a diner across the street and a gas station down the road, yet the motel is far enough from Tucson to see miles and miles of desert. I stood at the edge of it this morning, looking out into its emptiness. Being a city girl, I'd never seen such a sight, and its beauty made my heart swell with appreciation for nature, but there was also fear. It's a harsh and ambivalent place, one that could swallow me up and never let me go.

Like Kian.

Like any man, really.

Just as I think that, my phone vibrates with a text from him.

Pick up the phone and talk to me!

Bastard. I scroll back. He called me over twenty times while I was in the pool. Guess he knows I left him.

My gut twists, part of me getting a rush that he's frantic, the other side of me sickened by my response. This thing between me and Kian feels too much like the relationship my mom had with my dad.

Texts pop up, one after another.

Come on, talk to me.

I'm sorry. I fucked up. I never should have put my hands on you. It's been a hard year, you know that. With you by my side, I'll be better.

Be better by yourself, jerk.

Yes, he's had a tough year. He got two DUIs and was removed from the team's roster, then put money into a restaurant with a friend that later failed. He actually asked me to marry him this weekend. My stomach swirls with anxiety. Doesn't he know who I am? Marriage is the last thing I want.

Emmy. I was there for you when you needed me. I sat by your side when your gran died. I held you. I didn't leave. I'm sorry, baby. It will never happen again.

Oh, Kian. That's what they all say.

Come on, call me. You're messing with my head.

Nope. I'm done riding his roller coaster. I'm getting off and saying "See you in hell" to his amusement park.

I ram my phone in my bag but miss, and it skitters across the open-air walkway. Cursing, I bend down to swipe it up.

"Hey, gorgeous," a voice murmurs from behind me, and I whip around in surprise to see Clint Eastwood—not the real one, but a cheap knockoff.

Fake Clint showed up in the motel honky-tonk bar last night in a legit black leather duster, boots, and a hat. He lurked in the shadows cast by the flashing neon lights while I drank at the bar. He made the rounds, chatting up every woman in the place, and I left before he got to me. If he'd been interesting and less of a creep, I might have fooled around with him. Just to get over this awful feeling Kian has left in the pit of my stomach.

Gran said it best: *Darling, if he's no good, pick another pony.* Of course, she was talking about the racetrack, but still, it's a good reference for men as well.

I want to snap back a reply to Fake Clint, but an image of the last time I saw Kian flashes in my head, the shocking sound of his fist hitting the wall next to me, the pieces of drywall that flew into my hair, then the awful press of his fingers against my throat. I couldn't breathe. I could only fight and slap and scratch at his face. Nausea bubbles as I recall the smell of lemon and butter from the fish we'd had for dinner.

He shoved me away, overturned the room service tray, then stomped out of the door.

I glance around the empty breezeway as my unease rises higher. A knot forms in my gut, and my breathing quickens. I'm alone here. Best to not engage with Clint. I make a noncommittal sound and start to my door.

"Hey, wait, don't run off," he says as he follows on my heels. "I saw you at the pool. You were swimming laps like it was your job."

His eyes linger on my breasts, and I groan inwardly, regretting I didn't pull on a shirt. I'm in a black rash-guard shirt and bikini bottoms I bought from the dollar store in town.

"Thought I'd join you, maybe get a few laps in, but now you're done. Too bad." He holds up a longneck beer. "I've got more of these in my room if you want one?"

"I'm in for the day," I say as I rummage in my worn patchwork bag, searching for the motel key.

"You're alone here, right?"

My warning radar spikes. "No," I reply slowly. "My boyfriend is asleep in the room."

"I didn't see him last night."

"He doesn't like crowds. Or guys hitting on me."

"Hard to believe he'd let you drink alone." He stares at my navel ring peeking through my rash guard, then gives me a smarmy grin. "I noticed your room is next to mine. Talk about some cardboard walls. I heard you crying this morning. Did you have a fight with him?"

Play nice, the angel on my shoulder says, while the devil . . .

I find the motel key and grip it tight. "Should I wake up my boyfriend and tell him you're being a dick?"

"I like your spunk, but I'm just trying to get to know you. No need to involve your man. If that's even true." He eases around me until he's blocking my door.

His bloodshot hazel eyes hold mine. He's older than my twenty-eight and reeks of beer. Today he's wearing cutoff shorts, a faded shirt, and flip-flops. I guess the duster and boots were too hot for day attire. With a buzz haircut, a weak chin, and beady eyes, he looks like a mean hamster. And now I'm picturing a hamster in a cowboy outfit riding a horse in the desert and having a gunfight with Darcy the Iguana.

I'm five-nine and can hold my own, especially in heels, but he towers over me.

"Ease up. Just have a drink with me. I'm bored here. Where are you from?"

"Get out of my way, or my boyfriend will kick your ass."

"Yeah? What's his name?" His lip curls.

My brain scrambles for a name. "Darcy."

"Weird name." He touches a strand of my hair, and my heart thunders, part outrage, part fear.

Scenarios dance through my head. He's bigger than me. He's intoxicated. His door is currently open, and he's blocking me from mine. He could push me inside his. He could drag me. Flashbacks of my father dragging my mother burn inside my head.

The air thickens with tension. Sweat beads on my upper lip as my muscles quiver with the instinct to flee.

The sounds of footsteps arrive on the walkway, and relief hits like a tidal wave.

Lambo strides our way as he tucks his sunglasses into the pocket of his shirt. He seems to weave on his feet, then rightens himself by clinging to the balcony rail. His head turns to us, and he pauses, his eyes tightening, flicking from me to Fake Clint.

"What's going on?" he asks, his tone a dark velvet rumble.

Fake Clint takes a step back and holds his hands up in a placating manner. "I'm just on my way to the pool. You checking in?"

Lambo ignores him and comes back to me, his face expressionless. "You all right?"

It's as if I've manifested him. Give the man a cravat, and he's Darcy! As in, the guy from *Pride and Prejudice*, not the iguana. Well, him too.

A surge of adrenaline hits. Pasting on my brightest smile, I drop my bag and rush forward and wrap my arms around his waist in a bear hug. He grunts as we collide, his body a solid wall of hard muscle. My head hits him midchest. Oh, he must work out twenty-four seven, and kill me now, but he smells intoxicating, like dark cherries, expensive leather, and cedar.

My head tilts back as my eyes implore him, hoping he catches on quick. Swallowing down the pain in my throat, I manage to say the words in a husky (hopefully sexy) voice. "It's okay, honey bunny, he didn't mean anything. Honest. No reason to get upset—you don't want to violate your parole. I know how jealous you get. Remember in Chicago, when you beat that man to a pulp for dancing with me? We can't repeat that. It was *carnage*."

"What? I don't—" he starts.

"Oops, I shouldn't have brought that up. You don't like me to talk about your time in prison. It was so hard to be away from each other. Your passionate letters were the only thing that kept me going." I stretch up on my tiptoes and brush my lips over his cheek. The scruff on his square jawline tickles my lips. "Don't worry, I told this guy I was taken."

His hand lands on my ass and tugs me closer—instinct, I suppose, when a woman claiming to know you throws herself in your direction.

I burrow into the curve of his shoulder. I'm aware that my body is damp, and I'm probably getting him wet, but needs must. My finger doodles little hearts on his chest. His dress shirt is silky soft and obviously expensive. Now *that* would be nice to sleep on, instead of the scratchy sheets on my bed.

"You surprised me," I say. "I thought you were taking a nap."

"I wasn't," he says as his eyes flash at me. A thrill dashes over me at the intensity in them. They're an icy gray, surrounded by extravagantly thick black lashes. The color is striking, startling against his sun-kissed face. I see striations of blue and gold around his pupil. Mixed with the gray, his irises are like storm clouds with flashes of lightning. Straight brows slash over a face carved like granite.

My gaze moves lower, tracing the strong muscled lines of his throat to the gold necklace around his neck, a pendant hidden in the folds of his shirt. Men who wear necklaces are a little sleazy, in my opinion, but he carries it off like a champ. My man has style.

His face darkens. "What the hell is going—"

Shaking myself out of my detailed perusal, I pretend to hold him back as I whip my head around dramatically at Fake Clint. "This guy was just being neighborly, honey bunny. He said he was sorry for talking to me. Don't let him ruin our vacation. What we have is a unicorn romance."

"'Unicorn'?"

"Yes, honey bunny. *Our love.*"

Fake Clint bobs his head. "Yeah, sure, whatever, sorry, man, I don't mean to get in the way of, um, whatever. Just saying hi to my neighbor. No need to . . ." He looks at Lambo, then at his bag, his eyes narrowing with suspicion. "But wait, aren't you just checking in—"

"Oh good, you bought it," I interrupt as I try to take the duffel from Lambo's hand. He refuses to give it up, so I end up patting it awkwardly. "Thanks for getting this for me. My luggage is worn out." (Not even here. It's in Vegas.)

Fake Clint darts his gaze between me and Lambo. I'm not sure he's buying this charade.

Time to go for the gold. "Did you get the other thing, honey bunny?"

A few moments tick by as Lambo glares at me.

Come on, Lambo, help me out. Geez. Keep up. You are *my honey bunny.*

A dark eyebrow rises in question, annoyance just barely under the surface.

I ignore it.

"Lube. The cherry," I say playfully, nudging him slightly. "It's my favorite because it smells like you."

He scowls.

"You forgot," I say with a heartfelt sigh. "You're just so *big*, honey bunny."

His mouth parts, and before he can ruin my performance, I crook my arm through his and herd him to my door, unlock it, and tug him in. Surprisingly, he doesn't give me much trouble.

I slam the door with a bang—take that, Fake Clint—then engage the dead bolt lock.

Leaving Lambo to his own devices, I tense my shoulders as I peek through the blinds.

Fake Clint leans against the rail and lights up a cigarette, and I huff. *Go away, you rat.*

"Okay, what . . . the . . . fuck?" Lambo calls from behind me.

I turn, and he looks angry.

Sadly, it does nothing to hamper his attractiveness. On a scale of one to ten for hotness, Lambo is a million. He's truly a mountain of a man and stands with authority, his feet spread and arms crossed, calling attention to the roped muscles on his forearms. He doesn't have that pumped-up steroid look with a short neck; no, his muscles fit his frame perfectly.

"Well?" The sharp word hangs in the air, and I get it, totally. This man is *someone*, and I've just messed with him.

I note the Rolex on his wrist, the Gucci belt, the Italian loafers. La-di-da. He knows how to dress. Men like him are a dime a dozen in Manhattan. I can walk out of my building and see ten. Carry on, Emmy.

I sigh, nudging my head back at the door. "Clint was right; these walls *are* thin. I can practically hear him exhaling his cigarette. Keep your voice down."

Disbelief flits over his face. "I don't even know *who* you are."

I raise my hands, my voice going back to the terrible scratchy one. "I know, I know. I'm sorry for the drama. Truly. He was being weird; then you showed up, and I just went with it."

It was as if I was possessed.

I didn't even recognize myself.

I could have just told Lambo the guy was bothering me from the get-go. Maybe Fake Clint isn't even that menacing, but with Kian doing what he did, I may have gone overboard.

I'm not an impulsive kind of girl. Okay, that's a lie. Obviously.

"Lots of weirdos at the Golden Iguana," he says tightly.

"I hear the sarcasm."

He grunts as his eyes rove the messy room, taking in the clothes that drape over every surface, my books, the packages of tart candy. I have several from an emotional binge run to the gas station. I move to stand in front of the nightstand, hiding the copious number of empty miniature prosecco bottles. I bump into the table, and several fall to the floor, clanking together and confirming that yes, as a matter of fact, I do have a slight hangover. I've named my headache the End of a Relationship Throb. I thought a swim might help. It didn't. I rub my head absently, and he watches me.

The air-conditioning clicks on, and the room chills—and my nipples threaten to rip through my rash guard. His gaze drops to my breasts like they're beacons, and I imagine he can see right through the material. Right. I'm barely dressed. I grab a white button-up shirt off the bed, one of Kian's I snatched, and slip it on, thankful it comes to my thighs. I close a few of the buttons. "Sorry for the mess. I didn't know I was going to have company."

"Jesus. I'm not company," he says as he nudges his head at the door. "I need to go to my room, lady."

"Of course, but first, let me explain . . ." I offer him a tiny bottle of prosecco, one that isn't empty, and he frowns.

"A little early, don't you think?"

I shrug. "Depends on how one's morning is going."

"Today is totally sucking. You're. Annoying. Me."

Oh, I can see that. There's an angry glint in his eyes, and his stellar cheekbones are flushed. "Fine, okay, I see what you mean. The guy out there, the one you rescued me from, was hitting on every female with a heartbeat last night, and today he was watching me swim, and when I came up the stairs, he cornered me. He asked if I was alone, and I told him I had a boyfriend in the room, but he didn't believe me."

"Where is your boyfriend?"

I wince. "That's the thing. I *don't* have one. Well, I did, but that's another story. That's why I needed you."

"I see."

"What Kian did was beyond reproach. I left Vegas and came here to get away from him. I should have just flown home from there, but I wasn't thinking. I needed time to process. That's how I ended up in the middle of the desert."

"Uh-huh."

"I'm never dating again. I'm going to get a cat. A rescue one. The ugliest one they have, the most pathetic creature, the one that no one else wants. It'll love me unconditionally."

"I really don't care, lady. I despise cats."

Jeez. He's a tough nut. And a man who hates kitties? Concerning. Sure, a man (or woman) is allowed to like what they like, but cat haters are a good way to find out which humans to avoid.

Men who like cats, in my opinion, are usually kind and gentle, important qualities for a relationship. Men who don't like them can be quick to judge and impatient. On the other hand, Kian loved cats, and he's currently the king of douchebags. Dammit. There goes that litmus test down the drain.

I refocus. "Anyway, the guy outside is in the room next to mine and claims he can hear me. See, when he says that, I'm picturing him with a glass to his ear on the other side of the wall to spy on me. Or—and this is scary—maybe there's a tiny hole in my wall, and he can actually *see* me. I'm not saying he's a serial killer, but you seemed the better option." Anxiousness rises. I've judged Lambo safe, but hell, what do I know? "Um, *are* you one?"

"One what?" He rubs his eyes with the palms of his hands.

"Serial killer. You have to tell me if you are."

"Let's see, let me think. No! I've never killed anyone, but if I had, I wouldn't say, now, would I?"

"Guess not. I mean, how ironic would it be if I evaded Clint, only to end up being murdered by the hot guy?"

"'Hot'?"

"I misspoke. You're a troll." I smile tightly.

"Hardly."

I shrug. "Whatever. Guys like you are a dime a dozen. It takes a lot to impress me."

"What if *you're* the serial killer?"

"You'd twist me into a pretzel in a heartbeat." I snatch up one of the prosecco bottles. "Guess I could kill you with some miniature prosecco."

"So you might kill a man if you had a better weapon? Please tell me you're not armed."

"I only kill scorpions," I say. "Better check your bed tonight."

"I'd prefer a scorpion to this."

"I'll send them all your way," I snip.

Ten seconds of silence pass. It's so quiet I can hear the drip of the faucet in the shower in the bathroom. The air buzzes with tingles of electricity. Oops. Perhaps I should have been nicer.

"You're brave," he says softly, dangerously, as he studies my face, roving from one feature to the other. His piercing gaze makes the hair on my arm rise, goose bumps popping up. His eyes seem to see dig under my skin, right to the heartbreak I'm trying desperately to hide.

Gray eyes land on my mouth and linger. My tongue darts out to wet my lips as he watches avidly. Oddly, his perusal doesn't make me feel exposed, like Fake Clint's did.

I look like something the cat dragged in. I saw myself in the mirror when we walked in. My hair falls in a wet tangled mess down my shoulders, my face is angular, with high cheekbones, and my eyes have dark smudges beneath them from a lack of sleep—and crying. The freckles across my nose and cheeks look stark against my pale complexion.

His gaze hits my neck, and his eyebrows jerk down as he sucks in a sharp breath. Eyes flash back up to mine, and I fidget as I pop the collar on my shirt to hide the bruises. He opens his mouth to say something, and I just know he's going to ask about them, so I cut him off.

"Ever read *Death in the Desert*?" I ask, my brain scrambling. "It's a true crime story about a serial killer, Wayne Hopper. He murdered women staying at a motel like this one and buried them in the desert. Absolutely chilling. I wanted to go for a walk earlier but couldn't stop thinking about the book. Clint gave me Wayne Hopper vibes."

A few tense moments pass; then something about him softens as if he's come to a decision about me. His lush lips relax. The furrow leaves his forehead as he uncrosses his arms and tucks his hands in his pockets. Body language is an art, and I've perfected it at the bookstore by people-watching.

"I haven't. Is it any good?"

"Yes." I nod an affirmative as I offer a tentative smile. "Look. I'm sorry, really. I practically jumped on you, then dragged you into my room. You have every right to be upset with me, and I'm sorry for that."

"I get that a lot."

A laugh bursts out of me, more nerves than anything, but wait, he's serious; this isn't a joke. I straighten my face. "You've had women pull you into motel rooms before?"

"It makes me sound like an ass, but yeah. None were as wacky as this one, though." He shrugs, avoiding my gaze.

Is he famous? A celebrity? There's a familiarity to his features, but before I can place him, he pulls off his ball cap and rakes a hand through his hair. My thoughts stutter as thick raven waves settle around his face as if they had been choreographed. No man should have hair that shiny and layered, with soft curls that glint in the light.

"So, back to this guy outside . . ." He nudges his head at the window.

I clear my throat. "Right. He wanted to know if I was here alone. He blocked my door so I couldn't get inside. He could be a killer."

Anger tightens his eyes. "Fucking asshole. I hate guys like that."

"I have a younger brother, and he's a sweetheart. I've tried to teach him better manners."

"He really scared you, huh."

"Normally, I wouldn't be on edge, but . . ." I look away and brush my fingers over my throat.

"I see. Should I go out there and put my fist in his face?" His voice deepens to that dark velvet, and I shiver.

"Nah, I hate violence, and you don't want to go back to prison, honey bunny."

His lips twitch until it spreads into a slow, wondrous smile, turning him from a cold, handsome guy into a sexy AF man.

"That's cute," he drawls. "Never been called that before. Your 'unicorn love' was, um, something. Did you see his mouth gape?"

I chuckle. "I should have added a Scottish accent and said 'wee' a few times. I never took a drama class, but hey, maybe I missed my calling."

"You deserve an Oscar." He hands me an empty prosecco bottle. "Wanna make a speech?"

Warmth spears me as I laugh shyly and take the bottle. The tightness in my shoulders finally eases completely. He's all right, once you get past the exterior. I pretend there's an audience and put my hand over my heart. "Thank you for this award. It means everything to me. If only it wasn't empty." I bow.

He smirks. "Had a big night drinking, huh?"

"Just drowning my sorrows. Bad breakup and all."

"Hmm, if I'd arrived earlier, I could have joined you."

"Bad breakup for you too?"

He shakes his head. "Just life."

"Maybe we can meet up at the honky-tonk later and swap stories?" I ask.

Without answering, he peers over my shoulder and out the window. "It looks like he's left."

A tinge of disappointment hits—and that is just downright silly. Do I want to keep talking with Lambo? Maybe.

"I'm Emmy, by the way."

"I'm . . ." He stops, his brow furrowing as he debates.

"Ah, it's okay," I murmur. "Names have power. No need to share."

"No, it's fine. Call me G." He sticks his hand out, and I place mine in his. It engulfs mine and it's warm. Tingles race up my arm, and I laugh nervously as I pull away.

"Is it short for Greg?"

"No."

"Grant?"

"No."

"Geoff?"

"Is this the name game?"

"It could be. You already know my name and you won't tell me yours, so now I'll have to guess for the rest of my life. I'll be wandering the shelves in the bookstore, thinking, 'Who was that guy that saved me from a grave in the desert?'"

I bite my lip to stop the rambling. "Again, I'm sorry I pulled you into this . . . spectacle. You should have seen your face. Me, a complete stranger, jumping at you like a wild woman, talking about lube. The horror." I wave my hands.

"Hmm. Not so much a horror now." His eyes brush over me, his gaze pausing for a long moment on my lips again.

My breath catches.

Who are you, really?

What are you doing in this shithole?

"Thank you for the rescue," I say softly.

The moments tick by and the silence builds up, for what I'm not sure, but it's as if—

A horn blows outside, interrupting the moment. I start, and he blinks. He picks up his duffel and room key. He'd set them on the desk chair when he walked in. Curious eyes linger on my throat again. "Um, you need me for . . . anything else?"

"If you see Clint later, give him a menacing stare, maybe bump chests, but nothing violent. I don't want you to get into trouble because of me. Oh, FYI, I told him your name was Darcy."

An eyebrow rises.

"The hero in *Pride and Prejudice*," I say.

"Guess that makes you Elizabeth Bennet?"

Kill me now. He knows Jane Austen.

"Yes," I squeak. "You read?"

His face softens into a smile. "*Pride and Prejudice* was my mom's favorite book."

Was? I hear the ache of loss in his voice. Already I feel an affinity with him.

And before I can reply to that, he hitches his duffel back to his shoulder and seems to think about his next words carefully. "I'm on the other side of you. If you need anything, bang on the wall or come over, yeah? I'll protect you."

I'll protect you.

From a deep well inside me, unbidden, emotion rises up.

No one has ever protected me except Gran, and she's gone.

I've been the protector of myself and my siblings ever since the day they came home from the hospital, bundled up in their little blankets. I took on the role of their mom with a ferocity that came from instinct. I kept the three of us safe by doing whatever it took to survive. Sometimes that meant climbing up the rickety steps with two babies and hiding in the attic. We'd sleep there in a cramped storage area surrounded by Christmas decorations and old dresses until the rage had cooled in the house.

"You okay?"

I nod, kicking away those thoughts. "Actually, do you mind if I make some loud noises later, just to show him we're, you know, having a good time?"

He gives me that ten-thousand-yard stare, the gaze almost tangible, the intensity of it seeming to reach out to me and pull me closer. My body tingles as tension swirls in the room, thickening with possibilities.

I picture him pressing those luscious lips over mine, his hands on my breasts . . .

What? Worst idea ever.

I just broke up with a guy. *Get in the game, Emmy. It's cats from here on out. Meow.*

Not that Lambo's interested. This is probably his regular stare.

"I just don't want you to think I'm actually being murdered when I start screaming 'Oh, Darcy, yes, yes, yes!'"

He laughs! The man laughs! His entire face changes, his eyes crinkling as two dimples pop out on his cheeks.

I nearly melt into a puddle.

"Making me sound good, huh?" he says.

"My honey bunny is always good." Jesus. Why did I say that? "Guess you should go now, so I can scream into a pillow with embarrassment."

He smirks. "Gotcha. See you later."

I want to say something clever. I give him a thumbs-up. "Keep it real."

That wasn't it.

Without saying anything else, he makes sure the coast is clear, then waves goodbye and steps outside.

I still have my thumb up as I shut the door. I lock the dead bolt and engage the chain.

I bury my face in my hands. What in the world. He thinks I'm a prosecco-drinking, name-game maniac!

I flop back on the bed as my head tumbles through our encounter. I can't believe I threw myself at him like that. It just . . . happened.

He was a little hostile at first, completely understandable, but then he offered to fight Fake Clint. I give a one-two punch to the air. Cat hater or not, he's a good one.

Hours later, I awake and watch from the window as the sun sinks below the horizon. Half the sky is still dark, the other half tinted with pink and red. It's pretty, but I can't wait to get back home. I don't want cacti. I want Central Park, my little family, and the bookstore.

I grab clothes for a shower. I don't have much to choose from but find clean panties, a pair of gray sweats, and an "Arizona Rocks" shirt I picked up yesterday. I stand under the hot water and contemplate my dinner options, either pizza delivery or Chinese. I've picked Chinese by the time I get out and dry off.

As I stand in front of the mirror, my eyes snag on the small scars on either side of my rib cage from the surgery. I trace the raised red surfaces, then put my hand over my heart. Luckily, they didn't have to do open-heart surgery. Going in through my ribs was the best option for the mini-maze surgery, with a shorter recovery time. I sigh, thankful for normal, steady beats.

I part my hair in the center and brush it out. There's no motel dryer, so I scrunch the strands. When it dries, I'll have a riot of loose blonde curls spilling to the middle of my back. If I stretch it out, it'll reach my lower back. Pulling out my makeup bag, I dab foundation on my face and blend it in. Mascara is next, just enough to take away some of the paleness. Shimmery lip gloss coats my lips.

I laugh when I realize I have nowhere to go.

Maybe I'll go next door and chat with G. I could buy him dinner, considering what I put him through. Ugh. I wish I had nicer clothes with me.

My phone rings as I come out of the bathroom, and dread fills me when I see it's Missy. I debate answering but end up plopping down on the bed as I pick up. She's Kian's PA, and we've had some good times, but in the end, she's his minion.

Her voice is hushed. "Emmy! Thank God!"

Alarm hits. "What's wrong?"

"Where are you?"

"I'm not saying."

She rushes through her words. "I'm in the restroom at a gas station just outside of Tucson. Kian's in the car. He's tracked your phone, Emmy. He knows where you are."

"I turned off his tracker." Two days ago in Vegas when I found it.

I'd been shopping for a dress to wear to Kian's friend's wedding. Back in New York, I'd packed one, a black number with cutouts, but I'd forgotten to try it on. On my flight to Vegas, I realized it would show my surgery scars and perhaps rub against them.

I'd left Kian sleeping and went shopping. I was in a boutique in Vegas when I heard him calling my name; then he barged into the dressing room where I was. When I asked how he knew where I was, he admitted he'd put a tracker on my phone.

You were gone for so long that I was worried, Emmy.

I didn't buy it. It wasn't just about being concerned for me. He invaded my privacy and kept up with my movements so he could hide what *he* was doing.

"He reinstalled and hid it under an app," Missy says.

My teeth grit. "Do you see a motel outside the gas station?"

"Yeah. I think that's where he's going. I keep asking him, but he won't answer. He's really pissed because you won't answer the phone."

"Doesn't he have the rehearsal dinner tonight?"

"He told Danny he was sick. His best friend is getting married, and he's skipping it to look for you. He should be giving a toast right now."

"It's not my fault he makes dumb decisions."

She huffs. "If you want to end this, then leave and turn off your phone. I'm sick of your 'on again, off again' thing with him."

"Yeah, you'd love for us to be over. You'd just slip right in and take my place in a heartbeat." I pause, my voice thickening. "He hurt me, Missy. Beware of him. Please."

She huffs. "I don't know why I'd need to know that. He's my employer."

No, he's more than that.

As soon as I arrived in Vegas and met them at the hotel, my hackles rose at the undercurrent of tension I sensed. The way she fidgeted, her eyes darting to him over and over. The way he *didn't* look at her. They'd arrived a few days before me, and I smelled something rotten. Sure, Kian and I had a tumultuous relationship and had broken up a few times, but I always trusted him to be faithful when we were together.

Finding a pair of women's lacy white underwear under his bed had cemented my suspicions.

Then the awful fight that ensued afterward—the final straw.

"I'm throwing my clothes into my bag as we speak. You're literally giving me seconds."

"He's been with me in the car. I couldn't call you. I texted."

I was asleep.

"He can't focus when it comes to you," she adds, her tone annoyed. "He needs to be getting ready for next season—"

I hang up on her and turn my phone off. I fly around the room, grabbing candy and water. My hands shake as my head runs in circles, trying to hatch a plan in seconds.

There's no time to call a taxi or Uber; plus, I don't want to use my phone until I can delete the app he installed. I could use the one in the room, but there's no phone book, and I'd need to turn my cell on to find the listing for a taxi company. I could call from the front desk for information, but I wouldn't have time if they're just down the road. I could hide in the stairwell or a dark corner, but knowing Kian, he'll walk every inch of this place. I picture him walking the outskirts of the desert around the motel with the flashlight on his phone. Right now, he's thinking he'll get me back by showing how much he cares by sacrificing the wedding to look for me.

Look at me, I've traveled hours to get you back in my arms. That underwear was left there on purpose—to break us up.

I'm almost out the door when I spot a set of keys on the desk. For the Lamborghini. G must have left them by accident. I snatch them up, dash out my door, and dart to his. I knock and call out his name.

Mayday. Mayday.

Please. Answer. Let me hide in your room.

"It's Emmy, G!" I knock rapidly.

My reaction isn't just about Kian being angry; it's about my weakness. The man knows how to grovel. He'll beg my forgiveness, say that he's sorry for the tracker, that he never touched Missy, that he's sorry he put his hands on me. He'll make heartfelt promises with tears in his eyes, and I might just get in his car and go back to Vegas with him.

My heart thunders as a wild idea swirls.

Wait.

Could I "borrow" Lambo's car?

Gran's voice dances through my head. *If it feels wrong, then it probably is . . .*

I pull a notepad from my purse and scribble a barely legible message.

G

I'm in the middle of an emergency! You left your keys in my room, and I borrowed your car. You'll find it in Tucson at the airport. I'll leave cash for gas and the keys tucked on one of the tires. Thank you again for helping me. SORRY!!

Emmy

I slip the note under his door and dash down the breezeway.

After taking the stairwell farthest from the main office, I run through the parking lot. I click the fob to the Lamborghini, and the car unlocks. Relief hits as I open the fancy door and slide inside. It looks like a spaceship. And, wow, it smells like him, a spicy masculine scent mixed with rich leather.

I'm trying to figure out how to start it when a black Escalade pulls into the lot. Grunting, I duck down in the seat, recognizing Kian's rental. He parks in front of the office and gets out.

His jawline tics as he strides to the doors. He's dressed in black, from his Doc Martens to his expensively ripped shirt. Thick silver rings adorn his fingers as they tap the side of his thigh. I used to think his anger aura was just the result of him being a hot guy with inner demons. Which is true. He is angsty.

My eyes shut to erase images of him holding me when my grandmother passed away, his soft voice telling me he'd take care of the arrangements, that he'd make sure she got the service she deserved. Then there was the wake. While I was a mess, he arranged for a meal to be catered at the apartment and filled it with white calla lilies, her favorite flower. A few months later, I recall him carrying me into the ER, his face torn with anguish. I can still feel the brush of his lips on my forehead, the wetness of his tears—

I push him away. I have to end it. I'm *not* my mother.

The Lambo's engine roars to life, and I creep slowly out of the lot, then hit the accelerator as I head toward the airport.

I'm sorry, G.

Chapter 3

GRAHAM

Another day crossed off in my odyssey across the desert. I exhale heavily as déjà vu pricks at me.

I've missed something, somewhere.

Was it the encounter with Emmy?

My head circles back to the bruises on her throat, dark spots on either side that looked suspiciously like fingerprints. Sure, she sensed my awareness of them and popped the collar on her shirt, but I saw. Once the initial shock of how we'd "met" had worn off and I focused on her, I sensed the fragileness she held together beneath her bravado. I grimace. Kinda like me.

I almost knocked on her door to see if she wanted to come to dinner but decided I needed to be alone to figure out what's next on this trip.

The two things I know for sure are this: I've seen enough roadkill armadillos to last a lifetime, and this place is lonely as fuck.

Yes, I came out here to be able to drive my car in the desert, but the real idea came from a dream where I saw an endless highway in a barren wasteland. It's my theory that the images I saw while being "dead" on the field come when I'm asleep, or maybe it's just my subconscious conjuring up random ideas to compensate for the frustration I feel for not being able to recall them.

Except for that iguana on the motel sign. My intuition said, *This, this.*

I jerked the wheel and pulled in.

Pain ripples inside my head, and I massage my temples, willing the ache to disappear. I fumble in the pocket of my jeans and tug out my meds and pop one in my mouth. I pick up my coffee and take a hasty sip.

My diagnosis is postconcussive syndrome—headaches and dizziness, two things a football player does not need. It's not uncommon for players to have them, and they usually resolve in a few months, but mine still linger.

I'm inside the Roller Diner across the street from the motel. Patsy Cline sings from the jukebox. Above me, ceiling fans turn slowly, creating a soft whir over the clang of plates and silverware. The place smells like grease and coffee. I came in and picked out the darkest part of the restaurant to sit.

"Here you go, our special today," the waitress says in a sugary voice as she places down my honey chicken, rice, and egg rolls.

"Great." I barely read the menu.

"Can I get you anything else? More water? Coffee?" Her hand goes to her hip, calling attention to a curved body that fills out her pink uniform. She's attractive, with dark hair and red lips.

"I'm good."

She smiles, lingering.

I raise a brow.

"I almost forgot your fortune cookie." She takes it off her tray and places it down, then gazes at me expectantly.

Mom loved fortune cookies and horoscopes, and I never pass one up for her. It's almost as if she's talking to me through them. I crack it open and pull out the tiny piece of paper. I never was one to wait until the end of the meal.

Come out of the dark and embrace the sunshine. I blink away the sting of emotion that pricks my eyelids. It sounds exactly like something she'd say. I've been in the dark ever since my tackle on the field.

The waitress still hasn't walked away. She giggles, and I glance up. "Um, are you Graham Harlan, the tight end for the Pythons? See, the fry cook said you were, but I said, 'What on earth would he be doing in Old Town?' He bet me five bucks it was you. Are you him?"

Normally, I am not the most recognizable player on the team. That's reserved for quarterbacks and wide receivers, but the entire team has been on the TV since the Super Bowl. I've picked up some rabid fans, a lot of them female, plus more requests for interviews, and while that's great for the franchise, I'm not one to share publicly about my life.

"Yeah, that's me," I mutter.

Her eyes widen. "Wow! We never get famous people in here. Thank God your team won, right? I mean, after—"

I pick up my chopsticks. "Do you mind—"

She sits down. "Can I ask you a question?"

"No."

"Is it true you died?"

My jaw tics.

Yes, my heart stopped beating. I wasn't breathing. The used a defibrillator to bring me back. I was in the hospital for a week while they monitored me. My symptoms on the field represented what a "clinical death" can look like. Most experts say that after four minutes of no oxygen to the brain, your cells begin to die as parts of your brain expire: first the temporal lobe, where memories are stored.

I was out for under two minutes.

I'm about to tell her to mind her business when my phone rings.

"May I have some privacy?" I say to her.

"Oh. Sure, yeah. It was worth losing the bet just to meet you. We'll talk later. I get off at ten." She winks as she slides a piece of paper across the table with her number written on it. She flounces away, and I crumple the note.

"Hey," I say to Brody.

"Hallelujah, my big brother is alive! Tell me all the things. Did you figure out your dream?"

I laugh as I picture him in his apartment in Manhattan. He's probably on his balcony, sipping on a martini and taking in the views of Central Park. I bet he's wearing slacks and a tweed blazer. His socks will be color coordinated. At twenty-seven, he's three years younger than me and a replica of our mother with his sandy-blond hair and smile. He inherited her fun and spontaneity, while I got our father's dark looks.

"I've seen coyotes, roadrunners, snakes, and a tarantula as big as my hand. You'd be shitting your pants."

"Gross. But did you figure out your chat with God when you were dead? I'm picturing His Holiness as Queen Elizabeth in pearls and a powder blue suit."

"Your God is a British monarch?"

"Isn't yours?"

I chuckle. "I did find an interesting motel called the Golden Iguana. I've stayed in better tents."

My head tumbles back to the motel. I consider telling him about Emmy. My lips quirk. She ran into my arms like a long-lost girlfriend, and damn her acting was good. I'd been fighting a dizzy spell from the stairwell, and when she launched herself at me, I'd been stunned and a little confused, then angry. I'd assumed she was someone who recognized me and wanted to meet me.

He pulls me back to the present. "How's the head?"

"Fine."

He lets out a gusty exhale. "The desert sun has to be killing you. I'm sorry, G."

I tap my fingers against the side of the coffee cup. "There was a woman. She pulled me into her room."

"Now we're talking! Roarrr!"

"Nothing happened."

"*So* delicious! Was she hot? Blonde, nice tits?"

Yes. "I didn't notice."

"But you felt a tingle in your pants?"

"Jesus. No, Brody."

"You lie. In case you want to know, I'm twerking in happiness on the balcony right now."

"She wasn't my type."

Yet . . .

My fingers drum the table, thoughts drifting to her heart-shaped face and big green eyes. Her ass in that bikini was luscious. And she'd smelled like sun-kissed skin and vanilla.

Doesn't matter.

The last thing I need is a hookup.

I can barely take care of myself.

He sighs, clearly disappointed. "At least get some pics of the iguana. Maybe make a vision board. Remember when I made a board for us to move to California?"

"Hmm, you had the Hollywood sign, plus a bunch of hot guys."

"That's when Mom figured out I was gay."

"She hung it in the foyer like it was a Picasso."

He hums under his breath. "I miss her."

Same. My hand tightens around the cell, and my throat clogs with banked emotion. Regret pierces me. I adored my mother. She was taken too soon in a skiing accident when I was fifteen, but the pain of losing her never diminishes.

I change the subject. "How's Cas? Has he found a spot for the gym?" Cas is an ex-MMA fighter and Brody's spouse.

There's silence on the other end, and I frown. "Hey. What's wrong?"

He groans, frustration evident. "We got turned down for the loan. We applied at three different banks and got the same answer. We don't have the equity."

"How much do you need?"

"At least two million in assets. We have the apartment, but it's already mortgaged against loans for the initial business. I have some of

Mom's art pieces and jewelry, but it's not worth two million, plus I can't imagine selling things she adored. It's all I have left of her."

I frown as I draw circles on the wood table. Brody and Cas want to open a luxury gym that specializes in working with athletes. Cas can pull in his MMA friends, and Brody was a damn good tennis player in his early years before he gave it up to teach. At the moment, they're co-oping a warehouse, but with their client growth, they need a new space with all the bells and whistles.

I pulled in twenty million last year. I've got my fingers in Manhattan real estate. "Let me give you the money."

"No. You bought us the co-op spot plus some of the equipment. I can't let you. You may not be as set as you think. What if you can't . . ." His voice stops.

"Can't play again?" My stomach pitches. Just the idea of not being able to play makes me feel soulless. Empty and dark. I wasn't good enough to get into an Ivy League law school like my father wanted, but I'm a damn good football player. It's all I have. I have more than plenty to retire on, but I get it. Brody and Cas are proud. They want to do this themselves.

"What about Dad?" I ask, knowing the answer.

Brody's voice lowers. "No. We'll keep saving. Maybe we'll be ready in five years."

The waitress sashays by and gives me a sly smile, nothing like the sweet one Emmy wore when I told her bye at her door.

I look away, my head tumbling with ideas. "Wait . . . maybe we could get the money another way, money that *should* be rightfully yours anyway."

He scoffs. "Don't say it."

"I'm almost thirty. I could get married, get my inheritance, and hand it over to you."

Our father's mother arranged an inheritance for the grandchildren before she died. There's three of us, all males. When we turn thirty, we receive ten million. The only caveat is we have to marry a woman, and the language is very clear.

At age thirty, a grandson (with a wife) will receive the inheritance. Once the youngest brother reaches forty, any brother who isn't married to a woman will have his inheritance split.

"You don't even have a girlfriend," he tells me.

"I know plenty of women."

"Models and wannabe actresses? No way. I'll get married for a day."

"Hmm, but you won't be thirty for three more years, and you're *already* married to Cas."

He exhales an emotional breath. "Which I wouldn't change. I love him. He's my rock."

"Grandmother didn't even consider that our father might have a daughter someday," I say. "And she was homophobic. I'm sorry."

"She was mean as hell. I still shiver when I think about her razor eyes."

"Yeah. Same." Conservative and prickly, she had iron-white hair and a vicious gaze that scrutinized everything you did. I recall formal family dinners where I wasn't allowed to speak. Brody and I were required to wear jackets to dinner, even as young kids. Heaven forbid we'd use the salad fork to eat the entrée. She had a way of clicking her tongue or scoffing that made you want to crawl away and hide.

She died my first year in college and already knew that Brody was gay.

"We were never her favorite grandsons. That was reserved for Holden, the precious firstborn," he mutters.

I grunt. Holden is our half brother, five years older than me and our father's son with his first wife. After Dad's marriage fell apart, he married our mother, the younger and prettier wife.

That woman is a gold digger, Grandmother would say about our mother, just loud enough that we could hear.

He continues. "We could contest the will, but Holden will drag it out in court, and then there'll be attorney fees. I can't risk that. Teaching pays shit, even at a private Manhattan school."

I change the subject. "Back to this marriage . . . I can find someone."

"Phone an ex-girlfriend, huh?"

I ignore him, mostly talking to myself as my head swirls. "Just a business arrangement. Get married, get the money, get a divorce."

There's a long pause. "G? You're scaring me."

"Maybe I need to do something scary." My life is at a crossroads. I don't know what's going to happen next. The universe kicked me in the teeth when my mom died; then it pounded me in the kidneys when I got the concussion. I can't get Mom back, I can't fix my head injury, but I can help Brody.

"I know it's not something we like to think about, but what if I'd died on the field that day? Holden would have gotten my share of the inheritance, not you. That scares me. Hell, it makes me angry all over again at the will." I pause. "Mom would approve of this. She'd want me to help you."

He sputters: "Come on. She'd hate it! She'd want you to marry someone you cared about, not get involved in some arrangement."

"Listen to me—ten million dollars. All. Yours. Think of what you can do with that kind of money. You could add saunas and hot tubs. You could hire a nurse for your staff. You could do the nature elements you and Cas wanted, like water features or even a damn tree in the middle of the place."

He doesn't say anything, but I can feel him thinking.

"If you don't take this chance, then Holden will get part of it when you turn forty. Do you want him laughing his ass off as he gets your inheritance?" The mere idea of our half brother getting any part of what should be ours makes my hands clench.

"No." His breath hitches. "G? Maybe . . ."

I rap my knuckles on the table. "I'm doing this. You deserve your share."

"Oh my God? Oh my God!" He lets out a shaky breath.

"Wait, are you crying?"

He sniffs, blubbering. "No. You are. Okay, okay, let me think. If you do this, who will you ask?"

My brows lower. This needs to be a nonromantic arrangement. Strict rules. My former girlfriends won't work. I've parted amicably with them, but it's been months since I dated anyone. I don't have female friends.

"Just as I suspected—you're running headfirst into something without considering the consequences," he murmurs. "It's like that time when we were kids and you convinced me to go camping in Central Park. Just us and a box of Nilla Wafers. No plan on where to sleep or go to the bathroom."

I scoff. "Can't you let it go?"

"I had to shit in the woods, G, and a dog chased me and bit my ass, so no, I won't forget it. I'm traumatized every time I see anything brown and furry. You forgot my sleeping bag. You forgot water. I hate Central Park, and it's your fault."

"It was a chipmunk! No teeth. It *might* have gummed you."

"Don't care. I'm a delicate creature who needs two-ply toilet paper and a pillow for my pretty head. Without vermin."

"You came with me. I didn't make you."

"You said it was an adventure! You knew I'd follow my big brother into the woods!" He chuckles, then sighs. "For real, if you do this marriage thing, I insist on helping you pick the girl."

"Why?"

"You have terrible taste in women. Divina. Hello, cheating bitch."

My heart jerks at her name, my hands clenching around the phone at the rush of anger inside me.

"You need someone sweet," he continues.

"We need someone discreet. Someone who can pretend to be in love with me. We'll need to convince the family."

"I've got it!" he calls out. "Our drama teacher, Wynona, is a knockout and isn't dating anyone."

Witchy Wynona? "Isn't she the one with the cats and that mole on her chin?" I ask.

"Only three."

"Moles?"

"Graham!"

I grin. I love getting him riled up.

"She only has three cats, and they're trained to poop in the toilet. I have videos. I'll send them to you," he says.

"Don't. She's got facial hair that shouldn't be there, like *in* her mole. And she's got a crush on me. At our Christmas party last year, I walked into my bedroom, and she was touching my bed."

"She was tipsy!" he huffs.

"Let me be clearer—she was stroking my duvet. Pretty sure she was moaning my name. A minute later, I might have caught her masturbating."

"She's a drama teacher. She gets a pass."

"Yeah. Pass on Wynona."

"Okay. There's a trainer at our gym," he says. "Her name is Cinder. Very pretty."

"Met her and no."

"You're being picky about a fake wife."

I lean in and eat some of the chicken. "It needs to be someone I can at least get along with if we're living in the same apartment." For some reason, I have a vague image of a woman in my kitchen. She hums as she cooks, her hips swaying to the music in her head as I watch from the stool at the island. A waterfall of blonde hair spills down her back, teasing the bare skin between her cropped shirt and cutoff shorts. She tosses a look at me from over her shoulders, and her eyes are—

I chuckle at the absurdity, shutting down that little daydream. A woman hasn't made me dinner in years. Usually we order in or go out.

"Okay, so what's her incentive? Why marry you?" he asks.

"You act like I'm ugly."

He snorts. "You're moody."

"True. Movie stars and celebrities, they date and marry people for various reasons. This is no different. We just need to cover all the loopholes legally." I make a mental note to call my lawyer.

"Wait! There's a girl at A Likely Story Bookstore, you know the one off Fifth Avenue?"

"No."

"She also works at the bar across from our apartment. Surely you've been inside."

I've seen Marcelle's Martini Bar, but if I'm drinking, it's at the Baller, a private membership place for athletes. "Never been. Any moles?"

"Shut it. She's perfect. And fun. You need fun." He hums. "Jeez, what's her name? It starts with an E . . . Esme? No, wait, I've got it—Emmaline Darling. Isn't that adorable?"

"So adorable," I say dryly. Brody collects friends like lint, and if I give him time, he'll name at least fifty women. "All right. I'll peek in the bar."

A squeal comes from him, and I hear Cas in the background ask, "What the hell is going on?"

"Just planning the wedding of the year!" Brody calls back, and I grimace.

"Civil ceremony."

"Whatever. I'll change your mind. Oh my God, I love you, G! I'm dancing again!"

I smile at his exuberance and remember Mom doing one of her "happy dances" with us when something good happened. It usually involved her twirling us around in circles.

He keeps chatting, mostly to Cas, as he relays what the plan is. It's going to take at least another fifteen minutes to get off the phone.

Out of the corner of my eye, I see something yellow moving at the motel.

"*What the hell?* Somebody is taking off with my car," I shout as my hand instinctively checks my pocket for the key fob.

Not there. Shit. Did I leave it in the room?

"Wait! What? Are you sure it's yours?"

"There aren't any Lamborghinis here but mine," I say grimly.

My car pulls out onto the highway and accelerates away.

It's practically brand new. I had it on special order for two years, and it only arrived a month ago.

"Maybe it's part of the queen's plan!"

"Later, bro." I click off and jerk up from the table, drop a hundred on the table to cover the cost of my food plus tip, and race out the door. Breathing heavily, I run into the empty road and watch the red taillights disappear. Cursing, I dial 911.

"911, what's your emergency?" asks the operator.

"Someone stole my car from the Golden Iguana in Old Town. It's headed east—"

She cuts me off. "Is anyone in the vehicle, sir?"

"What? No! I mean, yes, someone is driving it, but—"

"Sir, to your knowledge, is anyone's life in danger? Is there a child in the car or another loved one?"

"It was *stolen*," I call out.

"I'll transfer you to our auto-theft division," she says without any change in her tone at my anger.

I reach the stairs of the motel and climb to my room while soft jazz plays on the phone.

I fumble for the key and go inside to see if anything else was taken. My duffel bag is still on the bed. My Rolex is on the desk. My clothes are in the closet. Nothing seems to be missing.

I see a folded piece of paper near the door and yank it up.

My jaw tightens when I finish reading it. I toss it on the bed and glare daggers at it.

Un-fucking-believable!

The girl I thought needed protecting is a thieving minx. I curse as I scrub my face, my palms digging into my eyes as I rub them. Was Emmy's entire story a lie, just an opportunity to get me in her room? Hell, maybe Clint was in on it.

I pace around the room, my jaw tensing as I remember how she'd looked at me with those innocent eyes, desperate for help. I let my guard down. I believed her story.

But she wasn't what she seemed.

Nope.

People disappoint you. Lie to you.

My father when he cheated on Mom and walked away from us.

Divina when she dumped me for my half brother, Holden. Five years with her, and she betrayed me. My throat tightens with emotion as my teeth clench to hold it in. The most bitter part of my memory of her is that when I proposed to her, she said yes. Little did I know she was already fucking my brother.

The music abruptly ends on the other line.

"This is Officer Tolbert. How may I help you?"

"My car was stolen," I tell him. "And it's headed to the Tucson airport."

I fill him in with more details. *No, I don't know her last name, but they can check with the motel. No, nothing else was stolen. And, yes, I'm sure I didn't give her permission, even though I left my keys in her room—which was an accident.*

I'm still bristling as I slam my room door to go downstairs and wait for the police. I halt when I see a man banging on Emmy's door. There's a pretty petite brunette with him, her expression tense as she wrings her hands, then tugs at his sleeve to pull him away from the door.

"She isn't here," she tells him. "Let it go. Maybe we can make the end of the rehearsal party."

"Her phone said she was here," he snaps.

"Maybe she found the app and deleted it," the girl says.

He turns to me. Dark kohl underlines his eyes, and his bottom lip is pierced. Brown hair falls into his face, and he shoves it back. "Hey, you there, wait a minute." He juts his chin out. "Did you see the girl who's staying in this room? Emmy?"

I open my mouth to tell him she'll soon be in jail but stop. "Kian? Kian Adams?"

He frowns and lowers his head, scanning me. "Yeah. Who the fuck are you?"

A short laugh comes from my chest. I've let my hair grow into an unruly mess during the off season, and my jawline is covered in scruff, but surely I'm not that unrecognizable.

Built like a truck, he's a defensive player for our rival New York team, the Hawks. In his position, he's the guy who wants to tackle the tight end—me.

He's a few years younger than me and was a real talent when he was first drafted, but not so much lately. You have to be an idiot to get a DUI. Every player in the NFL has access to a driver twenty-four seven, provided by the league. All it takes is a phone call. The Hawks' PR said he was benched for an injury, but the gossip is it's more about his personal issues.

I step into the light, and his eyes widen. "Graham Harlan. Shit. Sorry." He tucks his annoyance away and flashes a quick smile. "What are you doing here?"

"Passing through. You?" I glance at Emmy's door.

He tucks his hands in his jeans. "Looking for my girl. Have you seen her?"

His girl? I keep my face impassive as realization dawns. She mentioned she was through with the guy she'd been seeing. She might have even said Kian's name.

I take in the scratches on the tops of his fingers, others on his cheek and under his eye. He's the one who choked her, and she must have defended herself.

Rage rises like a wave inside me, but I keep my tone steady. "Nope. You guys have a tiff?"

"No. We get along great." He assesses me, eyes hardening. "It's funny that her room is next to yours."

"Small world."

42

"Very small."

"Minuscule," I drawl.

"Uh-huh. I mean, we're in the middle of nowhere. What are the odds." He opens the flashlight on his cell phone and roves his gaze over the parking lot, scanning the lobby area, then the pool. It's lit up but empty. He rechecks the parking lot, shining a light into the interior of the vehicles. He comes back to me, eyes narrowed. "She hiding in your room?"

I smile. Dangerously. My hands tighten as I speak slowly, enunciating my words slowly. "You're . . . welcome . . . to . . . check."

He rolls his neck. "Nah, nah, just messing with you. I believe you. She likes to play games with me, is all. If you see her, tell her I came by, and she needs to call me."

"Sure. Hope to see you on the field soon."

"You're coming back? After what happened? I mean, I hear your head is messed up."

"I hear you drink too much."

His jaw tics as he glares at me. "Yeah, looks like we both need to straighten our shit out."

Stuffing down my anger, I whip around and head downstairs. As I'm leaving, I hear him pounding on the door again, his voice pleading with her to come out.

I reach the clerk at the desk. Grinning, he's looking down as he counts out several hundred-dollar bills.

I see how it is.

It doesn't take a genius to figure out Kian paid the clerk to get her room number.

I move closer. "The girl in Room 307. What's her last name?"

Just noticing me, he sputters as he tucks the wad of money into his pocket. He clears his throat, face reddening. "Sir, I can't give out that information."

"But you gave out her room number for that money in your hand?"

His mouth opens and closes like a fish's.

I lean in over the counter until our faces are close. My words are soft as I grip the counter. "Name. Now. Or I'll come behind that desk and make you regret it."

He goes white and practically jumps at his computer, eyeing me as he types away. "Um, it's Emmaline Darling. Do you want her home address?"

I nod, and he scribbles it down and hands it to me.

"My car was stolen from your parking lot. Did you see anything?"

He frowns. "I saw a girl running. She had blonde hair."

I glance out the window, a part of me hoping my car will magically appear. I see that Kian has sat down outside Emmy's door, while the girl paces back and forth in front of him. It looks as if he doesn't plan on going anywhere for a while.

I smirk. *Sorry, Kian. She's in my ride.*

"When the cops show up, put us in an empty room on the first floor. I don't want anyone knowing my business."

"Yes, sir."

I glance down at the paper he gave me, and her name jumps out at me. *Emmaline Darling.* I heard the clerk say it, but it didn't click until now with what my brother said.

Jeez, what's her name? It starts with an E . . . Esme? No, wait, I've got it—Emmaline Darling.

Emmaline. Emmy. Of course.

I dial Brody, who answers on the first ring. "What's up with your car?"

"Forget that. What was the name of the girl you mentioned, the one I need to meet?"

"Emmaline Darling. Pretty. Nice boobs—not a D cup, but who needs mountains when you can have gentle rolling hills—and long legs. Will look fantastic in Vera Wang."

"She stole my car."

He gasps. "What? No way. That's a crazy coincidence. Impossible. Plus, she's a sweetie."

"And a thief."

He sputters: "Are you sure?"

"I have her name right in front of me."

A groan of disappointment comes from him. "But I already had a Pinterest board going for her—"

I cut him off as I pace, chopping the air with my hands. "She's the one. She's my fake wife."

"What? How? Wait, is she the one who pulled you into her room? Did you have sex with her? Are you still in the 'pussy glow'?"

"Hardly. What matters is she owes me."

"Um, not seeing it. She's a thief. Why would—"

"Let me handle it. I gotta go. Bye."

"Graham, wait—"

I hang up and watch the cops pull up.

Gotcha, Miss Darling.

Chapter 4
EMMY

It's barely seven in the morning when the wailing starts. Dragging myself out of bed, I rub my eyes and pad out into the hall. I pass Jane's room and peek in. Snoring softly, my sister has a sleep mask on, ear plugs in her ears.

In the next room, Andrew stirs and stretches his arms. "Better get her before she wakes up the whole neighborhood," he says with a crooked smile.

"I will. You have an early class?" I ask, lingering at his door as I tug my robe around my sleep shorts and shirt.

He scrubs his jaw. "Meeting a girl at the library. She's been taking notes in philosophy. I haven't."

"Hey, NYU isn't cheap." His tuition (sixty thousand a year) weighs heavily on my shoulders. "Keep those grades up."

"All right, Ma. I promise."

"Not your mama." I cross my arms and pretend to glower. "But I am your elder by eight years."

Wearing pajama pants, he's chuckling under his breath as he gives me a jaunty wave and disappears into his bathroom, then pokes his head back out. His mahogany curls frame an angelic face with dimples. He looks exactly like our dad, yet they have completely different personalities. "If Kian shows up, call me."

I groan. He says it every morning, as if I'll forget. "Don't worry about that. Besides, the building has been warned." All twenty-five residents. I went door to door to make sure everyone knows to never open the door for him. "No one will buzz him in."

He glances at my throat, nose flaring. The bruises have faded, but it's as if he's picturing them the day I came home, over a week ago. I've since blocked Kian's number, and he's only shown up once. Through the speaker box, I threatened to call the police, and that did the trick. The last thing he needs is bad press.

He sighs. "Maybe you should have filed a report."

"And have a media circus outside our apartment? Reporters taking pictures and following me? Dragging up what happened with our parents? Yes, there'd be support from people, sure, and I appreciate that women are believed these days, but there are also assholes who'd exploit every facet of our past. So, no. He won't come back. Not if he wants to play football."

His expression hardens. "It's what the fucker deserves."

My head dips as I stare at the hardwood floors. Something snapped in Vegas, like a rubber band that had been stretched too thin. He hurt me.

"You aren't getting back together with him, are you?" His eyes search my face.

A panicky feeling tugs at me. "Of course not. Go. Shower. I'll make coffee and breakfast."

Leaving him, I walk down the hall to the nursery. Painted a soft lilac color, the furniture is white French country. I lean against the doorjamb as Londyn struggles to push up to sitting, her cry changing to coos when she sees me. She manages to stand by gripping the wooden rail of the baby bed. Delighted at her accomplishment, she squeals loudly enough to wake the family in the apartment below us. At nine months, she is freaking adorable.

I tug her up and press my nose to her head, inhaling the sweet scent of her skin as joy ripples over me.

"Good morning, baby girl," I murmur as I sway with her in front of the window, where the sun is starting to peek over the Manhattan skyline. The city is coming alive as the first rays of sunshine reflect off the skyscrapers and brownstones. The tranquility is layered with the rumbling of the subway and the honking of yellow cabs. It's like music to my ears compared to the vastness of the desert.

"Bu, bu, bu." She watches a bus screech to a stop at a red light and points.

"Yes, the bus is going too fast, but it stopped. Everyone's got somewhere to be." I rub my hand over the tufts of wispy blonde hair on top of her head. "How was your night? Any dreams?" I love talking to her, and I've read all the baby books. Communication is key in helping her develop language skills, and she's going to be a little genius.

She grabs my hair and tugs. "Daaa."

I rub our noses together. "Yes, my love. You want a fresh diaper?"

After changing her, I sweep her up in my arms and head to the kitchen of our apartment. Located in Manhattan and bordering the East River, it's over three thousand square feet and takes up the top level of the six-story Bradford Building. It's not posh or fancy—in fact, it's old and needs updating terribly—but the apartment has been in my family for five generations, counting Londyn. My grandmother was born here. My great-grandfather helped build it.

A shadow creeps into my thoughts. When Gran passed away, she left us a hefty second mortgage. My teeth worry my bottom lip as I prepare Londyn's milk, then sit with her at the table.

After I've fed and set her up on the floor with some toys, it's another half hour before Jane walks into the kitchen. My hair is more platinum, while hers is honey colored. Like me, her eyes are a bright green, slightly tilted, and thickly lashed. Taller than me, she's the kind of beautiful that makes you blink to make sure she's real.

My eyes snag on a family photo framed on the wall across from the kitchen table. My father stands with an easy smile on his face, although he was never easy. My mother gazes down at Jane, her expression blank. Gran holds baby Andrew. It's the last photo of all of us.

Grief blooms like a rose in my chest. You'd think I'd be better after a year of Gran being gone, that I would have been prepared for it, since she'd been dealing with a series of strokes, but the sorrow crushes me over and over. I blink tears away and swallow thickly. After her first stroke, six years ago, I took over caring for her and also made sure Jane and Andrew had what they needed. Andrew was fourteen, Jane fifteen. I was twenty-two, fresh from college, and in charge of everyone. My world shrank as I focused on my family.

Jane gets her coffee, then plops down at the table.

"Morning," I say as I set down creamer for her.

She douses it in her coffee, her eyebrows lowering.

"You had a late night," I murmur. She didn't get home until two in the morning. "You could have texted."

"I wanted to see friends. We had dinner and drinks, then went dancing. Not a big deal." She pauses. "I feel your eyes on me. Don't judge me, Emmy. You aren't raising a baby alone. I needed a break."

"You aren't alone," I say as I study the tightness around her mouth, the bend in her shoulders, as if she's curling in on herself. We have seven years between us, and that space has only widened since she had Londyn. I don't know how to stop it. She used to smile more, used to laugh. Two years ago, her modeling career was blossoming, with exotic destinations and layouts in high-end magazines. Then she got pregnant. The final nail was her boyfriend dumping her. Gran died right after.

Her bottom lip trembles. "You're right. I'm sorry. I should have texted. Forgive me?"

"Of course."

"I'm glad you're back. I felt so . . . lost when you were gone."

I rub her shoulder. "I'm back. We're gonna be fine."

She chews on her lip, then says, "Look, Emmy, I've been thinking . . . even with both of us working, this apartment is sucking us dry. Each month, it's hard to make the payments. We could sell, then cover the mortgage and make money."

"What? No."

"A bill collector called me while you were in Vegas."

My hospital bills. They aren't terrible—thank God for insurance—but it's still money I've been putting elsewhere.

I'm not a quitter. Gran left us the apartment with the understanding that I keep it. "I'll call them back and take care of it. We can't sell, Jane. This is our *home*. If we did, we'd have to find something, and housing is expensive everywhere."

She waves her hands around. "The stove doesn't work half the time, we need a new water heater, and the electricity bill will skyrocket this summer. I miss Gran, too, but she isn't here. She's gone."

My hands clench. "I can't give up our home."

Andrew waltzes in, grabs a plate of eggs and a bagel, then stuffs half of it in his mouth. "Yo, did I interrupt NATO negotiations?" He darts his eyes between us.

"No," I say.

"Morning, Tiny," Jane says, calling him by his childhood nickname.

"Aaaa, aaaa, aaaa" comes from Londyn as she holds her hands up for him.

He picks her up and dances with her around the room. "At least Londyn adores my company," he says as he puts her down in front of her toys, then takes my hand and laces our fingers together. "Your turn, Ma. Let's salsa."

Setting down my coffee, I try to follow his lead but can't keep up with his beat. "I recall a time when the only dance you knew was the pee-pee dance. Who's teaching you?"

He waggles his eyebrows. "The girl at the library. She's a dancer."

"Stripper?" Jane snarks as she nibbles on a protein bar.

He dances us close to her and pops her on the arm. "No, dumbass. She's in a show."

"Don't say 'dumb a-s-s' in front of you-know-who," I remind him.

He swings me out, dances back, then dips me until my hair trails the tile.

"Help, Londyn. Your uncle thinks he's Patrick Swayze," I call out. She claps her hands. "Eeee, eeee, eeee."

Andrew bows. "And my job here is done. All the women are smiling."

Jane sticks her tongue out at him. "You never dance with me."

He pours himself a cup of coffee and clinks his cup with hers. "Next time I'll teach you how to moonwalk. You can't do it, and frankly, it's embarrassing. For a model, you're very uncoordinated and, dare I say . . . clumsy."

I giggle. "Oh, the drama. Those are fighting words. We better give them some room, Londyn."

Jane points a finger at Andrew. "You're a turd. I walk a catwalk like I was born on top of it."

"Anyone can strike a pose." He throws his shoulders back, puts his hand on his hip, then struts across the floor with big steps. He stops and levels us with a haughty, squinty look.

I smirk. "Blue Steel. You've got it."

Jane snorts. "You wish you were me. Oh, I forget, you're too short to be a model, Andrew."

"I'm six foot!" he calls. "And I never wanted to be a vapid model."

"I'm not vapid, you Neanderthal," she snaps back, "but I am taller."

"By a quarter of an inch," he retorts. "I've grown. Come on, let's see who's taller. Put your back to mine, and let Emmy measure."

"Your head is bigger. Big, fat, ugly head," she calls out.

I roll my eyes. "Children, please. Stop or I'll put you both in the corner."

"All right, Ma," Andrew murmurs, and I push him back, laughing.

The doorbell rings, and Jane jumps up. "That's the sitter. I've got a meeting with my agent today. Maybe it's about a job."

When she leaves to let Sasha, an older woman who lives downstairs, in the apartment, Andrew follows me out into the hallway.

"Emmy, look, I can drop out of school. NYU isn't going anywhere."

He must have heard us talking.

I cross my arms, drawing an obstinate line. "I went to college, Jane had acting lessons, and you'll get your turn. Plus, you help out with Londyn." He watches her at night if neither Jane nor I are here.

"What about a school loan?"

"You're only nineteen," I insist. "School debt like that will follow you the rest of your life."

"I'll quit."

"No, Andrew, stop saying that. You've dreamed of NYU for years."

He sighs, his face uncertain. "You had heart surgery, then picked back up with two jobs. It makes me feel like shit."

"It was minor surgery."

"No, it wasn't. You could have died, Emmy. It was the scariest thing I've ever been through."

"Oh, sweetie. People as young as me rarely die of A-fib. I'm going to be fine."

Atrial fibrillation is a rhythm disorder caused by irregular heartbeats in the upper chambers. When the too-fast pounding in my chest and shortness of breath started a few years ago, I thought it was just panic attacks or PTSD from my childhood. It wasn't. After getting an official diagnosis, I tried meds, which worked for a while, but then I stopped. What followed was me at the bookstore doing my job, when my heart started pounding out of control, as if I'd run a marathon. I tried to breathe slowly and soothe myself like I'd been taught, but nothing worked. My chest wouldn't stop roaring like a train. My head swam, and I stumbled into a bookshelf and passed out. They rushed me to the doctor, and a week later, I underwent mini-maze surgery.

I give him a fierce hug, tell him that everything will be okay, then shoo him out the door. Later, I go to my room and sprawl out on the bed and rub my face.

Yes, I'm running out of options when it comes to keeping the apartment, but at the top of my worries is the fact that I *stole* a car.

Every time the doorbell rings, I imagine it's the cops. Yesterday, I was alone when someone knocked on the door, and I forced myself to look through the peephole. I expected NYPD, but it was the neighbor downstairs selling cookies for her school. I was so thankful that I bought ten boxes.

I chew on my lips. Yes, I gave Andrew valid reasons for not filing a report against Kian, but I'm also scared that going to the police station will only end up in me being arrested for theft; then I'll be sent to rot in some desert prison in Arizona. I'll never get to see my family.

Last night, my dreams featured me in a cell in the middle of the desert, naked and freezing as I slept on the bunk. Millions of scorpions crawled on the floor, up the walls, and over my face. That's when I woke up, screaming, as I tossed covers in every direction to fight imaginary scorpions.

Obviously, my meandering subconsciousness worries for my future as well, and if dreams come true, I'm screwed.

Chapter 5
EMMY

After showering, I blow out my hair and arrange the strands into a sleek bun on top. The air-conditioning isn't great, so I have a fan pointed toward the bathroom to keep me cool. From the closet, I grab a black shirt with a corseted lace bodice and pair it with a layered long tulle skirt cut into strips. Louboutins that Jane bought me are on my feet.

I give myself a pep talk. I've got enough in savings to get us through the year. Jane's modeling will pick up. Andrew will finish this semester soon.

Half an hour later, I'm on Fifth Avenue, headed to work, when my neck prickles, a malicious tingling that skates down my spine. I toss an anxious glance over my shoulder. There's only a hundred or so people milling around, but I don't see Kian's head towering above them. Still, I can't help but think someone is watching me.

I brush it off as I arrive outside A Likely Story and linger at the large window display, featuring two mannequins, a woman and a man. She's standing in a floor-length empire-waist dress, and he's in a replica early nineteenth-century suit. He's down on one knee holding a book up to her in the palm of his hand. A sparkling diamond (fake) sits atop the book, Jane Austen's *Emma*. Fluffy clouds, angelic cupids, and white doves dangle from the ceiling with wire. It took weeks to put that together, and it's freaking glorious.

"Look at that window," a little girl gasps as she points it out to her mom.

"We feature romance in May," I explain with a wave. "You should see us at Christmas. Last year we did rabbits hosting a winter tea party for the forest. Come see us!"

They've already gone, but satisfaction lingers. Of course we aren't as famous as some of the other displays in New York—at Bergdorf Goodman, Macy's, or Bloomingdale's—but we're getting there.

The bookstore is my bright star that never dims. Built over a hundred years ago, the four-story building used to be a dance hall. There's even a gold plaque inlaid in the bricks that says **MYRON'S JAZZ CLUB, 1920**.

"What the hell?" comes from me at seeing the **A LIKELY STORY WILL BE CLOSING SOON** sign posted on the double oak doors. Sure, I took two weeks off, my usual summer vacation, and I knew Terry had the store for sale, but he would have told me if he'd found a buyer.

I shove inside, the bell jangling. I enter the marble-tiled rotunda and rush past book displays and cozy seating areas. The air is thick with the smell of coffee, warm croissants, and ink. The comforting buzz of conversation between customers and staff reaches my ears. Normally, I'd stop to chat with the regulars or tinker with the display, but I stride to the main counter, where Babs, the assistant manager, waits.

Petite, she's in her late fifties, with red hair in a stylish blunt cut. Her makeup is expertly applied, with sweeping eyeliner and thick false lashes. Her chin quivers when she sees me.

"What's with the sign? Is this a joke?" I ask.

"Oh, Emmy! Thank God you're back. As for the sign, ask the jerk in his office. He's the one who put it up this morning." She bursts into tears as I fumble around the counter to find a tissue. There's not a box, so I grab a wad of napkins from the coffee station.

"I swear to God, I hate Terry. I'm tempted to get a knife and"—she grabs one of the stir sticks for coffees and bares her teeth—"march in there and cut his balls off."

"Whoa, there's no need for cock cutting." I remove the stick as a customer walks by the counter and gives us the side-eye. He asks where the used books are, and I point to the beautiful wrought iron spiral staircase and explain they're on the third floor.

"But he hasn't given us any warning," Babs wails after he's gone. "I love the smell of books, the feel of a hardcover in my hands. I can't exist without this job!"

I *need* this job as well. I've worked here for years, first as a barista, then as a manager.

"Who did he sell to?"

She dabs at her eyes. "I'm not sure, but a man came in about a week ago, in a divine suit. It was a summer style, maybe linen or something, and a cream color. Can you imagine it? *Cream.* Few men can carry that off. Anyway, he sauntered in like he owned the place. He looked like a movie star, Emmy." Her eyes glaze over, and I nudge her.

"Did he buy it?"

"I don't know but thought I should mention it, because he asked if *you* were working, and when I said no, he asked to see Terry. Weird, right?"

I frown. I hadn't even realized Terry was back from his fishing trip. Even when he is in town, he only comes in maybe twice a week. "Did he know Terry, or was he just asking to see the owner?"

She shrugs. "I didn't put much thought into it at the time. Your name is on the door as the manager, so the mystery man probably wasn't looking for you specifically."

He could have been a rep from one of the publishers.

Or a detective with a sense of style. Ugh.

She sniffs. "Anyway, he might be a potential boyfriend, you know, since you and Kian are kaput."

"Nope. Men suck."

She completely ignores me. "I'm finding you a guy."

"God, no, please." Before Kian, she introduced me to three nephews, a couple of cousins, and her own son.

"I'm never fucking Terry again, that's for sure. Never." Her voice rises, and I take her arm and steer her toward the kitchen before the customers overhear.

Her shoulders dip. "That's a lie. I'm weak willed; you know this. I love the feel of warm skin, dirty talk . . ." She whimpers. "And Terry knows how to work it. Ever since his hip replacement surgery, he's got this swivel thing—"

An image of Babs and a sixty-year-old Terry going at it threatens, and I interrupt her by clearing my throat.

"I guess I could be one of those professional cuddlers. I hear they get fifty bucks an hour, plus the dopamine your brain releases. It's like free drugs, but I'd be worried I'd get horny; then I'd have to booty-call Terry, and girl, his D is capital D for delicious—"

"For the love of everything, please stop. I'm trying to have a tea." I take a hasty sip of the caffeine-free peppermint drink I made.

"Fine. The bakery on Seventy-Sixth is looking for a taste tester. I mean, I'd probably need some kind of culinary experience. I made snow cones in my teens."

My mind is halfway listening, twisting with how to deal with the store closing. I never imagined he'd sell it so fast, and I assumed whoever bought it would keep it open.

She heaves out a long exhale. "Whatever. I'm more worried about you! I mean, I have money from Freddy. I work here because I love getting out of the apartment."

Freddy was her late husband.

"If you need me to help you job search, I will." She nudges her head at her laptop, sitting open on the counter. "I've been looking. There's a place in Alaska that needs women. The entire town is hiring, pretty much any job you want. Give me a day, and I'll find you one. We could go together, since I hate Terry now."

She'd never leave Manhattan. But she enjoys talking, so I let her go on.

She pops her compact and gasps at her face. "Good God, one of my lashes have come unglued. My life is officially over."

She carefully sticks it back on, then reapplies her lipstick. She waves at one of the baristas, a young man, who then rushes over. "Be my favorite and bring me a scone and a chamomile tea with a touch of honey, please. I need something calming."

She needs something calming at least twice a week. Once a customer couldn't find his money to pay for a book. After rummaging for a while, he reached inside the front of his jeans to his crotch. She took it with a stony expression, but as soon as he'd walked out the door, she did a hyena/banshee scream, then ran to the bathroom to throw up. Now she wears surgical gloves if she works the register.

Once she had a fifteen-minute stare-down with a kid who'd broken all the crayons (over two hundred) in the kid area and was throwing them in the store. He told her crayons were ugly, and so was she. She kept inching closer to him—who knows what would have happened—so I ran to the PA system and announced that someone needed help in the ER section, code for erotica. She snapped out of it and dashed to help a customer with one of her favorite genres.

Another time, a man came in dressed in a black-and-red cape and asked for a vampire cookbook. She hung crosses and tossed garlic around the next day.

"Where are you going?" she asks as I head down the hallway to the back of the building, where the offices are located.

"To talk to Terry." And get to the bottom of this.

"Tell him we're over, but if he calls me repeatedly and tells me I'm pretty on my voice mail, I might pick up," she calls.

I flip her off behind my back and hear her laugh.

I knock at his door, and his raspy voice tells me to come in.

While Babs is coiffed and sophisticated, Terry sports a full head of gray hair that's a mess. Tall and slim with a rugged face, he's wearing rumpled jeans and a vacation shirt. This one is a faded peach color, with a "Bimini Beach" logo on it.

With a heavy sigh, he studies my face. "You're pissed."

"Some kind of notice would have been appropriate. I *am* the manager." I lift my hands in frustration, my words clipped as I plop down in the leather chair across from his desk. The surface is scattered with messy papers and a half-eaten muffin from the bakery. I add, "I thought it would take a few years before you found a buyer." And I was hoping my financial situation would be better when the time came.

A long exhale comes from him. "You had dreams of buying it someday, but we both know the situation your gran left you in. I should have called you, and I'm sorry. It was very sudden."

My throat tightens. "I have artists who have their work here, authors scheduled, and we talked about expanding to comics and vinyl records . . ."

My voice trails off at the resignation on his face. My breath catches. Shit.

"It's hard to compete with online stores. Bookstores close every day, Emmy."

But we're different. We make money.

I straighten my shoulders. "*Jaws* is the theme for summer, and I've got a papier-mâché shark and fake shark teeth ready to go. We're more than just a bookstore. The *Times* called us a 'truly religious experience.' They love the displays, the staircase, plus Babs is perfect to start a book club. I've been meaning to bring it up in a meeting—"

"Emmy. Please," he says as he interrupts me, then sighs, his voice softening. "The offer . . . it's more than I planned to retire on."

I deflate like a popped balloon. How can I be angry at a man who wants to retire?

"Dear, I'm sorry. Truly." He stops at a bookshelf and gazes at a picture of a fishing boat he bought a few years ago. "I want to get away from the city. I want to drink tequila and watch the sunset."

"Are they going to keep the store? The employees?" My hands clench, preparing for the worst.

"No. And the buyer wants to remain anonymous. I'm going to have a meeting with the staff in a few days with the particulars. Everyone will get a nice severance package."

I don't care about that right now. It feels as if I've just lost an arm. "What if they tear it down?"

"It's a historical building."

"They can still gut it. If they've got the city in their pocket, which they probably do, with that kind of money, then who knows what will happen. Was it the man who came in wearing a cream suit? I heard he asked for me."

He sits down in a chair next to me and pats my shoulder. "Emmy, nothing changes if nothing changes—you know that. Maybe you need something different."

He didn't answer my question.

I rub my face. "My life is blowing up. Scorpions are after me."

He gives me a worried glance. "Is that a gang or something?"

"No. I'm just in shock."

"And it's my fault." He rubs his jaw. "You should take the day off."

"What? No. I-I just got back."

"I insist," he murmurs, giving me a squeeze on the shoulder. "I feel terrible for not telling you before putting the sign up. Freshen your résumé and look for a new job."

Oh God. This is really happening.

Numbly, I mumble an agreement and leave. I make my way to my office, my eyes drifting over the store. Owning it was just a pipe dream, something to keep me going. Part of me always knew I'd never have the money, but to not even work here anymore—I can't fathom it.

Sitting at my desk, I cover my face with my hands. The anxiety that's been growing in my chest ever since I saw the sign claws at me.

It's all hanging over me, the bills, the Lamborghini, and now the bookstore.

In that moment, I wish desperately for Gran to appear at my side. She always knew what to do. She'd give me a hug and say, *When the Darling women get lemons, we make lemon drop martinis.*

A knock comes, and I start. "Yeah?"

A young man in a bike helmet and a messenger outfit eases in. He throws up a hand. "Hey. Babs sent me back here. I've got a letter for you. Can you sign for it?"

"Sure." I scribble my initials and take the white envelope, frowning at the lack of a return address.

Sitting on my desk, I rip it open and pull out a handwritten note.

Emmy,

Got your note and thought I'd reply. Look at what you did (see enclosed photo), and you're going to do something for me to make up for it. Because you stole my fucking car.

I'll be in touch.

G

With shaky hands, I reach in the envelope and pull out a four-by-six photo. A gasp comes from me. No way. I can't believe it. I've imagined his car at the airport, all nice and shiny and waiting for him.

It's his yellow Lamborghini—only it isn't at the airport. The once sleek and aerodynamic lines of the car are barely recognizable, twisted and curled up on a street. One of the doors is gone. The windshield is busted. A wheel is off.

Blood drains from my face. Holy shit.

I start when Babs appears in the door, carrying a tray loaded with cupcakes. Pink icing coats her lips. "I've been thinking . . ."

I tuck the letter and photo away and clear my throat. "Yeah?"

"My ma always said that life changes come in threes, especially the bad ones. Kian, the bookstore being sold, which means you've got another thing coming."

Funny. It just arrived. By messenger.

"So beware. Also, I sent one of the guys to the bakery on Seventy-Sixth." Her eyes flick down at the tray. "I'm practicing being a taste tester. You want a green one? They call it the 'grasshopper.' I think they can improve on the naming process." She frowns, lowering the cupcake as she searches my face. "Hey. What's wrong? Your face looks like that time we thought we'd lost that first edition of *The Great Gatsby*."

A faint smile ghosts my lips. An employee accidentally shelved it when it should have been locked behind a glass display in the rare-books section. We ransacked every floor looking for it, then found it next to the antique manual typewriter we keep on a table in the rotunda for customers to type messages and notes to people.

She comes closer. "Was Terry an ass?"

I shake my head. "No."

G has found me. He knows where I work. Probably where I live.

It's time to face the consequences of my actions. Karma has circled back to sting me.

I gather myself. "Question: Is there a vacant place here where I can go scream?"

"Basement. Nothing there but boxes and a papier-mâché shark. The art girl made it while you were gone, if you want to take a look. It's quite massive. You'll love it."

I sigh sadly. No one will see our shark. No one will see our summer window display.

"I gave Terry a blow job in the basement once. It was a good one. He blacked out."

"Thank you for letting me know. How do you think I'll look in orange? Maybe in scrubs?" I ask.

"No one looks good in orange. Why?"

"It's what they wear at county lockup."

She grimaces. "Are you in that much trouble?"

I nod as I think about his vague letter, anger curling inside me. Just send the police, already. Bring on the handcuffs and interrogation.

I'm not doing "something" for G. Scenarios dance in my head. Who exactly *was* he? Wealthy, yes, that was evident by the car and clothes, although he was staying in a shithole motel. He could be mafia or some kind of international thief. Maybe he wants me to kill someone, smuggle drugs, or steal art from museums.

I rub my temple. Maybe he just wants an apology?

Chewing my lips, I think about the twisted remains of his car. Somehow, I think "I'm sorry" isn't going to cut it.

"Where are you going?" she asks as I grab my purse and walk out of the office and into the bookstore. She trails behind me on my heels like an overeager puppy.

"Wait. Are you going job hunting? I want to go. Please . . ."

I grab one of the cupcakes from the tray she's holding and take a big bite, savoring the burst of sugar. "Stay. I'm going to find a man about a car."

"You can't just say that and not explain. What car? You don't even have a license!"

And that didn't stop me from stealing one.

I give her a wave and head out the door.

Chapter 6
EMMY

I walk into Marcelle's, a martini bar near Central Park. I try to get at least two night shifts a week here.

I didn't find out who G is because I have nothing to go on. I called the motel and asked if they could tell me who the man was in 306, but it got me nowhere. The clerk told me that it's illegal to give our personal information about their guests. I knew that but tried anyway.

The sound of low pop music greets me as I push open the door. Dimly lit, Marcelle's features a curved wooden bar, leather booths, and industrial-style pendant lights that hang from the ceiling.

Ciara is behind the bar, her face scrunched in concentration as she aligns bottles on the mirrored wall. A transplant from Nashville, she moved to New York for ballet but gave it up professionally after hurting her knee.

"Hey! I'm here!"

"You're early—" Her words stop when her gaze lands on the small head poking out of the backpack I'm wearing. I can see the animal in the mirror behind the bar, big amber eyes and a feline face with overly long whiskers.

She starts, then giggles. "A cat in a backpack? Holy . . . turn around and let me see that crazy carrier."

I turn and give her the back view, which is a clear, popped-out bubble, perfect for cats to see the world. "The rescue place said he hated his cage, so I grabbed one of these but couldn't bear to zip it, so I let him stick his head out of the top and see the city. He put his paws on my shoulders and stayed there the entire way here."

Twisting the backpack around to my shoulder, I ease him out, and his paw curls around my finger. I bend my arm to give him a resting place. He purrs, his back arching as I stroke his black fur. The rescue didn't know his origins, only that he'd been delivered to them under-nourished and bleeding.

"Bless his heart, what happened?" she asks. "He's missing an ear. Oh no, is his tail . . ."

"Yeah, it's been cut off midway. People can be so cruel."

"I see what this is. You wanted a Kian distraction?" She gives me a knowing look.

I wave his paw at her. "Meow. Say hi to my new boyfriend."

"Hi, new guy, you're gorgeous. What's his name?"

I hold him close to my cheek. "No clue."

"We had a cat when I was a kid. He chewed hair and licked my armpits. Midnight would be a cool name for him, or you could be ironic and call him Snowball. Oh, how about Lucifurrr," she says, drawing out the name for effect.

"Hmm, maybe. He needs an IG account. Put a bow tie on him, maybe some little glasses, throw some books in, and let him hang out in the bookstore window . . ." I let out a frustrated groan. "Never mind. The store is closing."

"I got your text. So sorry, Emmy. I know how much you wanted to own that place."

"Just a dream." I'm barely keeping a roof over my head.

She pats me on the shoulder. "How about a cat joke?"

I groan.

"I just made it up on the spot."

"Uh-huh."

She rubs the cat's back. "You know where you can go to get him a brand-new tail?"

"Where?"

"The *retail* store. Booyah. I'm so good at this."

"Somebody, please, save me from Ciara's jokes," I call out teasingly.

Mason, the manager, comes out from the kitchen with a towel over his shoulder. Carrying a tray of freshly cut fruit for the drinks, he's tall, with dark-red hair swept back on top and shaved on the sides. Our friendship goes back to my NYU days.

"Hello, health violation," he says when he sees the cat.

"Can I leave him in your office?" I say as the kitten scrambles up my arm and perches on my shoulder like a skilled acrobat. His short tail whips as he balances on my shoulder and blinks at Mason with an innocent expression.

Mason grunts. "He looks like he's about to pounce on me."

"He adores you," I say. "He just told me. Telepathically." I wink at him. "Come on—I brought some litter, and I can find a box in the back for him to go potty. Your office? Please . . ."

"Come on, Mason," Ciara begs as she bats her lashes at her boyfriend.

He lifts his hands and smirks in defeat. "Like I could ever tell you two no."

Squealing, I kiss him on the cheek and head to the back.

After getting the kitten settled in the office, I change into my uniform of wide-legged black pants and a white silk shirt. The shirt has ruffles and a long tie that goes around the neck. I let my hair down and brush it until it gleams.

Two hours later, the place has filled up. Mason manages the middle bar, I get one end, and Ciara takes the other. Waitresses in skirts and white shirts with bow ties roam the tables.

I'm mixing a Bellini when a familiar face drops down in an open seat.

"Brody!" I smile. "What's up? How are things?"

He's dressed handsomely in a tweed jacket and slacks. Black-framed glasses are on his face. He waves a hand. "Funny you should ask. Fate has been good to me recently."

"Nice." I rim a glass in sugar, pour in the shaken mixture, toss in sugared raspberries, slide on a lemon curl, then hand it to the woman next to him.

"Where's Cas?" He's usually with his husband.

"He's on his way."

"How's the search for a gym location going?" He's talked about buying property to expand their business.

"Oh, it's going, only not in the way I expected." His eyes sharpen. "How are you?"

"Great. What do you want tonight?"

"I'll have one of those things you just made. It looked refreshing." He rakes a hand through his blond hair, and I pause at his diamond-cut jawline, the set of his lips, the bottom one noticeably fuller than the top. Hmm, something about him is familiar—

"I've got a question: What are your thoughts on marriage?" he asks after I set his drink in front of him.

"Whoa, deep question. I've never been close to tying the knot." Thinking of my parents' marriage only brings memories of horrible nights wondering if my parents would kill each other.

"Are you a fan of our football teams in New York? My brother plays for the Pythons."

"Not really." I saw some of the media coverage, sure, but I had other issues to worry about in February, namely my heart.

Kian was on the roster for the Hawks, but he hasn't played since we met.

Cas arrives. He has cropped dark hair and is built like a brick house. Even his muscles have muscles. I grab him a draft beer and put a napkin under it.

Brody gazes up at him adoringly, then gives me a look. "Cas and I are considering a trip out west. How was your trip?"

Tingles of unease make the hair on my arm rise as I wipe down the counter. He must mean my trip to Vegas, because no one knows about me going to Arizona but my siblings. "I don't recall telling you about Vegas."

"Vegas?" A puzzled expression flits on his face until he smooths it out. "Yes, um, that's what I meant."

"It was fine," I say as I move to make several chocolate martinis for a group of people.

"Are you dating anyone?" is the next question from him when I come back.

I frown. "What's with the twenty questions? And I'm sure I never mentioned Vegas to you."

He gives me a seemingly innocent expression. "Oops."

Before I can ask what that means, Cas rolls his eyes at him. "Leave Emmy alone. She's trying to work."

Brody scoffs. "But she's so fascinating."

"I'm really not," I say warily.

"You're being nosy," Cas tells Brody as he tugs him close and lays a sweet kiss on him. Little hearts practically dance around them. I swoon a little. Magic.

"What was that?" Cas asks me, and I realize I must have said it out loud.

"Magic. You two have it. Few get it. Everyone wants it." I point out Edgar, one of our regulars, an older man with a sad face. He's sitting in a dark booth, his hand cupping his face as he peers down at his drink. "His last wife left him, but he's going to find the next one soon. Makes me wonder if he's never had magic and is still searching." I nudge my head at Margot, an aging Broadway actress, who's laughing up at her husband at a table. "She married Tom when she was nineteen. High school sweethearts. They never come in without the other, and they never look at anyone else. They have all these cute little inside jokes. True magic." My parents didn't have it, but Gran did.

Brody lights up. "I met Cas online. It wasn't exactly love at first sight."

"You thought I was a pumped-up steroid user," Cas drawls affectionately at his husband.

Brody chuckles. "It was the MMA thing."

Cas tosses an arm around him. "We texted for two weeks before he agreed to meet me. We met in this very bar."

"Had to make sure you weren't going to murder me," Brody says softly as he threads his fingers with Cas's. He glances at me. "I'd love for you to meet my brother. He might be your kind of magic, Emmy."

"The football player?"

He nods.

"Sorry. Not interested. I got a cat instead." I pause and slap the bar. "Magic! That's his name, guys, Magic!" Something I'll never have in real life.

Brody and Cas look confused.

Ciara and Mason whoop as Mason rings the bell we keep for big tips and announces to the bar, "Hey, everyone, Emmy has named the ugly cat who's taken over my office! He's also her new boyfriend. Magic, it is!"

Everyone claps.

"Purrfect," Ciara calls, and Mason hip checks her and chuckles.

Brody leans in. "My brother adores cats."

Cas groans. "Oh my God, you have to stop."

Brody shushes him. "Are you writing his dating profile? No, I am." He takes a careful sip of his drink as his eyes hold mine. Something in them causes me to stop mixing the gin and tonic I'm making.

Unease washes over me.

Alert, alert. Something is wrong! a voice inside my head whispers . . .

He smiles. "Besides, you met my brother in Old Town. I heard there were sparks—and cherry-flavored lube."

Old Town?

Cherry-flavored lube?

I gasp. "What?"

"Yeah, Graham Harlan—or G. That's my little nickname for him. I couldn't say Graham when I was little, and it sort of stuck."

My breath quickens, doom closing in.

It clicks. Brody's lips, his familiar jawline . . .

"Wait. Your brother is . . ."

A tall, broad shadow enters the bar and appears behind the couple, and my eyes move up to take in the man who's sucked all the air out of my lungs. He's wearing a blue shirt with the sleeves rolled up and a pair of navy slacks. His jaw is shaven, calling attention to his razor-sharp jaw and stark cheekbones.

Tension in the bar rises, buzzing around me as he towers over everyone at the bar, his chiseled face set in hard lines, not that the iciness affects how soul-crushingly gorgeous he is. Stormy gray eyes pierce me. A rush of electricity zaps me like a live wire. I'm a frozen deer in the headlights as he rakes over every inch of me, taking me apart.

The bar noise fades, and it's just me and him in the bar.

My heart jumps in my chest.

What is this awful thing I'm feeling when he looks at me? Fear? Attraction? Both?

Shit, whatever it is, it's not good.

His gaze drifts to my lips, almost caressing them; then his nose flares as if he's angry.

I fight the urge to run out the back door of the bar.

"Me," he says darkly, answering my question earlier to Brody, the one I'd already forgotten about. "Remember?"

A long breath comes from me as I cling to the edge of the bar.

This is impossible, yet there he is.

I swallow thickly. "G is for Graham. I get it now." Now that he's shaved and has trimmed his hair, I recall seeing his photos in the media.

I must have been blind at the motel, but he's the kind of person you'd never expect to see at a place like the Golden Iguana.

"It's getting hot in here," Brody murmurs as he fans himself, his eyes flicking from my face to Graham's as he twists to get a view of both of us. Cas chuckles, but I'm barely registering the people around me.

He sits on the stool next to Brody and straightens his collar, then leans in until his muscled forearms are on the bar. I see a peek of tattoos, a flock of birds that disappear up his arm. The name Hazel is written in script around his wrist. I hadn't noticed it at the motel, but then I wasn't completely myself then.

The overhead light glints off his raven hair, giving it golden highlights. The loose curls soften his jawline. He twists the Rolex on his wrist. "Give me a Blanton's, neat."

I whip around to the whiskey shelf, my hands shaking as I pull the bottle down. Usually I'd make the drink in front of customers, but I don't, instead grabbing a glass and pouring it with my back to him.

Mason slides in next to me. "What the hell is up with you and Graham Harlan?"

"Nothing." I wince, darting my eyes at Mason, then away. "Okay. I accidentally stole his car."

He rears back. "What? How? Why didn't you tell us?"

"Because I feel terrible. I'm a thief, ugh. I haven't told anyone," I mutter. "But he hasn't called the police yet. I think. I don't know. He sent a note by messenger to the bookstore. Why is he in my bar? How is he Brody's brother and I never knew? What are the chances? Am I losing my mind? Is he still there?" My brain darts in a thousand directions.

He glances back and scrubs his jawline. "Yes. Sorry. Do you want me to toss him out?"

Ugh. I wish. "No." He sent the note. Obviously, he wants something.

He glances at him again, his voice lowered. "He's looking at you like he's going to eat you for dinner. Did you have sex with him?"

I watch in the mirror as a blush sneaks up my face. I might have thought about having sex with him. "No."

He whistles under his breath. "Emmy, he's rich as shit, and his dad is a powerful man. Be careful."

"Who's his dad?"

"Big-time lawyer, old money."

A lawyer! Hello, jail cell.

I finish making the whiskey and slide a napkin under Graham's glass as I set it down in front of him. He barely notices. A pretty young redhead in a tight black dress has taken the stool next to him, and they're engrossed in conversation.

Brody catches my hand, his face earnest as I glare at him. "Ah, don't be mad at me, Emmy. He was going to find you one way or another. I thought this would be neutral ground for a second meet-cute."

I pull away. "Are you kidding me? There's nothing romantic about me and your brother. There was no *first* meet-cute."

His eyes gleam. "Be patient. Magic takes time. Especially with my brother. Go easy on him, yeah? He hasn't had the easiest road."

What? Hell no.

"What do you mean?" I ask a few moments later, my curiosity urging me on. "What happened to him?"

Brody leans in. "He needs magic, Emmy. More than anyone I know."

I shake my head and move on to make more drinks. I'm not buying anything Brody says.

Time crawls by as Graham orders a drink for the redhead, an espresso martini, then goes back to her. She asks for a photo of them, and he poses for a selfie, his face aloof. She flirts, even going so far as to dance her fingers down his arm. He barely even speaks, just nods or shakes his head while she talks. Seething, I turn away. He's torturing me, biding his time until I'm a nervous wreck.

"You should break them apart," Brody whispers in a conspiratorial tone.

I point at him with a stir stick. "You. Stop. And not on your life. Maybe she'll soften him up."

"She won't," he murmurs. "And I did my best to talk him out of this plan. Even today, I told him to let it all go, and I'll figure out the money side of things on my own, but once he makes up his mind about someone . . ."

I have no idea what he's rambling about.

"Another whiskey" comes from Graham, and I ignore him and mix a lemon drop.

"You okay down there? Need help?" Mason asks me.

"I'm good," I say, watching as Graham locks eyes with him, then comes right back to me. He arches one of his straight black eyebrows as if to say, *Hello? My drink?*

Uh-huh. He used the eyebrow at the motel. It says more than he does. It's a smart-ass, know-it-all eyebrow.

Huffing, I make the whiskey, then slam it down in front of him.

The redhead gives me a rude look, then sparkles up at him with a winsome smile as I linger to eavesdrop. She tells him she's headed out to a club and invites him to go with her and her friends.

Go, Graham. Have fun. Forget about me.

I audibly groan when he tells her he can't, that he has business to handle at the bar. Without a prompting from him, she writes her number on a napkin and gives it to him. With one last adoring look and a kiss to his cheek, she sashays away and out the door. He crumples the napkin in his hands, then drains his whiskey.

"Can we talk?" I ask him, my voice quiet.

"Oh yes," he says in a dark tone.

"Mason, I'm due a break," I call out to him. "Fifteen minutes, okay?"

Mason gives Graham a steely once-over. "Sure, Emmy. Want me to go with you?"

"No," I say.

"She's fine with me," Graham says, his tone curt.

Mason holds my eyes. "Yell out if you need me."

Graham stands to follow me as I walk around the bar and head to the exit outside. Pushing the door open, I look around, half expecting blue lights and sirens.

Brody's voice calls after us. "Be sweet, guys."

The wind whips my hair as thunder rumbles in the distance, a late-spring storm brewing in the air. Fitting. *Face the storm you've made,* I tell myself as I duck under the overhead canopy next door to the bar to wait for him.

He stalks to me, and I'm struck again by his massive height, his broad shoulders, the way his shirt stretches over his muscles. He crosses his arms to match mine. We're two feet apart, and the air wafts with the scent of his cologne.

I chew on my bottom lip, and he notices, his eyes landing there and staying. Two spots of color flare on his cheekbones, and he darts his gaze to a point over my shoulder.

Here goes nothing. A long exhale leaves my chest. "Graham, I'm truly sorry for the mess I made. Taking your car was inexcusable and wrong and impulsive. Extremely stupid. I'm old enough to know better. I've regretted it every day since it happened. I've had massive guilt over it. I am so sorry. So sorry. I can't say it enough. You have every right to be angry."

He grunts, unmoved.

Several moments pass, and I nod nervously, tension escalating when he doesn't reply.

"If it matters, I wasn't pretending in Arizona. I didn't know who you were. I imagine a man in your position, you're used to being recognized, but I was clueless. I missed it. My head was . . . all over the place at the motel."

"Your boyfriend is a player."

"My ex. He didn't play while we were together, and I don't follow sports. And how do you know?"

"Kian was waiting for you at the motel." Steely eyes narrow. "I can't see you with him. You . . . don't . . . fit."

He pauses between those last words, making it somehow more meaningful. I don't know if it's the cadence of how he speaks when he's emotional or if he's underlining that he knows what happened between me and Kian. My breath hitches. Of course—he saw my neck at the motel. Touching my throat, I drop my gaze to the ground as my insides twist. I'm deeply embarrassed about having been at Kian's mercy in Vegas. And the truth is that I was at his mercy in Old Town, because I didn't stay and face him. I ran instead.

"If you hadn't stolen my car, I might have had time to beat the shit out of him."

I glance up in surprise.

His eyes blaze with anger, not at me, but at Kian.

"I'm still angry with you, though," he mutters. "I'd had that car for two weeks. It was a Lamborghini Aventador."

I cringe. "I don't know what that means, but it sounds really expensive."

"Yes," he says grimly. "It was."

"How much?"

"Over four hundred."

"Thousand?" Nausea bubbles, and I put a hand to my stomach.

"Yes."

Oh my God. I can't even . . .

I might pass out. I lean against the brick of the boutique and cover my face with my hands in horror for a few moments, then drop them. "Why would you spend that kind of money on a car?"

He cocks his head. "Really? That's what you want to say after stealing it? You *drove* it. It has 740 horsepower, goes from zero to sixty in less than three seconds, with a speed up to 220 miles per hour. It's fucking beautiful."

"Where on earth would you drive that fast?"

"The desert. Until it was taken. By you."

Right. "I just wanted to borrow it. You weren't in your room when I knocked, but you'd left your key, and then my mind went off kilter, and I was convinced Kian would talk me into going back to Vegas. I needed to get away from him as fast as possible. In hindsight, I could have run to the diner or hidden in the desert, but then I'm really scared of scorpions and wolves. I should have just faced him."

"Why did you run away from him?"

I inhale a deep breath, debating my next words. "To give you some background, my parents had a very turbulent relationship. My dad drank, used drugs, couldn't hold a job. He hurt my mom." I glance away from him, my head swirling with memories of my mom with black eyes, a broken arm, ribs. She'd eventually forgive him; then they'd have this honeymoon phase, with flowers and candy and vacations. "As a kid, watching the abuse happen in front of you, it changes you and never leaves. When they'd fight, I always ran and hid. And I guess that's what I did in Vegas."

"I'm sorry that happened to you."

I nod as my throat prickles with emotions. Images flash through my head of my father dragging my mother across the floor by her hair that last night. I hear her sobs, begging him to stop. Jane was only three, and Andrew was two. I pulled them into the hall closet and watched through a crack in the door as it unfolded.

"Are you okay?" he asks.

"When I was ten years old . . ." My words trail off.

"Yes?"

I feel color rising in my cheeks, and I put my hands there to cool them off.

It's okay.

I'm not *there*.

I'm here.

I'm fine.

I'm good.

I'm a fighter. A survivor.

"What happened?" he asks, his brows lowering.

A tangled knot builds in my chest, then releases. "My mom shot him." I say the words woodenly, keeping emotion bottled up inside. "She was beaten down, broken, and afraid for her life."

His mouth parts. "What?"

I nod. "She was charged with manslaughter but was acquitted." Gran hired the best lawyers, researchers, and psychologists to help Bryony, my mom. Gran brought in advocates of domestic abuse, organized marches, and did radio shows and podcasts. The truth is many domestic abuse women end up serving long sentences for protecting themselves against their abuser, and Gran didn't want that to happen for my mom.

"And now? Your mom?"

"She moved to Costa Rica." She didn't even come to Gran's funeral. The only communication I have with her is via text, and that is rare. I haven't seen her since I was ten years old.

Part of me understands that she left to cope with her own trauma. She felt the sting of his fists, and perhaps she even kept him from hitting us, but the other side of me feels abandoned by the person who was supposed to always protect me.

Pushing those memories away, I raise my face to his. "I told you this deeply private thing because when Kian hurt me, it reminded me of my childhood. I just wanted to run. It's not an excuse, just an explanation."

He studies me intently, his gaze lingering over each feature as if he is trying to see into my soul. I have to glance away.

"I swear I parked it at the airport and left your keys on the tire—"

"And someone saw you and stole it."

I gasp. "What? No."

"It's on a surveillance camera. A man was in the garage when you pulled in. He grabbed the keys and took the car for a joyride and wrecked it. No clue who he is. Which brings us to you. You're responsible. You stole my car first."

I grimace, picturing the scene in my head, me getting out of the car, stashing his keys, then darting for the elevator to get to ticketing in the airport so I could leave Arizona. I wasn't paying attention if anyone else was around me.

"So you've confronted me. Do I need to pay for damages?" The mere idea of more debt makes me want to drop to my knees and weep.

"You have that kind of money?"

"No. Do I need to turn myself in? Be handcuffed? Get fingerprinted?"

"About that. I have"—he looks away, his hands flexing—"a proposal."

If he says he wants some kind of sex thing, I'm going to freak. "I'm listening."

"I'm in need of a wife."

Chapter 7
GRAHAM

Emmy Darling stares at me in shock, and I tear my gaze off her parted lips. Her chest rises rapidly as she grapples with my words. Just like at the motel, her delicate features make her look incredibly young and innocent. But she has a glint in her eyes, an inner fire, and she still smells of vanilla, the sweet scent lingering.

The story of her parents has gotten under my skin. I understand it. I know what it's like to be hurt or forgotten by those who are supposed to love us. My father put me and Brody in an all-boys boarding school in Connecticut a week after my mother's death. It cut me to the bone to lose the only home I'd ever known.

Pushing that aside, I roll my shoulders, trying to relax. I'm not myself because a lot is riding on this. It's a lot of pressure to marry a stranger and do it in such a way as to not raise red flags to the rest of the family.

Brody is depending on me, and I'm going to deliver.

"Are you messing with me?" Her voice is soft, layered with hesitation.

"No."

Her slender arms cross. "Is this a sex thing, where you keep me prisoner in a dungeon?"

I groan and press the tips of my fingers to the bridge of my nose. "Jesus, your imagination is off the charts, and no, I don't force myself on women. I don't want to marry, but I need a wife. We never have to have sex."

"Are you gay?"

"If I were, I'd live it proud, like my brother and Cas."

"But . . . why me?"

"Because you owe me. You'll be motivated to be the best wife you can be, and apparently you're a great actress. You fooled the asshole at the motel, and that's what I need—someone to convince the world that we're . . . in love." It sounds lame out loud, and the truth is, I'm not sure why it has to be *her*. I exhale.

"Are you in the mafia?"

"No."

"Do you want me to steal drugs or art or jewels?"

"Fuck no."

"Do you plan to put me in some sick game where I get chased on an island by people who hunt humans for sport?"

"What? That's . . . I don't even know what that is. Wait, is that from one of your books?"

"Short story, 'The Most Dangerous Game.' A big-game hunter falls off a ship and gets stranded on an island run by a Russian aristocrat who's been hunting humans as sport. The big-game guy, Rainsford, becomes his next human, very ironic, but back to you. What do you get out of marrying me? What are the benefits?"

I rub my temple. "A headache, probably."

"So why do it?"

"I'll get an inheritance if I'm married."

"So it's true. Rich people only want to be richer."

I groan. "It's for Brody, because he can't claim his." I hadn't planned to admit that, but . . .

"Why not just give him the money yourself?"

"I tried. He's proud. His inheritance won't go to him because he's married to Cas. It's about conservative family politics."

"Because he's gay?"

"Yes. Brody came out right before our grandma died, so she left him out on purpose."

She exhales. "That's awful, but why would you want to get married just to help him?"

Because Brody needs justice.

Because I detest Holden.

And maybe because I met Emmy.

"He's my brother. I take it you aren't a fan of marriage?" My eyes drift over the curve of her cheeks, the way her pouty lips press together.

"I'm more of a bookish spinster type."

A beautiful one. I take in the long wavy blonde hair, the arch of her golden brows, the high cheekbones.

I also see the shadows that play over her face, and a cold realization dawns on me.

Kian.

"I'm not . . . I'm not a cruel person. I wouldn't hurt you like Kian." I may have a temper on the field, but I'd never put hands on a woman. Another reason to marry her flits through my head. I could protect her from him.

"Were you following me today?"

I frown. "No."

"Never mind," she says as worry flits over her features. "It was just a feeling I had."

"Was it Kian?"

"It was probably nothing. Just my paranoia." She chews on her bottom lip. "Look, I don't want to go to prison. But I also don't like being put in a corner. This is very sudden, and I can't just upend my life and get married. What would people think? What would we tell them?"

I wince that she thinks I'd actually send her to prison. Yes, the police came to the motel after I called, but once they arrived, I left her name out of it. Some part of me didn't want to implicate her. Maybe it was the memory of the bruises on her throat. Maybe it was seeing Kian and realizing he was the one who'd put them there.

"It'll be easy," I reply. "We'll get married for a few months, then get a divorce. We'll never have to see each other again."

She narrows her eyes, searching my face as if trying to figure me out. "The question is: Will you send me to prison if I don't marry you?"

I exhale heavily.

She studies my face, seems to make up her mind about something, then pulls out her phone. "Go ahead, then—call the cops, have me locked up, let the scorpions eat me alive. Just remember that I didn't wreck your beloved car; I only *borrowed* it—"

"Police would say felony theft."

"—and left it at the airport. Yes, it was stupid and impulsive, but it wasn't malicious."

My jaw pops.

"I ran when I should have faced Kian, I know, but knowing it and doing it are two separate things. I'm sorry. Just know that you'd be sending a woman to jail who takes care of her siblings and a baby."

Twenty seconds pass, the air crackling with tension.

"Don't you think you owe me this, Emmy?" I glare at her. Of course I don't want to call the cops.

Several tense moments pass as neither of us drops our gaze.

A small laugh comes from her as she tucks her phone away. "Did insurance cover your car's damages?"

"Yes," I say tightly.

"Thank God," she says as she blows out a breath. "I have enough money problems as it is."

I rake a hand through my hair, trying to find a way to convince her. "I could help with your money issues."

"No thanks."

"And Kian. If you marry me, he won't be bothering you."

She curls her lips at me. "I don't know anything about you, other than you're a football player. Where are you from? Are you a creep?"

I list them off on my fingers. "I played football in Seattle, then got traded to the Pythons. I'm a creep. Obviously. I'm asking a stranger to marry me."

She huffs. "Don't you want to get married for real someday?"

From deep inside me, an unexpected yearning hits me. I recall being on the field, dead, and seeing a woman showing me a beautiful life, of how I could be alive in a way I'd never experienced before. I remember the feeling of peace and tranquility. Of happiness.

She smirks when I don't reply. "Guess you're not a believer in the fairy tale, either, huh?"

"Nope. Which makes us perfect." I pace around the sidewalk, shoving my hands in my pockets. I'm sure she's seen how I clench them, and she probably thinks I'm ready to pounce on her. I'm not. I'm fucking nervous. More nervous than I should be. I never dreamed I'd ask a woman to marry me after Divina.

I grab a business card from my wallet and hand it over, avoiding our fingers brushing. "My number is there. You aren't the only person I'm asking, so don't take long. I'd like this handled by the end of the week. I also expect discretion. No one can know the details of what I've asked you—even if I marry someone else . . ." I let my words trail off as I raise an eyebrow.

She rubs the card between her fingers. "I have competition. Hilarious."

The silence builds between us. My heart picks up. I expected her to say yes on the spot, but she's got fire in her.

Which I admire.

I rub my jaw as unease trickles over me. I'm weirded out by what I've proposed, and I need to breathe some Emmy-free air.

"Don't take too long to call me." As I turn to leave, my hand brushes hers, and an electric thrill ghosts down my arm. I push it down and walk away.

Chapter 8

GRAHAM

Jasper throws me the ball, and I run for the goal line as the other team barrels toward me. I do a fake and dodge, but a beefy linebacker catches up and tackles me to the ground with a crash. My head explodes with pain, and the impact reverberates through my bones. The world spins in dizzying circles. A body rolls over mine. And another. I'm crushed, like I'm in a giant iron vise, being squeezed and twisted until my insides beg for mercy.

I can't breathe.

I clutch my chest.

Icy tendrils of terror take over. I'm dying. And no one is here to help me.

I scream, but no one hears me, not a single soul.

But her.

Beautiful girl.

Green eyes.

Long blonde hair.

Champagne and sunlight—

I jerk away, my chest heaving as I shove away the dream. My hands clench the covers on the bed, grappling for reality. Sweat drips from my forehead. That feeling of dread from being tackled still clings to me as I get up and head to the bathroom. I splash water on my face and look at myself in the mirror. I look ashen. That's the second time this week. How am I supposed to play in a real game if this shit is in my head?

After putting on joggers and a hooded Pythons sweatshirt, I pad out of the bedroom and walk to the kitchen with its orange cabinets and psychedelic yellow-and-black flower-themed wallpaper, giving it a frozen-in-time look from the seventies.

The carpet in the den is shag, and the furniture is avocado green, from the couch to the club chairs. Which are newish. Someone wanted this place to look like Elvis might have lived here. The dining room table even has a disco ball over it.

I recently bought this particular apartment because Brody and Cas live on the same floor, in a smaller two-bedroom. Jasper lives here as well, but his apartment is on another floor.

After coffee, I'm at a neurologist's office on the Upper West Side, a doctor recommended by River Tate, our wide receiver. Apparently, Dr. Moreau is a superstar brain lady.

I pull my hoodie down over my sunglasses. Not exactly a disguise, but I don't want to be recognized in the office, or worse, videoed. There's already enough talk about my injury.

A receptionist smiles as she opens a door to a posh exam room. "This is our VIP room, Mr. Harlan. Dr. Moreau will be with you in just a moment."

The room has a couch and two leather chairs. On the coffee table is a to-scale model of the human brain on a stand. Made of silicone, it jiggles.

"Please don't fondle my brain, Mr. Harlan," says a voice with a heavy French accent.

I jerk my hand off the model like a kid with his hand in the cookie jar and turn around to see a petite woman with short white hair. Small wire glasses frame intelligent blue eyes. Her back is slightly bent, but it doesn't stop her from hurrying over to me.

I pull my sunglasses off and tuck them into my pocket. I feel massive next to her. "Sorry, I . . ."

"I'm Dr. Moreau," she says, cutting me off as she holds out her hand, limp wristed.

Do I shake it or kiss it? I take her fingers in an odd embrace.

She sits in one of the chairs.

I look at the other chair and then back to the couch.

"Should I sit there, or over here, or . . ."

"Just sit. There is a couch, but this is not therapy."

Yes, ma'am. I take the couch because it's bigger, and I need more room than she does.

She pops open her laptop. "I have looked over your most recent charts and scans. You've seen some of the best neuro-specialists in the city. I also see we managed to fit you in today after a cancellation. Lucky you. Some people wait months. I am, what do they say, a little unorthodox but brilliant. I speak my mind and expect you to do so as well. Now. Why see me?"

I clasp my hands together, the tension in my shoulders making me twitch. "My team cleared me to play football, but I'd like a second opinion."

The tight end coach, Marlon, gave me the news a week ago, while I was working out with Brody and Cas. I'd nearly wept in thankfulness. Being cleared was the best news I could have hoped for, but that night, doubts crept in, and the dreams.

She nods. "I am happy to do this. What's their latest opinion—in your words?"

"That I'm healed from the concussion."

"You want to play very much, yes?"

"Of course," I say, eyeing her warily.

She taps her chin. "I saw your injury on television. I lost money on you; I bet your team would lose. You did not."

A prickle of irritation buzzes in the back of my head, but I squash it down.

She looks down at her tablet and types a quick note. "I see my insensitive comment did not bother you much."

I lean back in my chair. "Not everyone is a fan."

"Would you say you are easier to anger now?"

Not really. I mean, sure, I wanted to pound on Kian a while back, but I would have anyway. "No."

"Good. This is very good. I like this. So now continue. Tell me about the physical issues you suffered."

"Headaches and dizziness mostly. I'm off the pain meds I was on, mostly Tylenol, and working out. I feel great." I haven't had one symptom since my headache at the diner in the desert.

"I see you were diagnosed with postconcussive syndrome, very common among athletes."

"It made me want to punch a hole in the wall," I say grimly.

"Don't do it in my office. And your heart?"

"Passed all my tests. There was never an issue with it."

She types in rapid fire. "I suspect your heart issue on the field was because of the violent collision to your brain."

I wince. "I wouldn't say 'violent.'"

Surprising me, she stands, picks up the brain model on the table, and slams it down on the coffee table. It makes a horrible smacking sound, ripples vibrating through the silicone model for several seconds. "This was your brain at the Super Bowl."

"Right, but I had a helmet on. Our protective equipment in the NFL is better than in any contact sport." I tap my temple. "And I have a skull."

"And I'm just a little old lady throwing a brain model on a table, and you got yanked down by a three-hundred-pound lineman. Are we going to argue over this?"

I exhale. "All right, I get it. I hit my head hard."

She sits back down and studies me from head to toe. I feel like a specimen under a microscope. "No bullshit with me, Mr. Harlan. I've seen people suffer the effects from this type of concussion for more than a year. We cannot know how long it will last. Just because you have no headache today does not mean it is gone."

My jaw tics. "I am healed."

She points a wrinkled finger at me, eyes keen. "So your brain looks good on scans. They clear you to play. Big whoop. So far you pay me for things you already know. What else should I help you with? Ask me your questions, and I will be brutally honest."

Dread coils tighter. "I'm worried about CTE, chronic traumatic encephalopathy."

She narrows her gaze. "What did your other doctors say about CTE?"

"They told me to get off the internet."

"True. CTE is a brain disease from repetitive trauma." She picks up the brain model and slaps it on the coffee table three times, each smack making me cringe. "Your doctors are correct: there is no documented evidence about how many concussions increase the risk of CTE or even if the *severity* will increase the risk. Why is this?"

"Because they don't know if you have it until you're dead."

She nods. "CTE can only be diagnosed with autopsy, so it is difficult to gather data because people usually do not want autopsy while alive. So, we have no good answer."

She stands and shuffles over to a poster on the wall that shows two brains. Surrounding the brains are microscopic pictures and little lines pointing back to the diagrams. She points to the poster. "Two brains are here, one good, one CTE. In an MRI, you see no difference, both good brains." She points a finger in the air. "*But* in autopsy we take tiny slices and look under the microscope."

I grimace, aware that many athletes donate their bodies to science after they pass away.

She points at the microscopic pictures of the CTE brain. "This is where we see tiny black splotches between and around the cells. These areas, they do not work anymore. They have atrophied. They died because they don't have blood flow or have a damaged neurological pathway. When you have lots of these black spots in your brain, you think differently, sometimes depressed, sometimes angry, sometimes forgetful. Maybe this is caused in a football player that has one big concussion. Maybe this is caused in a football player that has many, many little concussions. We can't tell."

I twist my Rolex, anxiety rippling.

She shrugs. "There are many autopsies of players that had many concussions in the record, and the doctors see *no* CTE. On the other hand, do you know story of Jonah Truman?"

Jonah died when he fell out of the back of a boat while on vacation. "Wide receiver for Atlanta. It was terrible what happened to him."

"How many years did he play?"

"Not too long—I just met him a few times."

She twirls her wrist in the air. "Four years is the right answer. He had *no* documented concussions in high school, college, or pro. They don't hit Jonah so much because he was very fast on his feet. His autopsy showed CTE, minuscule, yes, but there. He never knew he had it or probably never felt any issue from it. So the correct answer is, no one knows how many concussions will be bad."

That sucks. "So what advice do you have?"

Her gaze rakes me up and down. "I can tell you are an athletic man. You need exercise. You need to feel worthy. The most dangerous sport in the world is surprising. It is cycling. Then, football and hockey. Basketball and baseball are next. I would tell you to try swimming, but then you might hit your head on the diving board or the bottom of the pool. All sports leave you open to CTE, even going for a jog. You might trip over the sidewalk and bang your head on a fire hydrant or a street sign. Bang. Concussion. Possible traumatic brain injury, or TBI."

"Shit."

"Yes, merde. Lots and lots of shit. But we cannot hide in a hole to protect ourselves from getting injured, because all life is a risk. You walk out of the house, and boom, you might die from a piece of the space station that falls from the sky."

"Unlikely."

"Anything is possible, Mr. Harlan. Do not joke."

"Sorry." This is what I came for. She isn't treating me with kid gloves like the team doctors.

"You only have three recorded concussions," Dr. Moreau continues as she glances down at her laptop. "You are not experiencing quick anger. You are not forgetful. Your brain scans are normal. If you were symptomatic, then I would say, no, that you need to heal, but you say you have no headache, no dizziness, so I say okay, fine, take a risk. It is up to you. There's a baseball saying: you can't steal second base without taking your foot off first."

My breath quickens.

Football *is* worth the risk.

I'm already picturing myself in my uniform and on the field, Jasper passing me the ball.

"But I am *not* God," she declares as she points at me. "I do not know what will happen to you in life. So, I can only give facts. The truth is, you suffered a severe concussion, Mr. Harlan. You may have the beginnings of CTE right now, even though you aren't symptomatic." She folds her hands in front of herself. "This is the end. Do you have questions?"

My eyes shut briefly. "Thank you. I can't tell you how relieved I am."

She frowns. "No, no, don't be relieved. *Be wary.* Be afraid. I do not know the future, Mr. Harlan. That is the entire point. As a doctor, I must warn you about playing this sport. I cannot see the *inside* of your brain. I wish I could, so I could give you a definitive answer, but it is impossible. Your next tackle might be the end."

"Yes, I got all of that, I did, but the odds are in my favor. I've only had a few concussions in my life."

"Jonah had *none* on his record, Mr. Harlan, and he had CTE."

Sure, but she's being cautious. Most doctors who aren't affiliated with sports will always warn you against playing.

She sighs. "Life is a game of chance. Some win, some lose. I hope you win. Anyway, I promise not to bet against you next time."

My smile is lopsided. "Right, thanks for that. Actually, if you have some time, I do have some other questions for you . . ."

She nods and motions for me to sit again.

After we get settled, I take a deep breath, hoping she doesn't think I'm imagining what happened to me. "When I was on the field and I was . . . dead . . . something happened. It wasn't like a light at the end of a tunnel or some kind of religious experience like you see in the movies. It was strange and weird. I'm not into any kind of psychic stuff or woo-woo science or whatever you want to call this, but . . ."

"Interesting. What was it?"

"Visions, like I was on acid. I saw my brother, my parents, a girl I used to date, but the rest of it, the part that eludes me, or comes in dreams, I don't know, was different, almost peaceful, like another possible life I could have had. The images are hazy, and if I concentrate hard enough, I might be able to see them, but I can't."

"Ah, very odd. Was there a feeling associated with it? Did you think it was heaven?" She gives me a smirk. "Hell?"

"No, nothing like that, but it made me want to wake up, like I had to come back because there was someone waiting for me . . ." I sigh. "I can't explain it. My question is: Is it normal to see things when you're clinically dead?"

She slides down her glasses and peers at me. "I do not talk to many people who have died. You are special like this. Gold star."

"Thanks," I say dryly.

"This is not my field of study, but in my opinion, it is possible it was your brain gasping, much like a computer shutting down, but instead of going black, it flashes with images from your life. We refer to this phenomenon as NDEs, or near-death experiences. People who experience them often say they see scenes from their childhood, even going all the way back to being in the womb, but again, it is hard to study because there are few people who this happens to, and it is also hard to *believe* people. Most of us want to discount this because it seems impossible. But I do not know. What you have in common with these people is two things: it usually happens after head trauma or cardiac arrest, and they usually occur in cases where emergency medical help is required to survive."

She gives me a tiny smile. "Like I say, no therapy here. You will find many books about the topic, about people who claim to have experienced it. Are they true? I do not know. I cannot advise on what happened when you were clinically dead, but I believe you saw what you saw. It happened. It was your experience. It is valid. There are many things we do not know about the brain—or life—after we die. Was it a sign from a higher consciousness or lack of oxygen to your brain?" She shrugs. "I do not know, but I like this peace you described. That is something, yes?"

Maybe.

It just . . . feels important.

"I want to call you and check up on you soon. I'd like to know how you are doing. Also, I'm going to find some studies about CTE and send to you."

I tell her to call me whenever she wants.

Later, I leave her office, my mind churning. She scared the shit out of me, smacking that brain around, but my scans *are* fine.

I'm not having anger issues.

I'm not forgetful.

My headaches are gone.

I'm fucking fine to play.

My phone buzzes with a call from Jasper, our quarterback. "What's up?"

"Where are you?" he asks. "I'm outside your door to see if you wanted to hang, maybe grab some fajitas."

I smile. "I get it. Since we're neighbors now, you're gonna be popping by my place all the time."

He makes a scoffing sound. "If you're lucky. Everyone wants a piece of me. Why would you be different? Besides, you're my bestie. Me and you are lightning on the field, baby. Just don't be like Tuck and get married. He left me, and I never see him anymore. Marriage is for pussies. Me and you, bachelors to the end."

Tuck Avery was the Pythons' star wide receiver, but he'd retired by the time I was traded to the team.

"I'm second choice?" I ask. "After winning the Super Bowl? You bought Tuck a friendship bracelet. Where's mine?"

"Fuck right off. And you're *convenient*, so don't get a big head. Proximity is good for friendship. Are you in your apartment or not?"

I picture him stalking outside my door, curly blond hair sticking everywhere as he searches for a lunch partner.

Jasper grew up in a close-knit middle-class family from Utah. His four older sisters petted him rotten and lavished attention on him. Over Christmas, the entire family flew to New York to stay at his place, and he hired two interior decorators to make the place look like a winter wonderland. He had seven Christmas trees, each one adorned with decorations for every person in his family, including himself. He took them everywhere, the zoo, ice-skating, shopping. I tagged along when Brody and Cas were too busy for me and watched his sisters treat him like a precious doll, playing with his hair and feeding him special treats like an overgrown puppy.

"Are you ever alone, Precious?" I ask. "Do you do things by yourself?"

"I *am* fucking precious, so I'm not gonna fight you about the nickname. I'm a social animal. I love people. People love me. I'm pretty much a superstar. I am adored."

"So last's night date has already gone home, huh? Needing to feel validated?"

"Seriously, cut the shit—my stomach's rumbling. Do you wanna grab a bite or not? I'm starving after my workout, which you missed. Where you at?"

I exit the office building, slip on my shades, and flip the hoodie back up. No way am I admitting I went to see another doctor. It would make me look scared. "Out."

"Where is out?"

I huff out a laugh. "Do you ever give up? I'm at the dry cleaners." I am walking past one.

"I call bullshit. You have your clothes delivered to you. What's going on?"

I stop at the pedestrian crossing, my mind buzzing with thoughts of Dr. Moreau and all the what-ifs. I could get hit by a car today, be mugged, or come down with cancer. A subtle fear creeps in, of all the things that could happen that are out of my control, but I shove it away.

Life is about living.

Enjoying the moment.

And I don't want to have a world without football.

Like a kid, I raise my face to the sun in appreciation and feel a slight breeze. I inhale the smells of the city, mostly oil and asphalt, but there's also the subtle scent of flowers growing in windows and planted along the sidewalk.

New. Fresh. My injury is healed. The world is my oyster.

I cross the road, lightness in my step. I don't know what the future holds, but I'm ready to tackle it head-on.

And . . .

There's something else—someone—I can't give up.

Emmy Darling is the one. My gut knows it. Perhaps I was too overbearing last night, but it was a slap in the face to see her again. Something about her . . . pricks at me, like a ghost dancing down my spine. I know her from somewhere.

Regardless, it's time for a new strategy, and I have the perfect idea.

I clutch the phone. "I'd love to eat with you, but I'm going to see my lawyer."

"Oh shit, now we're talking. See, this is what I mean. We need to share. What did you do? Want me to come with? I'll be your backup."

"Nah."

"What's it about?"

I stare at the sky and chuckle. Jasper is a nosy son of a bitch. He's always poking his head in where it doesn't belong, but his heart is golden.

"I'm planning the future."

Jasper lowers his voice. "You're not getting traded, are you? Fuck. If you are, I'm quitting the team."

I laugh. He'd never. He *is* worshipped in New York.

"Nah, man, I hate to break the bad news over the phone, but . . ."

"What? Tell me!"

I grin. "I wish I was with you because I'd really love to see your face. I'm getting married, Precious. Don't be mad. It happens to all of us at some point. See ya later."

He lets out a vivid curse and yells, "*Nooooooo.*"

Still smiling, I click the phone off and start the walk to my lawyer's office a few blocks away.

Chapter 9

EMMY

"Um, book lady on the floor, hello, are you listening?" a voice says behind me, and I start as I look up and see two teen girls, one brown haired, the other a strawberry blonde. I'm literally on the floor as I reshelve books left in the reading area downstairs. I assume the girls tried to get my attention before, but my mind has been distracted since meeting with Graham a few days ago.

"Yes, how can I help?" I brush the dust off my red dress. It's a little retro number with a black velvet collar and buttons down the front. Sadly, there's a splash of coffee where my breast is and a hole in my fishnet hose, right on the knee. The coffee happened this morning while serving a customer, and the hole occurred minutes ago. I don't usually reshelve books, but we're down three employees.

Magic perks his head out from the top shelf above me. His stubby tail swishes.

The strawberry blonde, maybe fifteen and dressed in a preppy school skirt and blazer, knee socks, and saddleback shoes, steps forward. "Hi, we're looking for an autographed copy of William Shakespeare's *Romeo and Juliet*."

I do a little clap. "Oh, wow. Please tell me if you find one."

She scowls. "Don't you have those? Any good bookstore would."

I exhale, not in frustration, but in glee. I *live* for these bookstore moments. Girls, it's time for a trip down memory lane . . .

"Well," I say with a smile. "You're not the first student to come in and ask for this, but I've got some bad news for you."

"Are you out of them?" asks the other girl as she does a little hair flip. "Do we need to go to Lottie's Bookstore? They do have better coffee."

How dare she?

"I assure you, we are the best bookstore in Manhattan, but back to your book . . . Shakespeare doesn't have any autographed copies in any bookstore, and if he did, they'd be worth about, hmm, six to seven million dollars." My hand rests on my chest dramatically. "What I'd give to come across one."

They glance at each other, still confused, then almost in unison say, "But our teacher said to get one."

"Right. Follow me." They fall in line behind me as I lead them to the other side of the third floor to the fiction section, my thigh-high heeled boots clicking against the tile. "FYI: there are no original copies of his manuscripts, signed or not. There's not even a couplet written with his name under it. In fact, there are only about six items in the world with Shakespeare's signature, and none of them relate to his plays. They're on things like wills and deeds. What's really crazy is when we stop and think about the absence of this signature, we have to ask ourselves: What if he *wasn't* the author of those plays? Shocking, right?"

"Seriously? We didn't come for a lecture," the strawberry blonde says with a long, aggrieved sigh.

I nod and keep going. "I love a good lecture. What we *do* know about William Shakespeare is he only went to primary school, his parents were illiterate, and so were his children. I mean, why wouldn't a man who'd written such moving pieces of literature educate his own children? And, when he died, there was no public mourning, even when people had flocked to see his plays. It's just baffling."

"I'm not baffled. Are we there yet?" one of them says.

I trudge on. "Almost. If you're into conspiracies—I am—some believe that Christopher Marlowe, a writer of the same time period, was really Shakespeare. Did you ask how? No? Let me explain. Marlowe was despised because of his antireligious works, and nearly *everyone* in the late sixteenth century was religious. So, the theory is that Marlowe faked his sudden death—supposedly stabbed in a bar—because he was also a *spy* for the Tudor court, plus there was a warrant out for his arrest. Marlowe was in deep shit. Then, two weeks after his *supposed* death, voilà, the first work of William Shakespeare goes on sale. How's that for intriguing?"

"You need to take a break from Shakespeare," one of them mutters.

"Right. To each their own. 'To thine own self be true,'" I say.

"What are you even saying?" one of them says.

I wave her off. It's over now. The moment has passed. They didn't get it.

"Anyway, your teacher meant for you to buy one of these. Just a regular copy." I indicate the correct shelf and grab two paperbacks of *Romeo and Juliet* off the shelf and put them in their hands. "I hope you learned something today. Enjoy the play. Mercutio is my fav. Oh, and it's a real tearjerker."

They smirk. "We know how it ends, book lady. They die."

"'Parting is such sweet sorrow.'" And with those words, I mosey away, and Magic meets me at the end of the row. *What fresh hell were you spouting?* his eyes convey. I give him a pet and head to the staircase as he follows. He's fit in well in our apartment, and the expression on Londyn's face when she first saw him was priceless. Pure amazement.

The PA system clicks on, and Babs's voice blares: "Emmy, we have a cream situation. Emmy to the main floor *for the cream.*"

Cream? Then it dawns, and I groan. Last month our coffee station got knocked over, and a large plastic container of french vanilla shattered when it hit the marble tile. Sticky, sugary white stuff oozed everywhere, and the floor squeaked for days. It took multiple moppings.

I'll need the big yellow bucket from the maintenance closet. Magic follows me as I hop on the elevator and take the ride to the basement and grab it. Ugh. The water is murky and hasn't been changed, so I refill it, wrestle the mop back in, get back on the elevator, and push the button for the first floor.

"Attention, Emmy, please hurry! We need you to *see the cream*," Babs says over the loudspeakers.

"I heard you the first time," I mutter as I shove the mop and bucket out of the elevator and onto our main floor.

A man catches me before I get too far. He's older, maybe fifty. "Do you have any books on . . . erotica?" he asks as he blushes. "It's for . . . a friend."

If Babs were here, she'd clasp his hand in hers, gush over her favs, and skip with him to the sexy books. I smile. "Sure. Second floor, on the right. You can't miss it."

I turn back to the bucket, and instead of bending over to push it, I shove it with one of my heels. The motion causes the wooden handle of the mop to whip back and bang my nose. Tears burst from my eyes at the pain. The inconvenience of not having a cleaning person ratchets up, and I curse vividly.

Babs dashes over. "You move like a tortoise. Why are you trying to break your face? You splashed water out on the floor."

"You try rolling this thing. It's heavy, and one of the wheels is wonky." I wring out the mop and rub it over the spilled water. "There."

"You shouldn't be doing this."

"Our maintenance person didn't show. Guess who's going to be here all night, cleaning? Me and you." I push the pail forward, this time by the mop handle. She keeps pace with me as we reach the condiment area. "Where's the creamer? You didn't mean the cream soda, did you?"

"There's no spilled creamer," she hisses. "Is that why you're dragging around this mop bucket like a bedraggled waif?"

Only booklovers use words like "bedraggled" and "waif."

"Babs. What's going on? Why are your eyes darting to the left?"

"Mr. Hottie in the *cream* suit is here. Remember? I told you all about him when you got back from your vacay. He's near the window. Don't you dare look, or he'll know we're talking about him, and it's bad enough that you're pushing a mop." She gives me an exasperated look. "What am I going to do with you?"

"The PA system isn't your personal alert system for good-looking guys."

"It is."

"No, it's not."

"Whatever. Pretty soon it won't even matter because we're closing for good. It's *him*. The one who asked for you."

"Jeez, stop hissing," I say. "I understood you the first time. He's the man who came by, and boy was he hot, blah, blah, blah. Where is he?"

Her eyes roll so hard I think for a moment her fake lashes might flop off. "I already told you. He's near the display. He asked for you to serve his tea."

A snort comes from me. I enjoy reading Jane Austen, but I don't pour your tea, my lord. "The nerve. I'm not a waitress. At least not here."

"Okay, well, he didn't really say, 'Tell her to serve my tea,' maybe I sort of added that part because it sounded exciting, but Emmy! He's interested in you. I'm telling you: there's a gleam in his gorgeous gray eyes, and—"

"Wait. Gray? Like storm clouds?"

"More like the polished silver of a spoon. The man is dripping in sex pheromones *and* money. Not that you're a gold digger, but, well, you are in a precarious sitch right now," she says, then winces. "I may have mentioned some things about you to him, so forgive me in advance, but you're my bestie and I knew your gran, and the truth is she'd want what I want, which is something wonderful in your life and someone—"

"Stop. What did you tell him?"

Her eyes flare, and her nose twitches like a rabbit's. She takes a bite of the scone in her hands. "I just told him how sweet you are, which isn't true today. I also told him you're looking for love."

"Babs! I am not! I have other things to worry about."

Her shoulders slump. "I know. Everything is falling apart. The store is closing. Anyway. He's waiting for you. Fix yourself and leave the mop bucket in the corner."

Magic twines between my legs and gives me an *Are you okay?* look. Yes, sweet cat, something is indeed brewing in the air, and it's not tea but an arrogant jerk who thinks I'd marry him because I took his car to the airport, and then it got stolen. And yes, I feel enormous guilt and remorse for taking his Lambo, but marriage? Never.

Holding the pastry in one hand, Babs scoops Magic up with the other and snuggles him. He seems to adore her and Terry and the rest of the staff.

"I'll feed the Prince of Darkness. You go see him—oh, and there's a woman with him, which I can't quite figure out, so there's that."

I'm muttering as I straighten my dress and head to the front area of the bookstore. I glance in a mirror on the wall, and sure enough, my nose looks like Rudolph. Merry Christmas.

There he is, looking like he just stepped out of a magazine, wearing a fitted long-sleeved pale-blue shirt and slim navy slacks. Dark hair is swept off his face, and his inviting lips are currently smiling at his companion. Combined with his broad shoulders and a chest that tapers to a trim waist, he's gorgeous.

He sits at a table with a petite brunette in a yellow dress with her hair swept up on each side with gold barrettes.

Pretty snazzy for a weekday.

Babs slides in next to me, vibrating with excitement. She must have fed Magic in record time. "Act nonchalant," she tells me. "Don't run him off with your 'romance only works in books' spiel."

I inhale a deep breath, steeling myself. "Guess that's his other possible fake wife . . ."

"What?"

"Nothing."

"So you know him? He isn't a stranger?"

"Graham Harlan, football star, mega wealthy, possible mafia or international art thief on the side."

"What?"

"Kidding. That's just my imagination."

Graham must feel the heat of my stare. He glances over at me and quirks one of his eyebrows. *Well,* it seems to say. *Fancy seeing you here. Come meet your competition.*

I feel a blush rising up my cheeks. At least I put on makeup today: total skin coverage, plus winged eyeliner and crimson lips. And my dress is hot. A little too short. A little too tight. Just perfect.

Maybe a tiny part of me hoped he'd stop by the bookstore. Pfft. I don't need a love interest, not that that even matters, since he's only proposing a marriage of convenience.

I approach the table, intent on keeping a smile plastered on my face.

He watches me with lowered lids, as if trying to make sense of my movements, my expressions, *my feelings.* His eyes brush over my hair, taking in the messy bun, the wisps that linger around my cheeks, and when he ends on my lips, my smile falters.

His gaze is so heavy and intimate that I almost forget to breathe.

His stare needs to be outlawed.

When he sees the coffee stain on my chest, everything inside me itches to grab a napkin off a table and wipe at it, but I hold back the urge, my heart thumping a little too fast for my taste.

Why is the air more alive around him? Crisper?

"This isn't Marcelle's," I say lightly when I reach them. "I don't wait tables here; in fact, no one does. Hello, Graham."

He merely nods, but the woman lights up with a beautiful smile, eagerness on her face. Her eyes are midnight blue, her teeth like little pearls. Dang, she's pretty.

"Of course not," she says, then sticks out her hand. "Hi, I'm Mina. Babs mentioned how hard you work on the displays. It's so . . . cute."

"Cute" is a word for kittens. Our windows are freaking divine. "Thank you," I murmur as I release her hand. "We'll have a new one up for the summer. The *Times* comes by for the reveal." I stop, a heaviness sinking in as I realize I forgot for a moment that we're closing permanently. I shake my head. "Sorry. That's incorrect. The store is closing soon. Sometimes I forget."

"Oh, that's disappointing," she says. "It's my first time here, and G mentioned we should stop by."

You don't say. How interesting.

He shrugs. "It's near my apartment at Wickham."

Ah, Wickham, an exclusive apartment complex that overlooks Central Park. Of course he would live there. How nice for him.

She gives him a secret smile. "We just came from his place. It's horrendous and totally needs to be renovated. He actually has a statue of a giant penis." She laughs, a dulcet sound. "Have you been, Emmy?"

Well, no, but I have stolen his car. It drives like a dream.

"No," I say sweetly, then turn to him and raise an eyebrow. *She's perfect,* my gaze says.

"Thanks," he replies dryly; then I get flustered because, hello, do we have some kind of mind connection?

"And for the record, the statue was in my apartment when I moved in," Graham says. "As was the shag carpet and weird sunken living room. I'm hoping someone can help me redecorate." He raises an eyebrow at me, which I ignore.

Mina laughs. "It's lime green and bolted to the ground—the penis, that is. You really must go see it."

"How fun," I murmur. *I'll never see his apartment, Mina. Because you're going to marry him, not me.*

I put on my customer smile. "So nice to meet you, Mina. The girl at the counter will be glad to take your order. Please try one of our pastries on the house. Now, if you'll excuse me, I need to get back to work—"

Before I can leave, Graham takes my hand. "Wait a moment, Emmy. Please," he murmurs.

Oh. Shivers dance over me.

It's hard to resist a "please" from him.

Mina rises from her seat with the grace of a swan. "I'll let you two chat while I take you up on a muffin. I'm going to try the pomegranate tea. Same for you, G?"

"Sure," he replies absently, eyes on me. "Thanks, Mina."

She glides away to go to the counter, and he says, "Will you sit for a moment?"

"Okay." I loosen my hand from his grasp and take a seat.

"Have you considered my offer?" His gaze lingers on my face.

It's all I've thought about. Instead of replying, I lean in and cup my chin, giving him my full attention. "What are you holding over Mina to get her to marry you?"

"Nothing. She adores me. Isn't it obvious?"

"So you're going for the romantic angle? Love and devotion?"

He leans back in his chair, a relaxed smirk on his face. "You remind me of Brody, as if all women hate me. It really isn't true. You stole my dream car, and now you're breaking my heart, Emmy."

"You're different today," I say. He's softer. Sexier. More relaxed. It must be Mina. "What's going on? Got an ace up your sleeve? Are the cops waiting outside for me?"

His lips twitch. "Your imagination is adorable. I'm enjoying watching you work. Nice dress."

My breath quickens as I realize I'm playing with one of the buttons, and his eyes are following me.

He leans in on the table to match my pose. "And who says Mina's my fiancée? Jealous?"

My teeth click together as Mina arrives with a pomegranate tea for Graham. She places it and a croissant in front of him, then says she's going to wander around the store for a bit.

Pain twinges in the center of my skull, one I can no longer ignore, and I rub my temple.

His brows pull down. "Headache?"

"Hmm. I thought it would disappear by now, but it seems to be getting worse. Sorry if I'm not the best conversationalist right now."

He takes a napkin from the dispenser and hands it to me. "It's fine, but your mascara is running, and the bridge of your nose is turning purple. What's going on?"

I dab at my eyes. "I banged my nose on a mop. You might have enjoyed it." A rueful smile crosses my lips. "I'm shocked it isn't bleeding."

"Come with me." He stands and holds out his hand, and I hesitantly put mine in his.

"You want to look at it? Why?"

"I'm a football player. I know my injuries. The first thing we need to do is put some ice on it and make sure it isn't fractured. I also want to make sure you don't have a concussion."

"From a mop handle?"

"Trust me, anything is possible, plus nose hits sting like a bitch. I've taken a few of them just messing around with the guys. Where's the kitchen?"

"Um, behind the counter, through the swinging doors."

He doesn't release my hand as we pass a wide-eyed Babs at the counter, checking out the teen girls from earlier. Eyeballing Graham, they squeal in excitement, then take their purchases and rush over to us. One of them grabs his sleeve, and he disentangles himself and tells her that he's on his private time.

"Does that happen a lot?" I ask as we leave them behind.

"Hmm, you may not know this, but I'm famous."

"Did the player that pulled your face mask get fined or what?"

"Technically, the defense would have gotten a fifteen-yard penalty, but since I crossed the goal line anyway, it didn't matter," he says. "We won. It was a high-pressure game, and people react on instinct. Sometimes the caveman takes over on the field."

I stop, surprise flickering over me. "Wait. You actually have empathy for him? Even after all the problems it must have given you?"

"I believe he didn't mean for what happened to happen. It's a risk we all take when we put on the uniform. I'm angry it's fucked with me for months, but I've been cleared to play. I'll start this fall."

I frown. After discovering who he was, I watched the video of his tackle several times. He'd fallen into a tangle of arms and legs, then lay on the field while everyone else got to their feet. He didn't move. Not an inch. The crowd hushed. The other team prayed. His team formed a wall around him for privacy as the paramedics used a defibrillator to bring him back. I've had a similar thing done, to shock my heart back into normal rhythm.

We walk into the kitchen, and our hands drift apart. Tilting my chin up, he searches my face. With surprisingly gentle fingers he touches the top of my nose. Concern etches his features. "I don't feel a break, and it doesn't look misshapen. Your eyes look fine but might bruise later. Do you feel nauseous or dizzy?"

"No."

But my heart is suddenly thumping like a snare drum.

Dammit, I like this vulnerable side of him, his care. True, he's a towering man with muscles, seemingly invincible, but there's a gentleness about him that makes my heart tighten.

He smells intoxicating, and with our faces this close, I notice the feathery lines at the corners of his mercurial eyes. I see a small scar on his temple. I take in the strong muscles in his throat, the light dusting of dark hair I see below his neck. I wonder if there's a lot of hair on his chest. My mind wanders, and I imagine his abdomen, if he has a six- or an eight-pack; then I'm tangled up in thoughts about his penis—is there a curve, which direction does it point, is he circumcised, if his height and broad shoulders suggest a girthy cock, and what color the spring of hair would be—

And nope. I have a cat.

"Yeah, I don't think I have a concussion," I say as I ease away, grab a ziplock bag, and fill it with ice from the machine.

Leaning against the stainless steel counter, I press the bag to my face, focusing on the bridge of my nose and not the man next to me.

"So, tell me about this fight with the mop. You lost?"

"I banged it while pushing the bucket we use to mop up spills. Some of our employees didn't show, so I'm doing odd jobs."

"Ah."

I exhale. The mop incident is just another reminder that the store is going away. My stomach churns all over again. "I guess you saw the sign on the door. We're closing for good. Our people are skipping work to look for other jobs. My gran worked here for years. My siblings and I ran around, had meals in the kitchen, played hide-and-seek . . ." My voice trails off. I even got to first base with my crush on the velvet settee upstairs.

Just memories from the past, written on my heart.

I lower the ice pack, thinking. He and I don't know each other, but we've been through *something* together. I can't unload on Babs because she'll try to fix things, like find me a job in Alaska. I can't with my siblings, because Jane is going through her own issues, and Andrew is already on the verge of quitting school. "It's like, losing the store is just another piece of her gone. Pretty soon I won't have anything left."

My chest rises. "Then, there's the apartment where I live. My gran took out a second mortgage to help my mom. I know selling is the right thing to do, to get out of debt, and start fresh in a cheaper place, but it's hard to let go after all the sacrifices Gran made for us, you know? She is, was, my mother."

"I'm sorry," he says softly.

I give him a wan smile. "Sorry for venting. Bet you wished you hadn't shown up to taunt me with Mina."

He takes the ice from my numb hands and places it on the counter. His words are whisper soft. "She's not my fiancée. That position is only for you."

My breath catches.

A myriad of expressions flit over his face, ones I can't decipher. "It must be you."

I take in the diamond cheekbones, the beautiful lines of his jaw, and the way his eyes peer into mine with that deep, intense look.

"My answer is no. I don't want to get married. And about the car . . . I think you're the kind of person who would forgive me." He has empathy for the guy who tackled him. Maybe he can spare some understanding for me.

Seconds tick by as he stares at me, emotions flitting over his face. Then he turns and walks out of the kitchen, leaving me there.

Shit. I groan. Maybe I've misjudged him, and he's calling the police.

I start when the kitchen door flies open, and he stalks back inside, his chest heaving out an exhale as he stops in front of me. "You're infuriating, you know that?"

I dip my face and hide a smile. "Welcome back. So you aren't going to put me behind bars?"

"I never would have, and you know it."

I touch his arm, and the act sends a buzzing hot zap down my spine. His muscles are taut and hard. I let my hand fall away. "So let me help you out with Mina. What can I do? She clearly likes you. And she is sweet, even if she did say my windows are 'cute.'"

He rubs his face with both hands, his tone exasperated. "Of course she likes me. She's my cousin. She thinks I'm interested in *you*—romantically. She came along to be my wingwoman."

I can't hide the smile anymore and giggle. "You dragged her in here to push me into making a decision?"

"Yes." His eyes narrow. "But with you, I need to be a bit more . . . persuasive."

I rub my hands together. "Let's hear it, then."

"I have a confession."

My stomach pitches in hope. "What? Your car is perfectly fine? That photo you sent is a fake? Please say it's so."

"No, it's wrecked, completely totaled." He spears me with his steely gaze, the one that makes my hackles rise. "*I* bought the bookstore."

I take a step back and gasp. "You found out where I worked, then decided to pull the rug out from under me . . . in what . . . revenge? All because of a stupid car?"

"A four-hundred-thousand-dollar car," he growls as he crosses his arms. "Think about it, Emmy. Of course I was going to find out who you are, especially when I discovered Brody knew you. I came into the store to talk to you, and when you weren't here, I thought I'd check in with the owner to see what kind of person you were—seeing as I had so little to base my knowledge on."

"Terry knows I stole a car?"

"No."

Thank God. He's like the uncle I never had. And I never want Jane and Andrew to know I made such a dumb mistake. I'm supposed to be a role model for them.

"But when I saw his fishing boat, we had a conversation about retirement, and I said I might be interested in buying the store. We exchanged numbers, and I called him the next day." He stuffs his hands in his pockets. "I do invest in property, Emmy. It happened organically."

I shake my head. "You wanted leverage. You knew you wouldn't press charges about the car, so you bought the store. You're a diabolical devil."

"I only found this place because of you. You're the common denominator in this."

"Thanks for reminding me this is all my fault." I turn my back to him and stomp to the door.

"Dammit," he mutters as he catches my arm. "Wait, don't walk away. Just listen to me."

I flip around. "What?"

He struggles with what to say, brows lowered, then lifts his hands. "Christ! Fine. I wanted leverage, and if it didn't work, I could have resold it."

"But how did you know that I loved it so much?"

He sighs. "Terry mentioned that you'd wanted to buy it someday, so . . ."

It's too absurd. "Why go to such lengths? For me?"

"Because my mind is set on you," he murmurs.

"Why?" I search his face, looking for clues as to what he's thinking.

He debates internally, then says, "I'm in a rush to get married, and there aren't any other options I like. Brody adores you. You're . . . beautiful." His words soften as he averts his glance and drags a hand through his dark hair. "I'm not terrible to live with. I have training camp soon, and I won't even be around. I'll *keep* the bookstore for you. Brody doesn't want me to buy him anything anyway."

I inhale sharply as hope flares, burning like a beacon.

Keeping the store would solve so many issues. I'd still have the memories of Gran here, and I could continue to take care of my family.

But at what cost?

I can feel a tiny thread of *something* between us. Chemistry, most definitely. Heat, oh yeah. From the moment he got out of his car at the motel, something about him caught my attention.

But . . .

I don't want to get entangled with him. Haven't I been through enough with Kian? I don't want to jump right back into something else, especially something that feels . . . exciting.

Gray eyes search mine, trying to gauge my reaction.

What I want to do is run and break this spell he has on me, but instead, I stay rooted. My mind tumbles his words around, running different scenarios and outcomes.

"We'll be professional," he says. "Roommates in my apartment. Perhaps friends."

"For how long?"

"A few months, maybe three; I'm not sure. Until the lawyer approves the inheritance. Then we'll make up a story about why we're getting divorced."

I swallow, remembering how my heart jumps whenever he's nearby. Obviously he doesn't have that issue.

And buying the store? I don't get it. Sure, he could use it as leverage, but that would be entirely overboard. Why not just find someone else? What is it about *me* that he wants?

"What happens to the store after we divorce?"

He studies my face. "I swear I'll sell to someone who'll keep it open."

My throat tightens. It's everything I could want.

Unease rises.

I shake my head. "What if . . . I mean, it would be easy to . . ." *Get attached to him.*

Which is the last thing I need.

A moment passes, then: "I see."

"What?" I put my hands on my hips.

"You're worried about falling for me."

I scoff. "Jesus. Please. That was the last thing I was thinking. Save me from the egomaniacal asshole."

"You won't, I promise."

"Why not? Just curious why you'd say that."

He shrugs as he leans in, until our faces are close. The scent of ripe cherries and leather wafts in the air. If I moved a few inches, I could kiss him. His lips are perfect for kissing, like pillows.

"There's armor wrapped around you so tight it might never come off, and I get it. You still have feelings for Kian. Am I right?"

Of course I have *feelings* for Kian, but I'm not clarifying exactly what they are to Graham. I shrug nonchalantly. Let him believe what he wants.

"What about you? Is there an ex-girlfriend I should be worried about?"

His jawline tightens as he glances away from me with a faraway look, one that makes me want to ask what's wrong. The strong column of muscles in his throat moves. "We're alike in that. I love someone I can't be with."

I inhale, an inexplicable pang of jealousy hitting me. "What? Who?"

"Doesn't matter." He eases away from me, as if he needs distance. "Both of us have our guard up. We've both been hurt. Neither of us hold any illusions about love or each other. We're perfect. So . . . deal?" He glances at me.

"I'm in charge of the store?"

He nods. "Make it profitable."

"It is already, but I can make it better. I'll need a raise. After all, you don't want your wife bartending at Marcelle's part time, do you?"

Amusement glints in his eyes. "Did you ever consider law school?"

"No."

"You might have missed your calling. So. Yes or no?"

The sounds of the bookstore fade, muffled by my heart racing and my shallow breaths.

"Hello. You had me at 'bookstore' five minutes ago." It means I can stay here for a little longer at least.

We gaze at each other, the seconds ticking by as heaviness lingers in the air around us, a tautness buzzing around the space.

Maybe we're both feeling the weight of the decision we've made.

I'm thinking back to that moment when I ran from Kian by stealing Graham's car.

We wouldn't be here if it wasn't for that. I *am* the common denominator.

"Hmm, yeah . . . just . . . guess I should . . ." He reaches inside his pocket and pulls out a velvet box. He opens it and reveals a ring. "This was my mother's favorite ring. It's an antique, and if it's not to your taste, then we can get something else."

I gasp at the square-shaped solitaire surrounded on the sides by smaller diamonds. "It's . . ." Beautiful. Everything a girl could want.

He takes my left hand and glides it on my finger.

"It fits your finger."

My stomach flutters at the sight of the ring on my hand. I trace my fingers over it. "You have to say the words." Mostly I'm kidding, to lighten the mood, but another side of me yearns for it. Weird.

"What words . . . oh, I see. Really? You're serious. Why?"

"We'll need a good story. The truer it is, the more real we'll sound."

"I didn't think you were a romantic," he says.

"Can't a girl just want something, and there's not a label on it?"

"Is that any way to talk to your future husband? Also, your hand is shaking."

"So is yours, Mr. Cream."

He pops that eyebrow. "Mr. Cream?"

I wave my hand at him. "You wore a cream suit. Babs noticed. That's why she was on the PA system earlier, telling me about the 'cream situation.'"

His lips quirk.

"Come on, do it. Take the ring off and start all over."

He takes the ring off as he growls under his breath, "Hardest proposal of my fucking life . . ."

"How many have you done?"

"Jealous?"

"No."

He rolls his neck and shoulders. "I'm kinda sore from my workout. It's hard to get on the floor. Let's skip that part."

"Ah, I see, the usual. You've never been on your knees in front of a woman."

"Oh, I have, my darling."

Sexual tension swirls in the air as I imagine him going down on me. My breath hitches as my body quivers—

Nope. One, I have a cat. Two, this is fake. Three, catch the fuck up, Emmy.

"Your face is flushed, Emmy," he says, lids lowered.

I check my wrist for a watch I'm not wearing. "Look at the time. Guess I'll see you later—"

He grumbles. "All right, all right, I'll stop teasing, and if you really insist, I'll get down on my knee . . ."

"I do."

"You'll be saying those words very soon."

"I need to close up the store in ten minutes, Mr. Cream."

He shakes his head. "'Mr. Cream' makes me sound like I sit around and masturbate all day."

I have to bite my lip to keep from laughing.

With a deep exhale, right there in the kitchen of the bookstore, surrounded by a bag of ice and dirty dishes in the sink, he gets down on one knee, looks up at me with a gaze I can't decipher, and says, "Emmy, will you marry me?"

I cock my head. "You sound like a robot. I'm a woman. We're *in love*. You can't wait for us to be together forever. Put some soul into it, some excitement. I want to feel tingles over every inch of my skin. Give me some va-va-voom." I shimmy my shoulders to make the point.

"My God. You're the diabolical one. You're being mean."

I stifle down a laugh. "I admit, I'm enjoying messing with you. It's not my problem you have thin skin. You're the one who wants to get married, Creamy."

"All I see is a giant pile of cum—or mayo—when you say that."

I giggle.

"Stop giggling."

"I'm nervous! This is a big deal, okay? You need to stop getting flustered over getting on one knee."

"Jesus. I'm nervous too." His top teeth keep chewing on his bottom lip, and he keeps his eyes downcast as if searching for what to say. "Emmy, from the moment I saw you on the balcony of the motel, I knew you were an extraordinary woman. I want to spend the next few months with you. Will. You. Marry. Me."

The words, which ring with truth, hang in the air, and the moments stretch like a rubber band. The faux tenderness of his expression, the pretend glint of hope in his eyes, the way his fake smile gives me the shivers, I commit it all to memory.

"All right," I say, and that's when the kitchen door flies open, and Babs rushes in.

Chapter 10

EMMY

"Emmy, I'm sorry to interrupt, but your family is here and our shipment of dark roast hasn't arrived and we need to clean since the maintenance person quit—what's going on here?" Babs says as Graham rises to his feet and brushes his pants off.

Her eyes bug out. "Wait. D-did you just get engaged? Right here? Right now?"

"Um, yes?" I smile.

She has the reaction I expect. She drops the cupcake she was holding. Then her face crumples as if the entire world has imploded, her tears spilling over. She boo-hoos in full-on Babs style with her entire body.

"Y-you minx," she says to me once she's gotten a good breath and wiped her face. "Pretending you barely knew him, and all the while . . . congratulations!"

"Thank you," I say dryly.

"I'm so happy to have you as part of our family!" she tells Graham as she rushes forward and tackles him in a bear hug. He staggers back as she plants a kiss on each of his cheeks, smearing them with pink.

His eyes meet mine over her shoulders, and I lift mine. *Babs is just Babs.*

She pops him on the arm. "You wily fox! You seemed so blasé earlier when you asked about Emmy, pretending like you didn't know her. How long has this been going on? Wait. Is there a secret baby? Please say yes!"

"No," I say with a groan, and she harrumphs in disappointment.

Meanwhile Graham has leaned back against the counter, all casual, smirking. The devil is smiling like he just won the lottery.

"So how did you two meet?" she asks, eyes lit up with delight.

"Now that's a story. I'll let Emmy tell you," Graham drawls, and I send him a glare. *Really? What's the plan?*

She grabs my hand and peers at the ring. "But first . . . I love diamonds. They symbolize love and commitment—"

It dawns on me what she said when she came in the door. I interrupt her. "Did you say Jane and Andrew are here?"

"Yep," Babs says as she slips my ring off and tries it on her finger.

"Shit," I mutter under my breath, just as Andrew and Jane sweep into the kitchen.

Here we go . . .

Londyn squeals when she sees me. "E, e, e, e!"

"Hello, my love," I call out with my arms open as Jane waltzes toward me. She hands her over to me, and I tug her close as the world settles on its axis.

Andrew is staring at his phone as he goes for the pomegranate tea, pours himself a cup, grabs a croissant, then does a quick hop to sit on the counter. "Hey, Emmy, how was your day?" he murmurs absently without glancing at us.

"Oh, you know, this and that, the usual," I reply.

Jane pulls out a bowl from the cabinet and mixes together some microwavable pasta baby food. "We thought we'd meet you here for dinner, since you said you had to work late. The stove isn't working anyway." She gives me one of her rare smiles. "Londyn saw the store from across the street and started chanting your name."

"Good girl. She knows where I work." I rub our noses together. "And she knows Magic is here somewhere."

As if on cue, the black cat appears in the kitchen and pounces on a piece of crust Andrew drops for him. Londyn jabbers at him, and he watches her warily. They had a bit of a tussle last night when she yanked on his half tail. He hissed and ran straight to my bed and got under the covers.

Jane pauses enough to notice Graham, who's currently talking to Babs a few feet away.

She cocks her head. "He looks familiar. Handsome. One of your book guys?" she asks.

"No."

She shuts the door to the microwave and hits the power button. "And he is . . ."

I can't make myself say the words. "He's my . . ."

"Fiancé," Graham murmurs as he eases next to me. He must have been listening.

Butterflies dance wildly in my stomach when he wraps an arm around my waist. A nervous laugh comes from me. "Oh wow, just like that, you told them, honey bunny. I see, well, um, okay, guys, this is Graham, and he just proposed to me. Isn't that awesome?"

Crickets. The silence, the shock, is palpable.

"I think it's wonderful!" Babs says.

I lean into him, gazing up with what I hope is a rapturous expression. Londyn, on the other side of me, looks at him with intensity. "Graham, this is Jane and Andrew, and the little one is Londyn, Jane's daughter. Remember me telling you about them? My sister is a model, and Andrew goes to NYU." Catch up. This is the Darling Family 101.

"Hi, it's good to meet you. Emmy talks about you guys all the time," Graham lies smoothly as Babs shows a shell-shocked Jane the ring—that she's still wearing.

Andrew drops his pastry midbite on the floor and walks over to us as if in a daze. He blinks as he rakes his gaze over my fiancé. Then back to me. Then back to Graham.

There's a comical look on his face. "Graham Harlan? What the fuck? You want to marry *my* sister?"

"I'm right here, and language," I hiss.

"Fu, fu, fu," Londyn squeals as she jumps up and down in my arms.

"See what you did," I tell Andrew. "She knows when it's a bad word."

Andrew lets out a laugh, half amazement, half awe. "But . . ." He glances at me. "You're marrying the best tight end in the country. He's All-Pro. His team won the Super Bowl."

"She's lucky she found me. My little thief," Graham says with a glint in his eyes.

I boop him on the nose. "Of your *heart*, honey bunny."

Babs sighs, smiling. "Oh look, they're so cute."

Jane takes Londyn from me and makes a scoffing sound. "I didn't know you were dating anyone." The subtext is clear: *You just broke up with Kian! What the fuck?*

The microwave dings, saving me from a reply. Babs has already pulled out the high chair we keep in the kitchen, and Jane moves to get Londyn settled.

"Um, well, you see . . ." My voice is breathless. Sure, I acted my ass off at the Golden Iguana, but this is my family I'm lying to.

"We met in Vegas," Graham finishes.

Andrew frowns. "But you went to Vegas because of Kian. You were going to a wedding."

I say the first thing that comes to mind. "Right, of course, then everything happened, and thankfully Graham, er, saw me upset outside the Bellagio. We'd met previously, at some event Kian took me to, and he offered to give me a ride in his Lamborghini."

"You said you took a taxi to Arizona," Jane says.

"Hmm, well, I wasn't sure if I wanted to talk about Graham because . . ." I trail off, and he finishes.

"Because it felt so new, almost too good to be true."

Jane searches my face, as if looking for a lie. "So you went from one football player to another?"

"I like the way they look?"

Babs grins and gives me a high five. "Same, girl, same!"

Graham picks up the story. "She wanted to get out of town. I'd just gotten my car and wanted a road trip, so . . ."

"We drove to Arizona and stayed at a place called the Golden Iguana. The place was full of scorpions, wasn't it, honey bunny?" I smile.

He shrugs. "You were so terrified. Poor thing."

"Well. I killed one."

He nods sagely, laughter in his eyes. "You're very brave, darling."

"Thank you, honey bunny. So are you," I say adoringly.

"And?" Jane asks, looking at us. "What else?"

Graham smirks, then: "Well, Emmy was crazy about me from the get-go. Apparently, she'd had a huge crush on me for years. I could hardly drive for her wanting to kiss me. We got to the motel, and she sent me out to buy cherry—"

I elbow him as I force a chuckle. "What? Stop that. No need to go into detail. Basically, we went swimming, we checked out the bar, and there was a little gas station where we loaded up on champagne. Not exactly the Four Seasons."

"This sounds like a Hallmark movie," Babs says with her hand over her heart.

Jane snorts. "Why do you like those awful things?"

Babs sniffs. "Maybe they're predictable, but I like happy endings."

"Not everyone gets a happy ending in real life," Jane replies.

"Well, Emmy and Graham are," Babs retorts, clearly miffed that Jane isn't buying into her happy-ending love affair. "Freddy and I had a wonderful marriage, and he was taken too soon. The same for your gran."

Jane's face tightens. Number one, this is a total shock to her, and number two, she's been down on love ever since her boyfriend dumped her.

"Then there was the guy, remember, darling?" Graham says, ignoring Jane much better than I am. "Fake Clint, your little nickname for him. He tried to hit on you, and I was jealous, and then you got between us and yanked me into the room like a wild woman. I wouldn't have hurt him too bad. I don't want to go to prison, after all. What was that word you used? 'Carnage'? Yes. You didn't want me to create carnage."

"You are the jealous type," I reply sweetly.

"It sounds weird to me," Jane says, her eyes darting from me to Graham. "Almost as if you're making it up on the spot. Also, I don't see how she'd had a crush on you for years when she doesn't follow sports. Totally not her style."

Graham blinks. "Believe it or not, truth *is* stranger than fiction. *Someone* stole my Lamborghini—"

"Which was fine, because you didn't need that car," I say, interrupting him. "It's a gas guzzler and entirely too expensive. Do you know what other things you could do with that kind of money?"

Graham's hand slides under my hair to the nape of my neck as he brushes his fingers over my skin. "Oh, but I didn't care. I just love beautiful things." He presses his nose to my hair. "Like you," he whispers.

I swallow.

"So you were there when Kian tracked her phone to the motel?" Andrew asks Graham.

Graham turns to my brother. "Yes. I drove her to the airport."

"But your car was *stolen* . . . ," Andrew says.

I roll my eyes. "What he meant was he called an Uber and rode with me. I mean, it was the plan all along for me to fly home."

Andrew seems to accept our story as he grasps Graham's hand and pumps it, then proceeds to tell him how he was thrilled when Graham got traded to New York.

Jane feeds Londyn a bite of mac and cheese. Londyn, who's been darting her eyes from one person to the next and is probably understanding all of it because she's a little genius, grabs the spoon to do it herself, smearing pasta all over her face.

I laugh at her, and she grins and slaps the high chair.

But Jane isn't distracted. "So basically, you reconnected in Vegas, then went to a random motel in the desert, had an argument with some man named Clint, and now you're engaged? Sorry. It's nice to meet you, Graham, but Emmy, this is not normal for you."

Andrews makes a humming noise. "Emmy can be odd."

"What? Give me an example," I say. "And remember, I've seen you bite your own toenails as a toddler."

"Gross," Babs says as she makes a gagging noise. "I can find you a self-help book for that."

"I don't do it now!" He points at me. "Emmy only eats broccoli when it's flat. You smash it with your fork until it's like a pancake, then stick it in your mouth. Same for cauliflower and potatoes. It takes you an hour to eat."

"They tickle the top of my mouth," I say as I nudge my head at Jane. "Jane puts pepper on her ice cream." I direct my eyes at Andrew. "I have a list of weird stuff you did as a kid, so shut it."

"Like what?" he asks.

Jane smirks. "Oh, you've done it now, Tiny. *Ma* never forgets."

"For one, you ate toilet paper like it was chocolate."

"It was clean, at least," he mutters.

"Two, you also ate Bubbles the goldfish. You put your little hand in the fishbowl and gulped him down before I could stop you."

Jane gasps. "You told me Bubbles was different because he lost weight!"

I sigh. "No, I just bought a new fish for you, Jane."

She shakes her head. "And you never told me?"

"Sorry. I replaced Bubbles every three months like clockwork because Andrew was addicted to eating raw fish. Shall I continue?

There's the time you stripped down and ran around naked in the children's section of the store—"

He holds his hand up. "All right. I've heard enough. You are completely normal. Cross my heart."

"Well, the broccoli doesn't make her odd, but a sudden marriage does," Jane retorts. "What event was it where you met Graham, the one where you were with Kian?"

Graham squeezes my fingers. "It was, um, a charity ball."

Finally, he comes through with an original idea.

Jane snorts. "Kian at a charity ball. No way. The only person he cared about was himself."

Graham deflects like a pro. "I understand you're worried about your sister, especially after Kian, but I'd never hurt her . . ." He turns to me and tucks a piece of hair behind my hear. "She is too precious. Just when you least expect to find the woman of your dreams, there she is, right in front of you . . ."

Cheesy. I roll my eyes so only he can see them.

Jane's lips tighten, her gaze darting to Graham and then me. "It would be nice if you'd let us in on these things, Emmy."

"It was sudden, yes, I know," I say, deciding to stick close to the truth. "I didn't expect Graham to propose. Actually"—I sigh dramatically—"he asked me a few days ago at the bar. I told him I had to think about it. And I have. This is the best thing . . ." *That could come out of this particular situation.*

I hesitate to mention that he's bought the store until we can figure out the details. I don't want any more questions to arise.

Graham smiles as his eyes sweep the room with the look of someone who is a little on edge and preparing to exit. "It's been great to meet you guys, but I have to go. I'm sure I'll see you all soon."

"Running off already?" Jane says. "Not surprised. Her guys never last long."

"Don't be so weird," Andrew mutters at her.

"He's a stranger," Jane hisses under her breath, but we all hear her.

Graham and I keep walking as he escorts me to the door.

"Is there a date for this wedding?" Jane calls out behind us, her tone prickly.

He glances down at me. "As soon as possible. We're thinking a week."

I inhale a sharp breath as Jane puts her hands on her hips and shakes her head. "No freaking way. That's . . . she doesn't even have a dress. She hasn't prepared anything. What's the rush?"

I give her a reassuring smile. "It'll be okay. Be right back," I say with a wave as we leave the kitchen.

"A week?" I mutter as soon as we're out the door and into the store. "Are you crazy?"

"Yes. Fast. Before you change your mind. Or I change mine. None of this makes me happy. And your sister is a pit bull."

"She needs to be questioning this. I raised her well."

Mina sees us coming out from the kitchen and rushes over. "I wondered where you two went. You're both pale as paper. What's up?"

Whoa. I'd completely forgotten about her.

"I asked Emmy to marry me, and she said yes." He's got the robot voice again.

"Oh! I-I didn't know it was so serious. Congratulations!" She tries to hide her shock as she gives us hugs.

Eventually, after nodding my head and saying things I don't mean or won't recall later because all I can think about is *a week*, I tell them that I've got to finish closing the store.

First, I walk them outside and inhale the night air. People bustle past us on the busy sidewalk. Mina tells us she's heading out to meet a friend for dinner, and it's just me and Graham left on the street.

He scrubs his face, his eyes tired as he watches her leave. "That was harder than I thought. Good job in there. Are you okay?"

"No. I don't like lying to my family. Things tend to come apart when people lie. It turns into a tangled mess."

"I get that, but if one person suggests our marriage isn't real, then the inheritance might not come through for Brody. My half brother, Holden, is a lawyer, and he'll be suspicious. You can't tell anyone, not even your brother and sister. Promise me?"

I nod.

"Eventually you'll have to meet my family and prove to them that we're in love—not something I'm looking forward to." He tips my chin up. "How's the nose?"

"It's fine—wait, are those calla lilies?" I ask as I walk to a bouquet of about two dozen flowers leaning against the brick of the store beneath the window display. I pick them up, my fingers stroking the beautiful creamy-white trumpet-shaped petals. A yellow spike with tiny flowers is in the middle of the petals. The scent wafts, sweet and delicate, and memories of Gran wash over me. Out of all the lilies, she'd say, this one is the most fragrant, the most elegant, the hardest to find. She carried them at her wedding. She wanted them at her funeral. Mark, my grandfather, bought her a bouquet each month. He died before I was born, but she'd still bought lilies each month.

"Who do they belong to? Is there a card?"

I shuffle through the flowers, a cold feeling settling in my chest. "No, but Kian must have left them for me. He knows they were Gran's favorite—and mine. Ugh."

I hurl the bouquet to the ground, anger and fear mixing together, over Kian, over this fake marriage and lying to my family. Jane knows something is up, and I hate not telling her the truth.

Why did I steal that damn car?

"So much has happened, so fast . . ." My chest rises rapidly, and tears prick my eyelids. I'm supposed to avoid stress with my heart issues, but with everything going on, it feels impossible. "I'm sorry for being emotional, but . . ."

"Hey, Emmy . . ." Graham pulls me into his embrace, and I fall into him. It's the sort of comfort I haven't experienced in months. My worries slip away for a moment. Maybe because we're in this predicament together.

Moments pass as my heart settles. I'm not sure how long we stay like that, but it feels as if I've been here before, my face tucked against his chest. His hand runs softly through my hair.

When we finally break apart, the warmth of his proximity lingers.

He gazes down at me, his eyes searching mine as his hand slides over the collar of my dress to the back of my head, where he palms my scalp. "Are you okay?"

I nod.

He tugs down my messy bun, his fingers trailing through my hair. "So beautiful," he murmurs as he tips my face up. He fuses his lips to mine, tasting me with soft, hesitant brushes.

My hands curl around his waist, and his sensual mouth deepens the pressure. His tongue tangles with mine, stroking against it. I feel the warmth of his hand as it heats my nape, tightening. I hear the pounding of his chest. He kisses like a dream, and oh Jesus, his hand is trailing down, across my arms, to my elbows, to my hips. I smell and feel everything, the scent of his hair and skin, the scratch of his jawline. His fingers dig into me, tugging me closer and closer as his lips suck on my bottom one tenderly. My nipples harden, aching. His hands brush my ass, sparking heat between my legs. I melt into him.

Oh.

This feeling.

Heat.

Desire.

My fingers tangle in his hair, tugging him closer as the kiss intensifies. A rumbling, needy sound comes from his throat, one that urges me on.

Fire licks in my veins.

Suddenly, he pulls away, both of us breathing heavily as his forehead rests against mine. He brushes a thumb over my cheek, seeming to gather himself faster than I do.

"That was for your family," he whispers in my ear. "They have their noses pressed to the windows, watching us."

So that's why he kissed me.

It stings. It shouldn't. I'm a tough girl who's had plenty of relationships that didn't go anywhere, so this one shouldn't be any different.

When I look into his face, he's wearing a bored expression.

I swallow thickly, shoving away the desire still burning in my veins.

He tucks his hands in his slacks, hardness settling over his features as he glances at the flowers. "I'm going to take care of Kian."

I stiffen. "What? No. Don't do anything."

He chews on that, his eyes dangerously mercurial as they flash. "Why not? Because you're in love with him?"

"No. Because it'll only cause more trouble. Graham—"

"He hasn't let you go yet. And you thought someone was following you recently."

"I'm overly paranoid since Vegas. It's probably nothing."

"You need to text me or call me if something happens."

I shake my head. "Nothing is going to happen. Maybe he didn't send these."

His jaw tics, and he spears me with a look, one that says he isn't backing down on this. "Your favorite flowers just magically appear at the bookstore. I don't think so."

"I don't need a guard."

He drags both hands through his hair. "I'm taking responsibility for you, Emmy. No one will hurt you."

"You're taking responsibility for me for a very short time. We're pretend, remember? And it will end. We'll end."

His hands flex as he frowns, searching for something to say; then: "I think about him choking you, and I get very . . . angry. Those bruises were dark, and you must have been terrified. I saw the scratches on his hands, ones that you must have put there. God damn it. I regret not beating the shit out of him at the motel." His nose flares. "What did you ever see in him?"

I look away, not sure how to explain me and Kian. Some of the best people I know have broken bits, and I'm usually drawn to them in some fashion, as a friend, as a lover. Perhaps it's part of the reason I let things get too far with Kian. I sensed the danger in him, just boiling beneath the surface, and a side of me wanted to fix him. But some wounds run too deep. People have to pick up their pieces, slap them back on, and carry on, all by themselves. I'm not sure Kian can.

We'd been on a slippery slope for a while, and part of me knew we were over before I even went to Vegas. He and I had run our course. The phone tracking and the underwear only cemented my conviction; then he had to go and propose marriage to me to distract me, and when I didn't agree, he lost his temper in a horrible way.

"Once he touched me, it was over. He knows about my parents. He knows I can't go down that road with him. He's been to my apartment, yes, when I first got back, but he hasn't shown his face since."

His eyes search mine, and he says gently, "I'm glad. And you're strong, I can see that, a woman who's capable of taking care of yourself, but I *want* to protect you. Let me."

"Why?"

He gives me an exasperated look. "I don't know. Because you're going to be my wife."

Not forever.

"Just don't go looking for trouble, Graham. Violence isn't worth it. Trust me, please. I've been there. I've seen it firsthand. It's awful and ugly."

He groans, understanding dawning on his face. "Of course. You've seen it up close. I get that, but I'll never let him fucking touch you again, feel me? I have every right to protect you, and I will."

I give him my cell number. He takes my phone and types in Brody's, his, and some guy named Jasper's numbers.

"One of us will be around if anything comes up with him," he says. "Don't hesitate to call."

He tucks his hands in his pocket, changing directions. "We need to go public. I'm calling my publicist tonight, and they'll arrange for an announcement on socials. We need a real date. I'm thinking Borelli's on Wednesday. Are you free?"

I tell him yes, and he turns to go, then switches to face me, walking backward. "I hear you have a cat. Was he the one in the kitchen?"

I nod. "Magic. Or Stubs. Or Prince of Darkness. He answers to all three. Jane likes him because he's a mouser. Andrew mostly ignores him. Londyn thinks he's her new toy."

"You'll have to leave him behind when you move in with me."

"Magic and I are a couple. He's my man."

"I'm your man," he drawls.

I wave that aside. "When can I tell them about the store?"

"You're the manager. Do it when you think it's best."

My heart flutters as the reality of it settles in. The store is staying. I'm staying. The best part is I'm totally in charge now. I can implement new ideas Terry wasn't interested in. A thrill courses through me.

"I'll make arrangements for the marriage and call you tomorrow," he says, then turns back around and strides away.

I watch him walk away long after he's disappeared, my mind swirling with who exactly Graham Harlan is. And what it's going to be like to be married to him . . .

I glance back to the bookstore, and Jane still stands there, her arms crossed and a drawn expression on her face. Babs waves and points to my engagement ring, still on her finger. Andrew looks ecstatic and gives me a thumbs-up as he grins.

Right. I inhale a steady breath as I head back inside to finally close up.

Chapter 11
EMMY

I walk into the store the next day with my head down. I got here earlier and opened, but once the staff arrived and we seemed slow, I popped down to the secondhand store a block over to look at summer baby clothes for Londyn. I found a sturdy pair of sandals for when she starts walking and a pink ruffled-bottom bathing suit. I'm smiling when I hear Babs calling my name.

I come to a dead stop in the rotunda, my mouth gaping at the flowers. Bouquets are everywhere: on the steps leading up the stairs, in the sitting areas, on tables, on the checkout counter, on top of the bakery case, overflowing from every corner, and spilling out into the aisles. Roses, carnations, daisies, gardenias, and a whole host of other flowers I can't even begin to know litter the space with vibrant colors. It's like stepping into a garden in the middle of the store. The sweet scents mingle together and waft up around me in a fragrant haze.

"What the hell?" I murmur under my breath as I do a spin. I was only gone for half an hour. One of the delivery guys brushes past me and sets another vase on the staircase, then heads back outside to the van.

I grab one of them by the arm, a young guy in his teens. "Excuse me, who sent these?"

"They're for some guy's fiancée, Emmy."

"That's me."

He grins. "Congrats. We've got another van coming, miss. I gave the note he sent to Babs."

Everyone seems to know Babs. I'm not surprised he's already found out her name.

"Did you say there was another van?" I ask loudly, then take a breath and settle. "No. Just no. It's already a forest in here. We can't take any more flowers. I need room for customers. I need room to work."

The delivery guy fidgets. "Um, you don't want them?"

I wave my arm around the store. "I have enough. What do you think?"

He gives me a lopsided grin. "I think someone must be crazy about you."

Hardly. He's just making a point. And all because Kian left me calla lilies.

Babs dashes toward me, smiling for all she's worth as she waves a white envelope. "Aren't they just *gorgeous*? Girl. What did you do to that man that he sent these? You must be a tiger in the sack. Roar!" She claws the air and does a little hip thrust.

Oh dear. I rub my temples as I turn to the delivery guy. "Do me a favor, please. Deliver the rest of them to the nearest hospital, and ask them to give them to patients who don't get visitors."

He looks uncertain.

"Please. They're my flowers, and that's what I want."

He nods and turns away from me to make the phone call.

Babs pouts. "What? You're not taking all of them? Are you crazy? The man loves you. He just wants you to know."

Not true.

"I need some decaf tea," I say as I head to the kitchen, with her following on my heels.

"Do you want the note?"

I take it from her hand and rip it open.

> Darling,
> You need another favorite flower. No more calla lilies.
> Your future husband

I whip out my phone and send him a text.

With what you spent on flowers, I could have bought a small car.

But not a Lamborghini. Did you pick a favorite yet?

No.

Then I'll send more tomorrow.

I groan aloud as I grab a croissant and take a bite. My future husband is a stubborn man.

I sent the last of them to the hospital for the sick people. Flowers eventually wilt and die, and then I'll have a huge mess to clean up. I think you might be jealous of the secret flowers someone left me, I send.

Please. He's not worthy. Pick. A. Flower. Darling.

I've been called Darling my whole life. Is that going to be your nickname for me?

Yes. It suits you.

Okay, Creamy.

Which flower?

I go back out into the store and gaze around. A large pink-and-orange bouquet full of roses and peonies is on the counter, and I touch one of the silky petals. It smells divine.
Peonies, I text back.

Why?

I groan louder this time as I type. They make me happy. I like their shape. Enough?

Peonies it is. See you soon.

Shaking my head, I go to my office.

◆ ◆ ◆

It's late in the afternoon and I'm going through invoices when Babs pokes her head in. her shoulders slumped. Her makeup is a complete mess from crying, and one of her lashes is missing.

"Everything okay?" I ask gently. Even though the sale isn't final yet, Terry cleaned out his office earlier today and left to go fishing. She hasn't recovered.

"Are you free? Your sister is here."

Jane sneaks through the door. "Of course she is. I don't need an appointment. And why does the store look like a florist? I could barely get in the front door."

"Yes, they're from Graham. It's fine, Babs. Thank you," I tell her.

Babs nods, sniffing. "All right. Do you still want me to give away a bouquet with each fifty-dollar purchase?"

"Yes," I say. "And tell the staff they can take whatever they want home."

She sighs. "Fine. I'll bring you both some tea."

My office is a good size, with a couch, my desk, and two big filing cabinets. Jane plops down on the couch and picks up a decorative pillow, her fingers threading through the tassels on the corners. She looks pale and ashen, as if she didn't sleep well. Still, she manages to be pretty, even in joggers and a ratty Clash shirt.

"What's going on?" I ask, settling back in my chair. She barely spoke to me last night after we came home. She read some books to Londyn, put her to bed, then went to her room. Andrew, on the other hand, forced me to watch football on ESPN. Apparently, if I'm going to marry Graham, I need a better grasp of the game.

She looks down at her hands. "I just wanted to see you. And talk. I was bitchy yesterday, and not cute, sisterly bitchy but ugly, bitcherly bitchy. I'm sorry I was rude to Graham. You are your own person, after all, but I don't know him very well, and it makes me nervous."

"Graham was an unexpected surprise. You reacted."

"Hmm, yeah." She chews on her lip.

"So? He sent me lots of flowers. He's rich. I could do worse." I shuffle papers around on my desk so she won't realize my anxiousness.

"Let's forget about him for a moment."

"Okay. What's up?"

Her eyes get a faraway look in them. "I woke up this morning, thinking about the past. Remember when we were little, and you played those hiding games with us—to protect us? I mean, I was a toddler, but I knew you were taking us to safe places."

My throat tightens. "Yes." The closet, the attic, under the bed . . .

Her hands clench around the pillow. "I remember the night you ran with us to the neighbor's shed. I only recall it because *Charlotte's Web* was on TV, and I didn't want to miss it."

"Your favorite book."

Her eyes flick up at me. "It's *our* favorite, me and you and Andrew."

"If the Darling family had a crest, it would be a pig and a spider."

"Even though you'd read the story to us tons of times, I kept thinking that Wilbur was going to die in the show, and you kept telling me he wouldn't." Her lip quivers, and tears glisten in her eyes. "Then Dad hit Mom right in front of us. I couldn't see the TV because of them, and then you did what you always did—you snuck us out of the room and went to the shed next door. It was dark and cold and smelled like gasoline."

Oh, sweet Jane . . .

My heart breaks.

"Mr. Brenner kept his lawnmowers there," I say softly.

"You cleared us out a spot, or maybe it was already cleared out, but you made us a bed out of something . . ."

My lashes flutter as I recall the wooden shed that thankfully never had a lock on it. "Drop cloths, I think. He kept paint in there too."

A wry sound comes from her. "Somehow you'd managed to grab my stuffed pig on the way out, and you gave him to me and said that as long as we had Wilbur, we'd be okay."

I nod. It started a tradition with us. The pig went where we hid. As long as we had Wilbur with us, he'd take care of us. To this day, we still have him, and if any of us need bolstering, he gets to be in our room.

"You hugged us so tight while you talked about Charlotte and how wise and clever she was and how she saved Wilbur's life. She was a self-sacrificing, devoted friend to those she loved. She taught Wilbur about life, how to appreciate it. She taught him about friendship. You kept telling us that story for years." A tear escapes and traces down her cheek. She hurriedly wipes it away. "You *are* my Charlotte. You're my friend, my confidante, my mother. Bryony left us. I don't even think of her, you know. She's like a ghost in my memories, and I know Gran helped us, but without you, I would have seen terrible things, and you saved us from that."

She takes a tissue off my desk and dabs at her eyes. "I know other things. That you've done your best to take care of us, especially after Gran had her stroke. You came to every PTA meeting, you went to every baseball game of Andrew's, and you nursed Gran, all while trying to work and have a life of your own. You were there when I started my period, when Andrew got his tonsils out, when we both got lice. You cried with me when I got dumped at the middle school dance. You've barely dated, and you never let your heart get too involved. Maybe because of us. Maybe because of our parents. I don't deserve you, I don't."

My breath hitches. "You're my little Janie. I'd do anything for you."

"I know you would, and I'm sorry I haven't been myself since Londyn, but I'm trying my hardest." A shuddering breath comes from her. "I saw my agent a few days back. She has nothing for me, and I don't even care about the lack of modeling gigs. I just want . . . I just want to be as good with Londyn as you were for me. I want to be a good mom. I want to make good choices. I'm afraid I'm not good enough."

I'm not even aware that I'm crying until I feel the wetness on my cheeks. "I love you, Jane, and you're a wonderful mother. You're giving Londyn a real, solid family, something we didn't have. She's going to have a better beginning than we did." Regret is bitter in my mouth. "I'm so sorry you remember that night. I really hoped you and Andrew missed most of what happened in that house."

"No, don't be. Please. I don't want *you* to feel bad. I want you to know that I've watched you my whole life. You give and give to others, sometimes to the detriment of yourself." She pauses. "Which brings me to Graham. Something was just off last night in the kitchen with him. Maybe no one else would notice, but I'm the girl you raised. I know when something isn't right with you. And since when have you ever called any guy 'honey bunny'?" She spears me with her eyes, a fierceness there I haven't seen in months. Part of me is thrilled, but the other side of me senses danger.

She stands and paces around my office, a determined look growing on her face. "You agreed to marry him *in a week*, and I can't figure out why. You barely know him. Kian asked you, and you knew him for a year."

"Kian cheated, tracked, and choked me."

"I know, I know, and I'm glad he's gone, but the thing is you didn't even tell me you were dating someone. Please. Emmy. I need you to tell me what's going on. I need to know if you're sacrificing yourself somehow . . ."

I glance down at the gorgeous diamond on my finger, and my hands clench. I can't find the words to answer her—without lying.

"How does he take his coffee?" she asks me abruptly.

I sputter. "I, um . . ."

"Not fast enough. When is his birthday, and you have to give me the right answer because I googled it."

My stomach drops as we stare at each other.

"I have no clue," I admit ruefully.

"What's his middle name?"

I groan inwardly. Dammit. I twist a piece of hair around my finger. "Graham and I, we got caught up in the physical side of things and haven't really talked much about the little things."

"Why are you twisting your hair? No, don't answer that because I already know why. You only twist your hair when you're lying."

I huff. "I don't."

"You do, Ma." She smirks. "I knew something wasn't right. What is so special about Graham that my beautiful, kind sister would marry him—without really knowing him?"

My eyes meet hers. "Jane—"

I stop when the door opens, and Babs brings in a tray with teas and blueberry scones.

She eyes us both. "You two need anything else? Shot of vodka? I've got some in Terry's office."

I shake my head. "No, we're good."

"Are you sure?" She probably sees the traces of our tears.

Jane and I nod.

Babs fidgets. "Um, wanna hear something funny?"

"Sure," I say. Anything to deflect from me and Graham.

"Someone just came in and asked for a book on how to turn himself invisible."

Jane squints. "No way. Was he an adult?"

Babs smirks. "Oh yeah, and totally stoned. He smells like wacky weed. I told him we have a book called *The Invisible Man*, and I may have told him that we have an invisible section, but he'd have to find it on his own. Last I saw, he was feeling along all the walls on the second floor."

There's a beat of silence; then we all three burst into laughter. "God, I adore this place," I say.

Babs's eyes grow misty. "I hate that Terry is leaving, but I'm happy the buyer is keeping the store open. I gripe about some of the customers, but they're still lovely and make my day, except for the man who only comes in so he can poop in our restroom. I guess I need to go tell the stoned fellow to stop looking for the invisible part of the store." She sighs. "I'd really rather sit in here with you two and chat, but we're still down employees."

Jane's eyes flare as she looks at me. "Do you need help here?"

"Yes, please," I say in a pleading voice. She's worked here on and off a few times.

Babs squeals and claps her hands. "Can you start today?"

"Andrew has Londyn for a few hours, so yes," Jane says.

Babs sighs. "The two Darling sisters together. It's almost two perfect, especially since Graham is the owner of the store—"

She halts her words with a wide-eyed look in her eyes. "Oops. Sorry, Emmy. You said to keep that under wraps until it was time to announce to everyone, but I figured since she's your sister, she'd want to know that he bought the store."

Jane blinks. "Wait a minute. Graham *bought* the store." She glances at me, searching my face for answers.

Why does my sister have to be so tenacious?

"The sale goes through next week."

Babs nods. "Yep. He bought it for Emmy."

"Did he?" Jane murmurs, watching my face.

"Can you give us a minute, Babs?" I say, and she tells me yes and then heads back out into the store.

As soon as the door shuts, Jane turns to me. "Are you marrying Graham because he's buying the store? What is going on?"

I exhale, my mind churning with how to lie to her.

"Charlotte would tell Wilbur if she needed help. I'm here, Emmy. Let me shoulder this . . . whatever it is with you. Please. Please. I can't take the worry inside of me. I know something is wrong."

I rub my face with both hands and groan. "Sit down. I'll explain everything."

Chapter 12

GRAHAM

Fresh from a shower, I walk out of practice, and the evening air feels good to my wet head. Our strength coach complained about my conditioning this morning and made it his top priority. I nearly threw up while running the stadium steps before he was satisfied.

I'm pulling out my keys to unlock my Range Rover when I look up and see someone lingering in my peripheral.

Still wearing a suit, he's obviously come from the office. I notice his Mercedes in the lot a few spaces over. I pop the back door open and toss in my duffel bag. "Hey, Dad."

He nods, tucking his hands into his slacks. In his early sixties with dark graying hair, he's tall and built like me. "Hello." He offers a small smile, his granite face solemn. "Sorry to track you down like this. I tried to call, but you didn't pick up. As usual."

"Guess you saw the engagement announcement," I say as I lean against the car and cross my arms.

He moves to stand in front of me. "Yes. Congratulations. I can't wait to meet her."

He does sound eager, almost hopeful, but I shove any feelings away that that might give me. "We're doing a civil ceremony. Nothing fancy."

"Will I be invited?"

"No."

He takes that in stride as if he expected it and looks away, hiding his expression. "I called you on your birthday, too, but you never called back. I wanted to take you to dinner."

My thirtieth was two weeks ago, and usually I do have dinner with him, but with everything going on, there wasn't time. "Sorry. I've been busy with getting back in shape for the season. Jasper threw me a party at his place. Nothing big." Jasper and a few other guys from the team came over.

He swallows. "Your mom always made you a German chocolate cake."

My lips tighten. I refuse to acknowledge him when he brings her up.

He fidgets. "There are some things we should discuss."

I check my watch. "I really don't have time right now."

"Please."

I stare at my father for a long time. He's a man who rarely offers compromise. I exhale and say, "Two minutes, all right?"

He straightens his back, a tough expression slipping into place as I watch him transition into lawyer mode. "You can't play football—"

I throw my hands up. "Forget your two minutes. I don't have time for this."

He inches closer. "Sorry, sorry. That was the wrong way to start." His shoulders drop a little as he rubs his temple. "Please, I just worry about you. You have nothing to win and everything to lose by playing. I'm worried that if I don't say something to you now . . . I just . . . I don't want to miss the opportunity to speak. We talked in the hospital, but I've barely seen you since then."

My jaw tics. He was at the hospital. According to Brody, he only left to shower every other day.

"I'm doing great. My scans are great. My life is great. I've even seen a specialist. Don't worry."

His hands clench. "They had to restart your heart. Do you realize how terrifying that was for me?"

"First of all, I'm healthy. The team doctors say there's no reason not to play, and their concern has more credibility than yours. I'm sorry if my injury caused you stress. In the future, stop watching the games."

His eyes narrow. "I watch every game. I'm proud of you. For your success. You're amazing on the field."

I rub my jaw. Yeah, maybe, but he never was into sports. He wanted me to go to law school, only it wasn't what I wanted; plus, I couldn't get into his alma mater anyway. "Thanks."

"I may not have always been there for you, but this time—"

I scoff, interrupting him. I hadn't wanted to get into this with him, but he's gone and said the one thing I can deal with. "You were *never* there for us."

He blows out a breath. "I know."

"Were you concerned when Brody and I took turns sitting with Mom because we were freaked out about her depression? How about when you shipped us off to boarding school before Brody and I had even stopped crying about her? Your expectation for me to give one shit about your concern evaporated years ago."

His face dips as he stares at the ground, then looks back up at me. "Is that what you think? That I didn't care? I was devastated when she asked me to leave. I didn't *want* to go, and then she died before we could fix it."

Yeah, I've heard this before. "You cheated on her. That's what matters."

"I made a horrible mistake. Once. I admitted it immediately. I loved your mother, Graham. Right before you went skiing, we'd planned to meet. She was finally going to see me again . . ."

His eyes well up, and I wince. The only time I've ever seen my father cry was at my mother's funeral, but his tears that day made me furious.

But today my chest tightens, and I look away, fighting the emotion the memories bring. My head goes back to those images I saw when I was clinically dead, of him walking away from us with his suitcase.

"Then you shipped Brody and me away. You didn't want us."

"That was the second-biggest mistake of my life. Your mother died because of me. I know that. If I had been there, if I had never cheated, she wouldn't have been alone . . . It's easy for a lawyer to fill his time with work, and by the time I lifted my head up and decided it was time to get back to life, you were a star football player. Neither of you needed me."

I shake my head. "You taught us to live without you."

"But you still won't let me be a father."

Because I saw the hurt my mother had experienced. I saw her fucking tears. I was there the day she skied off the mountain. I can't let go of *his* mistake.

"What about Grandmother's will? Brody will be cheated out of his marriage share. If you want to be a father, why've you stayed silent?"

He cocks his head. "Unfortunately, my mother wrote her wishes, which excluded Brody. Legally, it's cut and dried. I didn't have anything to do with that."

I shake my head. "You could've said something."

"Of course I'm angry for Brody. I've offered him money, but he won't take it." He exhales. "I'm not here to argue. I saw your announcement and thought we could touch base. I don't want to regret not making my feelings known now. I don't want to watch you get hurt on that field again."

Football is my life. It's what I clung to like a life support when Mom died, when he sent us away.

I stare at him for a minute, trying to build my anger inside again to respond, and it does come, but something about it tastes of regret too. In thirty years of life, this is the first real conversation my father and I have ever had.

"Fine," I say grudgingly. "It is good to see you."

His eyebrow pops up. "Do you really mean that?"

I shrug. Things aren't perfect between us, but it does mean *something* that he hunted me down. "Yeah."

He pats me awkwardly on the shoulder, then steps out of my way to let me open the car door.

He starts to walk away but turns. "If I'm not invited to the wedding, I'd like to host a get-together afterwards at the brownstone. What do you think? Would Brody help?"

I will need to show Emmy off, so it's pretty much perfect for my plans. I tell him that's fine and get in my car, watching him walk away. He's a taciturn man, stern, and decidedly moody. Like me. And he's never married again, nor has he ever brought another woman around us. Maybe that means something, I don't know.

I shut the door and hit the call button on the dashboard and hear the line ring for Brody.

"Hey, bro. What's up?"

I answer, "You would not believe the conversation I just had with Dad. Also, I need you to help him plan a party after the marriage. Nothing fancy. Plain and simple. Can you get in touch with him?"

"You're moving fast. I'm getting tingles. Sure I can't talk you out of this?"

"Nope. Emmy is going to marry me. You're going to get your money, and everyone will be happy."

There's a silence on the phone.

"What?"

He groans. "I want you to be happy. You."

"I will be as soon as football season starts, baby bro."

Chapter 13

GRAHAM

The night air feels thick with anticipation as I open the door of the Range Rover for Emmy a couple of nights later. She's waiting for me outside her apartment, and I inhale a sharp breath at how beautiful she is.

Fierce.

Sexy.

And very, very unavailable.

There's no option where I let her in close.

I simply . . . can't go there.

I invited Divina into my heart, gave her full access, and she destroyed it.

That wound hasn't healed. It's a scar that still burns.

I'm not allowing anyone to make a fresh one.

But, damn, I can appreciate her beauty and take care of her the way a husband should. Protection. A home. She'll resist me helping her, but part of me wants to see Emmy happy. Can't deny it. Can't explain why, but I'm trusting my gut on this and going on instinct.

I open her door, and she steps carefully into the car, her long legs delicately grazing the leather seats.

"You look gorgeous." My words are husky and deep as my eyes eat her up.

"Oh. Thanks. Jane did my hair." A blush steals up her cheeks as I take in her red dress. It's silky, with one shoulder, a Grecian style, the clingy material skimming her hips and thighs. Her hair is up in a fancy updo, and her green eyes pop with dark makeup.

I get in on the other side.

She nudges her head to a lamppost down the street. "There's a man there. He snapped pics of me leaving for work this morning and was here when I came back. Should I be worried that he's here?"

I squint at the middle-aged man who's trying to look nonchalant. He keeps his head down but gazes up at us every few moments as he toys with a camera. "I imagine it's one of Holden's guys. The family law firm employs several private investigators. And the engagement announcement came out already."

She frowns. "Holden's checking up on us?"

"Unfortunately, yeah. To make sure we're legit."

"Why does he care so much?"

"Because if neither myself nor Brody marries by the time we're forty, then he gets our inheritance. That's twenty million in his pocket, plus him gloating over it when we're at Christmas dinner."

She winces. "Your family sounds . . ."

"Horrible?"

She laughs. "You aren't so bad."

She truly is sunshine—with a steely edge. I pretend an aggrieved look. "I guess we need to give him a show, yeah?"

The air thickens as I lean over the console to her.

"Another kiss?" she murmurs.

"Hmm." I touch the curve of her cheek, tracing my fingers over the top of her dress, my eyes hungry, my cock hardening.

"No objections?" I ask.

"None," she breathes, and I pull her close, my mouth seeking hers. The kiss is soft and slow, full of yearning. For me, it's the innocence in her I ache for, her sweetness, even though I know she's tough.

I like her.

The truth is, I lust.

For her.

But I'm gentle, my tongue tracing the contours and ridges of her lips, nipping delicately at her lips, every nuance amplified as I stroke my fingers over her dress, grazing her pebbled nipples.

Our lips together are pure sin, and as long as I keep my feelings locked away, this is cool, fine, I can do this, I can kiss her, I can take her in my arms, and I can fuck her—

Nope.

That's a dangerous path, one I don't want to travel down.

Take the path! the lizard side of my brain yells.

She pulls away, her thick lashes fluttering as she touches her lips. "Was he looking?" she asks.

I don't even glance that way. I'm too busy staring at her. "I'm sure he took pics. Let's get out of here."

I keep my gaze on the road, but it doesn't stop me from inhaling her sugary-sweet vanilla scent. Then I shove it away and think about football plays. I think about how being on the field this week for practice has been good. She plays with the hem of her dress, and I glance down at her legs.

This heat for her is damn inconvenient.

Don't want it.

Don't need it.

I shove those thoughts away as I whip into a parking spot at an office building.

Emmy gazes around. "What's this place?"

"I should have mentioned it earlier. It's my lawyer's office, David. He's waiting after hours for us. We'll get to Borelli's on time."

A little frown puckers her forehead. "Okay. Why are we here?"

"Prenup. A man like me doesn't get married without one."

Realization dawns on her heart-shaped face. "Ah, gotta protect those millions. I've never been wealthy, so I hadn't thought about it."

"Getting everything on paper is the smart thing to do, although money doesn't make a person happy," I say gruffly, my hands tapping out a beat on the steering wheel as I wonder what her reaction is going to be when she reads what's in it. I called David earlier and adjusted a few items.

"It's a cliché, but only people with money say that."

We're still talking as we get in the elevator. She's telling me about her day at the bookstore. Apparently Babs had an altercation with a customer who insisted on taking a book into the bathroom with him, when the sign clearly said that merchandise wasn't allowed. He'd been coming in a few times a week to go to the restroom—always with a book that he never paid for. She'd have to toss it in the trash after he left. She told him he could poop without a book, and he argued that his IBS was better with the smell of ink. She finally let him go to the restroom after he'd agreed to buy the book afterward.

I chuckle in the right places, but I'm on pins and needles as we reach David's office and walk inside. He greets Emmy, ushers her to a leather chair, and pulls out the papers I've already signed.

She scans the pages for several minutes, confusion growing on her face. "Okay, hold on. I understand the NDA, it's what we discussed, but this prenup agreement is . . ." She trails off as her green eyes rise to meet mine, incredulous as they search my face. "What's going on, Graham? We should have discussed this."

I'm standing next to the window, as far from her as I can get in the room. I actually feel my heart beating in my chest.

Damned inconvenient. She reminds me of the girl in my dream, the one who appears to me after I've been tackled on the field. I shove it away.

"What's the issue? Once the inheritance comes in and our divorce is final, once you put your signature down that we're over, you'll receive a million dollars, hopefully enough to pay off the mortgage on your apartment—or do whatever you want with."

"It's enough. Graham . . ." Her throat moves. "Is this a trick?"

"No."

She sputters. "You agreed to keep the store and only sell to someone who'll keep it, and now this. I-I don't understand why you'd do so *much* for me . . ."

"To make sure you're happy when you leave. I'll need your silence forever, Emmy. You can never go public, or we'd have to give back the inheritance."

She nods slowly. "Okay, I get that."

"Plus, you'll need somewhere to go after we divorce. You'll need a home. What would people think if we divorced, and you got nothing? It's not just about your silence; it's about appearances."

Her face dips, hiding her expression as she reads the papers. "You could have just started with all of this from the get-go."

But that was before I learned you were having trouble making your mortgage.

I want her to have this safe harbor, a landing spot once we're over. And I don't even know why. Perhaps because she is achingly familiar to me in a way I can't describe. Every fiber of me wants to take care of her. It happened the moment I got down on my knees. It felt *right.*

"Just sign the papers, Emmy," I murmur.

She shakes her head. "I can't. You're handing over money to me when you could have used it to buy Brody a place for his gym."

"I've never come across a woman who didn't want a gift from me, if you can even call it that. It's for services rendered in the future." I put my back to her, my hands tightening as I stare out into the city. "Making sure you're happy ensures your silence. If you break the contract, then you'll be in court, and I'll take the money back."

There's a charged silence as I watch her in the reflection in the window, tracing over her features. Her brows are pulled down, and her teeth nibble at her bottom lip. It's the expression she gets when she's considering something impulsive. Like dragging me into her room, probably the same one she had before she stole my car, and she certainly wore it when I "officially" proposed to her in the bookstore kitchen.

Luscious mouth.

I don't trust myself around her.

Because a part of me—shit, a serious part of me—is starting to wonder if she's . . .

No.

Football.

Football.

Football.

That's what I want.

With an exhale, she signs the papers while I stare out the window, grappling with how to endure a marriage to Emmy without, fuck, *getting feelings*.

Chapter 14
EMMY

We tell David goodbye and get back on the elevator. Several more people get on, mostly workers going home for the day, and Graham and I are pushed to the back. He stands behind me, and I'm acutely aware of him and how sinfully delicious he looks with his face shaven and his hair swept back.

"You okay?" he whispers in my ear, his jawline grazing over my skin.

"Hmm," I say as I nod. Which is a lie. I'm trying to suss out just exactly who Graham Harlan is. He certainly isn't the person I imagined when he stalked into Marcelle's.

The elevator opens, and more people get on. He's leaning against the back wall, and I shift toward him, the touch of his chest against my back making me warm. I shouldn't be playing with fire, but I can't resist.

A low gasp comes from me when he brushes his thumb over my nape in a soft caress. My chest rises as tendrils of desire flicker to life. "What are you doing?" I whisper, but I don't move away.

"Are you angry with me about the prenup?"

"I don't understand why you'd be so generous, especially after taking your car."

"I've forgiven you. Your actions were understandable, given how you coped with horrible things as a kid. You ran and hid. Trauma from your childhood triggered your response. You were repeating what you did in the past that always saved you. I get it. My past has taught me to trust no one."

I notice one of the women in the elevator darting her eyes at us. She glances at Graham, does a double take, then gives me a wink.

His hands encircle my waist to steady me—or to hold me? My breath catches, even though it's barely even a touch.

"Are we pretending right now, for the elevator people?" I murmur.

"I don't know anyone here, so . . ."

I lean my head to the side to give him access, and he groans quietly as his teeth nip at my neck.

What am I doing?

Do I care?

Abruptly the elevator stops, and I start to head to the door, but he pulls me back. "Not our floor," he rumbles in a sexy voice in my ear.

"Graham?" I say as I turn to face him, my chest against his. Nervous butterflies do flips in my stomach. I slide my hands up to his beautiful hair, tugging on the ends. "What is *this*?"

Because it's definitely something.

And it's hot.

"Emmy—"

The door opens to the first floor, and he blinks as if gathering himself. "We've got a dinner reservation," he says coolly.

My heart flutters at the contrast between what he did and now. His mood has shifted, from teasing to all business. We get back to his car, and he opens the door for me, watching me as I slide my legs in.

I get myself the mini pep talk. Cats, cats, cats. No men. Except for fucking, but okay, so why can't I fuck Graham? I mean, it would be fine, totally fine. I could keep it light and breezy and not let my heart get entangled—

My thoughts stop when he gets in the car, pausing before he cranks it.

It's all the time I need. I grab his tie, making him grunt as I pull him to me and kiss him. He makes a sound in the back of his throat, and his mouth parts eagerly to return the touch. His hands cup my face, his lips hungry and hard. Heat washes over me, curling and wrapping me in a fog.

I pull back, leaving *him* wanting more. "Thank you."

He settles back in his seat, his chest rising rapidly as he yanks his eyes away from me. He cranks the car. "You're welcome."

A photographer snaps a photo of us as we exit Graham's car and walk to the entrance of Borelli's. I try to act natural, as if being on the arm of one of the most celebrated players in New York is an everyday thing.

He curls an arm around my waist tenderly, and my body responds by melting against him. "The photographer is a guy from Page Six," Graham whispers in my ear. "My people gave him a tip that we'd be here."

Ah, right. I kiss his cheek, then smile for the next photo, being sure my ring is visible.

Borelli's is an elegant place, filled with tables and booths covered in crisp white linen. Dimly lit chandeliers dot the ceiling, and a pianist plays softly in the corner. There's a back deck, with double doors that lead to a stone terrace with a long narrow fireplace, currently not burning since it's nearly June. The place is packed, and it feels as if we're on display, especially when the room quiets as we follow the maître d' to a booth.

Graham nods at a few people, ones I don't know. He lets me sit first, then slides in across from me. I search his face, trying to see if the smile he wears reaches his eyes. It does, and I feel my shoulders relaxing. It feels as if we really are on a date.

"You like this place?" he murmurs as the waiter leaves with our drink order. Sparkling wine for me and a bourbon for him.

I nod. "I've never been, but I love Italian."

"You don't have to mash your pasta?"

"Andrew was exaggerating. Annoying little brothers tend to do that."

He laughs, highlighting the crinkles in the corner of his eyes and the dimples in his cheeks. "You just sighed. Why is that?" he asks.

I hadn't even noticed. "Truthfully?"

"I always want the truth."

"I was thinking how happy you look. You have cute little dimples when you smile."

"'Cute.'" An eyebrow rises.

I nod. "Hmm."

He leans over the table. "Tell me—why did you kiss me in the car?"

"Does a woman really need to explain that? Should I apologize?"

His eyes lower to half mast. "No."

Our drinks arrive, and I take a sip, noticing that his brow is furrowed.

"What?" I ask.

He takes a sip of his bourbon, seeming lost in thought as his eyes intently follow someone or something in the restaurant. There's a vicious look on his face, and just when I'm about to turn around and see who is deserving of such a look, he refocuses, smiling broadly as he glances back at me. "Nothing. We need a crash course in getting to know details about each other."

"Agreed." My talk with Jane solidified that I know very little.

He grins boyishly. "Let's pretend we're speed dating and just go for it. Ready?"

I prop my chin up with my palm and place my elbow on the table as I gaze at him. "Sure. Me first. I need to know how you take your coffee, your middle name, and your birthday."

"Black, Bernard, and my birthday was two weeks ago, which is why the earlier we're married, the better. I turned thirty and can inherit. What about you?"

"I drink caffeine-free tea with honey. My middle name is Grace, and my birthday is January first. I was a New Year's Day baby. Now, hmm, tell me five things you can't live without."

"Fast cars, football, hanging with Brody and Cas, a good whiskey, and travel. You go."

"Books, my family, Babs, Mason, and Ciara. Where have you traveled to?"

"Everywhere as a kid in the summer with my parents. Europe, Asia, South America. One of my favorite places is Greece: the Acropolis in Athens, the laid-back islands, especially Santorini. That's the one with the blue-domed buildings."

"I've seen pictures in books. It's beautiful."

"The villages have these crazy paths and quaint shops. Cats are everywhere—which you'd like, not me. Time seems to just stop there. Brody and I used to run around on our own, swimming in the ocean, chasing each other around the alleyways. Someday, I'd like to own a house there, right on top of one of the mountains so I can see the ocean."

"Those were happy times for you."

"Travel was important to my mom, Hazel. She grew up on a farm in Upstate New York. She didn't come from money like my dad. Her parents died when she was ten, and she was raised in foster care."

"That's her name on your wrist?"

He nods as he shoves up his shirt to show me the flock of birds on his forearm. "Yeah, I got this to remember her. The birds remind me of her because she flew away too soon."

"How did your parents meet?"

"She was playing piano in a bar in Manhattan. He says he fell in love with her the moment he saw her."

"What's your favorite song ever? Not just today but for all time?" I wave my hands around for effect.

He smiles, flashing white teeth. "Oh, that's easy. 'Stairway to Heaven,' by Led Zeppelin."

"Nice. Why?" I take a sip of champagne.

"First, it's kick-ass as shit—the guitar riff, the organ, the lyrics. My mom used to play it on the piano, and it sounds fucking amazing on piano . . . it grabs my heart every time I play it. You?"

I cock my head. "Wait a minute. You *play* it?"

A sheepish expression flits over his face. "Mom taught me. I'd come home from school and sit down next to her on the piano. It's where I felt the closest to her."

"Wow. You play piano. See, now that is something I needed to know. I wish I was that talented."

He looks down, his lashes fluttering on his cheek for a moment, and it's so entirely sweet and boyish that my heart squeezes. I like this side of him, the unsure look on his face, the slight embarrassment at my praise. "I have a baby grand at my place. I haven't touched it in years, though."

"You can play other songs?"

"Yes. What's your favorite song—of all time?"

I study his face, trying to mesh the image of him as a tough football player with a man who plays the piano. "'Hey Jude,' by the Beatles. Do you like art?"

He pops an eyebrow. "I wouldn't know a Rembrandt from a third grader's masterpiece. You?"

"I appreciate it but can't afford it."

"I like books. Always have. Thrillers especially. I've read *Pride and Prejudice* a few times, mostly because my mom adored it."

Funny. He's the embodiment of Darcy for me, arrogant and broody, with hidden depths of compassion. "Good to know, since you're buying a bookstore. Okay, so, what are you most afraid of?"

He leans back as he ponders my question. "You go first."

"Oh no, is the wee little football player afraid of telling me his secret?"

"Didn't know you were Scottish."

I laugh. "Okay, what am *I* afraid of? Not being able to take care of my family, and then I guess losing the people I love. My parents are gone, my gran, and someday Jane and Andrew will find partners and leave." My throat prickles with emotion. "I mean, that's what they need to do, but . . ." I pause, clarity settling in. "I'm afraid I'll never have that."

"Why?" he asks softly. "Kian is just a blip on your radar. There are good men who'll worship you like the queen you are."

My face heats. "'Queen'? Seriously?"

He brushes his fingers down my cheek, and my heart stutters. "I'd treat you like a queen."

My lashes flutter as my body heats. "Oh."

"In all the best ways." His voice deepens. "Darling."

He's totally pretending.

I roll my eyes. "Stop messing around. You're trying to deflect from telling me what you're most afraid of. You're a chicken."

"Noted." He lifts his glass to me and takes a sip.

"Fine, let's switch gears. What's the first thing about me that you noticed the day at the motel?"

"Your tits."

I sputter. "Figures. Couldn't you have been a little more original?"

He smirks. "No, I mean, okay, yeah, you've got a nice rack, but I could tell one of your nipples was pierced. Your bathing suit was thin, and it poked out."

I scoff. "I thought you'd be a better conversationalist."

He huffs, but there's a teasing look in his eyes. "Don't give up on me. Tell me. What do you have on your nipple?" His eyes drift down my neck to my chest.

"You'll never know."

He chuckles. "Come on, don't be mad. It's not like I knew you were a spinster wannabe, did I? I didn't have time to notice your brain because you hijacked me into your little intrigue, and there I was, pretending to be your prison boyfriend."

"There was no intrigue. Fake Clint was a mastermind serial killer. I'm convinced."

He laughs, and I nearly spit out a mouthful of champagne as I laugh with him.

"You're funny."

I bow my head. "Thank you, my king. I'll be your queen, the one with the pierced nipple," I declare, perhaps a little too loudly, since the older couple next to us send me a withering glance. "Oops."

I glance down at the ring on my finger. "Tell me more about your mom. You said this was hers."

His face softens. "She was several years younger than my dad. She taught music at a private academy, the same one where Brody teaches."

"When did your parents divorce?" His description of them traveling the world sounded idyllic, but something went wrong somewhere.

"Technically, they were separated. My dad walked out when I was fifteen. Six months later, my mom died in a skiing accident. She went the wrong way on a trail and went off the mountain." The thick muscles in his throat move as he toys with his glass. "Brody and I were with her. She was behind us on the slope and must have gone the wrong way."

My heart clenches. "I'm sorry. That's terrible."

"She was an excellent skier. Sometimes I think maybe it happened because she was . . ." He trails off as the waiter comes by to take our order.

As soon as the waiter disappears, he says, "I've never told anyone that, besides Brody."

"You think it wasn't an accident?"

His eyes search mine. "It must have been—I mean, she'd never leave us on purpose. It's just, sometimes my head gets caught up in wondering if she did something on impulse."

I squeeze his hand. "The what-ifs in the world can drive us crazy."

"Tell me how you met Kian?" I notice that his eyes darken as he mentions him.

"He came into Marcelle's and asked me out. I told him no, but he kept coming back. I admired his persistence."

"Do you still love him?" Gray eyes capture mine.

My forehead wrinkles.

He tips my chin up, searching me, trying to read me. "You don't, do you? Still love him?"

"I care about him as a person, but he wasn't good for me. Maybe if I cared enough, I'd try to get him help."

He exhales.

"You don't like my answer?"

"He needs to find his own help. You don't need to be near him," he says with fierce eyes.

"Tell me about this woman you can't have. Who is she?"

He stiffens as his eyes scan the part of the room I can't see, his face hardening for a moment as he seems to settle on something or some-one. "Divina. I met her when I was twenty-two and a rookie playing in Seattle. We fell in love and were together for years. We were engaged." He says the words in his robot voice, as if they mean nothing, but I hear the bitterness in his tone.

"What happened to break you up?"

His eyes go back to that certain corner of the restaurant, then come back to me. "We'd come to New York on holidays and during the off season, mostly to see Brody and sometimes my father and half brother, Holden. She got along well with them, especially Holden." He exhales. "We came back to Seattle after spending a Christmas in New York. She'd been distant over the holidays, spending time with friends in Manhattan and sightseeing. It didn't click until we got home, and I saw a text pop up on her phone from someone called H. He was begging her to come back to him. I scrolled through and saw where they'd been sexting for months. She'd sent him photos of herself nude. He sent dick pics. The usual sordid shit." He takes a sip of his drink, anger tightening his eyes. "I pieced it together. Holden couldn't take his eyes off her at

Christmas. Turns out, she'd been fucking him behind my back for a while."

"Double betrayal."

His jaw pops. "Yeah. Exactly. She packed her bags and moved to Manhattan and married him six months later. Holden always wanted everything Brody and I had. He was jealous of us from day one, maybe because we got more of Dad. Holden was only five when our dad left his family and made one with my mom."

"How long ago did they get married, Divina and Holden?"

"Three years ago."

I nod. "And then you got traded to New York." To be close to her?

"Not for the reason you think. Moving here was always the plan, so I could spend more time with Brody."

I take in the vulnerable glint in his eyes. I'm not sure I believe him.

"And now you have to see her with him?"

He takes a drink of his drink. "Occasionally."

What would that be like? To see the love of your life married to a sibling?

He leans in over the table. "Holden is a creature of habit. He comes to Borelli's on Wednesdays."

I stiffen. Ah, I see what tonight *really* is.

Graham wants to flaunt me in front of Holden.

The heat from his kisses, the way we've been opening up to each other, it doesn't mean anything. It's been leading up to him seeing his half brother.

A slow simmer heats in my chest.

This is just a game to him, a charade.

We're a fake couple. Yet, I let myself get swept up in the date and forgot.

Don't get close to him, Emmy. Just play the game like you promised.

Fortunately the server brings our food, and I look down at it, not wanting Graham to see the growing frustration on my face.

Chapter 15

GRAHAM

Emmy and I are waiting for the check to arrive when she tells me she's going to the ladies' room. She rises gracefully as I brush my fingers down to her hand to give it a squeeze for the crowd at Borelli's.

A few minutes later, I've paid the check, and she still hasn't come back to the table. I walk to the back of the restaurant area where the restrooms are. Minutes tick by slowly. Finally, an older woman emerges, and I describe Emmy and ask if she's inside. She shakes her head and tells me she was alone in the restroom.

Growling under my breath, I stalk back to the table, and the maître d' is there.

He nods his head at me. "Mr. Harlan, your companion is out on the back deck, sir."

Great. At least he's keeping up. She must have slipped past me when I was checking my phone.

I thank him and head that way, weaving through the tables. I step out into the stone terrace and see her standing near the edge of the landscaping—next to Holden. My nose flares at the punch that hits my gut. Motherfucker. He's probably been eye-stalking her ever since he saw her with me earlier. As soon as he walked into the restaurant, he saw us and sent me a haughty nod, which I ignored.

I study him while he's not looking. He's handsome, I suppose, in an oily kind of way, all full of bullshit charm. Tall and lean, he has brown hair and a square chin with a cleft.

Put us side by side, and we look nothing alike.

He's vaping, the smoke curling around Emmy as she talks to him. He reaches over and offers her a drag. When he touches her arm, jealousy bites so hard I have to clench my fists to steady myself.

I stalk their way, and Emmy must sense me approaching because she turns and smiles at me with her whole heart, her eyes fake adoring me as she takes steps to meet me.

"Sweetie pie, I met your brother. What a coincidence that we happened to be at the same restaurant."

"Careful with him, darling. He never plays nice," I say under my breath.

"I've got this," she whispers as she crooks her arm in mine, and we head back to Holden.

He watches us with eyes that drape over every inch of her, a smarmy leer on his face. He spreads his arms wide. "Graham! Well, look at this. The happy couple together on a date." He drops his arms when I make no attempt to touch him. "Ah, no brotherly hug, then?"

"Not today," I say coolly.

"Ah, whatever. I can wait for the holidays—or the wedding." He laughs.

My body tenses. I went to his wedding, an elaborate affair with over three hundred guests. Fighting the anger and bitterness inside me, I sat in the back, unnoticed, and watched him and Divina exchange vows.

"It's going to be a very private affair. Where's your wife?"

"Oh, she's around." He smirks at me, then shifts his gaze to Emmy. "Graham knows I come to Borelli's. What a coincidence that we're both here on the same night. It must not be much of a surprise to see me."

"It was actually my idea to come," Emmy says. "I adore Italian, and this place is close to Wickham, where Graham lives." She glances at me. "I hope you weren't worried about me when I disappeared. Holden bumped into me on my way back to the table and insisted I see the back deck and fireplace. We were just talking about our engagement. Apparently, he saw the announcement."

Holden raises his drink in a mock toast. "I'm so excited that I must insist the family throw a breakfast or a dinner for you after the nuptials. After all, I'm sure Dad will want to meet your gorgeous bride."

"Dad and Brody are already planning something," I say.

Holden curls his lips at me, a gleam of malice there. "About time you got married, and I promise to keep my hands off this one." He smirks at Emmy, then looks back to me. "You'll get your inheritance, of course. Not that you need it. I imagine Brody wants his, but that will never happen. Sadly, our grandmother made a will that doesn't include him."

Emmy narrows her eyes at him. "You don't sound disappointed by it. It's terribly unfair. Brody is married. He should get the same as the both of you when he turns thirty." She glances at me. "Has Brody ever considered contesting it?"

Yes. But there's no telling how long that would take. Or how expensive it might be.

Holden laughs. "Graham! She's a little spitfire."

"She is," Emmy says.

Holden sucks his vape, letting the smoke curl around us as he exhales. "I'm a lawyer, Emmy. The will *is* ironclad. New York has tough laws about wills, and our grandmother's was perfectly executed. I have no issue with who Brody is married to, but our grandmother would. The language is on purpose. She wasn't incapacitated, or unduly influenced. Believe me, I've considered the different angles."

Oh, I'm sure he has.

He continues. "It's sad for Brody, especially since I hear he's been shopping banks for a loan to open a gym."

"Not much gets past you, huh?" I arch a brow.

"No." He looks at Emmy. "Especially a hasty marriage to someone you hardly know."

"We're in love, Holden," I murmur. "It makes a man do crazy things."

"Right," he scoffs. "We'll see about that."

"Holden, darling? Are you ready to go?" comes a dulcet voice from the doorway that leads back into the restaurant.

We turn as a pretty woman with long red hair approaches us in a pantsuit, probably Holden's age. She moves to stand next to him, their arms grazing slightly. "Oh, I thought you were out here alone."

Holden tucks his vape pen away and kisses her on the cheek. "Pia, meet Graham and his fiancée, Emmy. Guys, this is Pia, one of the partners at our firm."

Emmy has stiffened next to me, and I sense her confusion about the fact that this isn't Divina.

Pia nods. "Nice to meet you. We were just celebrating a new case tonight."

A smirk rises on my face. "My brother is a creature of habit, I guess. He loves to do *work* at Borelli's."

Pia throws a glance at me, lingering. "I've heard of you, of course. Your dad talks about you. You're quite famous."

I take her hand and give her a smile. "Would you like an autograph?"

She blushes. "Oh yes! My nephew would go nuts over it. Let me grab something from my purse for you to sign."

Holden grunts. "He's barely famous."

"Don't be jealous. I get this all the time." I sign a notepad Pia presents from her purse with a flourish, relishing the fury emanating from Holden. I hand her pen back, then thread my fingers through Emmy's hand and kiss her fingers gently and gaze into her eyes as if she's the only woman on the planet.

"We should go," Emmy murmurs.

"Indeed."

Without saying goodbye to the other couple, I turn and guide us away from the deck and back into the restaurant.

Chapter 16

EMMY

Graham parks on the street outside my building, and before he can turn the car off, I'm out of the vehicle.

"Emmy. Wait," he calls as I hear him following me. He catches up with me as I reach the lobby doors.

"There's no need to follow me inside. There's no photographer. Go home, Graham."

"You're mad at me. You barely said two words the entire way here."

"I didn't have to say anything because we aren't a real thing. I don't have to pretend in the car. Acting is over," I say sharply.

I stab at the elevator button, and it opens. I walk inside, and he follows me.

"Did Holden do something? Touch you or make you feel uncomfortable?"

"He was a giant anus, and he was definitely waiting for me outside the restroom, but that's not the point. The point is you didn't tell me what was going on. I didn't realize that our entire evening was a performance for Holden and his coworker."

He exhales. "She's his mistress."

I lift my hands. "I don't care. If I'd known it was a spy mission to see if he's cheating on Divina, I would have liked to have been told. I knew you kept looking over at someone in the restaurant, but then we . . ."
Were having a good time.

I was beguiled by him. That's the damn issue.

The elevator door opens to my floor, and I march to it, then whip around. "This date is over."

"Let me explain at least."

Jiggling my key, I open my door and walk into the foyer. "Fine."

He rubs his jawline, a perplexed expression on his face. "I'm sorry I didn't tell you he was there. I didn't know for sure that he'd show, but he and Dad usually go there on Wednesdays. Brody and I have been invited several times, and we go sometimes, mostly when it's just Dad. I didn't know he'd show up with her, although I'm not surprised."

"And there's a party apparently? After we're married? I had no clue what was going on."

He groans. "I didn't have time to bring it up."

I shake my head. "I thought you were in the moment. I thought we were having a great time—"

Jane's hushed voice interrupts me as she appears in the hallway. "You both sound like a herd of elephants. Londyn just got to sleep and she's teething, and if you wake her up, you'll have to deal with it."

"Sorry." A long exhale comes from me as I toss my purse on the narrow table in the foyer and walk to the den.

"Hey, Andrew is still out, and I scheduled drinks with a girlfriend. Are you in for the night?" she asks me, her eyes darting to Graham.

He's right there in the den, of course, clearly not leaving.

I smile, noticing that she's wearing a miniskirt and a lacy blouse. "Sure. Go on. Have fun. I'm not going anywhere."

Graham plops down on the couch. "Neither am I," he says quietly, then narrows his eyes at me. "Not until we start communicating and figure out what this attitude is about."

My eyes flash. "'Attitude.' Oh. Just you wait."

"Is your temper always this hot?"

"Only when someone hurts my feelings."

"How?" he mutters, crossing his arms.

"Oh, one more thing. Mason and Ciara were in the neighborhood and dropped by," Jane says, interrupting us as she slips on a cardigan.

I wince. I left a voice mail on Mason's phone that I was going to be putting all my work into the store and would have to let the bar go, but if he needed me to come in this coming week, I would, but I didn't explain why.

"What did they say?" I ask.

Jane glances at Graham, who currently looks very comfortable on my couch. "They heard about your *engagement* and wanted to congratulate you. Mason, in particular, had lots of questions about it."

I rub my forehead, recalling that Mason knew about me taking the Lambo. He's probably worried.

"Why did you just put an emphasis on 'engagement'?" Graham asks her.

"I didn't," Jane says, then glances at me with an *I'm sorry* look, which only makes it worse.

"Yes, you did," he insists. "You said, 'They heard about your *engagement.*'"

"Didn't. Oops, look at the time. I've got to dash, or I'll miss the train. Bye, guys." With a little wave and a last look at me, she grabs her keys and wallet and heads out the door.

The silence builds in the apartment as Graham stands with his hands on his hips. "Dammit, Emmy. You told her."

Tension swirls, almost a tangible thing, as our eyes clash together.

He rubs his face. "I specifically asked you not to tell anyone, even your siblings, and you signed an NDA."

"I signed it *tonight* and I told her *yesterday,*" I snip, brushing past him to head down the hall. "Plus, she already knew something was up when Babs told her you'd bought the store. For me, apparently."

"I did buy it for you. You should be happy."

"You bought it to manipulate me."

He follows me. "What if she tells someone, then they tell someone? Holden already knows that Brody wants to open a gym, and he didn't hear that from me or Brody, which means he's always spying on us. You can't tell *anyone* my secrets."

I open my bedroom door and walk in. "'The best way to keep a secret between two people is if one of them is dead.' Mark Twain. Or someone. I can't remember because I'm pissed at you."

He shuts my door behind him and faces me, his cheekbones flushed with twin spots of color. "And for no fucking reason."

I take down the pins in my hair and toss them on the dresser. Threading my fingers through my hair, I release the chignon, and the strands fall to my shoulders.

Do I have a reason?

Not to him.

He's just playing a role.

I'm the moth who flew a little too close to his flame.

A small huff comes from me as I try to clear my thoughts.

He never said anything different tonight, but I got caught up in the moment, especially after his generosity with the prenup.

I deflate, my shoulders slumping. "I forgot, okay. It felt real, and I was getting to know you. I forgot that there was an ulterior motive for our evening out."

His expression turns quizzical, as if he's trying to decipher my words.

I huff. "I'm angry at myself, and then Holden surprised me, and then Pia shows up and you don't seem fazed at all. I don't like being kept in the dark. It was all too much at once."

He picks up a candid photo of Jane and Andrew and Londyn and me. "Who else have you told? Your brother?"

I shake my head. "No."

He's walking the perimeter of my room, taking it all in, from the Victorian doll collection I inherited from Gran to the mess of clothes on the floor to my stuffed animals. Magic abruptly darts out from under my bed, arches his spine, hisses at Graham, then runs from the room.

"He was just saying hello," I say.

"Your cat is temperamental," Graham says dryly as he gives me a look. "Like you."

I sigh, changing directions. "I used to read *Charlotte's Web* to my siblings. Are you familiar with it, Graham?"

"I wasn't born under a rock. Yes."

I grab the stuffed Wilbur off my nightstand and hold him out. About twelve inches tall with pink fur and gentle eyes, he's a little ragged from all the years. "Whenever one of us is going through a tough time, we take the pig and sleep with him. Sometimes Jane gets him. Sometimes Andrew. We still do it to this day, not nearly as seriously, of course, but Wilbur *is* meaningful. Jane has noticed that I've had him for a week. You see, we've been through so much together, and she knows when something isn't right. Wilbur is here to make it better. He's a hopeful, dreamy, soulful little creature."

He gives the pig a look.

"Don't doubt the pig. He is magic."

He rolls his eyes.

"I mean it. He knows you're angry with me for telling Jane. Do you want to hold him?"

He cocks his head. "So you're saying that she saw you giving extra love to Wilbur and deducted that you were faking an engagement?"

"Mostly. It's hard to explain, but sisters have a weird connection. Andrew? Clueless. Here, catch." I toss him Wilbur, and he catches him and stares down at the animal with a perplexed expression.

"How does he feel?" I ask.

"Like an old stuffed animal. Am I supposed to be getting some magic vibes from him?"

"Fine. I'm going to make you watch the movie. Maybe you'll get it."

"Now? No. I want to talk about you telling your sister. I'm angry."

I put my hands on my hips. "Yes, I told her. Why? Because she was crying in my office and asking me questions, like how you take your coffee and what your middle name was. I was clueless. She has been sworn to silence. She knows the stakes here. And I couldn't keep lying to her. I can't hide things from a sister who's so much like me already. There. Are you still mad?"

He lets out a big exhale. "A little. If you trust her, then I will."

I smile. "See. The pig worked."

"Here's an idea. We never go to Borelli's again," he says as he tosses the pig at me, and I catch him, then set him on my nightstand.

I run a brush through my hair. "Agreed. It wasn't even that good."

I put my back to him and place my hands behind my back. My fingers catch the midshoulder zipper of my dress, but from the angle, I can't get it to go down.

"What are you doing?" he asks, his voice husky.

I toss him a look over my shoulder. "Jane and Andrew aren't here, and I don't want to sleep in this all night."

I point to where the zipper is on the outfit. "Please?"

His fingers brush over my skin as he tugs down the zipper, and my dress falls to the floor. His breath catches, and I look in the mirror and see us, me in my white lingerie and him with his head bent, his eyes drinking in my skin.

I don't cover myself but stand with my spine straight. Gray eyes meet mine in the mirror, and when he speaks, his voice is rough. "We said we'd keep this professional."

"That's cool. I'm just breaking the tension between us."

"'Tension'?"

"Hmm, sexual. Very taut. Needs a release. That's it."

He rubs his jaw. "Sounds plausible."

"And you asked about my piercing. It's hard to describe, and I took you for a visual learner, so I thought it best to just show you." I ease down the straps of my bra and undo the clasp in the front. My breasts swing free. I look at the piercing in the mirror. "It's a curved titanium barbell design, with a half-moon shape on the ends. There's tiny diamonds inside the moon."

"Why did you get it? When?" I watch a pulse beating rapidly in his neck.

"First, hand me a T-shirt to sleep in, will you? They should be in the top drawer, on the right."

He swallows. Seems to think. Starts to the dresser, then comes back. "No. Let me see it. Your mirror sucks. Turn around."

"That wouldn't be *professional.*"

"God damn it, Emmy, nothing about you being nearly naked is professional." He scrubs his jawline.

"Hmm, I guess a little more wouldn't cross too many lines, then?"

"Turn. The. Fuck. Around." His hands clench in frustration.

Delicious shivers dance over my skin like tiny bolts of lightning. Yes. That's the real Graham. Big. Tough. Demanding. A man telling me what to do sends shivers over me—as long as I know he won't hurt me.

I turn slowly, our eyes holding. "Look."

He does, his gaze tracing a path of fire from my lips to my breasts. He lingers there for several seconds, then skates down to the curve of my hips and the wisp of white lace covering my pelvis. Awe and longing flicker over his face, and he rubs his lips with his hand, as if imagining it's my skin.

"Is anything else pierced?"

"Sorry, not brave enough for a genital one. This one hurt."

"Was it worth it? Does it make you . . ." He blinks, his words trailing off.

"Oh yes. One lick or tug and everything is sensitized. It goes straight to my clit."

He groans, the tent in his pants bulging out.

"I was twenty-five when I got it. Gran was sick, and I was taking care of Jane and Andrew. I needed something that was mine, like reclaiming myself. It's a symbol of sorts. I wasn't seeing anyone romantically because of everything I had to do, but I had this, and it made me feel feminine and sexy. It felt empowering, like I was saying, 'Hey, I don't need anyone to make me feel bold or beautiful—I just need myself.'"

I glance out the window and up to the sky, where the moon sends light shimmering into the room. "I got the half moons because they mean the changing of life, the coming and going like the tides. And I feel like the moon is a she. For me anyway. She might mean something altogether different to someone else. She changes every night, evolving and becoming something new. How fucking awesome to be her." I laugh softly as he comes closer, so close that I can feel the heat of him. "I'm not sure you're listening."

"Trust me, I'm soaking it all in, Emmy. Answer me this: Have you had too much champagne?"

"No, and I love that your voice sounds like it's been dragged over concrete."

"May I touch you?" he asks with his hand raised halfway.

I nod, but instead of his hand touching me, he bends over, and his tongue darts out and strokes my pierced nipple. He flicks the metal, exploring the hard titanium, his mouth searching my peak to taste every ridge and contour.

Tremors take my legs, and I gasp as he sucks it into his mouth, the metal clinking against his teeth. He tugs. Gently but precisely. Skilled yet careful.

He is hot. And he's built so broad and big, and I can't resist, and maybe getting undressed in front of him wasn't my smartest idea, but Jesus, his lips and tongue are maddening. My hands go to his scalp and bring him closer.

His other hand twirls my other nipple between his fingers, as if he knows the desperation I feel for his touch. His fingers roughen, and I groan as wonderful, sweet heat blooms in my pussy, and I bite my lip to keep from gyrating on his leg.

He pulls back, leaving me gasping, as his big hands cup my face, and he stares at me with the intensity of a laser as if reaching inside me to draw out all my secrets. His silky shirt rubs against my skin, and I swivel to get more friction. He licks his lips. "Emmy . . ."

"What?" I tug him up to look at me in the eyes. If I'm being honest, this here, this man lusting for me, is what I've wanted ever since the moment he got down on his knees for me. Maybe before then.

"I can't get serious."

"Why?"

He traces my eyebrow with his finger, his voice strained. "Because I need to focus on football. And a million other reasons."

It's what I expected to hear. "Are you going to kiss me or what?"

"Or what," he growls as he lowers his head to mine and takes my lips hard, his hand going to my ass to press my entire body against his.

He says my name on a groan as he kisses my neck, down to my clavicle and to my piercing. Deft fingers tease the waistband of my panties until finally he slides underneath and cups my ass.

"Darling," he murmurs as he eases down the wisps of lace.

I feel exposed and vulnerable in the best way. The air feels heavy and thick with desire as he gazes at my body with reverence. He kneels in front of me, then locks his eyes with mine. I'm gasping, waiting for his touch. Chills dance over my skin, anticipation rising.

His lips land on my navel, tasting the gold ring I have there, then slides to my hipbone. "You smell so fucking good."

I'm reeling in sensation when one finger enters me slowly, teasingly, barely there.

"Good?"

I nod, my body shivering as he goes deeper. I'm wet and hear him groan against my skin as he hears the sound his finger makes inside me.

I'm bracing myself against the bedpost, crying out with need, when he lifts my leg and puts it over his shoulder.

He spends a few moments staring at me, his gaze devouring the shape of my pussy, the contours, and the way I'm already clenching for him to touch me again.

He does. With his tongue. He eats at me with ferocious intent, his tongue flicking against my clit with an assault of emotion. Passion ignites even higher when his finger joins in, and he works in tandem with his tongue. I can't really move how I want because of the angle and the way I'm holding myself up, and I mewl out, wanting and needing more.

His fingers find the secret spot inside me, and he rubs, faster and faster. My head falls back, my breasts aching, as I surrender to his masterful touch, to the carnal moment, whether it means something or not.

I give in to everything that is him. My body tenses, my pussy clenching around his fingers as my orgasm races to the top of the mountain and explodes. I cry out, spasming around him with my hands in his hair, digging my nails into his scalp. His tongue continues to suck at me, his fingers still delving inside, and my heart jumps as I wonder if I can come again so soon.

"You can," he growls on my skin, and I shudder with the intensity of heat in his voice. He eases my leg off his shoulder, still finger-fucking me as he pushes me back onto the end of the bed.

"Keep your legs spread," he says, his eyes like liquid metal.

I whimper as he devotes himself to pleasuring my body, as if it is the only thing in the world he's ever wanted.

He moves to kiss my nipples, lingering on my piercing. He plays with my breasts, squeezing and molding them, drawing maddening circles with his fingertips, at first gentle and soft, then increasingly harder. The friction escalates as he adds two fingers to my pussy, fucking me like a cock, then grinding against my clit when he exits.

I'm a live wire. A pulse of sensation. I am on fire.

I ache. I need. I desire.

His teeth nip at my nipple as he taps my clit, then stops, then taps again in an uneven rhythm, making me squirm under the madness.

"Please," I call out.

He makes a noise in his throat and rubs his slacks against my thigh. His cock strains to escape the confines of his clothes, and my mouth waters at the thought of taking him down my throat.

Sensuous abandon takes me over as I eagerly try to undo his pants, but the angle is all wrong.

"Just you," he groans as he sucks my nipple, then bites.

It's as if I'm being uncoiled from a tense spring as I come with a sharpness that sneaks up and detonates like a firecracker. I shudder, my body arching up toward him, my hips pumping to wrangle out the last throes of passion.

Gasping, I fall back, sinking into the covers on my bed as I moan. He collapses next to me, his face slicked with sweat, his eyes heavy and burning with tempered desire. My chest heaves as if I've been running.

I huff out a laugh. "You still have your clothes on."

He smiles. "That's what happens when you strip in front of me. Wasn't time to really think." He pauses, his eyes lingering on my face, searching my features. "You are extraordinary."

Most men might have said I was "beautiful" or that I was "sexy," but somehow "extraordinary" feels more eloquent. "You aren't too bad yourself."

His fingers graze down my throat softly, tracing the outline of my breasts before dancing over my nipples. "I don't have a condom."

I feel heat flooding my cheeks. "I do. In my nightstand." They're there for "just in case," since Kian and I mostly had sex at his place.

A wailing reaches my ears, and I sit up, my head spinning from the movement. "That's Londyn." I wince. "I must have woken her up."

He gets off the bed and holds his hand out for me as I put my feet on the floor. Moving swiftly, I scramble around and find my underwear, then grab a tank top and sleep shorts.

"What's wrong with her? Doesn't she just go back to sleep?"

"Nothing probably, but she is teething, and once she's awake, she likes to let everyone know."

"Can I help?" he asks, following me as I open my bedroom door.

"Can you grab a washcloth from the bathroom, get it wet with cold water, then stick it in the freezer for a bit? It will cool down her gums and give her something to chew."

"I've never been around babies."

"You want kids?"

"I used to."

With Divina, I suppose.

"Do you?" he asks.

"Londyn is perfect for me, but maybe someday . . ."

"Even though you don't plan on marriage?"

I shrug. "Single ladies can have children."

"Oh."

She cries harder, and I leave him there and go to her room. She's standing, hanging on to the crib rail as she whimpers. Her little face is red, and the top of her sleeper is wet with drool.

"Poor darling," I murmur as I pick her up and cuddle, patting her bottom. I change her into a fresh diaper and sleeping outfit. So she doesn't get more drool on it, I put a bib on as I murmur soothing words. When I turn, Graham is at the door, watching me with an odd expression.

He blinks, seeming to come out from wherever he was. "I put the washcloth in the freezer."

Londyn quiets as she looks at him with big eyes. She sniffles and babbles something that I think is probably *Why are you here?*

I head to the den.

"What now?" he asks as if he's taking notes.

"You can bring me the washcloth," I say as I sit in a blue swivel rocking chair next to a window that overlooks the city. I prop her on my lap, and Graham hands me the washcloth.

"I, um, washed my hands first, you know, after . . ."

I giggle. "Okay. She appreciates it."

Londyn reaches for the cloth and promptly sticks it in her mouth and chews. Her back rests against my chest as I rock with her. Slowly, she stops her whimpering.

"Wow, that was easy. She really is adorable."

I laugh under my breath at his surprised tone. He saw her in the kitchen at the bookstore, but there was so much else going on that he probably barely noticed her. "Now we have to get her back to sleep."

"We?"

"You're here, and we just had relations, and you can't run off. It would be ungentlemanly."

He rolls his eyes.

"What?"

"'Relations' and 'ungentlemanly.' Your words crack me up."

I shrug delicately so as not to disturb Londyn, who seems wide awake as she darts her eyes between me and Graham.

"I don't want to say 's-e-x' in front of you-know-who."

"Hmm. I saw the scars on your rib cage. What's that from? Did Kian . . .'"

"No, no. I have A-fib. It's a heart condition where I have irregular heartbeats. Too fast. I took meds for a while, but they quit working. I had an incident at the store where I passed out, and my doctors decided I needed a cardiac ablation." I go into detail, explaining how I assumed it was panic attacks at first but realized later that it was a medical condition.

He's suddenly sitting at attention and walks over to me. "Let me see it again?"

Londyn pulls out her washcloth and watches Graham as he lifts my tank top and peers at the scar on my rib cage. He frowns as his fingers lightly trace over it. "Did surgery fix it forever?"

"Are you worried for me?" I ask, surprise in my voice.

"You're going to be my wife."

I shift the focus from me to him. "My heart issue is minor compared to what happened to you on the football field. Want to hear something crazy?"

He nods.

"I had my surgery the night of the Super Bowl. You and I were in the same hospital on the same night, Mount Sinai."

He studies my face searchingly, his gaze lingering on my mouth. "And then we met in the desert. Life is weird." His hands trail over the line of my cheek, tenderly, making my breath quicken.

"Yes."

"I think I'm going to stretch out," he says as he pulls away from me and settles back on the couch, adjusting the pillows as he lies back. It's not quite long enough to fit his frame, so he removes his shoes and props his feet up on the end of the sofa.

He taps his fingers against his chest, the only indication that he isn't completely relaxed. "Are you free Friday?"

"I can be. Jane and Andrew are helping out at the store."

He shuts his eyes, almost as if he doesn't want me to read his expression. "Good. Can you meet me in the afternoon. I can text you the exact time when I know for sure."

"Where?"

He's so quiet that for a moment I think he's gone to sleep. "Clerk's office at the courthouse, if that works for you? I can send a car to pick you up."

I continue to rock a now-sleeping Londyn. "Should I wear white?"

"If you wish. Just us. Me and you. They'll provide witnesses for us."

I nod, even though he isn't looking. No siblings at our marriage ceremony. And I get it. This isn't real. There's no reason to create a memory with our loved ones.

His breaths deepen as his chest rises and falls.

"What are you wearing? So we can match," I murmur.

"The mayo suit."

I kiss Londyn's head. "Mr. Cream," I say under my breath, and Graham doesn't seem to hear me. A soft snore comes from him.

I pick Londyn up, remove her bib, and cradle her on my shoulder as I go back to her room and put her in her bed. She rolls over with a sigh, and all feels right in the world.

I ease back into the den and cover Graham up with a blanket, then leave a note out on the door telling Andrew and Jane to be quiet when they come in and not be startled by the giant man on our couch.

Chapter 17
EMMY

The last person on my schedule to interview leaves my office, and I groan as I pinch the bridge of my nose. Only one of the applicants today would be a good fit, and she can't start for two more weeks.

The bookstore phone rings, and I pick it up. "Emmy Darling from A Likely Story Bookstore. May I help you?"

"Emmy! It's been forever. How are you?"

"Great." If I could just find more workers.

"It's Angela from the *Times*. I thought you guys were closing; then I heard you weren't. Good news. Does this mean you'll have a new window for us soon? I'd love to see it and feature it in our summer roundup photos."

Right, ugh. My anxiety shoots up. I've been so busy with Graham that I haven't thought about the window lately. I need to get the new display up. "Hi, and yes, we'd be so thankful if you'd feature us. We put a lot of time and effort into our displays. We'll have it ready by the second week of June. How does that sound?"

"Awesome. What time would be good to come by?"

I schedule a slot for her, and as I'm getting off the phone, a photo comes through on my cell. It's Graham, replying to the text thread I've entitled Things We Should Know About Each Other. We've been texting on and off since our date, usually first thing in the morning and then in the evenings.

I squint at the pic he's sent. It's one from a college party where he's standing on top of a bar inside a fraternity house as he holds up a trophy. A wide, broad grin is on his handsome face. His hair is short and spiky, his face young and free. He's wearing Florida State gym shorts and no shirt. His chest is a work of art, an eight-pack glistening.

You were trashed, I send.

We'd just won the national championship over Alabama.

Did you have a serious college girlfriend?

No. I was too focused on football.

Hmm, Divina was his first serious relationship. It lasted for years. And then she cheated on him.

Send me a pic of you from the past, he sends.

I scroll through my pics and send one of me from a birthday dinner at the bookstore, after hours. Whoever took it, probably Babs or Terry, caught me in the middle of an eye roll as I attempted to blow out candles on a four-layer coconut cake Gran had baked. Andrew and Jane, ages twelve and thirteen, sit on either side of me, laughing, and Gran is behind me, a serene smile on her face.

I dig the pink streaks in your hair. See you soon, he replies.

Tucking my cell away, I finish my tea, then check my hair in the mirror. It's up again, the length braided and twisted around a bun in the back. Little curly wisps dangle from the side. I reapply my red lipstick. I get on the PA system and ask for Jane to come to my office.

She waltzes in, and I smile nervously. "It's time. Will you help me?" I ask as I nudge my head at the dress hanging from a sconce on the wall.

She nods, her face impassive as she helps me change out of my slacks and blouse and into a tea-length dress that Brody insisted I get yesterday. He and Cas showed up at the store yesterday at closing time. Jane and I went with them to a bridal store in Tribeca. The place was appointment only, but Brody said his family knew the designer, and he was able to get us one after hours.

We lounged on a couch and watched as models showcased tea-length bridal gowns. I chose a champagne-colored, figure-hugging slip dress. Small sparkling beads adorn the material. My favorite part is the corset bodice with silk ribbons that tie in the back. I balked at the cost, but Brody insisted Graham wanted me to have a new dress. After a few alterations that only took minutes, we left the boutique.

Jane zips up the back, then turns me around. "You ready?"

"This dress is entirely too much for a civil ceremony," I murmur as I gaze at myself in the mirror and smooth down the fabric. It is the most beautiful dress I've ever seen.

"It's perfect. Now, get out of here before I lock you in your office so you won't marry him."

"Babs would just let me out."

She gives me a kiss on the cheek. "Good luck. I'm gonna go upstairs and straighten the shelves. Keep myself busy."

The rotunda is full of customers when I walk out, but no one seems to notice I'm overly dressed. Books can do that to a person.

"Emmy?" says a familiar male voice. Sucking in a sharp breath, I look up from the messages I was reading on the manual typewriter in the rotunda.

What is *he* doing here?

Standing near the door, Kian wears joggers and a Nike shirt, as if he's just come from the gym. His blue eyes laser in on mine. "Hey."

"You can't be here," I hiss as I walk over. "I told you not to come near me. That includes the bookstore."

"I would have called, but you blocked my number. I needed to talk to you."

My heart jumps in my chest as I remember our fight, his choking me, me being terrified beyond reason. I recall the rushed way I packed, hands trembling, the intense adrenaline rushing through my veins.

My father may not have hurt me physically, but his abuse and my mother leaving left a wound on my soul. That hurt, that awful wound, has kept me from truly giving myself to anyone.

"You. Need. To. Leave," Jane calls from the staircase as she rushes down the last few steps. Anger flashes from her eyes. Her voice has carried around the store, and a few customers openly stare at us.

I think she's going to bump chests with him, so I put a hand on her shoulder to hold her back. "That's enough," I say under my breath.

"Come on, Emmy, please. Just give me a minute. Outside," he adds. "It won't take long."

"Why?" I ask.

He exhales heavily. "I need to tell you about a visit I got yesterday. It's important, or I wouldn't have come."

Okay, he has my interest.

"It's about you and Graham." He practically spits his name.

I exhale. "No tricks, Kian."

He holds his hands up in a placating manner. "None. I'm sober. I haven't had anything to drink for weeks."

Ha. I've heard that before, but his eyes aren't bloodshot, and he does seem calm. But appearances can be deceiving. My dad would be easy one minute, then turn into a monster the next.

"Are you seriously going to listen to him?" Jane asks, her tone incredulous.

Yes, I'm curious. Plus, a ton of people are outside, milling around on the sidewalk. It's not like I'll be alone with him. And if he knows anything *real* about me and Graham, then I need to know so I can protect Graham.

"I'm watching from the window," she calls out as I follow him to the door, "and if he so much as *looks* at you wrong, I'm coming out with an axe."

What's scary is we do have an axe in the kitchen, next to the fire extinguisher. It's not big, but it could do some damage.

Kian holds the door for me, and we exit the store. He takes a seat on a bench that faces the window and sends a wry wave to Jane, who simply glowers. I sit next to him and wait for that tingle of attraction, for the tug I used to feel, but there's nothing but the bitter taste of regret.

He leans down and puts his elbows on his knees as a long exhale comes from his lips. "I really messed things up with you this time."

"Yes."

He gives me a glum look. "I put a tracker on your phone because I was fucking around on you."

As I suspected. My intuition is rarely wrong. I grew up with mistrust and fear and learned early on to be hyperaware.

"I hurt you, then chased you across the desert to convince you to come back to me."

"All true."

A few beats of silence pass as he mulls over what to say next.

"I'm a real asshole, Emmy, and I'm sorry."

Sincerity is in his tone, true, and I appreciate it, but . . . "Leaving bouquets of lilies won't fix anything, Kian."

Then his next words make me flinch.

"Missy admitted she called you and told you that I was coming to your motel. You must have been desperate to get away. You stole Graham Harlan's car to escape me." He cocks an eye at me, studying my reaction.

"Me? Hardly." I blink innocently.

"Here's the thing. This guy came around to my place and started asking questions about you and Graham. He claimed to be a reporter, but I know a PI when I see one. I saw your engagement post, by the way. Congrats. It's created quite a stir in football world. 'Kian Adams's ex set to marry Graham Harlan.' But whatever. I didn't deserve you, and I fucked it up royally. Too much drinking. Too much money. Fame. I've hit some rough patches in my career, and I was lashing out."

I tense. "There's no excuse for what you did."

His mouth twists.

"You're responsible for your actions," I add. "You caused harm. Don't do it to someone else. Don't hurt Missy."

"Forget her. You look beautiful," he says, his gaze caressing me.

My lips press together as I say nothing.

He inches closer. "Anyway, I thought you should know that this guy told me you stole Graham's car. He also asked me about your parents. That's why I came. I know how private you are and wanted to warn you."

Graham mentioned that he didn't file a report about me, just that his car was stolen, so the PI must have talked to the clerk at the front desk.

He makes a noise in his throat, a pained sound. "Tell me, Emmy, was it love at first sight—with Graham?"

I stare down at my beaded shoes. "Yes."

I feel him glancing at the ring on my finger.

"We were just over, and I thought you'd be more upset or at least wait awhile before going out with someone. I'm hurt that he's someone I know." He hangs his head. "Did you plan on meeting him at the motel in the desert?"

I glance at Jane in the window. She's holding the axe. Jesus.

The less I tell him, the better. "I never cheated on *you*, Kian. Sometimes it takes meeting the wrong person to find the right one."

He stands to his feet as he drinks in my features. "Baby. That bullshit doesn't sound like you. We had something good."

I narrow my eyes. "We weren't right for each other, or you wouldn't have been tracking my phone. You would have had more respect for me. And you never would have choked me. Also, don't leave flowers here. Don't be following me down the street. We're over. You know it. I know it. Graham knows it."

"I still love you, baby. Don't marry him," he says fervently as he takes my hand. I jerk back at the zap of fear that dances up my spine. I guess it will always be there when I encounter him.

Jane exits the store, axe in hand. "Let her go, motherfucker."

"I do love you. I really do!" He gives me one last longing look, then drops my hand and stalks away.

She slides in next to me, both of us watching his back as he turns the corner.

Jane sighs. "I'm mad at you right now for even talking to him."

"Hopefully not enough to axe me?"

Her shoulders release the tension she was carrying. "Meh. I guess not. It is your wedding day, and I'd hate to get blood on that dress; plus, you did give me a steady job. I'm actually really hungry. How about a cookie before you tie yourself to Graham?"

"I'll have to be careful in this dress."

"Oatmeal raisin. Fresh from the oven."

"Deal." We link our arms together and walk back into the store.

"So," she says as we head to the kitchen, "are you going to let him dip his stick tonight?"

"Excuse me?"

She smirks. "Technically, you aren't really married until you consummate the union. Do you want me to draw you a diagram?"

"I know how sex works, smart-ass, but it's a marriage of convenience."

"Well, it was awfully *convenient* to let him finger-bang you, so . . ."

I glare at her. "That was different. It just happened. It won't again."

"Uh-huh."

"What?"

She gives me a serious look as she sets down her cookie and takes my hands. "Taking care of us is who you are, and this is part of that—I get it, I do—but if he turns out to be a troll, just come back home."

Chapter 18

GRAHAM

"Civil ceremonies are so boring," Brody grouses as he adjusts my tie in my dressing room in my apartment.

He pouts as he finishes the final touches. He tries to fix my hair, and I slap his fingers away. "You're not doing my hair."

He cocks his head. "How about some mascara?"

"Not today." I smirk.

"Fine. Are you sure I can't come? I really want to be there. I'll be so good. I'll get behind a plant or stand in the corner. I won't make a peep. *Please*," he begs as he follows me into the bedroom, where I slip my dress shoes on.

I stand in front of the floor-length mirror and brush the lint off my three-piece suit. "No."

He plops on my bed, spreading out like a starfish as he grunts his disapproval. "All you say is no. You're mean. You should be wearing fucking Prada. You need a cathedral. Or a beach. Anywhere but the courthouse."

I ignore him.

He swivels his head so he can watch me put on my watch. "I'm still processing your prenup. I can't believe—okay, well, maybe I can because you're generous—but holy shit, you're actually giving her money after the big divorce. And let's be honest. You bought that store for her. You may have told yourself it was a good investment or that I might want it, but I'm not so sure." He jumps up off the bed, looking amazingly unruffled as every hair settles in place.

"Stop trying to cause drama."

He puts his hands on his hips. "I'm flummoxed because you're being so good to her." A sly expression flits over his face. "Hate to break it to you, big brother, but I'm starting to think you might care about the little thief."

I arch a brow. "Please."

He follows me out into the hall and through to the kitchen area. "That's right. I said it. 'Care.' You like her. You think she's sexy. You like her personality. You *want* to marry her—"

"Did you get the things I asked for?"

"The boutonniere is on the counter."

"Did you get the peonies?"

He nods. "Hmm. I did. I'm also wondering why you insisted on them."

I hear him making a hooting noise and turn to see that he's stopped at the formal parlor. With cheetah wallpaper. It's one of those rooms that will need attention at some point. "I can't believe you," he calls out as he snickers.

"What? The room came that way. I'll redo it eventually."

"It's not the horrible wallpaper, dear brother, it's the *cat litter box*." He sends me a wild look. "Who are you, and what have you done with my brother?"

"Not a big deal. Magic won't be here long. And it is kind of a cat room. Look at the wallpaper."

"And you know its name!"

"So?" I put my hands on my hips.

"When you were eight and I was five, a big tomcat from the neighborhood ambushed us on the steps of the brownstone after school. That cat was in full-on attack mode—I'm talking flat airplane ears, claws out, growling and hissing, with its whole body shivering. It was swatting and batting and pouncing around you like a damn tiger. It may have had rabies. You nearly peed your pants."

"You exaggerate."

He lets out a long whistle. "You *really* like her. Shit. Wow. I mean, don't get me wrong, you are marrying her, so maybe, just maybe, she is, like, the *one*—"

Cutting him off, I grab the items I need and say, "Let yourself out, and don't forget to pick us up for the party."

"Don't worry, I've got everything planned. Happy wedding day. Kiss her real good. With tongue," he calls out as I slam the door.

Chapter 19

EMMY

When things fell apart around me, like the time I didn't make the newspaper staff or when I found out my college boyfriend was cheating on me, Gran always told me to breathe, that this part of my life was just a prologue, and I had many other chapters to go. She promised me that good things awaited me in my story, regardless of who or what my parents had done. Ultimately, she said it was up to me. To go forth with my hopes up, to say yes when I shouldn't, and to live like it was my last day.

Gran was a wonderful soul. Will I ever be like her? To go forward with hope, to go all in without a backup plan? Maybe. The truth is, I'm entering unknown territory with this marriage. I'm scared that I may be in over my head with Graham.

I've been pacing in the lobby of the clerk's office for what seems like an eternity. The hallway has become a blur of people coming and going. Since seeing Kian, my energy level is kaput.

That changes the moment Graham steps off the elevator. He looks breathtaking in his suit. His wavy hair has been tamed, and his broad shoulders seem to expand the fabric of his jacket.

When he sees me, he stops and takes me in with determination on his face, as if he's ready to face the challenges ahead.

"Hi," I say weakly.

He runs his gaze over me, little electric sparks igniting the path he takes. "Hi."

I bite my lip.

"Nice dress. You look incredible," he says as his gaze lingers on my face, my lips, then the corset bodice of my dress.

"So do you."

He smiles. "And here we go."

We sign in and provide our marriage license, one that Graham was able to arrange quickly, along with our appointment. We take a seat in the waiting room alongside several other couples, ones who are giggling and holding hands. We don't. Instead I pin a small white peony to his lapel, and he thrusts over a bouquet of them. They smell divine, the sweet scent wafting in the air.

"Are you ready for this?" I ask, noticing that he twitches about every five seconds: adjusting his tie, pulling at his jacket, or raking a hand through his hair.

He grunts.

I look away from him. Clearly, he's dreading this.

The assistant at the desk calls our name, and we head inside the room. The chamber is cold and stark, and my tension amplifies. The officiant waits for us behind a desk, dressed in judge's robes. Two witnesses, employees obviously, stand by. There's no photographer, no family, no friends. It suits me just fine. Right?

The ceremony starts before I realize it, or maybe I'm in a daze.

The officiant speaks, his voice echoing off the walls. He speaks about love and commitment and the power of marriage. But I only hear the beating of my own heart pounding in my chest.

Graham and I turn to each other, and he repeats his vows. His lashes flutter, as if he wants to block out the words.

"I, Graham Harlan, take you to be my wife, to have and to hold, for better or worse, in sickness and in health, for richer, for poorer. I promise to love you and cherish you."

I was staring at the flower on his lapel, but at those last words, my eyes meet his. I read no emotion there, just fierce resolve.

He takes my hand and squeezes. "Emmy, it's your turn."

I blink, realizing I've zoned out. I swallow. "I, Emmy Darling, take you to be my husband, to have and to hold, for better or worse, in sickness and in health, for richer, for poorer. I promise to love you and cherish you." I feel the weight of the words inside every syllable.

The judge nods. "Today we unite two people in one of the most sacred ceremonies. What have you chosen as a token to seal the sign of your commitment?"

A knot forms in my stomach.

"Rings, Your Honor," Graham murmurs.

"Please exchange rings," he replies.

Graham slides a slender band on my finger, nestling it next to the solitaire.

The judge looks at me, and I throw a questioning glance at Graham.

"I have it," he says as he gives it to me, and I slide the band on his finger. There, it's done.

"Then, by the power vested in me, I now pronounce you man and wife. You may kiss."

Graham brushes his lips over mine for a second, and then it's done.

He threads his fingers through mine as we leave the courthouse and walk down the steps. There's a crowd of people at the bottom and a crew from ESPN. My stomach pitches. I'm still processing the wedding.

"Are they here for you?"

He heaves out a sigh, resignation in his gray eyes. "I thought it would be a good idea to have some photos of us leaving the courthouse. I meant to tell you, but . . ."

"You can't seem to think straight either."

A small laugh comes from him. "I was nervous as hell. You?"

"Absolutely terrified. Still am. We're really married." My chest rises. "I don't feel any different, do you?"

"I'm glad it's you, Emmy. You know that, right?" He glances back at the reporters. "It's better to rip the Band-Aid off, or they'll be chasing us around for photos for weeks. This way we can get it out of the way. Can you handle it?"

I school my face and drape my hand over my heart. "Sir. I won an Academy Award at the Golden Iguana. Of course I can manage."

He laughs, his dimples popping out. "Good."

"Graham, Graham!" calls a reporter with an ESPN lanyard around her neck.

He smiles at her. "Hi, Shelly."

She inches closer to us. "Everyone wants to know. Have you been cleared to play this fall?"

I hide my surprise that the first question isn't about his marriage but his football career. It reminds me of how important he is to New York.

"Yes," he announces as immediate cheers and claps go through the crowd gathered around us. I notice a few regular people with their phones out taking videos. Excitement etches their features. This is their hero, the man who won the Super Bowl, died, and came back.

Her gaze flits over me as she smiles. "We all saw your engagement post, and I see you're holding a bouquet. Does this mean you're married?" She directs the question to me, and I gaze adoringly up at Graham and bat my lashes.

"Yes, to a most amazing man."

His smile lights up, and part of me realizes that I mean those words, I do, while the other side of me is whispering in my ear to put more armor around my heart.

"Training camp is about to start. Is there a honeymoon planned around all that work?" she asks.

Graham and I have already discussed how to address this if it comes up, mostly in front of his family. He smiles at Shelley. "We're waiting until the season is over so we can spend some quality time together. Obviously we can't tell you where we'll honeymoon this weekend, because we'd like for it to be a private affair."

She nods. "Tell us—any qualms about taking the field again after what happened?"

Graham squeezes my hand harder as if he needs support, so I lean my head on his shoulder, trying to offer comfort.

"I trust the game. What happened to me was unique and won't happen again."

"What does Kian Adams have to say about your marriage to Graham?" a man calls out, jutting his way forward. I frown, recognizing him as the middle-aged man who hung around my apartment for days.

I keep my face blank while Graham visibly tenses, his eyes turning into slits. "You'd have to ask him," he growls, then whisks me down the steps and away from the man.

The man follows us, along with the crowd of people. "Is it true that you spoke with Kian today?"

Graham whips his head around. "No."

"I was talking to your wife," he replies snidely. "There are photos online of Mrs. Harlan outside a bookstore with Kian, right before the wedding. It's no secret they were a couple before she met you."

Graham stiffens and with great effort turns to me and pushes up a smile, but I see the fury in his eyes. "Brody's here. Let's go, darling."

Leaving the man and the crowd behind, he ushers me down the steps and opens the door to the back seat of a black Mercedes.

"Congratulations, newlyweds!" Brody calls from the driver's seat as Graham gets in on the other side of me in the back. Cas waves and smiles from the front next to Brody.

I say nothing. Neither does Graham.

Brody squints at me, then Graham. "Too soon, my turtledoves?"

"Just drive," Graham mutters as he stares out the window, decidedly not looking at me.

"All righty then," Brody murmurs as he pulls out into the traffic. We get three blocks before I finally break the silence.

"I was going to tell you about Kian, but there wasn't time." Not exactly true. I could have sent a text, but I just wanted the wedding to be over with, and then I would have told him. I didn't expect the PI to be on the steps of the courthouse. "You're angry," I say.

"Yes," he says as he whips out his phone, taps it, then shows me the photos on a website.

I exhale. The PI captured us just as Kian took my hand. Kian's face is earnest, yearning evident, while mine is slightly obscured.

"It's not what it looks like," I say softly.

Brody glances back at me at a red light. "What's going on?"

"Kian came to see me at the store. He wanted to tell me that a man had been asking questions." I pause, searching Graham's granite profile. "If I'd know someone was taking photos, I wouldn't have gone outside, but it seemed the better option than talking inside the store and making a scene."

Graham pinches the bridge of his nose. "I can't believe you talked to him. You should have sent him away."

"If this is about the NDA, I'd never tell him. I only talked to him to protect you."

Mercurial gray eyes pin me. "This isn't about the NDA. I don't want him near you, Emmy. You're my *wife*, and it worries me that he might hurt you. Don't you understand?" His gaze searches my face. Endlessly. He continues to trace my features before landing on my lips. His nose flares.

Tension sparks the air, making it potent.

I drop his eyes. "Jane had an axe. I felt perfectly safe," I murmur as Brody parks on the street in front of a brownstone.

Brody turns around to smile at us. "Okay, my little lovebirds, let's kiss and make up or put a pin in it. The marriage is done, and we've got to face the family and prove you're legit. We're doing drinks and finger foods. It shouldn't be too messy. Your honeymoon is a weekend at the beach, if anyone asks. I have your bags packed in the trunk. Now. Are you ready?"

Cas pumps his fist. "I'm ready for alcohol."

Same.

Graham gets out and comes around and opens my door, then takes my hand. He pulls me against his chest, taking my breath away with the sudden movement. I run my hands up the silky material of his shirt, my hands ending in his hair as I sweep some of it off his face.

"I should have told you about Kian. I'm sorry. Still mad?"

His jaw tics. "I'm putting it aside for now."

"If you two have finished your spat, we're waiting," Brody calls from the steps of the house.

Chapter 20

EMMY

We approach a four-story brownstone with ornate columns on each side of the door as Brody explains that this is the home they grew up in.

The door swings open to reveal a butler, who then ushers us in to the foyer of the house. I swallow at the grandeur of the hallway. Intricate carvings line each wall and corner, a telltale sign of the home's original features. A chevron hardwood floor stretches down the hall, dotted with plush Turkish rugs that cushion our feet. Exquisite high-end furniture fills the rooms: leather couches, sleek coffee tables, and glossy side-boards. Beautifully arched windows are everywhere. The afternoon sun streams through them, illuminating the place in a soft glow.

I mean, I've been inside ritzy homes before. Kian has a great apart-ment, and Mason, who's a trust fund baby, has invited me to his parents' beach house several times, but this—well, I have no words. It's the most opulent home I've ever been in. Suddenly, I feel like a pauper and very much out of place.

Brody and Cas tell us they're going to find the bar, leaving us alone. My nerves tighten.

Graham stops at a large, framed painting of a beautiful woman. The photographer captured her midlaugh, head tilted back as she plays a black baby grand piano. She's wearing a red dress, with sandy-blonde hair spilling around her shoulders, and her blue eyes have a knowing gleam as they look lovingly into the camera. This must be . . .

"My mother," he says gruffly. He hands me a champagne flute from a passing waiter. "My father is coming over."

A man approaches us, tall with broad shoulders, his dark hair peppered with silver at the temples. His eyes are a calm, introspective gray, and his brows are straight, like Graham's.

He hesitantly nods to Graham as he takes him in. "My son . . ." He stops, a weight in his voice. "It's good to see you. I'm happy you came to celebrate your marriage with us."

Graham shakes his hand. "Hello, Dad. This is my wife, Emmy."

His father turns to me. "It's a shame we haven't met before now, but my son doesn't return my phone calls. I'm Vale."

"Hi," I say, smiling. For some reason, I like him on the spot.

"And I hear you have a bookstore?"

"I'm the manager."

"Ah. How did you meet Graham?"

"A charity ball." I cling to my glass of champagne, needing something to anchor me as I lie boldly. "We recently reconnected, and things just fell into place."

Vale smiles. "Young love is the sweetest. Any plans on children? I know it's presumptuous to ask, but well, I'm sixty and don't have grandchildren yet."

Children?

I glance at Graham for guidance, but he's wandered off to the waiter to pick up another drink. Without looking back at me, he walks into a room on the right, where I hear the din of other guests and low music.

Vale crooks my arm in his, a disappointed look on his face as he watches him disappear. "He left you to fend for yourself. Trial by fire, I suppose. He's not subtle about his disdain for me, is he?"

"Hmm."

His eyes linger on the framed portrait, his voice softening.

"My wife," he says, "lit up a room. She was, is, the love of my life." He pauses, seemingly lost in the memory of her, and I remain silent, not wanting to interrupt him.

He turns and looks at me. "We separated when Graham was a teen, and she died a few months later. I blame myself for her death, and, well, Graham and Brody can't forget that I was the one who walked away." He exhales deeply and gives me a pained, searching look. "I'm sure you already know this."

I nod slowly. "I'm sorry. Families are complex. I could talk for hours about my own."

He guides me down the hall. "I'll hold you to that, but first let's give you a quick tour of the place. Everything you see, she decorated. Hazel had a flair for decor. She had many talents, really. Music was her first love, but she adored books, so I thought I might show you this room."

He opens a door, and we enter a library, the wall-to-wall shelves filled with books, several of the spines encased in leather. There's even a sliding ladder. In the corner is an oak desk, and a red chaise lounge is off to the side. An overhead chandelier lights the entire room with a glow.

"Wow." I ease out a first edition of *The Catcher in the Rye* and lightly stroke the cover before placing it back on the shelf.

"You're welcome to come to the house whenever you want. Graham and Brody only come during the holidays, but I'd love to have the house full of laughter again on any occasion. He deserves to be happy after everything he's gone through." A solemn expression flashes across his countenance. "The truth is, I made mistakes with them. I didn't handle things well after Hazel. I'm afraid there's not much to do to fix that. I'm glad he's found love."

I shift uncomfortably. Although I appreciate his candor with me, I feel guilty that our marriage isn't quite what Vale thinks.

He gives me a wan smile. "He needs family, something he refuses from me. I actually never believed he'd find someone after . . ." He clears his throat. "Well, none of that matters. I'm disappointed your brother and sister couldn't come."

"We'll have our own celebration soon. It's a busy time at the store, and it's a family business. Maybe we can all get together soon at Graham's place."

He gives me a quick look, seeming startled. "I'd love that. I don't see Graham nearly enough."

My throat tightens with apprehension. Did I just invite Graham's estranged father to hang out?

"I don't want to monopolize you. Let's find everyone else," he murmurs as he offers me his arm.

"I need a restroom first."

He points me down a hallway and up the stairs, and I go that way, grabbing another glass of champagne on the way and taking a deep drink.

From behind a cracked door, low voices reach my ears, and I stop, recognizing Graham's deep tone.

I peek inside the room, which appears to be some kind of office. What I see makes my breath catch. Graham stands with his back to me, arms crossed and feet planted firmly. In the corner of the room, a woman with beautiful auburn hair and a classical face sits in a chair in front of the fireplace. She stands and moves toward Graham, tilting her face up as if to search his gaze, longing in her expression.

"I thought the world might lose you, that you might die on that football field . . ." A lone tear spills down her face.

"Divina . . ."

"No, don't tell me to stop," she says. "Holden's already having another affair, this time with Pia. Am I just supposed to ignore it? Why can't I have you?"

"You get nothing if you divorce him, so your idea is for us to have an affair?" His tone sharpens. "I'm not here to be the revenge you get on Holden."

"It's not revenge. *It's love.* We spent years together, longer than I've been married to Holden, and it took you nearly dying for me to realize what a mistake I made. I want you back."

So this is Divina, the reason Graham has his heart locked away.

There's silence from the room as I stand with my heart hammering. I touch my chest, checking to make sure the fast beats are normal.

"Remember the night you proposed in Paris?" Divina says. "You promised to love me forever. You held me in your arms and swore. Just say the word, just tell me you still care, and I'll do anything." Another tear slips down her face, and Graham hands her a tissue from a box on the desk.

"I'm married," Graham says tonelessly as she moves closer to him and presses her body against his, her eyes searching his face. She runs her fingers through his hair, a gesture intimate and familiar to her.

"Which can be fixed, G," she begs. "Get an annulment. Be with me. We can go to Paris again."

Why isn't he moving away from her?

He bends his head toward hers—

I yank myself away so I can't see them kissing.

Should I really expect fidelity when we aren't even real?

My hands fist. *I don't know.* I really don't.

Brody appears next to me and guides me away from the room. I barely notice. My brain is grappling with visions of them, young and in love, in Paris. I imagine Graham promising to love her forever.

"Best to leave them alone," Brody says quietly as we go down the stairs. He stops at the bottom of the steps, searching my face. "Are you all right?"

I nod.

"Are you really?"

I blink away tears.

No.

And I can't even put my finger on the why of it.

"Oh, Emmy."

I stuff down my emotions, locking them away. I'll unpack them later and figure out what it means that I'm hurt and jealous. I take a deep breath, centering myself. "I'm fine."

He leads me into a giant open room, the walls hung with art, with a glittering chandelier in the center. About twenty or so people are here, all of them staring at me over their drinks. On one side of the room is a formal dining area with a wooden table surrounded by ornate chairs. On the other side is a formal parlor with cozy sitting areas and side tables. A harp player fills the air with gentle notes. I head to the bar in the back, where a server is making drinks. I grab another glass of champagne as Brody follows me.

"Please tell me there isn't a wedding cake anywhere?" I ask.

"No. Graham was very specific about this being low-key."

How can anything be low-key in this gorgeous setting?

Brody asks for a martini, and as the bartender is mixing it, he leans down to my ear. "I'm going to introduce you to a gaggle of cousins and the like, so just nod and smile."

"Of course."

He sweeps me around the room, and after a few minutes, I'm feeling the buzz of the alcohol, dampening the emotion from earlier. I smile and chat in all the right places, and when I see Mina, the only familiar face, I hug her. She asks me where Graham is, but before I can reply, he enters the room with Divina. There's a hush in the air as everyone seems to hold a collective breath.

I couldn't get a good look at her in the office, but there's no doubt she's an incredibly beautiful woman, almost fragile, with wide brown eyes and thick lashes. Her dress is red and tight, accentuating her petite figure. Her auburn hair is up in a high ponytail, with the ends curled delicately as it hangs over one shoulder. She gives the room a tremulous smile, then gazes up at Graham.

I feel as if I'm going to be sick.

Brody squeezes my shoulder. "Don't make assumptions about his feelings for her, Emmy."

"He told me he still loved her," I say as Graham nods to Divina and leaves her to talk to his father.

"Forget that. The bad guy approaches," Brody says conspiratorially as he nudges his head at Holden, headed in our direction from across the room. "It's not just that Holden slept with Divina behind my brother's back. He's always been jealous of our father's attention. Ten bucks says he'll mention how Graham isn't next to you right now or throw in the fact that our mother came from nothing."

"Is *his* mother here?" My eyes search the room.

Brody chuckles. "She won't step in this house because it's the one Dad lived in with us. It's always been my theory that my mother stole Father away from Holden's mom."

"Your mom was the other woman?" It would explain some of the animosity Holden feels.

Brody nods. "My mother was much younger." He waves his hand. "And you, my dear, are perfection. Tell me, when you yanked him into your room at the motel, did you have sex?"

I send him a pointed look, and he pouts.

"He won't tell me either. That aside, he does care about you."

"How do you know?"

"A cat litter box. I know it doesn't seem like much, but he bought one. It's waiting for your little pet."

We watch Holden get closer, and I feel the eyes of people watching him, watching us.

Brody smothers a breath. "It's like we're in some kind of court intrigue as he walks to us. You're the queen, and I'm your adviser, trying to protect you from the lord who's plotting to steal your throne."

I giggle. "He's greedy and wants to steal *your* inheritance. All he needs is some white hose, a sword, and a hat with a feather in it. Maybe a wig and some powder on his face. Oh, is this the French court or the English? Should we speak French, *mon ami*?"

Brody snorts. "*Ma chérie*, I adore you. And here his is, *le méchant* . . ."

The villain.

"Congratulations on your wedding," Holden says as he reaches us, wearing a smirk as he runs his eyes over me. "It seems your groom has left you alone."

"Bingo, ten bucks," Brody whispers to me, then says louder, "I'm here, dear brother. She's not alone at all." He tips his martini at him.

Holden dismisses him with a veiled look, then turns to me. "And where's your family, Emmy? Are you an orphan like Brody's mother?"

"Bingo again," Brody says as he lifts his glass.

I smile tightly at Holden. One thing I've learned is sometimes it's best to confront a prickly issue before someone else does; that way, they'll have no power over you. "I assumed you knew all about my family since you've kept a photographer outside my apartment. Yes, I grew up in the turmoil of domestic abuse, and in the end, my mother shot my father, then left us. That's it. You won't find much else about me."

"You've got a backbone. Some women don't." His eyes dart to his wife as his lip curls in distaste.

"How vicious you are," I say.

Holden smiles, although it doesn't reach his eyes. "You'll fit in well. Although I am concerned about how long you'll last."

A knot forms in my stomach.

He leans in too close, his lemony cologne wafting around me. "Be honest—what's he giving you to marry him?"

"Sweet, sweet love," I say as I put a hand over my heart.

His teeth flash. "There's going to be a big story coming out—your lovers' quarrel with Kian in Vegas, your mad dash to Arizona, then you stealing Graham's car. We'll add an eyewitness, of course, the clerk at the motel. Your past will be splashed around. In the end, it will convince everyone that Graham coerced you into marrying him."

Brody stiffens next to me.

I laugh. "And when you say all that, all I hear is a Cinderella story about a girl who falls for the guy she meets after a horrible ex-boyfriend experience."

"A random person stole my car and wrecked it," Graham says tightly as he joins our group. He brings my hand to his lips and kisses my fingers as his eyes search my face. "Hello, darling. Is Holden bothering you?"

I can't quite meet his gaze. "Hardly. Family is the same everywhere. Complicated."

We're saved from further conversation as Graham's father quiets the room by clinking a spoon against his glass.

He smiles at everyone. "Thank you for coming tonight as we celebrate Emmy and Graham." His eyes brush over me before landing on Graham. "Congratulations. I wish you both the very best in life and love." He pauses, his throat moving as he seems to gather himself. "I wish with all my heart that your mother were here tonight. Cheers."

"My turn," Brody says as he clears his throat and raises his martini. "For my brother and Emmy, may their love be as big and wonderful as mine for Cas."

Cas, who's across the room with Mina, smiles brilliantly at him.

"I'm next," Holden says dryly as he looks around the room before stopping on Divina. He raises his glass. "To Divina, for giving up Graham so he could find Emmy."

Graham tenses next to me as a rumble of uncomfortable laughter spreads around the room.

Graham clears his throat and gazes down at me. "And finally, to my beautiful wife. Life gives you what you want when you least expect it. Darling, to you."

And as everyone lifts their glasses to us, my eyes find Divina's across the room, taking in her sour face. Yes, he was alone with her in that room, but I'll think about that later.

Chapter 21
EMMY

I blink my eyes open to the darkness in the back seat of the Mercedes. My head throbs a little from the champagne that's now worn off. Something warm is under my cheek, and I realize I've leaned over and fallen asleep in Graham's lap.

The car is quiet as I slowly rise up, moving carefully so I don't wake Graham. His head leans against the headrest, his chest rising in deep breaths.

I pause, taking in his features in the dim light. His wavy hair is a mess, spread out like a halo of softness on the seat. His eyes are closed, and his full lips are parted slightly. His chiseled cheekbones and strong jaw are relaxed. My attention goes to his hands, resting on either side of him. They're big and strong, able to break and hurt, but my gut knows somehow that he'd never put them on me in anger.

I lean in closer to him, wishing I could freeze this moment forever, until I figure out exactly why I'm entranced by him.

He's my husband keeps flashing in my head.

It feels strange and unreal. That's why I'm fascinated.

He stirs and slowly opens his eyes—probably because he sensed my eyes—and I settle back in my seat, not wanting him to know I was inspecting him like a bug under a microscope.

My head goes back to the party at the brownstone. After the toasts, we spent at least two more hours there, mingling with the guests. I met great-uncles and great-aunts, cousins, and a few close business associates from Vale's law firm. Mostly, I enjoyed talking to Vale. We sat on a couch, and I confided in him about my parents. He was sympathetic and kind.

I look out the window and see a quaint, picturesque town, most of the businesses closed. It's nearly midnight.

Brody glances back at me. "You've been asleep for about two hours. We're almost there."

"Where is 'there'?" I ask. Brody told us it was a beach house, but he wanted the rest to be a surprise. He arranged with Jane to pack a bag for me, and he packed Graham's.

"We're in Montauk," Brody says as he makes a right onto a small gravel road. "I have a friend who owns a bungalow on a private beach. It's perfect for the weekend, and you'll be completely alone." A gleam glows in his eyes as he glances back at me. "Doesn't that sound idyllic?"

No. I really need to be back at work, but it would look suspicious if we didn't do something to celebrate.

Graham grunts, stirring as he rubs his face and eyes. "Are we there yet?"

"Almost," Brody says as he gets out to unlock a metal padlocked gate, then gets back in the car. He drives up to a pale-blue wooden gingerbread-type house with wind chimes hanging from the porch. It's one story and quaint, but probably worth millions. A thick line of trees is nestled on either side of the home.

After we've parked, Brody unlocks the door to the house, then hands over the keys to Graham. "I've arranged for a town car to pick you guys up Sunday."

Graham nods as Cas unloads the bags and carries them inside to the foyer.

The air smells like the sea, and I hear the distant screech of seagulls. A long exhale comes from my chest. It will be good to stare at the ocean and unwind.

I step inside the cottage and look around. It's cozy, with a large area that features an eat-in kitchen and a living area with worn couches. Artwork of the sea decorates the wall. Huge windows face the Atlantic Ocean.

"There's a hitch," Brody murmurs as he flits around the room and lights a few candles, making Graham scowl. "There's only one bedroom."

Tension fills the room.

"I'll take the couch," Graham says roughly, and I sigh. He'll be a pretzel on the couch.

"Whatever works," Brody says airily. "The fridge and pantry are stocked for you. Enjoy, my little turtledoves."

"Drive carefully," Graham says. "It's late."

I watch as they hug each other tightly. Graham ruffles Brody's hair. "Thanks for taking care of things."

Brody pats his back. "Anything for you. Be good." He slants a look at me and smiles.

After they leave, I grab my bag and head down the hall, checking for the bedroom. I find it, my eyes widening as I start.

"What is it?" Graham says from behind me, and I guess I must have made a sound.

"Um . . ."

Graham pushes past me and glares down at the peony petals shaped into a heart design on the bed. He shakes his head and pinches his brow. "Christ! I can see Brody dancing around as he arranged those petals just right."

I look at him. "Wait, are you laughing?"

He glances up, eyes crinkling as his dimples pop. "Yeah. I mean, I'm sorry if it makes you uncomfortable, but it's typical Brody. Here, let me." He bends over and moves them into a pile, then picks them up and throws them in a trash can near the door.

I look at them in disappointment, but he doesn't seem to notice.

"I'm going to find something to change into, then find us food," he says. "I'll use the bathroom down the hall."

After he leaves, I open my bag. My mouth parts as I gape at the contents. "Graham!"

At the same time, he says. "Fuck!"

I come out into the hall, and he's got his hands on his hips. "Okay. What did Jane pack for you?"

"A bikini and lacy lingerie. No clothes. Some lube. What did you get?"

He shoves his duffel at me, and I open it and take in the contents.

I giggle. "A swimsuit, boxers, and dildos. Wow, that's quite a collection of cocks. Are they yours?"

"No," he says with a glare.

I smirk. "They pranked us."

"I should have checked the bags before they left. Now we're stuck here for two days with no clothes."

I shrug. "There's a washing machine, and thankfully, I have a slip under my dress."

"I'm wearing a suit. It has to be dry-cleaned."

"Hmm, guess you're wearing a swimsuit all weekend."

"Dammit."

"Not laughing now, huh?"

He smirks as his fingers undo his tie, then the buttons of his shirt. I watch in rapt attention as he whips them off, his muscles rippling as he throws them over a chair.

He arches a brow, and I blink and flip around to the bedroom, where I quickly wash my face in the en suite bathroom, then hang my dress up.

When I come into the kitchen, he's only wearing his dress pants. His feet are bare as he stands at the stove, stirring something with a spatula. My eyes eat up the defined expanse of his broad tanned back, the way his pants taper down to a slim waist. My breath quickens. Just damn.

He's all mine now. My husband.

He glances at me over his shoulder. "I'm making us cheese omelets. There's fruit too. Want to set the table?"

We chat idly as I arrange the fruit on a plate and get plates and cutlery. He tells me he wants water, and I grab us two bottles from the fridge. Carrying the pan from the kitchen, he slides the omelets onto our plates, then takes the pan back to the kitchen.

We sit down across from each other. Neither of us ate much of the finger foods at the party.

"Ah, before we eat . . ." Graham gets up and opens his jacket and pulls out a small box. "A wedding gift for you."

Taking the box in my hands, I open the tissue hesitantly, and an awed gasp leaves me. Sitting nestled inside is an exquisite iguana bangle. The eyes gleam with emerald jewels, and his tail is curved with lines of glittering white diamonds. The tail thickens at the end and becomes the circular pattern of the bracelet. "Wow. Just wow. It's beautiful. Thank you." I slip it over my hand and up my arm. "Does it match my slip?" I smile.

"Hmm. You're welcome," he says gruffly.

"I didn't get you anything," I say, fidgeting.

"You showed up, Emmy."

I chew on my food. "I can't believe Jane went along with Brody on the luggage thing."

"Brody is smooth. He's good at convincing people."

"Like you . . . ," I say as I bite into a strawberry. He watches me avidly, his eyes following a trail of juice that escapes down my chin. I hurriedly wipe it away under his scrutiny.

"Hardly. I had to buy a bookstore to get you to marry me."

And he loves Divina. I cut viciously into my omelet.

"Is everything all right?" he asks.

"I saw you with Divina."

He pauses with his fork midway to his mouth, then sets it down on his plate. He leans back in his chair, and I battle to keep my gaze on his face and not his naked chest. "I know."

210

"Brody told you?"

"There was a mirror over the fireplace. I saw you."

That makes it even worse. Did he see the jealousy on my face?

His eyes gleam. "She found me as soon as I came in and insisted we talk. Are you upset?"

I swallow tightly. "I heard what she said. That she wants you back."

I wait for him to reply, but he says nothing.

I exhale. "I guess if you really want . . ."

A muscle in his jaw jerks. "Are you suggesting I take her up on her offer of an affair?"

I stare down at a blueberry on my plate. "If you want to be with Divina, I'm not here to stand in your way—"

I stop abruptly when he stands up from the table. With his hands on the table, he leans into me. "I . . . don't . . . want . . . Divina."

He rears back up, chest rising rapidly, then stalks to the deck door, opens it, and stomps outside into the night.

Why is *he* angry? He's the one who freaking told me he loved her.

An hour later, he still hasn't returned. I've cleaned the kitchen already and fiddled around the cottage. I've picked up books and set them back down, unable to concentrate on anything but Graham. I try to see the situation from his side. Divina betrayed him with his half brother, and he's never gotten over the sting of it. Now that he's married, she offers herself to him. Perhaps he could even marry her now, claim the inheritance, and get back at Holden.

I pace around before marching to a hall closet. I find an old cardigan and slip it on. I exit the patio door and find the cobblestone path to the beach. The moon is white and full, illuminating the waves rolling onto the beach. I reach the edge, letting my toes feel the cool water.

Graham is about fifty yards away, staring out at the waves. My feet press into the sand as I walk to him and then stand next to him, just letting the silence of the night wrap around us.

A crab darts out of the water and inches close to me, and I squeal and dart to the other side of him.

"It's not just scorpions, huh?" he asks.

"Just make it go away," I say, and he shoos it away from us and onto the beach.

I study him, taking in the furrows on his forehead. "Thanks. What are you thinking about out here?"

If he says Divina, then I'll deal with it. I'll be cool. I'll go along with whatever. I mean, who am I to ask him if what *we* have is something real?

I shake myself. Is that what I really want? No.

"Football, actually. Training camp starts Monday in Atlanta. It will give you time to acclimate to my apartment without me." His lips twist wryly.

"Do you have mixed feelings about playing?"

Instead of answering me, he bends down to pick up a seashell, studying it carefully. A wind blows, ruffling his hair as his scent fills the air, thick with cherries and leather. I inhale it deeply.

"Graham? You can talk to me."

He clenches the shell in his hand, and it shatters. "I saw a doctor, who warned me about CTE. Do you know what that is?"

We start walking, our shoulders side by side. "It's caused from concussions, right? Lots of famous people have had it. It's believed Muhammad Ali did. Brett Favre has admitted to over a thousand concussions and says he doesn't know what it is to be normal anymore."

His jaw pops, emotion flitting over his face as he tosses the crushed shell into the sand. "Yes. There's no way to diagnose it when you're alive; instead it's by symptoms—personality changes, anger issues, depression, suicide. Several players have even murdered people or committed suicide. Eventually, it can lead to dementia and Parkinson's."

The words settle around us heavily. I thread my fingers through his, and he starts. He stops, gazes at me, and then looks down at our hands. No one's here to see us pretending, but I don't care. I want him to know that he can come to me, talk to me. "And you're worried about it because you had a bad concussion."

"My headaches and dizziness are gone. My sensitivity to light. I'm great physically."

"Mentally?"

He pops an eyebrow. "What are you insinuating?"

"So you would have married a girl who stole your car anyway?" I tease.

"I'd do anything for my brother, so yes." He stares out at the ocean. "I'm the same as I always was, I think, except for *one* thing."

"What's that?"

He turns to look at me, and his eyes hold mine for several moments, until I'm breathless.

"Graham?"

"Nothing. Never mind."

My instinct senses that he just needs me to listen, so I stuff my questions away as he tells me more about his appointment with the French doctor, about MRI scans and autopsy reports. His doctor sent him more information after his appointment, about a famous player and sports analyst who recently passed away at age seventy-one. He donated his brain to science to raise awareness of the disease, and they discovered stage-four CTE, the most advanced, which presents as severe cognitive and behavioral issues.

In an interview, the player's widow said that in the last years of his life, he'd isolated himself from everyone, even her, and that he'd struggled daily with balance, memory loss, paranoia, and severe depression. He was terrified to watch football games with his buddies because he didn't know what was happening on the field anymore. When asked about how many concussions he'd had during his fifteen-year career, he'd said ten but possibly more, since he'd played at a time before the NFL kept an official count.

Graham picks up another shell, his fingers tracing it. "Boston University has a CTE center, where they do a lot of research. Five players who committed suicide, one of them only twenty-seven years old, had CTE. On the other hand, the NFL is making helmets stronger and making new rules about tackles. We aren't ignoring CTE."

A deep unease and anxiousness rises inside me as the enormity of his issue dawns. He wants to play, but he's also worried about the future, of getting Parkinson's, of losing his memory.

I study his profile, and he notices, stopping to gaze down at me.

"What?" he asks.

"If I were your real wife, I'd beg you not to play. Every time you go out there, you're taking the chance that you'll have another concussion."

His lashes flutter against his cheek. "You don't understand."

"I have the gist of it. You're playing a game that can potentially damage your brain."

He frowns. "I scored the last points of the Super Bowl. The Pythons took a chance on me, and I delivered. People are counting on me to come back, and it's not just that—who would I *be* without the game? I don't have anything else."

Brody. Cas. Me?

"I'm taking a risk, but every day is a risk. I could go swimming in the ocean tonight and drown. I could have a car accident. Yeah, I worry about knee injuries, and my head, but most pro players do. Some of us are terrified, but we shove it down and keep on going. When I win a game? It's the highest I get. The adrenaline, the knowledge that I'm the best at what I do? It gives me pleasure, a sense of belonging. The pressure from the team, the fans, the feeling that if I quit, then I'd be giving up the best thing I've ever had, the only thing that's been consistent and true to me. This is who I am. It's made me famous. Who would I be without football?"

"You'd be you," I say softly. "You could start over, do anything you wanted, belong to something else. The world is open to you."

"Are you?"

I start. "Am I open to change in my life?" I huff out a laugh. "I married you. That's a change."

His gray eyes capture mine, then look away. "That's not what I meant," he says as he turns away from me, looking at the ocean.

A lone seagull squawks in the distance as the tide rolls in over our feet.

"You told me in the kitchen at the store that you loved someone else. You meant Divina."

When he doesn't answer, I continue. "Not that it matters, because this is a marriage of convenience, but I'd like to know if you plan on being with her."

He stuffs his hands in his pockets. "I feel nothing but regret that she fooled me. I realize now how lucky I was to get away from her. Not only did she cheat on me, but she's ready to cheat on Holden, although he's never been faithful to her."

"Then you lied to me when you said you loved her."

"I knew you didn't want to get your heart involved, so I wanted to assure you that neither did I. And you? Talking to Kian on our wedding day?"

I huff. "I'm sorry, okay! I only did it to protect you."

He groans. "Emmy, never protect me. Always consider your own safety. Never see him again. Promise me."

"Okay," I say quietly on a sigh. "But you . . . you kissed her."

"So we're going to fight on our wedding night?" He sends me a wry smirk.

I kick sand at him. "Stop being cute. This isn't a real wedding night. I just want to know what's going on. If you want her, fine, fuck her, but you can be assured that I despise Kian."

"I don't want her," he mutters. "I thought I made that clear. You assumed I kissed her. If you'd stuck around, you would have seen me push her away. It's not the first time she's come on to me, Emmy. Last Christmas, she sat next to me at dinner and couldn't keep her hands off me. Touching my arm, my leg, whatever. She isn't a good person. She isn't you."

My heart dips, and I blink. "Oh."

Before I realize it, we're back on the path of the cottage and on the deck. The silence between us stretches like a rubber band as we rinse our feet at the outdoor faucet, then go inside.

I busy myself with cleaning the kitchen again, and when I finish, I turn to see him in his boxer shorts in the den. He's fluffing an extra pillow he must have gotten from the linen closet. He tosses it on the couch, then turns around to face me.

He is magnificent. All hard, marbled body muscles as if he's just stepped out of a Michelangelo painting. I lick my lips nervously, then clear my throat. "There's no way you'll fit on that couch. The bed is big enough for the two of us."

He rubs a hand over his jaw. "It isn't."

"It's a king-size bed."

His gaze lingers over my face, then down to my cleavage, peeking through my slip.

"If I get in that bed, I'm going to ask to fuck you, and you'll say yes, and we'll make up an excuse that it's to 'break the tension'; then . . ." He stops, an eyebrow raising. "You want that?"

My throat prickles with the word *yes*. "No."

He moves so fast that I blink when he's right in front of me. "Is that so? Then explain to me why those pretty green eyes are blown, Emmy."

I tilt my head up at him, ready for a comeback, but I have nothing, not when I see the desire on his face, the lascivious way his gaze drinks me in as if he's a man starved in the desert.

I press my hands on his chest, sliding them up until I curl my arms around his neck.

"What are you doing?"

"Kissing my husband good night." My lips lightly brush over his. It was barely even a kiss, yet I watch with bated breath as I pull back, and he brushes his fingers over his lips, as if savoring the taste of my kiss.

Part of me wants to fall into his arms, but I can't.

It happened once, but . . .

"Go to bed, wife," he says with hungry eyes.

I feel his eyes on me the entire way down the hall. I shut the door and lean against it, shuddering. Jesus. What am I going to do about Graham and these feelings? Wait for them to pass? Ignore this fantastical connection we seem to have?

Ugh. Whipping off my clothes, I step in the shower and let the hot water wash everything away. All of it. Graham, his family, Kian. I slip on the lingerie Jane sent and consider calling her and being pissy about my lack of clothes, but I figure Londyn is asleep.

I curl up in the bed and fall asleep, my dreams turning dark as Graham is on the football field underneath a pile of players.

◆ ◆ ◆

The next morning I'm awake by six as I try to remember where I am. The beach. I get excited when I find a fluffy white robe in the back of the closet. I slip it on and tiptoe out into the den.

He's not on the couch. In fact, it looks as if he hasn't been here at all.

I'm making coffee when I find the manila envelope with a note on top of it on the counter.

> Emmy,
> I left after you went to bed. I'm certain no PI followed us so no one will know. Enjoy the beach. In the enve-lope are keys to the apartment and cash for whatever pops up. I'll be in Atlanta, then I'm going to Seattle to handle some personal things. I'll text you soon.
> G

My heart thumps erratically, and I tense up, a chill running down my spine as I drop the note. Pressing my hand to my chest, I gasp in a deep breath and exhale slowly out of parted lips. Inhale, exhale.

Gradually, it steadies itself, and I'm unsure if the episode was simply due to the fact that Graham left me or something else.

Just enjoy the day. Bask in the sun. Fine, I can do that. Alone.

On Sunday, the car picks me up at noon. By three, I'm standing in front of the Wickham apartments, wearing the dress I got married in. Brody meets me and introduces me to the doormen and desk workers. Once on the elevator, he keeps darting his eyes at me.

He points out his smaller apartment, then shows me to Graham's. We walk inside, and I blink at the seventies throwback. In the den is the penis statue, about four feet tall and lime green.

"It's worth a few grand," Brody tells me. "Graham says I can have it, but it's bolted to the floor. Looks like you're stuck with it."

"I won't be here long," I murmur. "Just until your inheritance comes in. Do you ever wonder if all this was worth it?"

Brody's face grows serious. "Marriage was never my idea. Mostly because I don't want to see my brother hurt."

I say nothing.

"Guess the honeymoon wasn't so hot?"

"He left."

Brody nods sagely. "And if you think hard enough, you'd know why."

I swallow, looking away.

"Come this way, and I'll show you your bedroom."

We pass Graham's bedroom, and I peek in. It's huge and done in shades of white and navy. There's a balcony outside his room that connects to the one in the den. Brody tells me there are views to Central Park.

Across the hall is my room, the next-biggest bedroom. The white metal bed frame looks new, with a plush white duvet and velvet pillows in cream. I take in the white wicker dresser, a fancy armoire, and a big mirror propped against the wall. What makes my breath catch is a sketch of the bookstore, framed on the wall. I marvel at the detail, a smile coming from me when I notice that the woman in front of the store looks like me.

I glance at Brody, who's fluffing a pillow. "Who did this? When?"

"Oh, that. I put it up yesterday. The artist is Francesca Avery. She's super talented and happens to be married to a former player on the team, Tuck. Graham's friend Jasper put him in touch with her. Sketching buildings is one of her specialties."

"But when?"

"Graham sent her a pic of the store and the one of you at Borelli's. She works fast. She'd be a great friend to you. They stay in the penthouse on and off." He pauses. "Maybe Graham will let you keep it, you know, *afterwards*."

"Right. Is all this bedroom stuff new?"

"I picked everything out, and Graham approved it. I wish he'd let me redo the entire place, but he wanted to start with this room."

He could have just put a cot in here, and I would have been fine with it, but these little touches, the new furniture, the sketch, his bangle, the money after our divorce—he's done more than was required. I'm unused to someone else taking care of me.

In the kitchen, Brody gives me a paper with a schedule on it that tells me a grocery delivery is sent every Tuesday that I'll need to pick up downstairs, or they'll deliver it to the door if someone is here. A housekeeper comes every two weeks, on Monday mornings.

"If there's anything you want moved here, such as furniture, I can set that up," Brody says, and I tell him no, seeing no point in moving in anything but my toiletries and clothes, and Jane is bringing those to the store tomorrow in a duffel. I can get more as I need them.

He makes to leave, then pauses at the door. "Cas and I have cocktails in the apartment in the evenings. Come join us sometime if you want."

"Thank you. Wait," I say and then chew on my lips, my head churning.

"Yeah?"

"Your dad asked about my siblings and wants to meet them. He gave me his card. What do you think about a dinner with your dad, here at the apartment? I actually love to cook, but the stove at our place is always on the fritz. It might give your dad a chance to see that we're connected as a family."

He thinks about it, his hand tapping his leg.

"Super casual," I add. "Just letting him know how crazy I am about Graham."

"And are you?"

My hands clench around the paper I'm still holding, and Brody smiles broadly. "Fine, set it up. Dad would love to be invited here. He's never been."

After he's gone, I walk the apartment again, peeking in all the closets, except in Graham's room. I walk out on the balcony and take in the park.

A deep loneliness sets in.

My heart feels hollow and empty.

I try to ignore it but can't.

I wish Graham were here.

I wonder where he is. Most of all, I wonder if he'll be safe at camp. I can't stop thinking about CTE and the absolute unknown of the disease.

His absence leaves a strange void at the center of my being. I look at my phone, hoping for a call or message from him.

An undeniable feeling of dread overcomes me as I drop into a chair, my head in my hands. The truth is that I long for him with every ounce of my being, and I can't deny it any longer, not the sparkle in his eyes when he smiles, his dimples, the way his nose flares slightly when he's near me yet doesn't make a move. I relish in his banter, the way he opens up to me when I least expect it.

My stomach drops as the realization hits me. I'm falling for him. His warmth, his vulnerability, the way he wants to keep me safe at all costs, his unconditional love for his brother, the look of despair that lingers on his face whenever he speaks of losing football.

How do I navigate this and survive with my heart intact?

I won't. I can't.

Jesus. I need to stab this *feeling* right in the center of my chest and rip it out.

Needing a distraction, I call Jane, then the rest of my friends.

A few hours later, I've got enough Chinese delivery for a feast. Jane, Andrew, and Londyn arrive first, then Babs, Ciara, and Mason. Magic finds his litter box, does his business, then goes to sleep in my lap.

I've tossed a blanket over the giant penis for Londyn's sake.

Chapter 22
GRAHAM

Two and a half weeks later, I wake from a groggy dream, trying to figure out where I am. I rub my eyes. Right. Back in Manhattan. I arrived last night on a late flight during the middle of a huge thunderstorm. By the time I got to the apartment, it was midnight, and Emmy was already asleep with her door closed.

Once I'm dressed in gym clothes and out of my bedroom, the apartment is silent. Emmy's already left for work. As I drink a protein shake, I stalk around the apartment, seeing hints that my wife lives here: a cup of half-drunk tea left on a side table, several fortune cookies left over from takeout, and a blanket over the giant penis.

We've communicated briefly through texts, but I've done my best to keep my distance.

Is it wrong that I itch to see her?

Like it always does, a warning bell dings in my head, telling me that I don't need her in my life. I should be focusing on my game, on my dreams.

I shove it aside and call Jasper.

He answers with a groggy "Somebody better be dead, Graham. It's seven in the morning, and it's not a practice day."

"Does Precious have a hangover? Suck it up. I need a run through the park. Wanna join?"

There's a long silence, and I picture him in his mammoth bed he special ordered when he renovated his apartment. It looks like something a vampire would sleep in, all dark mahogany and fancy scrolls and tall elaborate posts at the ends. His bedding—as he so lovingly showed us—is black silk damask. The top of the bed has a canopy that matches.

"If we wait until later, it'll just be crowded and hot."

He lets out a string of curses. "You got married and I wasn't even invited, and now you're waking me up? I'm pissed at you. Tuck shared with me. He confided. It built a bridge between us. We can't truly connect on the field if you don't let me into your personal life. Whatever. I haven't even *met* this girl. You get me?"

He complained about this in Atlanta during camp. I sat through an offensive strategies class, with him ignoring me. When I said hello at practice, he'd just grunt. His hotel room was next to mine, and usually we'd go to dinner together, but he spent most of his time in the gym where we had our training.

"Ah, stop giving me the cold shoulder, Precious. Would it help if I said, 'Please go running with me? With a cherry on top?'"

"Fucker. You'd need a million cherries."

"And maybe we could get some Mexican later? Healthy? I'm thinking fajitas and no tortillas. No chips or cheese dip either."

"But I love the chips. They crunch so good," he says on a groan.

"Chips it is. Was that a yes?"

"No."

"What if I said we'll go meet Emmy afterwards. She can't wait to meet you. You know, I gave her your phone number in case she needed a friend to help out with Kian."

"Of course I'd help her. I'm awesome. Fine! Fifteen minutes. I'll meet you in the lobby." He hangs up on me.

After our five-mile run and lunch, we head to the bookstore. My heart beats harder with each step that gets us closer. I want to see her face. Those plump, delicious lips.

"Tell me about Emmy. Was it love at first sight, like you told the team, or was it more lust?"

I frown, my train of thought interrupted and fear crowding in when I see a fire truck parked on the curb and firemen milling around outside the bookstore.

I'm about to burst inside and see what's going on when Jasper grabs my arm in front of the bookstore. "Dude. Check out the window. Your wife is into some kinky shit."

The mannequins that were there before, a man and woman, have fallen. She's tipped backward and leans against the wall, her updo hair in disarray, while the male mannequin's head is shoved under her dress. To add to the scene, one of his arms is on her waist. The book and ring he was holding litter the floor.

Magic lounges on top of the male mannequin's chest, tail flicking as devious eyes narrow in on me.

"I like this store already," he calls on a laugh as we enter the store.

I glance around and don't see fire or smell smoke. I blow out an exhale. Everything looks normal, except that the floors are scuffed up in the rotunda, probably from the firemen.

I stop at the table with the manual typewriter and type a quick message, then move along.

Jane works at the counter as she checks out customers, her blonde hair piled up on her head. The line of people stretch all the way to one of the sitting areas. One woman huffs as she steps from foot to foot. A man grumbles under his breath.

I notice Andrew as he dashes back and forth behind the pastry counter, making coffees and slipping croissants into bags.

Jane gives me a smirk. "Welcome to A Likely Story. It's a wreck."

"Still can't find enough employees?" I ask.

She smiles at a customer as she finishes checking her out. "We've lost six total. She's hired us and two more, and they're still learning the ropes."

"What happened to the window out front?"

Jane sighs. "Magic got his claws stuck in the lady mannequin's dress. No one's had time to fix it. This entire day has been off-the-charts insane."

"What else is going on?" I ask.

"Our second cash register went on the fritz, there's a leak in the basement, a kid got locked in one of the restrooms upstairs this morning, and we had to call the fire department, and Andrew keeps burning pastries. If he burns another batch of cookies, I'm going to stick my foot in his ass."

Andrew snorts. "Touch me and see what happens."

"Oh, shut it. Get back to work," she snips.

He flips her off as he sings the chorus to "You're So Vain," by Carly Simon.

She pokes her tongue out at him.

The next woman in line clears her throat. "Excuse me, miss, but I'd like to check out now."

"So would I," someone else grouses.

Magic chooses that moment to dash out of the window display and dart between someone's legs. A small child squeals and chases the cat.

"Holy shit. This place is cool," Jasper says. "Wahoo!"

I inhale a deep breath. Okay, so things are a bit messy at the store. "How can I help?" I ask Jane.

She gives me a look. Assessing.

"I don't think she likes you," Jasper murmurs.

"She's coming around," I say back.

Jane cocks her head toward the kitchen. "Go bake some more cookies. We're running low, since Emmy gave the firemen several dozen. They're in the freezer, and directions are on the package. Set the timer, then come back out and work the back of the line. If you don't know what that means, it means being nice to them and asking if they've found everything they wanted."

Andrew huffs as he turns to the kitchen doors. "Jesus! You're asking Graham? He's a football player! Hey, Jasper, nice to meet you. I'm a big fan. You're fucking awesome." Andrew glares at his sister. "*I'll* do the cookies. You two help Jane by working the crowd. I'm not sure she knows how to be nice to people."

"Neanderthal," she says under her breath as he goes into the kitchen.

Jasper leans in on the counter. "Your hero has arrived. What can I do for you, beautiful?"

"Jane, this is Jasper, my quarterback."

Jasper gives her his killer smile and bats his lashes. "Hey."

She pushes a two-foot stack of books toward him. "Do you know how to read?"

His charming demeanor vanishes. "Don't throw shade because I'm a football god. I was cum laude at the University of Southern California"— he reads her name tag as if he's forgotten her name—"*Jane.*"

"Congrats," she says dryly. "Shelve these."

He picks a few of them up. "Did people change their minds and just leave them here?"

She nods. "Sometimes."

"I kinda feel sorry for the books that get left behind. Oh, look, here's one about Romanian folklore. Maybe there's a section on vampire tales. That's my kryptonite. I'll buy that one." He moves it to the side.

"You're into that?" I ask. It might explain the Gothic bed.

"You never asked. Tuck did. He asked me all kinds of things. That's why he got the bracelet." He gives me a pointed look. "My major was world history, with a minor in poetry."

"No one cares. Can you shelve them *now*?" Jane asks, interrupting us.

"In a hurry to get rid of me?" Jasper says as he sets the books on the rolling cart.

"No, I just want you to clean the toilets when you're done." She smiles slyly.

Jasper sputters and throws me a look. "No way. Uh-uh. I came to meet your wife, not clean."

I smirk, laughing. "That's what friends do. We help each other out when things go south."

"I draw the line at toilets," he mutters as he picks up a book.

I step closer to Jane, behind the counter. "Hey, any Kian sightings?"

She nods. "I've seen him walk past the store five times since you've been gone. I'm keeping tabs, don't worry. I hate that asshole."

My fists tighten. "Five?"

"He left another bouquet of lilies, which Andrew found when he came in early one morning. She never saw them. Truthfully, he probably walks by here once a day, and I just don't see him. FYI, I've been going to this axe-throwing place for fun. If he comes in, I'm ready." She points to an axe she has under the counter. "I can be a badass too."

I wince. "I can't decide if you're kidding or not."

She blinks at me innocently. "Not."

I exhale. "Don't worry about him. I've got it covered."

She rakes me up and down. "You have a plan?"

"Yes," I say grimly. "I'll let you know when it's time. I'm going to need you."

"I like you about twenty percent more than I did." She taps the PA system. "Emmy, we have a cream situation in the lobby. Please come see him."

Jasper cocks his head. "'Cream'? What's she talking about?"

"Long story that I don't—" My words come to a halt as Emmy approaches us in a white silk blouse and a black pencil skirt with heels. She's talking with one of the firemen as they come from upstairs. My iguana bangle encircles her arm. Her hair falls in loose waves and hangs around her face. Her makeup is dramatic, with arched brows and pouty lips. And she is . . .

"Fucking hot," Jasper murmurs from next to me, and a buzz of irritation hits.

"That's my wife you're drooling over. Stop."

He holds his hands up. "Just saying. If things don't work out between you two—"

Jane's voice cuts like a knife. "Of course it will work out. It's *Emmy*. She wouldn't commit unless she means it with her whole heart."

Magic struts behind her like a king, then detours and jumps behind the counter with Jane and surveys the customers with beady eyes.

I stick my hands in my shorts pockets and walk to meet Emmy as she shakes the fireman's hand. He flirts with her, an older guy with scruff and a bit of a belly. She laughs with him, but I see shadows under her eyes, as if she hasn't slept much. The fireman walks away, and she turns to the people at the end of the checkout line, explaining how they're short staffed and missing one of their registers. She offers them a free coffee with their purchases.

She turns around, and I'm there.

A long exhale comes from my lips. It's been too long. I should have come back earlier.

"Hi," I say, my tone soft as I study her features. "It's good to see you."

A blush rises up her cheeks. "Hi."

"You look short staffed. What can I do?"

She blows out a long breath. "Everything that could go wrong, went wrong this morning. The firemen just cleared out. A little girl locked herself in the bathroom. Her mom said she was epileptic, so I called the fire department to rush things along. They broke the lock, and the little girl is fine."

"Good."

"Plus, there's a leak in the basement." Worry flits over her features. "My shark was in the basement, and it's ruined."

"Show me."

We get on the elevator, and when it opens to the basement, I see the problem. A leak from a pipe has spilled onto a large worktable in the corner of the room. Water is under and on top of the table. Art supplies are soaked.

"We had a beautiful giant papier-mâché shark for the window. One of the sinks in the kitchen leaked, and this is the issue." She explains how she's already shut the water off for that sink.

"I have nothing to display to the *Times* when they come tomorrow. My brain is done with this day, and I . . ." She sways on her feet as she puts a hand to her chest.

I catch her and hold her into my arms. "Emmy! Are you okay?"

Her throat moves as she inhales deep breaths. "Fine. Just superearly mornings and late nights."

I search her green eyes, not letting her out of my grasp, but then she isn't pulling away either. "So you need a new display? You can't just set the mannequins back up?"

"It needs to be new. We were going to make an ocean and hang the shark about midway up. Our books were *Jaws* and nonfiction titles about great whites. The art girl I use and I planned it for weeks." She rubs her temple. "Guess you saw the mannequins getting freaky?"

"Horny mannequins. Trying to have sex in front of customers."

A small smile crosses her lips. "I'm glad you're back." She leans her head on my chest, her curves against my muscles, and I squeeze her a little tighter, resting my chin on her head. "How was camp?" she asks, anxiousness evident in her tone.

"We did some scrimmages with the Falcons, took a few classes, worked with our coaches."

She quiets for a few moments; then: "Did you get hurt? Any headaches or dizziness?"

"Training is gentle. We don't roughhouse. We're just getting ready, and no one wants to injure another player."

"Oh."

"Were you worried?"

"Of course not," she mumbles.

"Hmm."

"What's next on your calendar?" she asks.

"Training camp here, then preseason games. The first one is August eleventh, then the regular season starts September seventh."

"How many games do you play during the regular season?"

"Seventeen."

She exhales. "Dammit, Graham. That's a lot of chances to be hurt."

"You won't need to be concerned."

"Why not?" She tips her head and gazes up at me with big eyes.

Emotion makes my throat prickle. "By then, the inheritance should be here."

She inhales a breath and holds my gaze for several long moments. A vein near her temple throbs. "Right. Of course. We won't even be together. We never have to speak again—"

"Wait. Come on, Emmy. We can be friends after this is—"

She cuts me off and steps out of my arms. "While you were gone, I had your dad over for dinner, and he met Jane and Andrew and Londyn. Hopefully, I've convinced him we're real, so even if Holden tries to pull his tricks, then we'll have his support."

I nod, regret knifing into me at her cool words. Brody filled me in on the dinner. Apparently, she and Jane made a lasagna. According to Brody, Dad adored the Darling family, especially little Londyn. Emmy also confided in Dad about her upbringing and also told him that Holden had a PI following her and was planning on releasing a story.

"Thanks for doing that," I reply, studying the way she's holding herself, her shoulders curled in. "Dad called me last week. He had words with Holden. There isn't going to be any story about us."

She pushes out a nonchalant shrug. "Honestly, I always thought I'd be upset to see my name and my parents' past dragged in the papers, but that seems like a trivial thing compared to me nearly losing the book-store—or your concussion. I like your dad. He reminds me of you."

She pauses, seeming to consider her words. "Speaking of faithful, you left me at the beach. Why did you go to Seattle after camp?"

I needed some space from her, but I also had business. "I still had a condo there. It sold, and I was there to handle it."

"Brody keeps saying I should know why you left. I don't. Not really. Nothing definitive. I mean, you could have stayed. We could have hung out."

I don't reply.

She sighs. "Have you heard of Occam's razor?"

"Yeah. It means that a simpler explanation is more likely to be true than a complex one. One famous example is if you hear hoofbeats, think horses, not zebras."

She fidgets, the color rising in her cheeks. "So, the simplest explanation is you couldn't wait to get away from me."

I heave out an exhale. "Emmy—"

"No, it's fine." She gives me a tight smile. "I'm going upstairs to get back to work."

She turns to go, and I don't stop her. Part of me wants to comfort her, but the other side is wary of getting too close.

She didn't *want* to marry me.

She wants us to end.

And I'm afraid she's going to rip out my heart when she leaves.

I shove that thought away. This was the plan. Just stick to it.

Chapter 23
EMMY

Since the basement incident, Graham's taken care of dealing with the plumber, swept the rotunda, and helped an elderly couple onto the elevator. Both he and Jasper wear ball caps, and only a couple of people have recognized them.

Graham looks relaxed—that is, until Londyn squirms in Andrew's arms and points at Graham. Andrew hands her to Graham, who holds her from his body with outstretched arms until Andrew tells him to put Londyn on his hip. He bounces her around when she starts to whimper, and pretty soon he's walking around the store with her, pointing out different things for her to look at. She's sleepy and rests her forehead on his shoulder.

I take a bite of the grilled cheese Jane made me earlier. It's the first time I've sat down all day.

"Quite the view, right?" Brody says as he plops down next to me at the table. He arrived about an hour ago, after Graham texted him. Cas stayed behind for work but said he'd come by later.

I take a sip of my tea. "What view?"

"Graham with a baby. Giving you ideas?" He waggles his brows. "I'd adore a little niece or nephew. Cas and I have thought about adoption, but we need to get the business going first."

"Are you looking at places for your gym again?"

He nods. "I think we've found a great place in Brooklyn. It's in a fun part of town and has plenty of space for everything we want to do."

"The cookies are going off in the oven," Jane calls out to him.

Brody smirks and rises to his feet. "Sorry. I'm on cookie duty. Want me to bring you a hot one? It's chocolate chip in this batch."

I tell him no, that I don't eat chocolate because of caffeine, then check my phone as a text comes in. It's from the art girl who made the shark. I sent her a text this morning, hoping she might have some ideas for us on how to repair the shark.

Sorry I can't help you fix Mr. Shark. I got hired at Bloomingdales full-time.

I congratulate her on the job, then toss the phone down and want to cry in frustration.

Great. Now what?

◆　◆　◆

"Tomorrow is the big reveal for our window," I tell the staff and everyone else who's gathered in the rotunda. It's nearly closing time, and a few customers come and go, but Jane is handling them.

"The *Times* will be here to take a look at it. We'd planned a shark window, but that isn't going to happen because the shark is ruined, and the artist isn't available to help. I need quick and easy ideas, and whoever is available tonight to stay and help put it together. I know we've all been working hard, but this window is our biggest coup of the summer. We need something fantastic." I pause. "Also, in case you haven't heard the good news yet, our buyer of the store is keeping it open. He's also here today helping us. Staff, meet Graham Harlan." Apparently Graham met with Terry in Atlanta, and they officially signed the papers.

Babs claps excitedly.

The staff waves a hello at him. Some of them cheer.

"Graham, would you like to add anything?" I ask.

He clears his throat. "Good work, everyone. I'm glad to be here."

Andrew munches on a cookie as he flirts with one of the newly hired girls. "He bought it because he loves my sister. They're married."

Babs rolls her eyes. "We all know they're married, Andrew."

Graham's eyes find mine and glint with something. "Who couldn't love her?"

Brody smiles widely as he gives me a thumbs-up and claps. "Bravo, brother! The bookstore is your great new adventure."

Jasper elbows Brody. "Being the best tight end in the country is his adventure."

"With that settled, shoot me with your ideas for a summer display," I say. "Anything. Just something. Please."

Jasper's hand shoots up in the air, and I smirk. "You don't have to raise your hand, Jasper."

"Oh, well, you're in charge, so . . . How about a bunch of sand, giant beach balls, then toss some books in there about summer—"

Jane interrupts him as she arrives with Londyn in her arms. "Not exciting."

"It's a great idea," he retorts to her as she sits at their table.

Babs clears her throat. "Just rolling with the beach theme . . . we could put a chair in there, an inflatable palm tree, put the male mannequin in a Speedo, and let him read a book with a summery title. Oh! We could toss in a surfboard."

I jot down her thoughts on a clipboard.

"We could ask our owner or one of his friends to sit in the beach chair a few hours a day, you know, just to make it exciting," Jane says with relish as she sweeps her gaze over Graham and Jasper. "Gives them something to do besides banging against each other on the football field."

Jasper glowers at her. "We have busy lives."

"It must be so hard to put on a uniform and run around. Give the man a cookie," Jane says sweetly.

Jasper glares at her. "I'm going to get a cookie, then I'm going to shelve more books." He stalks away, and I sigh as I give Jane a *Can you settle down for a hot minute?* look.

She shrugs and mouths *I'm sorry.*

Brody raises his hand, and I groan. "You don't have to raise your hand."

"Is the shark completely ruined?" he asks.

"It has half a head. A few teeth left. The rest of the body is unsalvageable," Graham says.

Brody taps his chin. "Maybe have the mannequin—in his Speedo, of course—fighting off a shark, only you can't see most of the shark, just the mangled head. Blood is everywhere. His leg is gone. Maybe an arm. The girl mannequin—maybe a lifeguard—is trying to pull him out of the water. You could feature books about sharks and travel guides to sea destinations."

I nod. "I appreciate your idea, but the blood and loss of a leg might be a bit much for some customers. We try to keep our displays PG."

"Yeah, they don't want to scare people away, Brody," Graham adds.

Brody pouts. "I love gore. If I had a bookstore, it would be a horror one."

One of the staffs suggests summer hobbies like gardening. Another suggests a camping scene with a tent and a fake fire. None of them seem to take hold.

My shoulders slump. "We need to nail this down. Any other ideas?"

"I noticed you had a box of old vinyl records in the basement," Graham says. "Anything good?"

I shake my head. "Just some items Terry bought when we talked about selling records. What are you thinking?"

"Well, most windows will be doing beachy themes, right? We want to stand out."

I nod.

"I was flipping through the records, and most of them are from the seventies. You could do a 'Disco Summer of the Seventies' or a 'Fifty-Year Anniversary of Books' kind of thing. You could get a disco ball; well, actually I have one at my—*our*—apartment."

Brody nods enthusiastically. "Dude, yes! Hang the ball, dress the mannequins in seventies outfits—halter tops and bell-bottoms, head scarves, chokers, feather jewelry. I can get in touch with our drama teacher at the school. They'll have a roomful of costumes."

We have a few costumes we keep in storage for our mannequins, but not anything from the seventies. "Thanks, Brody. Could you get them today?"

He taps his phone. "Already on it. Might as well consider it done."

Jasper comes back over. "Graham, you mentioned the records. Maybe we could play music in the window, let it trickle out into the store. We passed an antique store on the way here. They might have one of those old record players to add to the ambiance."

I smile at him. "That's a lovely idea. Okay. Let's come up with a list of books. What books do we associate with the seventies?"

Everyone pops out their phones, and Graham is the first to say, "Judy Blume's *Are You There God? It's Me, Margaret.*"

"A favorite," I say as he holds my eyes intently until tingles dance over my skin.

"*The Joy of Sex,*" Jasper calls out triumphantly. "That's what I'm talking about, folks! Twelve million copies sold. Boom."

Jane smirks. "Typical that you'd go to the book about sex. Do you need a little self-help?"

Jasper narrows his gaze. "I don't, Joanie."

"It's Jane."

"Who cares," he replies coolly.

"I don't," she says.

Jasper narrows his gaze. "The book is about experiencing intimacy and having fun with sex. Maybe you need it."

"You know nothing about me," she mutters.

"Okay, enough of you both. Keep going," I say, rolling my hands.

"*Fear and Loathing in Las Vegas, All the President's Men, Roots, The Shining*," Babs says as she balances her phone and Londyn in her lap.

"*The Shining!*" Brody exclaims. "A creepy caretaker at a hotel in Colorado, ghostly twins, dead guests, and an axe! Oh, I want a window just with that."

"We have an axe," Jane murmurs.

"Enough with the axe," I tell her pointedly.

"It's a good list of classics. Great idea, Graham," I say. "You'll make a great bookstore owner."

He's bent over his phone, taking notes, and glances up at me. A long moment passes, or maybe it's just my imagination, but it feels as if we're sharing more than just ideas. Nope. We're just professional. A professional marriage.

"You're welcome, darling," he murmurs.

I shake myself out of my reverie and gaze around. "So . . . who's going to help us get this done tonight?"

Chapter 24
EMMY

Graham steps down from the inside of the window, sweat on his brow as he takes his hat off and rubs his hair. "The ball is up and turning. I'm not an electrician, so we might need to have it checked tomorrow."

"Good idea. Come on, let's go look," I say.

The air is thick with humidity as we dart outside and stand out on the sidewalk. Even though it's nearly midnight, people have been pausing to stop and watch us work in the window.

I gasp at the full effect. "So perfect," I murmur.

The iridescent ball sends sparkles over the window, highlighting the couple in a frozen dance beneath it. Brody's school's drama department did a parody of the movie *Saturday Night Fever*, and he managed to snag a John Travolta–style seventies dance outfit for the male mannequin and pink bell-bottomed pants and a crocheted halter top for the woman.

Jane used a curling iron and styled her hair into beach waves and added dangly feathery earrings. Jasper delivered with the record player, which is on a table in the corner, softly playing "Stayin' Alive," by the Bee Gees. Various records, ones Graham picked out, are strewn around the table.

We pulled two more mannequins from storage and dressed them in bright colors from the era. They sit propped against the wall on either side of the display. The girl has her head bent as she reads *The Shining*, in a nod of respect for Brody securing the costumes. The other mannequin, a teen girl, is reading *Are You There God? It's Me, Margaret*. The other titles, in hardcover, are suspended from wires from the ceiling.

"It looks damn good," Graham murmurs.

Emotion fills me as I look around at everyone. I blink away tears as the stress I'd been carrying ever since I came in this morning drifts away. "You guys worked so hard. Graham, you went and took down your light fixture. Brody and Cas, you ran around Manhattan and got us costumes. Jasper, you bought the record player. Jane has already left, but I couldn't have done it without her dressing the mannequins."

Brody shrugs. "Meh. I'm off for the summer anyway. I'd help my sister-in-law anytime she needs it."

Sister-in-law. Right.

"Guess we should take out the pizza boxes and soda cans we left in there," Brody muses.

Cas says he'll get them and dashes inside. He waves at us, does some disco moves, then comes back outside to where we are.

I kiss my brother on the cheek. "Thanks for keeping us fed and hydrated."

"I'm a cookie machine, Ma," he says.

Babs crooks her arm in mine, and I pat her hand. "You, too, Babs. You found the books and got them hung."

"Ah, don't get misty on us. We still need to clean up the kitchen," my brother says.

"You need to go home," I tell him. "I'll want you back in the store at eight to make more cookies."

"Nooooo," he wails, and I shoo him away.

"And thank you to Graham for the idea," I say as we move to head back inside the store.

I glance at him, and his eyes are already waiting, a heat there I don't want to acknowledge.

I can't.

My heart should be—*is*—stone when it comes to him.

Andrew gives me a hug. "I'm gonna head out, Ma. Call me if you need me, all right?"

We head inside and go into the kitchen. Cas says he's still hungry, so I grab croissants and pull some fruit and cheese out of the fridge for them to munch on. After sticking dishes in the commercial dishwasher, I leave Graham and them chatting as I go to Terry's office to check on Babs.

I open the door, and sure enough, she's sitting in his chair, looking glum. "Missing him?"

She dabs at her eyes. "It's not just the sex. I miss his messy office, his crazy hair, our trysts."

"Call him. I'm sure he'd love to hear your voice, Babs."

After she leaves, I wander into my office to get my purse, and just before I'm about to go, I see a small package on my desk.

"It's from me," Graham rumbles from behind me, and I turn around. He's leaning against the doorjamb, his hair a mess where he's been raking his hands through it. His shirt is damp against his chest, and I swallow. We have the AC set to automatically go off at five, and the store has slowly heated up.

"You don't need to keep getting me gifts. You've bought my silence forever already."

He straightens, with his arms crossed in front of his chest. "This isn't about keeping you quiet. It's personal." He pauses. "I'm sorry about before, in the basement. I know this marriage has been hard for both of us. I shouldn't have stayed away so long."

I glance down at the gift. Part of me wants to rip it open, but the other side of me doesn't want to know what he bought.

"Open it." His eyes caress my face. "I enjoy watching you."

I inhale a deep breath. Fine. I tear at the little string and unwrap the brown paper. My lips tremble when I see what it is. My fingers delicately touch the jacket on the paperback, an illustrated picture of a girl holding a pig as a spider dangles down on a web. Inside, the book features an aqua-colored page with a beautiful web. Little illustrations of the story are in each chapter.

My eyes find his. "You got me a first edition copy of *Charlotte's Web*, and it's signed." I want to clutch it to my chest and weep. "You shouldn't have."

"Why not?" He eases down on the couch.

Because it's breaking me.

He's chiseling away at my heart piece by piece.

Pretty soon he'll own it forever.

"You deserve that book. You deserve beautiful things, Emmy."

My heart swells with a mixture of emotions at his soft tone. Everything around me suddenly feels fragile and delicate, as if the slightest gesture might shatter everything into a million pieces.

I must resist giving in to these feelings.

I should put him aside and move on.

He is temporary.

We are temporary.

"You asked me once what my greatest fear was, and I didn't answer you," he says as he leans forward.

"Yeah?"

A gruff sound comes from him. "It's letting someone in. And you? It's yours too."

And it's too late for me.

Like a thief, he snuck into my heart before I knew what was happening.

He rubs his jawline. "We have something. I tried to push it aside. I tried restraint. It's not working. As soon as I saw you this morning, I . . ." His words trail off.

I swallow. "Too much tension."

"Perhaps we should just give in to it."

My stomach knots in anticipation.

He says the words quietly: "What would it take?"

Barely anything.

His eyes hold mine, a knowing there, a desire. I'm drawn into his gaze, being pulled toward him, an invisible force controlling my limbs.

He inches closer to me. "Do you want me, Emmy?"

I say nothing as he tucks a piece of hair out of my face and says, "Let's see what it's like between us if we face this fear together."

"What if it . . . ends badly?" My breath trembles in my chest.

"Focus on the good." His intense gaze is filled with hunger and desire, and my lashes flutter.

I want him. I want him to make me forget we're not real.

I feel his breath on my skin, and my whole body tingles with anticipation. His hands slide up my arms, sending shivers down my spine, and then up to my neck, pulling me close until our lips are just a breath away.

I close my eyes, savoring the moment, before his lips finally meet mine. His kiss delves softly, brushing me with little tastes, and I can't help but moan in pleasure. Our tongues intertwine, and my hands caress his shoulders, feeling the strength and power in his muscles.

His hands move to my hips as our bodies press together.

The heat between us burns like a fire, and passion rises with every kiss. His hands wander to my blouse, his fingers expertly undoing the buttons, eliciting moans from me.

My shirt is tugged from my skirt, and he tosses it to the couch. He kisses me hungrily, his lips growing passionate, his mouth open as he explores the recesses of mine. With a snap, my bra is off, and he groans as he finds my piercing and tweaks it between his fingers. His breath is in my ear as he kisses up my neck. "I've been dreaming about these tits."

I gasp, my head falling back to give him more access. "They're all yours."

"And this luscious ass." His big hands palm my butt as he pushes my skirt up to my waist.

I bite his bottom lip gently, and he hisses, burying his face in my neck. He sucks on a piece of skin, and I swivel my hips against the bulge in his shorts.

"Clothes. Off." I tear at his shirt until he pauses enough to rip it off. Holy mother of . . .

His bare chest under my hands is mind blowing, his tanned skin, the dust of dark hair on his pecs, his glistening eight-pack. I gasp his name, and he pushes me against the wall, caging me in as he takes deep breaths.

"Strip."

My core flutters at the command in his voice. I marvel at how safe I feel with him, how sure I am that here's a man who would never hurt me physically. He wants to protect me. He gives me gifts that speak to my heart.

Holding his eyes, I remove my skirt, unzipping the side with slow movements. My lace panties are next as I slide them down and let them fall at my feet. "You like?"

His eyes feast on me, his lids lowering. "You. Are. Extraordinary."

My throat moves as I trace my hand down my neck to my clavicle, to the tip of my breast, then to my core. I taste myself, my tongue rolling around my finger.

"Fuck." A long breath shudders out of him as he watches me. "You're a siren."

"It's been a while," I say as I shove down his shorts and boxers, and his cock jerks free. It's long and thick, the crown weeping. My mouth waters, and I fall to my knees and take him into my mouth.

He curses, his hands slapping the wall behind me. His body tightens beneath my hands as I massage his thighs, then reach up to his waist and chest.

He thrusts gently into my mouth as I press kisses up his length, my tongue sucking on his tip.

"Emmy, fuck, stop, stop . . ." He pulls me back up and hits me with his lustful eyes. "Once we start fucking, we aren't going to stop. No breaking-the-tension shit. I'm going to have you every day we have together."

"Promise?"

He smirks. "I don't have a condom, but I'm just back from a physical. You?"

I nod. "On the pill too."

"So, we're doing this?"

I kiss him, and finally he touches me again, his hands palming the back of my skull as his lips devour me.

He's a man possessed, giving me deep, passionate, hungry kisses that make me weak.

I am lost in him, in this deep need to have him inside me.

His hand touches the top of my mound as a finger glides inside me, testing the wetness. "Dripping for me."

"More."

He finger-fucks me, and I gasp out with each exit, itching for more of him, for endless touches. When his thumb brushes my clit, I writhe against him.

He picks me up in his arms, my back against the wall. He thrusts inside me, deep and hard as I cling to his shoulders.

"Emmy," he breathes as he squeezes my ass. His mouth sucks on my piercing, his scruff making excited tingles erupt over my skin.

There's no resistance as I accept him. He swivels his hips, finding a new angle, and I adjust. He takes me roughly, checking my eyes for guidance.

"Do you know what it's like to fuck you face to face?"

"No," I say around a moan.

"A dream, darling. A fucking dream."

Sensations spiral over me, a voracious need. And when he uses his pelvis to grind against my clit, I scream, trying for more, to get to the zenith.

"Graham," a voice says from the door, and I gasp, my eyes flaring wide when Brody pokes his head in.

"Get. The. Fuck. Out," Graham yells as I dip my head behind his chest to hide.

"Sorry to intrude. Emmy, dear, when we go out the door to leave, does it lock behind us?"

"Um, yes," I say, my face burning with embarrassment.

"I thought so but wanted to check. Bye, turtledoves. Enjoy." I hear a chuckle; then the door shuts again.

"You okay?" he asks me with a tender expression.

I nod as his hands move to each breast, playing with my nipples, then up my waist, each touch creating new waves. My breathing grows shallow until I'm dizzy. My legs tighten around his waist.

I shudder as he toys with my nub, pressing down with each stroke inside my pussy.

Over and over.

He fucks me.

Harder.

Wild.

Voracious.

Deep thrusts.

Like he's trying to crawl inside me.

Until the imprint of the drywall must be on my back.

My body winds tighter and tighter, the sensations building until I'm about to burst. I glance down to watch him slide in and out, my hips thrusting to meet his. He growls, a deep sound, and it makes me skyrocket. My hands claw at his neck as I pull him in for a kiss and dance toward orgasm. It rises and rises, then shatters into beautiful shards, my pussy clenching around his cock as ecstasy tingles under my skin, in my veins. I call out his name, and he groans, kissing me through the vibrations.

"My turn, darling." He kisses me hard, his hands digging into my hips as he repositions us and increases his rhythm as he pushes inside me with faster thrusts. I can barely keep up, my fingers around his neck as I hang on.

He groans out my name when he comes. Heavy breaths come from his chest as he grapples with the aftereffects, his body shuddering.

Maybe all we have is sex, chemistry, and pheromones that neither of us can resist.

But maybe it's something more.

I don't want to be temporary. I don't want to be pretend. I want *him.*

He pulls out of me and stumbles to the couch with me still wrapped around him. He kisses my shoulder as I lean on him, snuggling under his chin. I feel his lips brush my hair.

I pat his arm. "That was great, Creamy." I giggle when he huffs out annoyance. "You may as well accept the nickname. Mine is Darling, and yours is Creamy."

He twists a strand of my hair around his finger. "You wanna go home and do this again, only with a bed?"

"Mine or yours?"

"Who cares?"

I laugh. "I have to be back at seven to get the store ready."

"Is that a no?"

I ease off him and grab my clothes from the floor as he watches me with heavy-lidded eyes. "It's a 'Get your ass in gear so we can hurry.'"

He smiles, broadly, the effect of it nearly taking my breath. "Yes, darling."

Chapter 25
GRAHAM

Having a bachelor party a month after being married is a bit unortho-dox, but we're at the Baller, a private membership club for professional athletes, and they serve a mean burger and have great beer.

Technically, it really isn't a bachelor party. We're here for a reason.

The waitress brings another round of tequila shots, and I discreetly push mine over in Cas's direction. I need my wits about me. There's a special guest arriving soon, and I want to be fully aware. Just the thought of seeing him makes my hands clench. Zero alcohol for me.

We're inside one of the private rooms as Jasper chews on a french fry and gives me a baleful look from across the table. He nudges his head in the direction of Jane, Ciara, and Babs. "When I suggested we have a bachelor party, I didn't know girls we knew would be invited. I was expecting hot strippers, not *bookworms*."

"Sorry to disappoint," I murmur. "I'm not into strippers."

Jane flips him off. "We can hear you, meathead."

Jasper uses both hands to return her salute. "I meant for you to hear, Miss Model."

"Settle down, children. No squabbles," Brody says as he swirls his martini, takes a deep sip, then stands and glances around the room.

"Welcome, everyone, especially the ladies we have present tonight. Ciara and Mason, it's great to see you outside the bar. The time has now arrived for us to offer our dear friend and brother, Graham, marriage advice. If you aren't married, any good old-fashioned relationship tidbits will do. Let's help him out, yes?"

After Brody sits, River Tate stands. The best wide receiver on the team, he came to the franchise married to his college sweetheart. He was the one who recommended Dr. Moreau, and we've become close. "I'll go first. Never use the bathroom with the door open. Once you do, there's no mystery left. There's nothing more eye-opening than watching your loved one drop a deuce." He grins. "Of course, I have two kids, and you wouldn't believe the diapers I've changed. Pureed pears, man, don't feed them to your baby. Turns them into shitting machines."

"Here, here!" Brody says. "I concur! Not about the baby food, but the other. Cas and I have separate bathrooms for a reason. Namely, his bombs are death fumes." He kisses Cas. "It's okay, baby. I love you anyway."

Jasper blows out a breath. "I've been in a few, okay several, relationships. My main piece of advice is, if a girl wants an argument, just strip. Usually, my beautiful body halts everything. Also, angry sex is the best."

He leans in, a serious look on his face. "Also. Dude. I've got four sisters. Trust me when I tell you to keep track of her cycle so you can be ready with cuddles. And buy tampons for her so she doesn't have to. Might wanna get some candy. I buy out the Walgreens for my sisters."

"She might need her pig," Jane says.

Brody blanches. "God, don't tell me she has a pig and a cat?"

Andrew laughs. "Not a real pig. Wilbur, from *Charlotte's Web*. He's our stuffed animal that we share."

"Oh." Brody shrugs. "There's a story there, I guess."

Andrew does a fist bump with Jasper. "I've bought my share of tampons."

I exhale. "Let's move on from menstrual cycles."

"All right then, say yes more than you say no," Jasper replies. "And don't act disgusted if she burps or farts. It's gross, but don't let her know. It's fine if you do those things. It's manly."

"So manly," I reply dryly.

My mind drifts. I left her at home tonight, curled up on the couch with a book.

Being stealthy, I sneak my phone under the table and text her. What are you wearing?

She sends me a pic of herself in kitty PJ pants and a tank top.

Sexy.

Having fun yet? she asks.

Hmm, it's nice to see River outside of football, and I don't know Mason very well, but I've clocked the narrowed looks he sends me. He doesn't trust me. Maybe after tonight, he will.

I need to know when your period is so I can be prepared with chocolate.

There's a pause, and she sends, I enjoy champagne on my period.

I'm smiling as I envision myself buying feminine products and champagne.

"Are you paying attention?" Jasper asks, kicking me under the table.

I look up. "Yeah, what did I miss?"

"I was telling you to always tell her she's hot, even when she's got hairy legs and pimples. That's true love, man."

"Like you know what true love is," Jane mutters as she flicks back her hair.

Jasper slams down his glass. "I've had just about enough of your mouth."

She pops an eyebrow. "Yeah, big boy, whatcha gonna do about it?"

Jasper pushes his chair out of the way and marches around to her side of the table.

The low conversation of the table grows quiet.

"What's going on?" Babs asks as she straightens from a conversation with Ciara.

Jane stands up to meet Jasper and points her finger in his face, making me wince. That's like waving a red cloth at a bull. He grabs it, pulls her to him, and lays one on her. Her arms sneak around his neck for about three seconds; then she shoves him away and gapes at him.

"You're an asshole," she hisses.

Brody smirks at me. "Maybe a little magic there, heh?"

"Whoa," Cas says. "Is she going to slap him?"

"Yep," Babs says. "In three, two, one . . ."

Smack. Jane's hand lands on Jasper's cheek. Red prints flare on his face as he rubs it, grins, then waltzes back to his seat.

"That should work for a few minutes," he says as he takes a drink of his beer.

Jane sputters, then seems to gain her equilibrium and sits back down, huffing as she glances at the room. "Why is everyone smiling?"

We all go back to normal conversation, murmuring as we finish up our food.

The hostess peeks in the room and gives me a head nod.

Grim determination flows through me as I stand. "Everyone, thanks for the meal and advice. Now, we have other business to attend. Follow my lead."

"I can't wait for this shit," Jasper says, then does a few jumping jacks.

Babs cocks her head as River, Brody, and Cas whisper among themselves. "What's going on?"

Jane grabs her purse off the back of the chair, smiling. "We're going on a mission."

"Like spies?" Babs asks.

"More like ninjas with an axe to grind," Jane replies, grinning in anticipation.

Of course I let my guy friends know what's going to happen, and I felt compelled to let Jane in on it. She's Emmy sister, and this is important to her. Mason and Babs and Ciara are along for the ride.

I toss down several big bills to cover the tab and a nice big tip, then straighten my collar and crack my neck. "Let's go."

Jasper grins. "We aren't going to end up in jail, are we? I mean, I'm with you, but I need to call my lawyer real quick."

"You should have already called him," I say.

"Hell, yeah! I've never been in jail," Cas calls out as he hooks his arm with Brody's.

"I hope we can make bail," Jasper says as he helps a baffled and slightly scared Babs to her feet and offers his arm as an escort. He assures her that he'll take care of her if anything happens.

We exit the room and walk down the hall to the bar area of the Baller. Low music plays on the speakers, and a line of TVs on the wall show different sports games.

The place is half-full for a Monday evening. My tight end coach, Marlon, is here with some of the assistants and gives me a back slap as I pass by. Every table has a member of the Pythons team, from offense to defense. Deacon, one of the linebackers, whoops out a yell when he sees us, then gives me a thumbs-up.

Not that Kian seems to notice.

He's leaning over the bar and chatting it up with the pretty bartender as he tips back a glass of whiskey.

Jasper leaves Babs behind us as he and Cas ease up on either side of me. I stand behind Kian and tap him on the shoulder. "Hey, asshole. You aren't wanted here. I suggest you leave."

He flips around, his face tightening when he realizes who I am. "You don't own this place, Harlan. I paid my dues just like everyone else here."

I smile tightly. "Men who hurt women aren't allowed in here."

His eyes turn to slits as red colors his cheeks. Alcohol reeks from him. "Back off, Harlan. Who do you think you are?"

"Better. Than. You." My voice is low. Dangerous.

He shoves the barstool away and gets in my face. He's tall, maybe six-four, but I'm taller. And he's a big dude, but I'm bigger. Yeah, he's younger than me, but there's never a day in this world when he would overpower me.

I shove him with one hand, and he staggers back, his legs banging into the barstool. It falls to the floor with a clanging sound.

He juts back in my space, fists clenched. "Stay out of my way, Harlan. It's my bar too."

"Actually, it isn't. The owners are revoking your membership." All it took was a few well-placed phone calls about his abusive behavior toward my wife. I tap my chin. "Go on, take a swing. I'll give you one free shot."

He stiffens, his gaze taking in the crowd of Emmy's friends behind me. Jane glares death daggers at him. Even Babs looks a little scary as she takes her glasses off and tucks them into her purse like she's getting ready to rumble. Cas has his arms crossed, a lethal grin on his face. Mason even looks like he's ready to throw down. I look at him and point to Kian. "This is why I invited you. I don't know you, and you don't seem to like me, but we have a mutual enemy. You know what he did to her, yeah?"

"I like you now, Graham," Mason mutters with a head nod.

I turn back to Kian. "Come on. Don't be a baby. Hit me, Kian. You want to because I married beautiful, sweet, Emmaline Darling, and you can't have her."

Rage grows on his face, his hands twitching. He swings at me, and I let it connect, feeling my lip split. It's nothing.

I laugh as I wipe at the blood on my mouth. "You hit like you play football. Lazy."

He leans back for another punch, and I catch his fist, grab him by the throat, and maneuver him against the wall of the bar. My crew gathers around me. The rest of the place just watches.

My hand encircles his neck. "This is exactly what you did to Emmy, although honestly I'm being easy with you. Want to know why? Because Emmy doesn't like violence. She detests it," I grind out as I put my nose to his.

"W-what . . . ," he tries to say, then peters off.

I nudge my head to the people behind me. "They all know what you did. They also know that you've been following Emmy, leaving shit for her, and stalking outside the bookstore. It ends here and now. Gentle-like. I won't hurt you. For her. But give me a reason, any reason, and I will destroy you piece by piece and make sure you never play football again. If for some reason I'm not around to hurt you, the people behind me will be. Feel me?"

He struggles to pull my fingers away, and I tighten them. "My coach and my team are here to support me. This is a private club that you are no longer welcome in. I never punched you. You hit me. So go away. Live your life and leave Emmy alone or I'll have you arrested for splitting my pretty lips." I glance back at Brody. "Remind him of who our dad is."

"Powerful lawyer in New York," he says grimly.

I look back at Kian. "Don't call her, walk by her, look at her. If you see her coming, run in the opposite direction, and don't you ever fucking lay your hands on a woman again." I smile. "Say you will, Kian."

"Y-yes. J-just let me go."

I toss him away, and he catches himself on a table. The bar is silent, hard eyes on him as he stumbles through the place. The hostess opens the door for him as he walks away. She shuts it with a slam, and a cheer goes up in the crowd.

"How did you know he'd be here?" Jane asks.

It took some planning. "Several of the waitresses sent him a text that they wanted to see him tonight. He agreed to come. But he won't be back."

I raise my hand up to get everyone's attention. "Drink and food on me."

Whoops go up through the bar. "Now it's a fucking party!" I say as someone hands me a shot of tequila.

◆ ◆ ◆

It's one in the morning when I walk in the door at home. The room is darkened, with only a lamp illuminating the area.

Emmy is asleep on the couch, her hand curled up around her chin. I stroke a finger down her face, and her eyes open slowly.

"It's bedtime," I murmur as I help her sit up.

"Okay," she says around a yawn, then yelps when I swoop her up in my arms and carry her to my bedroom.

Life with her has been a blur of sex ever since the bookstore. I wake up and go to practice; she goes to the bookstore. Afterward, we have dinner with her family at the store or here, then fall into bed at night.

I'm not thinking about the future.

I can't.

I'm just taking it one day at a time.

My wish is for her happiness. To shelter her from anything that might hurt her.

"You smell like you've been dunked in a keg," she says as I ease her down, and she whips off her tank and pants and crawls under the covers with only her panties on.

I get naked and cuddle up to her. "I'm really tired," she murmurs.

"Which is code for 'I'm not down to fuck.'"

"Hmm."

My fingers stroke her hair, then trail down to her shoulder. "I'm gonna sleep naked anyway," I whisper.

"How was the party?"

"Lots of people. Drinks. Food. The usual." I smirk, then wince as my lip stings. "Tell me about your day before you go to sleep," I murmur, and she sinks deeper into my embrace.

"The new hires are great. Angela from the *Times* practically orgasmed over the window. There's not another bookstore in New York with the same concept. The fiftieth anniversary of those books just makes it all the more relevant. You, Mr. Cream, have great ideas. How about your day?"

I caress the line of her shoulder, my fingers gliding down her arm to lace our fingers together. "Practice was good. Our first preseason game is coming up, with Kansas City. You'll need to come."

She stiffens in my arms.

"Don't worry, darling. I'll be fine."

She doesn't say anything, but I can hear the wheels in her head spinning.

A long exhale comes from my chest. "Maybe we shouldn't talk about football."

"Okay. Wanna talk about the blood on your lip, then?"

I sit up and click on the lamp on the nightstand as she props her head on her arm and watches me. "You saw it? I thought I cleaned it up pretty good at the club."

"You don't think I inspect you from head to toe after you've been to a bachelor party? I was checking for hickeys and lipstick, and what I get is a busted lip."

I arch a brow. "Sorry?"

She moves and straddles me, her lace underwear rubbing against my hard cock, making me hiss. My hands land on her hips as she scowls down at me.

"Jane goes to a party, and you don't think she told me what happened immediately? In graphic detail. Then she admitted that Kian's been walking past the bookstore and leaving flowers again."

I narrow my eyes. "Minx. Were you really asleep when I came in?"

"Hell no. I was waiting to see your lip, you jerk! You could have hurt yourself or hit your head, messing with Kian. I was worried about you! Did you really plan the entire thing, for him to be there during your party?"

I grin.

"You *are* diabolical," she calls out.

I cup her face and brush our noses together. "You like me just the way I am."

She pouts. "Did you put some bacterial cream on it?"

"Yes, Ma. Jane had some in her purse."

She rears back. "Absolutely not. You do not get to call me Ma. That is wrong on so many levels."

"I was just kidding—come back here," I say when she tries to crawl away. I tug her back into my lap while she pouts. It makes me chuckle.

"Seriously. Are you mad at me for giving Kian a little taste of his own medicine? Eye for an eye—he deserved a hell of a lot more. I could have really hurt him, but I didn't. I merely let him know that you have family. And friends. And a badass husband who will protect you until the end."

Our eyes cling, her green to my gray, as the silence builds between us. "'Until the end'?"

I reach over and click off the light. I do not want to talk about *that*.

"Can we just cuddle?" I ask as I ease her back down to the bed.

"Anytime." She runs her fingers through my hair, then carefully inspects my split lip. Her eyes hold mine for a long time as she studies each of my features as if cataloging them for later.

"What?" I ask softly.

Her throat moves delicately as she swallows before she speaks. "No one's ever protected me before. No one has ever been this good to me."

"Darling, I'm yours. You never have to worry."

She dips her face so I can't read her eyes and snuggles into my neck. "You know my greatest fear?"

"Yeah," I say as my fingers idly drift down her shoulder to her arm.

"I'm not afraid anymore," she whispers. "Of this."

Silence fills the room as I digest her words. I get what she's telling me, and it makes my heart do somersaults in my chest. Her hand rests there as if she senses my own fear.

My throat tightens with words I can't say. My own fear still clings to me. My armor is still intact. Right?

"That's great," I say before kissing the top of her head. Eventually she slides away and turns over with her back to me. A long breath comes from my lips as I curl around her, my hand encircling her waist.

Chapter 26
EMMY

A chill runs over me, even though it's August. I'm in bed, my hands twisting the sheet as I grapple with the knot in my gut, trying to suss out where it's coming from.

Maybe it's because of Graham's preseason game. With each day that draws closer to him going back on the football field, I want to beg him not to play.

Maybe it's because I'm seeing my doctor soon. My hand touches my chest, checking the beats. Steady. Normal. But they haven't always been recently. Something isn't right.

I get up out of bed and slip on a slinky white robe and make my way to the window. I step out onto the balcony that overlooks Central Park. Even though I miss seeing Londyn in the mornings, I adore this view. I inhale a deep breath, trying to shake off the earlier feeling of trepidation.

Time has slipped by as the days have turned into weeks with us in the apartment. Each day brings new information about Graham. He's never tried watermelon. He eats his french fries with mayo. That one made me giggle for a full five minutes until he told me to try it, and it wasn't terrible. He loves warm weather and the sound of the ocean. He has a triangle-shaped birthmark on his hip and a tricky knee that he massages each morning, then ices down after practice. He still grieves from his mother's death. I know because I've asked him to play his baby grand, and he tells me he's not ready.

"Hey, sleepyhead. I made you a tea," Graham says as he steps out onto the balcony. He's wearing gym shorts and a practice shirt, and the sheen of sweat covers him. He's been on an early-morning run. Today is Sunday, and I slept longer since Babs opens today at noon. I'll pop in a little bit later.

Yesterday was a busy day at the bookstore; business is actually starting to boom. Of course, that could be because word has gotten around on social media that a couple of Python players frequent the store. Graham even works the checkout counter when he's there. It's fun to watch his earnestness as he asks customers if they've found everything they need. Maybe for the fall we can do a football window. Oh, perhaps we can twist the stereotype and have a girl baller and a boy cheerleader.

"Thanks." I take the cup from him as he moves to stand in front of me, leaning his back against the rails of the balcony.

"You look deep in thought. What's cooking?" he asks.

I inhale the smell of the peppermint tea, then take a sip. "I was thinking about the store. I've got so many ideas floating around. Babs wants to organize a book club, and I told her to go with it."

"Romance? That seems to be her fav." He smirks.

"Hmm, I was thinking about doing a singles event, like a speed-dating function where you bring your favorite book and talk to prospective dates about it."

"I've heard of restaurants doing them. Sounds fun."

"Plus, we could use the kitchen and make tapas."

"Ah, what about adding a theme to the event itself, maybe to fit the window, like an era in history or the theme from a book, like *Pride and Prejudice*."

A smile curls my lips at his obvious interest. "Only if you dress up as Darcy."

"Only if you're Elizabeth."

I blush. "Of course. I want to do more for the children's section too. Maybe let parents sign up to have a kid's birthday there."

"*Charlotte's Web*," he says, and I smile.

"Maybe do a display of the prettiest book jackets or the most unique. I also want to buy more impulse products and put them near the checkout—bookmarks, candy, magnets."

"Maybe magnets with the store's logo on it." A horn blows in the distance, and he looks away from me to check out the scenery.

I study the chiseled lines of his profile, the awful prickle of unease rising again.

He sees my frown. "Everything all right?"

I chew on my bottom lip. "Just a bad feeling when I woke up, like something terrible might happen."

He stiffens, his body on alert. "Like what?"

I shake my head. "I don't know."

"Do you get them often?"

"No, but Gran used to. She'd say it was a ghost walking through her and that I better watch my back that day. When Jane was a toddler she seemed to have premonitions of something terrible on a certain day, but most of that was because of the house we grew up in. Any day could be an awful day. I was always prepared."

He gives me a serious look. "You're coming to the game, right? I've got your tickets at the gate. Lots of wives will be there. Even my dad is coming."

We've spent time with Vale. On the Fourth of July, Graham rented a boat and invited my family and his, except for Holden and Divina. We sailed around the East River as Macy's did their fireworks show. Four barges stationed between Twenty-Third and Forty-Second Street set off over twenty thousand aerial effects. Londyn gasped in amazement at the vibrant colors in the night sky. Graham and I cuddled in a big chair on the deck, my hand over his heart as he held me. I'll never forget it.

"That bad feeling could be you. What if—"

"I'll be fine, Emmy," he says tightly. "Don't worry about me."

"Just telling me not to worry doesn't work," I insist, placing my tea down. "Life doesn't work that way. You're going to walk out onto that field, and *anything* could happen to you. A few days ago you came home with an ankle sprain from a tackle. What about all those studies Dr. Moreau sent you? Don't you think about them? Aren't you afraid?"

"No," he says curtly. "Bumps and bruises are normal. I don't want to be coddled like a child."

"If you'd just listen—"

"Nope. I came out here to bring you tea, not discuss my career. You don't know anything about football or how I feel. I'm going to eat breakfast." He turns and stalks away from me, his shoulders tense as a coiled spring.

I exhale. He's defensive because football is everything to him. It's true I don't know much about football, but he's the one who keeps avoiding any discussion of the risks he's taking.

A few minutes later, I step into the large tiled shower off Graham's bedroom, feeling the rush of warm water against my skin. I close my eyes and let the heat seep into my tense muscles. I'm shampooing my hair when the shower door opens, and Graham steps in with me.

My mouth dries. I'm not sure I'll ever get used to how gorgeous he is, those hard muscles toned to perfection. His thick cock bounces against his pelvis.

I arch a brow, and he shrugs and grins mischievously. "What? It's always like this with you around. Let me wash your hair for you."

"I can't say no to that," I murmur as he eases me so that my back is to his chest.

I shove my premonition and my worries away, burying them far away from this moment.

Without a word, he pulls me close, our bodies wet and slick against each other's. I lean against him, feeling safe from the world, as he pours my vanilla shampoo into the palm of his hand, then runs it through my hair. His fingers massage my scalp deeply, hypnotically. The steam of the water rises around us, cascading over our skin as he tips my head back to rinse me. He puts my hair over my shoulder, and his lips brush my neck as he kisses me. I melt against him, his cock hard against my ass.

His hands cup my shoulders. "I'm sorry I was short with you. Forgive me."

My heart swells with emotion as I turn and wrap my arms around his neck and stare up at him. I wonder if he senses the way I feel, if it radiates from me.

For a moment, emotion makes tears prick my eyes. He's that little piece of magic, that irresistible feeling I never imagined I'd feel for someone. I've fought it, but I can't stop. That's how love is, impossible to pack away and forget.

He smiles at me, his dimples popping as his eyes crinkle, and suddenly I feel lit up inside. I understand it now, why people do crazy things for love; the emotion of it is like a drug, intoxicating and addictive. And when he traces his finger over my lips as if memorizing the shape of them, I'm floating, safe and secure in his arms, with my protector.

"That's a very intense look you're giving me, darling," he murmurs.

"I want you to kiss me," I say as I push the hair from his face.

"You never have to ask." He bends his head and kisses me fervently, earnestly, as if conveying all his feelings and emotions in that one embrace. He captures my lower lip in his mouth and sucks on it as I tighten my arms around him. I savor his kiss, his touch. I revel in him, never wanting this, us, to end. I cling to him as he kisses down my neck, his teeth nipping and pulling at my skin.

Butterflies dance as he grazes his fingers over my piercing, tugging gently on my nipple and making me groan. My core heats, a need for him flaring like a lit match.

"Graham," I whisper as his hands caress my breasts, kneading them in his strong hands. My head falls back as he drops more kisses on me, his tongue sucking a pebbled nipple in his mouth.

"Am I making you forget about your bad feeling?" he rumbles against my skin, and I nod an affirmative, not able to speak as his fingers lightly play with my clit. He taps me gently, then draws intoxicating circles until I can't breathe.

"That's it," he growls when I straddle his thigh and rub against his leg for friction. "You need more, baby?"

A finger dips inside me, teasingly, softly.

"More," I whisper, and he chuckles as he picks me up as if I weigh nothing, and my legs wrap around his waist. We've had sex a hundred different ways since I moved in, and this is my favorite way, him displaying his strength while I get to look into his face and hold his eyes.

He pushes my back against the wall and stares down at me with yearning in his gaze. Firm hands hold my ass as his cock head slides into me, then out, just his tip, again and again until I'm writhing in his embrace.

Finally, he goes deeper, his shoulders shuddering as sensations whip over him.

"Darling," he growls and sinks deeper, his cock like steel.

My fingers grab his hair; then I clench my muscles around him, making him gasp. His body then owns mine with devilish intent, his hips thrusting into me as he presses me against the tile. He feels so good, and each time he exits, I beg for more, to feel every delicious inch of him, every vein and ridge, and he delivers, his dick pumping into my pussy over and over.

Groaning in satisfaction, he rocks into me, and I whimper with need, rubbing my breasts against his chest seductively, inviting him to go harder, to fuck me like he can't live without it.

I get lost in the sounds we make, the moans and groans and sighs of pleasure, the wet sound of our bodies in the water. He takes me with unflinching remorse, his eyes blown and dilated as he looks down at me.

He slows, his rhythm easing into long, languorous strokes as he draws out the intensity and my begging for release. He snatches my mouth with a deep kiss as his fingers circle my clit with each thrust.

I come suddenly, without warning, the sharpness almost painful in its glory, and it's the best fucking orgasm ever, making my body writhe and shake and tremble. My face goes to his throat as I scream out, my muscles contracting and spasming over and over. Emotion, deep and from my heart, overwhelms me. "I love you," I whisper into his neck, my lips tasting his skin, smelling his unique cherry-and-leather scent.

He pauses for a long moment, then resumes, his hands holding me tight, more tightly than before; then he goes over the edge to his own bliss.

Our heavy breaths are the only sounds uttered as he gathers himself. Then, with a pat of my bottom, he lets me down, shuts off the water, and tells me he's going to get dressed and head to the stadium.

Without meeting my eyes, he wraps a towel around his waist, hands me one, then leaves the room.

Tears prick my eyelids. I didn't mean to say those words. I didn't.

He didn't reply to them. He didn't even acknowledge them.

My throat prickles with tears, and I fight them down.

It's okay.

I'm fine.

It's just another day.

And nothing bad is going to happen.

Or maybe my confession *is* the bad thing that happened . . .

Chapter 27
EMMY

The stadium is alive with excitement as I make my way through the buzzing throng of spectators. The guard at the gate checks my lanyard before nodding toward the stands. I squint against the bright sun and make out Vale's figure in the packed seats near the fifty-yard line. He waves his hand to catch my attention.

Breathing in the smell of popcorn, burgers, and beer, I wing my way through the tightly packed bodies and reach the spot where Vale has saved me a seat. He pops an eyebrow at me. "You ready for this? Exhibition games bring out all kinds of fans. It's a good way to get used to real game-day craziness."

I nod in agreement, taking in the scene as players in their gold-and-black uniforms either run drills or talk to fans. People clamor around them, waiting in line for autographs and photos. Around me, everyone talks excitedly; I can almost taste the thrill in the air. I get why he loves the game. Unfortunately, I haven't been able to stop myself from reading about his injury.

I'm a bundle of nerves, my stomach in knots. I want to run to Graham and beg him not to play.

"Nice jersey," Brody says to me as he ambles over, holding a hot dog, popcorn, and a beer.

"Thanks. Graham got his number put on one for me," I say with a smile as he plops down next to Vale.

Graham breaks into a sprint, jogging over to us as he removes his helmet. His hair blows wildly in the breeze as he gestures for me to come closer and join him in the first row, which is taped off from the rest of the stands.

"Hey," he says when I reach him. "I'm glad you came. I wasn't sure if you would."

My chest tightens at his words. "Of course I would."

"Give me a kiss," he says softly, "for luck."

My breath catches in my throat as I lean in and crush my lips against his, willing him to see how much I care about him. He curls his fingers around the back of my neck, intensifying our kiss.

He slowly steps away, his gaze studying my features, before someone shouts his name from across the field. He spins around and takes off without another word.

When the game starts and the whistle blows, my hands ball up tightly.

Vale pats my shoulder. "It's hard to watch him, isn't it?"

I nod, willing myself to relax as I refocus. "Andrew has been testing me on plays and positions. He thinks I need to know what's going on."

He smiles. "You have a great family, Emmy. Thank you for inviting me to get to know them."

I nod.

Chewing my lips, I look back at the field.

It's just a game.

He's going to be fine.

He wants to play.

He wants *this*.

I'm remembering the morning I stood on the edge of the desert in Arizona, beguiled and yet terrified of the vastness, afraid of being swallowed whole. By life. By love for a man.

He didn't say he loved me this morning. He walked away.

I shove those feelings away and focus on the game.

We watch the first few plays, and I search for Graham's jersey, number eighty-seven, on the field. Maybe the coach isn't going to play him today. After a few minutes, the Pythons face third down and five around midfield. Their offense subs some players, and my stomach pitches when Graham runs onto the field. The crowd yells out a cheer.

The offense breaks the huddle, and Graham lines up in a blocking stance. Jasper looks over the defense and yells. Graham shuffles a few feet to the left as a linebacker shifts and lines up directly in front of him.

At the snap, Graham and the linebacker collide. Graham shoves the man away and breaks into the middle of the field. Jasper is barely able to throw the ball before getting tackled. Graham catches the wobbly pass and runs directly into the charging team. He's hit when the safety places his helmet in the middle of Graham's exposed chest and raises him off the ground.

"No!" I jump up as the thud of the impact seems to echo around the stadium. Graham falls backward, clutching the ball as he's driven into the turf. When the two hit the ground, there's a momentary hush from the crowd.

Vale's hand holds mine tightly as we watch the field.

I can't seem to breathe as I beg internally for Graham to get up. *Please, please . . .*

The safety moves to a stand, and Graham, still on the ground, clutches the ball in a death grip.

The referee signals first down.

Graham gets to his feet gingerly, seems to stagger a bit, then flips the ball to the ref and adjusts his helmet before raising a fist to the home crowd, who cheer wildly.

"That's what I'm talking about!" I hear from a fan behind me. "Toughest tight end in the league is back! Almost died last year and fucking fearless! YEAAAHH!"

He was weaving on his feet, and yeah, I get it, that's what football is, hard hits and catching the ball, but what if he hit his head too hard? What if he has a concussion and doesn't even realize it yet?

Vale and Brody and I sit in stunned silence; then more anxiousness rises as Graham lines up for the next play.

Nausea swirls in my gut as he tightens his stance, ready to take down the defense. The ball is thrown to a wide receiver, but my eyes remain on Graham as a defender runs for him. He jumps at Graham and takes him down again. They crash to the ground.

I want to vomit. I want to cry.

Somehow, I hold it together.

On the next play, Jasper throws to Graham again. The linemen chase him, almost catching him as he runs into the end zone for a touchdown. A strangled sound of relief comes from my lips.

The crowd erupts into victorious cheers, chanting Graham's name.

Vale grips my hand. "The game has just started, dear. We've got about two hours of this. Are you going to be able to make it?"

I swallow down the emotion in my throat as I nod an affirmative. Graham wants me here—for the pretend marriage—so I'll stay.

It's after eight in the evening by the time Graham arrives home from the postinterviews and catered meal the team had for them at the stadium with the owners. I've got a book in my hand and Magic in my lap when he walks in the door, dressed in joggers and a T-shirt.

Magic darts to him, hisses, then runs away. "Hey. Congrats on winning the game." I stand and give him a hug, a long one.

He smirks down at me. "Hey. See, nothing bad happened today."

"There's plenty of opportunity with seventeen games." My words are sharper than I want them to be. "Let me see your bumps and bruises. Any big ones?"

He cocks an eyebrow. "I've been iced down already. They're healing."

"Show me."

He lifts his shirt, and I grimace at the giant yellow-and-purple bruise on his side, from his rib cage to his hip.

"Jesus. Is anything broken?"

"Nope. Doc checked me out. No concussion, either, before you ask." He heads to the kitchen and grabs a beer from the fridge. "You want anything?"

"I'm good. I had dinner with Jane and Londyn at the store after the game."

He takes a sip from the long neck, his eyes carefully shielded as he asks, "Did you enjoy watching the game?"

I stiffen. "I enjoyed Vale and Brody."

"So you didn't?"

"Graham . . ."

"What?"

I lick my lips. "I was looking online. A new article recently came out. Boston University has diagnosed 345 former NFL players with CTE, out of 376. You're playing with fire. You may not have it now, but—"

He puts his back to me. His chest rises up and down rapidly. "I don't need a fucking lecture, Emmy."

I shove that aside and keep going. "Watching you play was one of the most terrifying experiences I've ever had. I know you're passionate about football. I know it's what you love, but you're literally playing Russian roulette every time you walk on the field." My hands fist, my emotions rising higher. In fear. In love.

He turns to look at me, his lips tightly pressed together. "I never asked for your opinion. I asked you to go to the game because this is a *fake* marriage, and it's part of your duties. This isn't real. Nothing you say really matters, does it? We'll be finished soon enough."

I feel as if he's slapped me. How can he be dismissive of all the time we've spent together? Could he truly just walk away once the inheritance comes in? I struggle to blink away the tears, bending to pet Magic so that he doesn't notice the emotion on my face.

He moves away to look down at some of the mail on the counter, his movements short and coiled as if he's keeping his emotions bottled up. "I won't keep you. I'm crashing."

"Graham . . ."

"Hmm?" He drains his beer and heads down the hall, seemingly nonchalant, but I know he's upset.

Did my declaration of love, combined with my fear of football, send us off the cliff? "Nothing."

He holds my eyes for a long moment, emotion swirling in those gray irises, anger and disappointment. He sticks his hands in his joggers. "By the way, I'm leaving in the morning for LA for the game there."

"What? I thought the game was a week from today?" It's one I hadn't planned on attending since it's so far away.

"Some of us are going early. Jasper wants to hang out in the city. Brody hasn't gone back to school yet, so if you need extra hands, he'll be around."

He's already to his bedroom door, lingering as he waits for me to answer.

He's leaving.

A harsh laugh comes from my lips. I want the truth from him, and sometimes the only way to get that is to put everything on the line. "You can't wait to get away from me. I told you I loved you, and you freaked out. You never acknowledged that I even spoke. Football is only for a while, but love and family . . . those last. They dig into your soul. All it takes is accepting it."

"I can't talk about this."

Something inside me rages. "Right. You're so afraid of hurting that you've chosen to not love at all. You can't even speak of it. You've given up. But then, maybe you aren't capable of love. Maybe you're so messed up from your past that you'll never give it a chance. I love you. Yes, it's messy and complicated to admit these things to you, but I'm here and ready to try this with you, to see where it goes, to face all our crazy fears together. I'm not Divina. In fact, I'm not like *anyone* you've ever met. I know my value, and it is fucking amazing. I am the person for you. *Your* person."

I pause, sucking in a steadying breath. "I'd never leave you. I'd never hurt you on purpose, Graham, but it terrifies me to watch you play." Not only is it dangerous for him, but the stress of watching him play made my heart erratic as hell. Sure, maybe it was normal heart stuff, but I don't think so.

I almost tell him, almost, but I can't. I'm not sure it would matter.

He flinches as his lashes flutter, then vanishes into his bedroom, leaving me there, alone with my heart on my sleeve.

My chest hurts, and I rub it. I laid it all out—and he walked away. Again.

Chapter 28

EMMY

The next day, I take off the paper gown and slip my bra and blouse back on. I've just gotten settled into the chair inside the doctor's office when Dr. Shultz, my cardiac surgeon, comes in. Around forty, he's balding and thin, with a kind face. He's holding papers in his hand, results from this latest EKG, I presume.

It's not my first visit here since my surgery. I did my postop appointment here and another follow-up. After my heart did something weird at the beach, I came back in for more tests, blood work, a urinalysis, x-rays, an echocardiogram, and a stress test.

He takes a seat across from me, and I clench my hands. "As previously discussed, we used cryothermal energy to make several precise modifications to your heart tissue in the left atrium. These cuts formed a web of lines that became scar tissue. This scarring works to block the irregular electrical signals from your heart. The ones we placed in the first procedure weren't adequate. It has improved your diagnosis, this is true, but there's a few places we missed. This isn't uncommon. Only about fifty to seventy percent of mini mazes are completely successful."

I nod, chewing on my bottom lip as the news sinks in. I swallow. "So what's next?"

"We could try medications, but they didn't work before."

"True."

"Several patients require a second mini maze, which are more successful. I don't recommend that you wait. Every day you experience an episode weakens your heart. At this time you've only had a few brief episodes, but you don't want to remain in an A-fib status for longer than forty-eight hours. We want you around for a long time, Emmy."

"Yes." My brain races with what needs to be done to get ready for surgery. I'll need to prepare Babs and Jane at the store. And Graham? He's got football season approaching. The last thing he'll want is an invalid wife. Not that it matters.

I study my hands in my lap, twisting them.

"A second procedure has a higher success rate, so that is what we'll focus on, yes?" He pauses. "Are you all right, Emmy? Do you feel light headed?"

I glance up. "No. I'm fine. Just other things going on in my life."

"I understand. It's not the news you wanted to hear. You do need to avoid stress. Is that possible right now?"

Ha. "I'll try."

"Like before, we'll make three to six keyhole-shaped incisions on either side of your chest, around your ribs and under your breast area. We'll insert the device through those holes to reach your heart. Your heart will never stop beating."

"I remember." It was a fear of mine that it might stop and never pick back up.

"The surgery will take about three hours, and then we'll put you in ICU for monitoring. If all looks well, you'll get a regular room and can be discharged in three days. Your risks are bleeding, infection, stroke, pneumonia, heart attack."

"Last time, I went back to work after a few days at home. Did I mess it up somehow?"

He frowns. "No, but you shouldn't have. Sometimes it takes a couple of days for the anesthesia to completely wear off. I suggest you wait and see how you feel, but at least wait a week before you go to work. The nurse will give you a list of things you shouldn't do, such as lifting, care of the incisions, et cetera. She'll also get your surgery scheduled, all right?"

"How many of these can I have? If this one doesn't work?"

"Some people have several over their lifetime. We'll get it right this time, Emmy." He comes over and pats me on the shoulder to reassure me, but that dread from earlier has settled deep in my bones. The bad premonition I had came true yesterday: Graham and I are over.

Chapter 29
EMMY

I'm browsing the third floor of the store when I hear a man clear his throat behind me. I turn to see who it is just as the PA system comes on. "Emmy, there's a situation. Headed your way. Long and slithery—repeat, long and slithery."

"Fuck," I mutter under my breath as I take in the man with a giant yellow snake coiled around his throat like a necklace. The snake's body is long, its diameter as thick as my leg. It rears its head, slithering, as its tongue darts out to taste the air.

The hair on my arm rises, but I make my face impassive, even though I want to throw the book in my hands at him and run screaming. I don't do that because one, the snake might chase me, and two, I don't want to scare the other customers.

The man appears older than me and rather handsome in a rough way, with a full beard and his wiry hair pulled back in a ponytail. He's wearing a New York Pythons jersey. A fan.

"Sir, you can't have that snake in the store."

"It's all right. She doesn't have any fangs, and she's nonpoisonous." He says it as if he's talking about the weather, then gives the snake a loving stroke down her skin.

"Can I help you?" Maybe he just wants a book, and I can escort him out without too much attention.

"Maybe. Just wanted to check out the place, see the store where Harlan works sometimes. He's my favorite player." He grins widely. "Did you see the game? Unbelievable play action. Our team is gonna win another Super Bowl. And little Veronica here watched the game with me."

I can't take my eyes off little Veronica. I wonder if she's hypnotizing me. Like I'm prey. "Indeed."

Babs shows up and comes to a halt next to me, her entire body vibrating. She leans in and whispers, "According to the staff, he walked in like it was no big deal and went right up the stairs. I was working on the schedule and didn't see him."

"How do we make him leave?" I say under my breath as the man strolls around the bookshelves, talking to Veronica the entire time.

"Police? Animal control?"

I shake my head. "He isn't threatening anyone. He's polite."

"He's wearing a python, Emmy. This isn't a petting farm," she hisses. "Those snakes squeeze you until you suffocate and die."

"The snake isn't coming after us. Mostly, it's just a legless lizard, right? Okay, let me try something," I say as I approach the man, and Babs follows me. "Hello, sir. Hope you like the store."

He grins broadly. "It's awesome. So much to look at."

"Great. Listen, I'll pass on your message to Graham, but unfortunately snakes aren't allowed in the store. We'd love to have you come back without Veronica."

His face crumbles. "But she's like a mascot. Harlan would love it."

"Tell you what," I say, "I'll take a pic of you here and pass it on to him. How does that sound?"

His shoulders slump in disappointment; then his eyes graze over Babs, then dart back.

"Babette?" he exclaims. "Is that you? By God, it is! It's Hank, you know, from Highstreet Prep. We had every single class together." A slow grin curls his face. "We had some fun times under the bleachers, didn't we?"

She blinks rapidly. "H-Hank Westbrook? It's been ages." She laughs. "Love the beard and ponytail. What are you doing now?"

I look from one to the other, noticing the flush on Babs's cheeks and the flirtatious smile on his.

"You're still as pretty as ever," he says. "I heard about Freddy on Facebook. My condolences."

"Thank you. How are you? Still on Wall Street?"

"Nah, I'm retired now, living in Brooklyn. You still on Forty-Seventh Street?"

She says yes, and then he offers for her to pet Veronica. To my amazement, Babs gives the creature a tiny head stroke, then coos about how unusual her skin is.

I watch as they continue their conversation. Another customer walks by, sees the snake, and darts for the stairs. I rub my forehead.

"Um, sorry to interrupt this little reunion, but Hank, you need to leave so we don't scare other people." I give Babs a smirk. "Can you handle this? Maybe put him and Veronica on the elevator to the basement, where you two can catch up? Also, take a photo for Graham. He'll get a kick out of seeing a fan in the store."

She smiles and bats her lashes coquettishly at Hank, her face bright. I'm glad. She's been lonely ever since Terry left. "Let's take a ride. We can talk more in the basement. We recently added a table and chairs down there for breaks." She waves her hand at me. "Can you have Andrew bring us some tea and scones, darling?"

"Of course," I say, amused, as I watch them get on the elevator.

An hour later, I'm in my office when Jane pokes her head in the door. She's wearing a concerned look, and I raise my brows, wondering what happened to put it there. "Hey, there's a David Spencer to see you. He says he's Graham's lawyer."

I straighten in my seat, a sinking feeling in my stomach. I check my lipstick and tighten the bun on my head. "All right, send him in."

To my surprise, David walks in wearing preppy shorts and a polo shirt with boat shoes. His brown hair is covered by a ball cap. The last time I saw him at his office, he was in an expensive suit.

He sits on the couch and smiles as he sets his leather satchel next to him. "Good to see you, Emmy."

I manage a smile. "What's going on?"

"The last time I met with Graham, he asked me to deliver the divorce papers to you as soon as the inheritance went through," he says as he opens his bag and starts to riffle through it. "Congrats, my dear. I spoke with the trustees of the will this morning, and everything's been approved."

I blink as my chest stings, horribly, as I process his words. My voice is breathless. "That was sooner than expected."

He grins, oblivious to my distress. "Yes, we can thank Vale Harlan for that. He urged the trustees to expedite the funds for Graham."

"I assume you've told Graham?"

I haven't spoken to him, but he did text me that they'd arrived in LA and were settling in and working out at one of the training facilities. I didn't reply.

"I'm sure he'll be thrilled," he says.

I nod. Yes, he will.

"He's got a preseason game this week in LA," I murmur as I clench my hands together, needing an anchor. "It's better to call him in the evening, after practice."

He stands and brings me a bundle of papers. I can't bear to look at them, so I don't, instead keeping my eyes on David. "That's the thing. I'm off on vacation with my family. We're doing one of those Disney cruises. Lots of characters and meals. I've got four kids, all under the age of six. I'm not sure how available I'll be, so I'm trying to take care of everything now. That's why I came over." His index finger lands on the papers. "Here's everything for the divorce. For a no-contest divorce in New York, we're looking at up to three months once we get it filed at the clerk's office. I suggest we go ahead and get the paperwork going, but no one has to know. We can file whenever you both think enough time's elapsed from receiving the check. I'll just need your signature and his; then my office will keep them ready."

My heart skips a beat. "I see."

"Are you all right?" he asks, his brow crinkling in concern.

My beats are fine. It's not my arrythmia; it's just heartbreak. The truth is, he sent David here with these papers. Graham wanted it this way. And I need to finish this.

"Has anything changed since we drew up the agreement?" he asks.

Jane pokes her head in without knocking. "Hi!" she says, obviously making sure I'm okay. "Just checking in to see if you two need anything?"

He looks at Jane and tells her he'll take a coffee to go.

Jane leaves to get his drink.

I pick up the papers and look at them without really seeing them. Anger, tied to fragile emotions, rises inside me. "Actually, yes, something has changed. I'd like to circle back to the prenup I signed. I don't want Graham's money. None of it." I married him with my eyes wide open, and I need a final goodbye to us, a period at the end of a sentence.

I clear my throat at David's stunned silence. "Are you sure?" he asks. "That's a lot of money."

And we'll manage without it. "Can you make it happen? Quickly?"

He nods. "Of course. We'll make an addendum to the agreement. I'll call the office and have them send it over for you to sign today."

"Good."

Jane comes in with his coffee, and he picks up his satchel. He gives us a nod. "All right. I'm headed to Orlando. Let Graham know the details, get his signature, then send it to my office, and we'll be set. The trustees should be sending the check today. Looks like our business with the marriage is concluded."

Graham and I just aren't meant to be. There's no magic. Not for him at least.

I nod at David. "Yes. It's done."

Chapter 30
GRAHAM

The LA sun sets in a fiery blaze over the edge of the stadium, casting long shadows across the field as I finish my stretches with the rest of the tight ends. The air is thick with anticipation for tonight's preseason game. I head to the end zone for a catching drill before the start of warm-ups, feeling the adrenaline pumping through my veins like a tiger ready to pounce.

"Hey, G, I was thinking," Jasper says as he jogs over, mischief dancing in his gaze. "If you could either be a cockroach or a rat, which would you be?"

"Neither. Both are disgusting." I take my helmet off to drink down some Gatorade.

"Come on. Indulge me. You have to pick one."

"Fine. A rat. They're tough bastards, especially in New York."

He makes a grunting noise as he picks up his water. "See, I think it's cockroach. I mean, sure you gotta look out for spiders and pesticide, but when the nuclear bombs start to drop, you'd have the entire city to yourself."

"Maybe rats could survive. They eat cockroaches."

He rears back. "No shit?"

I nod and chuckle as we head back to the field. I run a quick route in front of him and catch the pass he throws before lining up next to him again.

He backs up to throw the ball, then stops short. "How about this one. If you had a crystal ball that could tell you the truth about any one thing, like your death day, would you want to know?"

He finally throws the ball, and I catch it, toss the ball back to Coach Marlon, and then line up near Jasper again.

"You got a crystal ball in the locker room?"

"No, asshole, these are hypotheticals. I'm a thinking man. I like to consider life. But if such a thing existed, I'd say no to knowing my future. Ignorance of self is bliss. I don't want to know anything. I just wanna live life to the fullest, take all the chances I can, and be fucking happy."

I slap him on the back. "I think you've got that covered."

The whistle blows, and I follow the team into the locker room to finish dressing out. We'll have another pep talk before heading back out for introductions.

I'm stoked about the game, my body vibrating, but there's also apprehension dancing down my spine. I'm fully aware that each time I take the field, I'm taking a chance. Hasn't that been part of the message in my dreams, that feeling of being suffocated as players pile on top of me? And yeah, if I had a crystal ball to tell me something, I'd ask about my injury.

My head churns as I open my locker. No, fuck that, I'd ask about Emmy. My mind goes to her, circling round and round since our conversation. What is she doing right now? Is she okay? Happy?

A long exhale leaves my chest, and I scrub my face in frustration. I think—okay, fuck, I know—I hurt her before I left to come out here.

She wants *more* from me.

And me?

I admire her. I need her.

She's an image, always walking in the back of my mind.

She's natural and funny. Beautiful without being aware of it.

And her loyalty and self-sacrifice to others? It's hard for me to wrap my head around it all because I've never had someone like that in my life, except for Brody.

And the truth is, an empty space inside my rib cage has been ripping me apart, ever since I left New York. Something feels off. I've barely been able to concentrate since arriving. I seem to be doing things on automatic. Practice, work out, eat, sleep. And my dreams? She's there, smiling, telling me she loves me.

I grab my wallet and pull out the fortune I got from the diner across the street from the motel that night in Old Town. *Come out of the dark and embrace the sunshine.*

She's sunshine.

My heart sinks and my stomach jumps as I hold my phone and check my messages to see if she's sent one, but she hasn't. My breath hitches as I hesitate over what to do; should I call her, or should I maintain this wall of silence between us? My palms get slick with sweat, and my fist clenches so tightly that my knuckles turn white. An intense ache in my chest starts as an overwhelming desire to reach out to her pricks at me. Dread hits, for what reason I don't know. I shouldn't have left her without talking. I shouldn't. What if . . . what if something happens to her? Or to me?

I notice I have a few random texts and three voice mails. I rarely have voice mail.

I listen to the first:

Graham, it's your dad. Wanted to wish you luck, and I'll be watching tonight on TV. I just ask for you to be careful out there.

I click the save button.

The second message starts:

Graham. David here. I wanted to check in. Good news: the inheritance has arrived. The only way they could attempt to claw it back would be by lawsuit, and I highly doubt that would happen, especially with Vale supporting you. Whenever you're ready, you can transfer to Brody, or keep it, or whatever. It's yours. Since that came through, I dropped off the divorce papers with Emmy. I'm flying out tonight to join my wife and kids on a Disney cruise, so I wanted to get that done. Once I get back, we can get those filed. I'll reach out in a few days from whatever island they're dropping us at, just to make sure there's nothing else.

Fear spikes as thoughts zigzag in my brain. Yeah, he knew I wanted the divorce, but that's not how the papers were supposed to be delivered. I wanted to be there. Fuck. I wanted time to think first.

The third message is from Jane's number:

Dick move, jackass. You could have at least given her a heads-up that you wanted her gone. I've met some dumb men over the years and felt I was a pretty good judge of which ones were good people and which ones were trash. Congratulations, you actually fooled me. Apparently you're just like the rest, a professional narcissist that can't think of anything beyond your own bank account or prick. Well, I better let you go so I can go in and wish your ex-wife good luck with her HEART SURGERY tomorrow morning. Enjoy being rich and alone, motherfucker.

What?

My stomach jumps as nausea swirls in my gut. What is she talking about? What surgery?

What the hell is going on?

I call Emmy, and it goes directly to voice mail.

I switch to text: Is everything okay? Just got a voice mail from Jane. Please call me.

There's no response, and I try Jane and Andrew, but there's no reply.

Reaching over my neck, I grab my pads and pull them over my head and toss them to the ground. Snatching my joggers and a T-shirt, I start changing.

"Yo, Graham. Tight end meeting before we go out. Something wrong with your uniform?" Marlon asks.

"What? No, I can't. Sorry, I gotta go." I stick my feet in my sneakers. Was she having issues? Is this an emergency? Why didn't she tell me? A million thoughts dart through my head.

Marlon grabs my shoulder to get my attention. "What are you talking about? I know this is preseason, but it's important you get more live reps. I—"

"Fuck that, Marlon, I gotta go."

Jasper walks up, frowning as he searches my face. "What's going on?"

My throat feels so tight I can barely swallow. "It's Emmy. She's gonna have heart surgery tomorrow. I gotta get back."

Marlon shakes his head. "If you're part of this team, priority one is getting into season form. We'll get you home after the game. You can still make it."

I shove everything in my duffel bag and flip around. "Emmy's more important."

He gives me a blank look, not comprehending. And I get it. Sometimes players take the field regardless of what's going on in their personal lives, but not this time. One of our defensive linemen played while his wife was giving birth. Our safety played when his father passed away.

I pat his arm. "Tell Coach I'm sorry. I'll see you guys next week."

"Call me and let me know how she is!" Jasper yells out, and I give him a thumbs-up as I walk out the door.

The next morning I land in New York. I was able to get a flight last night and barely made it through LA traffic to the gate to board the plane. My thoughts were only on Emmy.

I head straight to the apartment, hoping she hasn't left. No one in her family answers my calls, even Babs.

I feel pushed to the brink of exhaustion as I rush into the apartment, and the silence is deafening. My heart jerks painfully when I find a neat stack of legal papers on the kitchen counter. The divorce papers. The last page is signed by her, and there's an empty line waiting for me. Dizziness hits me as I take a walk in the den. Her books are gone, her teacups, even the cat litter box. Shit. I head to the bedrooms. My bed is made, and so is hers. The entire place has an empty feel, as if she hasn't been here for a few days. Her toiletries aren't in the bathroom, and when I see that her clothes are gone from her closet, I feel sick to my stomach. I stalk back to the dining room, wincing when I see that she's left her wedding and engagement rings, her iguana bangle, and the signed *Charlotte's Web* I gave her on top of the table.

That light-headed feeling hits again, and I sit down and breathe slowly, willing it to go away. It isn't my injury. No. It's her absence from my life. She's left me. She packed up her stuff and walked right out the door.

A few moments later, I call Brody, who answers groggily: "Hey. It's early. What's going on?"

"Emmy's not here. She left all her stuff. There's divorce papers on the table, signed. I got a voice mail from Jane saying Emmy was going to have surgery. I thought you were keeping an eye on her." I sit on the couch, regret and fear sweeping over me. "What do I do?"

The sound of rustling covers hits my ears, and he must be sitting up in bed. "I have no idea what you're talking about. Where is she having surgery?"

My temples pound in frustration as I struggle to find my words. "Her last one was at Mount Sinai. She was there the same day I was in February."

"Okay, give me a minute to get dressed, and I'll be at your place."

"Hurry. I don't want to wait long." I lick my lips. "Can you call Dad? Please. I need both of you."

By the time Brody arrives dressed in shorts and a hoodie, I've made to-go coffees for us. He takes a deep sip. "Dad's on his way to the hospital and will meet us there."

My leg bounces up and down. I've already confirmed that she's a patient at Mount Sinai.

We leave the quiet building and catch a cab.

My head is throwing around ideas, and my eyes can't seem to stay off Google Maps as I estimate how long it's going to take us to get to the hospital.

Brody studies my profile. "You left the game? I'm assuming you aren't in trouble for that?"

I flick my hand. "I'll get back to football when I know she's all right."

A deep sigh comes from him, and I look at his face. "What?"

"Emmy, me, Dad, the people who care about you the most, it's hard to watch you play, G. I don't enjoy it anymore. It's a death match out there every time you line up."

I bow my head, the tic in my jaw working. "You don't have to like it. It's my passion."

He scoffs. "Maybe a year ago, but now? Have you thought any more about dying on the field, on what you might have seen? Maybe there was a message there."

"From a higher power?"

He shrugs. "Who can explain anything in this world? Why we're here and why we die and why we love? Your near-death experience ended with a mystery person. Sure, your doctor wants to say it could be your brain shutting down, section by section, using your own experiences, but we both know it wasn't."

"How do you know?"

"Because you saw someone you didn't know. She wasn't me or Dad or Mom or Divina. You saw *her*, and she pulled you back. Think about it, Graham, she was in the same hospital as you, you found her in the middle of the desert, and she stole your car and *I* knew her. These aren't random acts of coincidence. It's the fucking universe. Maybe sometimes, things really are meant to be."

I recall the girl from my dream, the long blonde hair, those big green eyes, the serene smile.

I rub my temple, a rough sound coming from my throat. "I don't know."

His words tug at me, digging up emotions that frighten me. We get out of the car, and I leave Brody behind as I run to the entrance. Dad is already there in the lobby.

The nurse at the front desk informs me of Emmy's room number in ICU on the eighth floor. We step off the elevator and enter the family waiting room.

The room buzzes with anxious energy. The smell of antiseptic lingers in the air, and the sound of beeping monitors mixes with the hushed conversations of visitors.

In the corner of the waiting room, I spot Jane, her face pale and drawn. She paces, her hands restless as she swings them, her brow furrowed in worry. I approach her, heart pounding and palms sweating. Her eyes widen in surprise as she says hello to us.

"So. You came," she murmurs, tidying up the jogging pants and fuzzy jacket she's wearing.

"Is she okay?" I ask. "What happened? Is she out of surgery?"

She does a hair flip and curls her lip at me. "Like you care."

"I do care. A whole fucking lot, Jane, so tell me what's going on. Please." My voice rises, and one of the nurses in the hall turns to look at us. I exhale and lower my voice. "Can I see her?"

She sighs and looks away. "She's still in surgery. Nobody knows for sure how long it will take." She glances back at me, eyes glassy with unshed tears. "The thing is, I don't know what I'll do if she . . ." She trails off, unable to finish the sentence.

I swallow thickly. Obviously this is a procedure she's planned. "Why . . . why didn't she tell me?"

Her face tightens. "You know why, Graham. She didn't want to bother you. You just fly off to your game and do what professional athletes do, even though it might kill you."

I sink down in a seat with my head in my hands. "I never would have left her if I'd known. Never. Not in a million years. Has the doctor been out?"

She shakes her head. "Not yet."

Dad tells us he's going to get us breakfast, and Brody tags along with him. They've just gotten back from the cafeteria with muffins and fruit and coffee when Jane gives me a hard elbow in the ribs. "Here comes the doctor," she says as we stand up together.

A small man wearing a white jacket over blue scrubs approaches us and smiles compassionately at Jane. Clearly, he's spoken to her before. "Morning, all." He shakes my hand. "Graham Harlan, right? Emmy's husband? I'm a big Pythons fan."

"Right, how is she?" I ask, brushing off the "Pythons fan" part. The last thing I want to do right now is talk about football. In fact, it feels pretty damn unimportant. "I'm a little out of the loop here."

He nods. "Everything went exactly as it should. A perfect procedure. We did a mini-maze surgery and targeted the upper chambers of her heart, the atria, with cold energy to create a maze of scars to correct the faulty electrical issues with her heart. We used a small camera through one of the incisions to direct us to her heart. A second tool was used to create small areas of scar tissue. She'll have stitches on her sides that will dissolve. I'll see her back in a week for a postop to make sure everything's okay."

"So it didn't work last time?" I ask, my tone insistent as I try to drag out the information.

"It's not uncommon to get another procedure. Emmy is a careful person. She was fully aware when she felt the signs of her A-fib recurring."

I frown, wondering when that happened.

"What if this doesn't work? What happens?" I ask.

Jane nods, agreeing with me for once.

"Her main issue is that most of the drugs for A-fib don't work with Emmy. Right now, we're giving her fluids and pain medication through an IV line. She'll also be given medication to help control the buildup of fluids. She'll do some deep-breathing and coughing exercises. This will help reduce the risk of fluid buildup in her lungs."

My hands clench as I commit every detail to memory.

The doctor taps on his computer, then looks up and smiles. "Hopefully, we can get her up for a walk today. She's young."

"And strong," Jane adds.

"She'll need to keep her regular appointments for checkups," the doctor adds. "There's always the possibility of other ablation treatments, but considering how young and healthy she is, I'm hoping for a successful outcome."

"Can I see her?" Jane and I say at the same time.

"Of course," he tells us.

Jane and I walk into her room, a large single room with beeping machines and an IV attached to Emmy's arm. Her hair is spread out on the pillow as she lies in a reclining position, sleeping.

A nurse is in the corner, sitting on a stool as she types information into a computer. She gives us a smile and tells us that Emmy hasn't woken up yet, but if all goes well today, they'll move her to a regular room tomorrow.

Jane rushes past me, grunting as she bumps my shoulder to get past me. She throws me a look over her shoulder. "Points for coming, but I'm the first person she's going to see when she wakes up. I love her, Graham. She is the toughest person I know. The most beautiful soul. And you can't see it."

My heart is in my throat. I do see it. Emotion claws at my throat with sharp nails. She looks entirely helpless lying there.

All those dreams I had, the ones where I'm tackled and can't breathe, and then she shows up, beckoning me to safety, to love. I've been so blind, trying to push her away, when she's everything. I've just been too afraid to face it head on.

"She's the one," I whisper under my breath as I grip the rails of Emmy's bed.

Jane frowns, rearing back. "Don't you dare fucking cry on me."

Ignoring her, I sit down and take Emmy's hand and thread our fingers together, and then I speak to her, even though she probably can't hear me. "I'm sorry, darling. I'm yours, I'm here, and I'm not leaving. I came back from the dead—for you."

Chapter 31

EMMY

My eyes flutter open, adjusting to the light overhead as I take in the room. I woke up a couple of times earlier, but only for a few moments before I drifted back asleep. The room has a small table in the far corner next to the window, with a bouquet of pink-and-white peonies. From the light coming in through the window, it looks to be late afternoon. Wilbur the pig is next to my leg. Jane is asleep on a cot, and on the other side of me Graham sits, his eyes wide as he stares at me. His face is unshaven, his hair sticking up and clothes rumpled. I remember him from the last time I woke up but thought it was a dream.

He leans forward. "Hey. I've been waiting for you to wake up. Everything went great. How are you feeling? Are you in any pain?" His gaze goes to the area on my side where my bandages are under my gown.

"Hey, um, I-I didn't expect to see you."

"Jane called me. I flew home as soon as I heard."

"Your game? How was it?"

Before he can reply, the nurse comes in to check my vitals and record them on her computer. She checks the incisions around my body with practiced hands. I suppress a wince as her fingers brush against one of the stitches. She asks me my pain level, which is moderate, and gives me pills in a cup to take.

Graham hands me a Sprite. "You asked for one earlier when you woke up. I got you several."

I barely recall. I lean back to the pillows, careful to keep my eyes off him directly, not wanting to get lost in his gaze. I take another sip of the Sprite, the cool liquid wonderful to my throat. "You didn't have to come. I'm fine."

"I'm not fine, Emmy," he says a few moments later as he turns my chin, making me meet his gray eyes. I note the haggardness of his face, the shadows under his eyes. "I didn't know what was going on. I thought something horrible might have gone wrong with your heart."

I play with my covers, threading them through my hand. "I left the divorce papers at your place. I'm not taking any of your money. Things are working out for the Darling family. Jane is working at the store full time, and Andrew is going to take a gap year and work at the store. It wasn't my idea, but it's his decision, and he wants to contribute."

He rubs his face. "David shouldn't have come to you without speaking to me first. He only did it because that was the plan from the start, to do divorce proceedings after the inheritance, but now that—"

"I'm really tired," I say, interrupting. "I need to rest."

He puts his hand on mine. "Will you at least look at me, Emmy?"

I hold his eyes, and his face is so tender that it almost hurts more than any physical pain could ever do.

A tear slides down my cheek unbidden, and he quickly wipes it away with his thumb before pressing my palm to his heart. He holds it there. "I'm sorry. For everything," he says quietly. "Let me be the one who takes care of you."

Emotion tugs at me like a weight. Seeing him like this only makes things worse.

I manage a smile. "There's no need to feel obligated. I'm exhausted. Can you go?"

"You want me to go? Truly?"

I nod.

He inhales a deep breath. "I'll be back when you're feeling better."

"Don't. I mean, I have Jane and Babs and Andrew. Besides, you have a life you need to get back to."

A vulnerable look flashes over his face, a brief moment, before he tucks it away, his throat moving.

"Call Jane," I say. "She'll tell you how I'm doing."

"Emmy—"

"Will you just give me some space?"

I stare at the TV on the wall, watching from the corner of my eye as he exhales, then walks out the door.

Jane, whom I suspect has been listening to us, sits up from her cot, her hair ruffled around her head. An exaggerated yawn comes from her. "These five a.m. surgeries are crazy. How are you feeling?" she asks as she checks me over like a mother hen. "Everything all right?"

I wince as I try to sit up more. "I told you not to tell him, and you did."

She shrugs. "Technically he's still your husband, Emmy. And I've witnessed for myself how he looks at you. He needed to know." She pauses. "And he dropped everything and came. He seems genuinely scared and rather pathetic."

My fingers touch Wilbur. "Graham feels sorry for me. It's who he is."

Jane watches me intently, her gaze softening as she takes in my expression. She reaches out and places a hand on my shoulder. "I'm not so sure I agree with you, but you are the one who just had surgery, so whatever you say, goes."

Chapter 32
EMMY

"Graham offered us a town car to take us home, and I told him yes," Jane says as she helps me get dressed a few days later.

"Fine," I say as I slide on a pair of joggers easily enough, but the loose blouse requires more movement and makes the incisions sting. I slip my feet into a pair of sneakers, and she brushes my hair and puts it up in a high ponytail.

The best way to deal with the things Graham has done since my surgery is to keep my emotions locked down.

"He's worked at the bookstore for the past two days," Jane continues. "He needed something to keep him busy, since you said he couldn't visit you here."

I take the brush from her hand and stuff it in my bag. "That's great."

She exhales. "I swear the man nearly cried when he saw you."

I shrug. "He's empathetic. Don't read into it."

"God, you're so annoying." She rolls the wheelchair up and pats the seat. "Now have a seat, and we'll escape this place."

The nurse arrives and escorts us downstairs to the exit for waiting vehicles. A driver gets out of a black luxury car and helps me inside. Jane slides in next to me and smiles. "Homeward bound in style."

I narrow my gaze at the gleam in her eyes. "Just to make sure, we are going to our home. Gran's. Right?" As much as she's been pro-Graham since the surgery, I'm starting to wonder if she'll slow the car down and kick me out in front of his apartment building.

She nods. "Yes."

"What's up with all the smiling? If there's a bunch of flowers in the apartment, call Andrew and tell him to give them to the neighbors. I can't deal."

She rolls her eyes. "I'm happy because my sis is coming home, and Londyn has missed you, and I'm thankful you're okay. Isn't that enough?"

"Hmm, I suppose."

We arrive home and head to the elevator. Jane opens the door to the apartment, and Andrew and Londyn come rushing toward me. He gives me a hug with her in his arms. I'm not supposed to lift anything, so I have to settle with giving her kisses.

"Graham had dinner sent over," Andrew tells me as we walk in the den. "It's pecan chicken salad with croissants and fresh fruit. I put it in the fridge for later. Can I get you anything?"

"I'm just going to make some tea." As long as I don't bend and twist much, I'll be perfectly fine.

I walk into the kitchen and stop, frowning. I feel Jane behind me. "Um, where the hell is our stove?"

Jane pats my arm. "In the dump, I hope. Maybe providing a home for some rats. We didn't want to raise your blood pressure, darling, but well, Graham sent a new one. He said if you're going to live here, then you needed a stove to make your meals on."

"He *sent* dinner. We aren't using the new stove."

"We will. Stop being a Graham meanie."

I grab my purse and root around for my cell. Jane knocks it out of my hand. "Don't call him. I doubt he'll answer anyway. He's probably busy with stuff."

I gape at my phone on the floor. "Who are you, and what have you done with my sister?"

She picks it up and hands it back, then tosses an arm around me. "Did I mention he sent someone over to check on the plumbing. He replaced the hot water heater."

"Ugh," I groan.

"Come on, relax. Let's go watch TV."

An hour later, I'm propped up on the couch reading aloud to Londyn when Andrew and Jane both come into the den.

"Turn on the TV!" Andrew calls out. "ESPN!"

I toss him the remote. "Go for it."

He clicks it on as I sit up straighter, positioning Londyn next to me. "What's so important, anyway?"

"News conference about the fall season for the Pythons," Andrew says excitedly, then sends me a glum look. "I really hope y'all work shit out so I can go to some games."

I throw one of Londyn's stuffed toys at him, and he ducks, still focused on the TV screen.

The screen shows a long table with several players and coaches. The Python emblem hangs on a wall behind them.

As Jane calls for Andrew to turn it up, my body tenses. I feel the energy in the room as the flashes from cameras illuminate the area. Graham stands confidently behind the podium wearing a Pythons polo and jeans; his smile is contagious, causing the crowd to erupt into cheers that go on longer than expected. He shifts uncomfortably but accepts their applause with grace.

"Thank you for that sweet reception. I really appreciate it," Graham murmurs as the people grow quiet. "There's nothing like New York fans, and there's nothing anywhere more incredible than the guys and coaches on the Pythons team. I've felt at home here from day one, and since last year, after winning the Super Bowl—well, it was one of the greatest highs I've ever experienced. There's no better way to leave football in style than after that win. Today, I'm officially retiring . . ."

I lose track of his words, the shock making my ears ring. I study his face, searching for signs that something is wrong. I search for dread, or dissatisfaction, on his features, but only see . . . relief.

"I suffered a serious injury last season that gave me reason to think about the rest of my life and what I wanted that to look like, and well, it's about health and family. I'm newly married and now own a bookstore. Formerly known as A Likely Story, we're renaming it the Darling Bookstore. Check us out on Instagram."

Several people cheer.

He pauses, and the crowd waits eagerly for his next words. He smiles, a wry expression softening his face. "It's been a long road to get here," he begins, "to find the person I need, and once you find them, it's not hard to figure out the rest."

"He's talking about you!" Andrew says with an awed look.

"Arghh" comes out of me. It's not a word. I don't know what it is. I'm trying to process if he means what he's saying.

Graham continues. "I'm so proud to have been part of the Pythons team, and I'm thankful for all the wonderful memories we made together. It has been an honor to be able to contribute to such an incredible team."

The reporters begin to call out questions, eager for more information.

"What motivated you to leave such a successful football team?" asks one reporter.

"I just want to be around my family. Enjoy them," Graham says and then stares at the screen. It almost feels as if he's talking directly to me. "I'm crazy in love with my wife, in case you haven't figured that out. I loved her before I even knew her."

A tear slides down my face, and I brush it away. Does he mean it? Is this for show? My mind races in a hundred directions. If this is true, has he given up football to make me happy? I'm not sure that's okay. I want him to be happy. I want him to make the right choice for him.

"What's been the most challenging part of owning a bookstore? Do you and your wife work well together?" asks a woman.

Graham laughs wryly. "You think football is wild. Bookstore life is different every day. Also, a shout-out to my friend Hank and his python, Veronica. You're welcome in the store anytime, but leave her at home, yeah?" He winks into the camera.

"How have your teammates reacted to your decision?" shouts someone.

"They respect me and understand why this is what I need."

"We're fine!" Jasper calls. "I support our guy a hundred percent."

Everyone laughs as Graham smirks. "Guess you all want to hear from Jasper now, am I right?"

More whistles reverberate from the crowd as Graham moves aside to hand over the mic.

I ease Londyn to the floor and get up to head to the bathroom.

Jane follows. "Well? That was a pretty awesome thing, right? He won't be playing football anymore."

I nod.

"I mean, he changed the bookstore name to Darling. He's creating a legacy for you."

"Yeah. Now, if you'll excuse me, I gotta pee." I ease the door closed, but not before I see her disappointed face.

I tug out my phone and sit on top of the toilet and send Graham a text. Hey. Saw the news. I hope you're happy, that you did this for you.

He doesn't reply, which isn't surprising, since he's still at the press conference.

I stay there for several minutes, waiting to see if he replies. When he doesn't, I go back out into the den, tell my family good night, and head to bed. Magic jumps up when I pull the covers down and slide inside.

Grabbing the extra pillow, I wrap my arms around it tight and somehow drift off to sleep.

Chapter 33

EMMY

A few days later, I announce I'm going to the bookstore, not to work but to hang out while Jane and Andrew do their thing. She makes me swear that I won't do anything strenuous. I can walk up the stairs and relax in my office or sit in one of the lounging areas and read a book. It's a relief to get out of the apartment.

Graham has called, but we haven't spoken. I just need time to process if what Graham said is actually true.

I can't resist helping a customer when I notice a man on the third floor. An older man, maybe in his seventies, he shifts from one foot to the next as he stares uncertainly at the books on the shelves and blows out a long breath. It's a cry for help.

"Hi, I'm Emmy," I say as I get up from the comfy leather lounger I was sitting in. I straighten my loose linen pants and matching peasant blouse. "I work here. Can I help you find anything?" I smirk. "It will actually make my day if I could find you a book."

The man smiles engagingly as he speaks in a slow southern drawl. "I don't want to bother you, but I'd appreciate it. I'm Carl."

"It's no bother." I go to stand next to him, and he tells me that he's in town to visit a friend of his, River Tate, a Python player who told him about the store. I reply that I saw River play once, at the preseason game.

Carl smiles and gives me his life story, about how he lives in Ellijay, Georgia, and knew River when he was in college. Then he describes a museum in Ellijay dedicated to UFOs. Apparently, the locals claim that part of Georgia is a hotspot for extraterrestrial activity.

"I was abducted once, you see, and I thought I could find some books about true-life stories of people who've experienced the same thing."

I nod sagely, keeping my expression blank. "I have just the thing. We have an entire section and even a brand-new book of interviews from whistleblowers who once worked for the government and have come forward with stories. I flipped through it when it came in, and it was fascinating. Follow me."

I escort him to the display we have on the second floor. He's chatting to me about aliens with big eyes, and I nod in all the right places. He's just wrapping up a long-winded story about how he hopes they come back and take him to their planet when the PA system goes off.

I start at Graham's voice. "Emmy, you have a cream situation in the rotunda. Please meet me there. It's me. I'm the cream. I'm waiting for you."

My breath catches.

I tell Carl to excuse me and head down the staircase. Butterflies dance in my stomach when I see him standing in the rotunda next to the manual typewriter.

Jane and Andrew are at the counter, all wide eyes and smirking, while Babs has literally taken a seat at one of the tables with Brody to watch me. I start when I notice Vale at the counter, a couple of books in his hands. He smiles at me, a knowing expression on his face as he looks from me to Graham.

I lick dry lips. Graham looks gorgeous, his dark hair swept off his chiseled face, his gray gaze watching every step I take.

"Hey," he murmurs when I reach him, his greedy eyes eating me up.

"Hey," I reply shakily. "Um, good to see you."

"How are you feeling?"

"Better."

"Have I given you enough space?" he says with an earnestness I can't deny. "I know things are happening fast—your surgery, my retirement. I wanted to give you time to think. I can't stop thinking of you, though. I want to be the one who takes care of you, Emmy. I want to protect you, from whatever comes, whether it's an old boyfriend who won't leave you alone or a health issue."

"Oh," I say, letting the words settle inside me. I bite my lower lip to keep the tears pricking my eyelids from falling. "I've missed you."

His warm hand cups my cheek. "Oh, baby, I've missed you. I want to show you something. Look." He points down at the manual type-writer, and I scan the various messages people have left. He picks up the three-ringed binder where we keep older messages from the beginning of the year. He flips back several pages to one dated in late June. "This is the day I came to the store after our honeymoon. I'd been gone for seventeen days, and I missed you for every one of them." He reads the message aloud. "'I am obsessed with you, Emmy. From the moment you stepped out on that balcony. From the moment you called me your prison boyfriend. From the moment I dreamed of you on the football field. You are mine. You are my saving grace, my reward, my happiness, my darling.'"

"You wrote that?"

He nods, a gleam in his eyes as he caresses my cheek tenderly. "I couldn't tell you that day, but I left you at the beach because I was terrified none of it was real, that I'd end up hurt and betrayed or alone with nothing, just like I did with Divina, but you're not her; you'd never be her. You're good. You're kind. And you're mine. When I married you, I meant it. I kept telling myself we were temporary, but inside of me, my heart knew the truth; I just had to let everything fall apart before I realized that I can't be without you in my life. I'm not a smart man when it comes to feelings. I've never had a good romantic relationship.

I've got massive flaws. I've never learned how to compromise, to resolve conflict, to express myself, but I love you, Emmy."

Happiness swells in my chest, and a tear falls as he gently wipes it away. "I love you too."

He smiles softly. "As soon as I saw you in that hospital bed, everything clicked together. I knew I never wanted *you* on the other side of that, wondering if I was going to be okay, or healthy. I'm sorry I'm an idiot and couldn't communicate how I felt."

"It's okay. I forgive you."

"We've got some living to make up for. The first thing I want to do is take you on a real honeymoon."

Uncaring of the crowd of people who've gathered around us, I lean my head on his chest as my arms wrap around his waist. "Will you miss it? The game? I don't want to be the reason you don't play."

He chuckles. "I'll miss the camaraderie and the test of my skill. I certainly won't miss two-a-day practices and bumps and bruises. I won't miss worrying if I'm going to get my next concussion. I've got faith that life is gonna be good for us. Life gave me you. I dreamed of you before I even met you."

He tips my face up, his eyes searching mine. "I thought I knew everything I wanted before I met you, but I was wrong. We're starting a new chapter of *our* story. We're going to write the book on being happy. The bookstore is ours, not just mine. You have to know that I bought it just for you. We're gonna make it the best place in New York to come and buy books and see fantastic windows. Are you in it with me? Do you still want me?"

I laugh, a flood of joy hitting me so hard I feel drunk. "God. Yes."

He laughs, and I smile. "I just don't want you to get bored."

"I've been talking to my coaches and players. I'm not the only one who's dealt with a TBI. It's a lot to think about, but I'd like to bring more awareness to concussions, maybe find ways to prevent them on the field."

"I could use some help at my luxury gym," Brody calls out. "I'll let you make the juice drinks."

Graham rolls his eyes. "Sorry, they tagged along. The three of us were looking at a place for the gym when Jane called me and said you'd be in today. They insisted on coming."

I wince. "So your dad knows about the marriage of convenience thing."

"Hmm. He's fine. Don't worry about it." He pulls my rings out of his pocket. "I've been carrying these around with me." His eyes meet mine. "I have a question for you."

My nerves flare to life. This moment feels momentous and beautiful. I swallow. "Yeah?"

He types out a message on the typewriter, then whispers in my ear: "I want this to be for us, something to remember. Look at what I wrote."

Emmy, will you stay married to me? are the words he's typed. Tears well over and slide down my cheeks as I pull his face to me and crush my lips against his. "Yes," I breathe when we come up for air.

Cheers go up around us, and I hear Babs crying in joy.

Graham gazes down at me. "We're gonna make some beautiful magic, darling."

Epilogue

A few years later

I stir from my nap, the soft sounds of waves crashing against the shore in the distance. My eyes flutter open to the sight of the Prince of Darkness snuggled up on my chest like a fuzzy, purring blanket. Yes, he came with us to Santorini. Our one-year-old daughter (Hazel Darling Harlan) loves him, and Magic travels well.

A smile tugs at the corners of my mouth. The damn cat has finally warmed to me, and all it took was Hazel crawling around after me at the apartment. Magic just trailed right along, and pretty soon we got used to each other.

"Hey, buddy," I say, scratching his head gently.

His eyes peer up at me, and he lets out a little mewl. Slowly and carefully, I ease myself into a sitting position, trying not to disturb him too much. He stretches lazily in a sunbeam before hopping off my chest and onto the cool, tiled floor of the villa Emmy and I bought after our honeymoon. Nestled into the side of the mountains, it overlooks the Aegean Sea and has a private grotto and lagoon below the house.

"All right, Magic"—I smirk—"let's get you that treat I promised for not shredding my shirt I left on the floor last night."

As I stand up, the light catches my wedding band, glinting, the weight familiar around my finger. It brings back memories of our honeymoon in Santorini, the laughter we had as we traced cobblestone streets, drank ouzo, and ate delicious local food. I recall her hand in mine, the way her eyes gleamed when she smiled up at me.

"Here you go, you little con artist," I say as I toss a treat to the cat. He leaps into the air, catching it midflight before landing gracefully on the ground. His half tail swishes proudly as he attacks the treat, then struts back to the couch.

"Show-off," I tease. "Just remember who keeps those coming, yeah? Emmy doesn't let you have them."

I swear he winks at me.

I glance around the bright, airy space of the villa, the sunlight streaming in and making patterns. The scent of sea and salt mingles with the aroma of blooming flowers outside. Emmy picked out this house on our honeymoon as one she'd like if she had the opportunity, not knowing that I planned on buying one. It was a great Christmas surprise that first year.

With a contented sigh, I walk down the hall to the nursery to check on my little angel. I tiptoe into her room, and sure enough, she's still sleeping, her arm curled around her own special Wilbur that Jane and Andrew picked out. Watching her tiny chest rise and fall, it seems almost impossible that my life could be this idyllic. I'm overcome with gratefulness. Emotion tugs at me as I slide a piece of white-blonde hair away from her face and behind her ear.

"Keep dreaming those dreams, my angel. Daddy will do everything he can to make them come true."

I can't believe it's been a year since she came into our lives. I recall the frantic rush to the hospital to deliver her, the worry I felt for Emmy's heart, even though the doctor assured us she was fine, as was the baby. Holding her in my arms, I knew my life would always revolve around her. Around Emmy. Around family.

Having a child has only cemented my confidence in leaving behind football. I *thought* football was everything. I *thought* it was my passion. Ha. I was so wrong. This. Here. Family is my passion. Being with the people who love me is what makes my world turn.

That circle includes my dad. We've spent more time together since his retirement. He enjoys popping into the bookstore to see us and even works at Brody's gym behind the juice bar.

"Every day with you and your mom is a gift, my darling baby."

Making sure the monitor is on, I head to our bedroom and change into a pair of swim trunks. I caught sight of Emmy down at the lagoon earlier, the light dancing on her long blonde hair, illuminating her fair skin like the goddess she is.

I take the path that leads to the water, past bright-green shrubs and pretty flowers. We try to spend several weeks a year here. Our staff at the bookstore is solid, especially now that Jane is a full-time manager with Babs. Andrew works there part time while he goes to NYU. He's determined to pay for his tuition himself and doesn't mind if it takes him several years.

"Hey," I call out to her, and she flips up her sunglasses and smirks at me.

"Hey. Nice nap? Is Hazel still asleep?"

I nod.

"Aw, you brought a friend."

I glance behind me, and Magic sits on top of a rock, peering around the sea as if he's a king.

"You need some lotion?" I ask as I flop down next to her and take in her willowy long legs and red bikini.

She nods, and I get to work, pouring out the coconut-scented lotion and rubbing it onto her sun-kissed shoulders, down to her spine, to the small of her back. My hand dips inside her bottoms and massages her ass.

She groans and tells me how good it feels, and I chuckle.

"Wanna race to the water?" I ask, winking at her as I stand up and stretch my muscles, still tight and toned. I work out at Brody's gym nearly every day.

"Prize?" She tips off her straw hat and smiles.

"Hmm, whoever wins gets to pick what's for dinner."

She checks me out. "I lost the last competition we had. I might have to cheat on this race."

"You can't win. I'll always be faster."

"Really? What about now?" She unclips her bikini and tosses the fabric over her head.

My tongue darts out and wets my bottom lip as I gaze longingly at her delicate face, those perfect tits, the curve of her waist. Damn, she is so achingly beautiful and sexy.

"You're really not being fair. You know I love your boobs! Hey—"

"Too late," she cries as she darts for the water.

Laughing, I take off after her, nearly catching her until she plunges into the lagoon.

"I win!" she calls out as she jumps in, hair slicked back.

I concede, panting slightly as I wrap my arms around her waist and pull her close to me. Our eyes lock, and I can see the tranquility there. The peace and happiness radiating between us.

"Victory is sweet," she whispers, pressing her lips against mine in a slow, passionate kiss that sends shivers down my spine. "And I want *you* for dinner, Mr. Harlan."

My cock hardens in an instant. "If you're in a hurry, no one will see us near the trees."

She glances around to ensure our privacy. We're completely alone.

"Not a soul in sight," I say.

I carry her to the shore and underneath the trees. We're close enough to still hear the baby monitor if Hazel wakes up.

I arrange the beach towels, marveling at how lucky I am to have her, to hold my darling under the sun as it dapples the palm fronds above.

"I love you," I say, my voice barely audible over the lapping of the waves.

"Same," she breathes as we surrender to the moment, to the passion that still burns between us like a wildfire.

The world fades as we make love, as I experience the life I was always meant to have.

The end

AUTHOR'S NOTE

Dear reader,

Called "one of the best romances of 2020" by *Southern Living*, *Dear Ava* is one of those powerful books that sticks with you and doesn't let go. I'm happy to share a small excerpt with you after *My Darling Bride*. Please see my website for a list of content warnings.

With over eighteen thousand reviews, it has a rating of 4.5 on Amazon. If you enjoy enemies-to-lovers, he falls first, zany friends, and a strong female heroine, this might be your next read.

Best,
Ilsa Madden-Mills

WSJ BESTSELLING AUTHOR ILSA MADDEN-MILLS DELIVERS A GRIPPING, ENEMIES-TO-LOVERS, SECRET-ADMIRER ROMANCE

The rich and popular Sharks rule at prestigious, ivy-covered Camden Prep. Once upon a time, I wanted to be part of their world—until they destroyed me.

The last thing I expected was an anonymous love letter from one of them.

Please. I hate every one of those rich jerks for what they did to me.

The question is, which Shark is my secret admirer?

Knox, the scarred quarterback. Dane, his twin brother. Or Chance, the ex who dumped me . . .

Dear Ava, Your eyes are the color of the Caribbean Sea. Wait. That's stupid.

What I really mean is, you look at me and I feel something REAL.

It's been ten months since you were here, but I can't forget you.

I've missed seeing you walk down the hall.

I've missed you cheering at my football games.

I've missed the smell of your hair.

And then everything fell apart the night of the kegger.

Don't hate me because I'm a Shark.

I just want to make you mine.

Still.

DEAR AVA

EXCERPT

Ilsa Madden-Mills
Copyright © 2020

The sun beats down on me as I get out of my older-model Jeep Wrangler, Louise, and give her a little pat. There's a dent on the driver's side—came that way—and the paint is rusted at the edges of the hood and over the wheels. I worked three summers waiting tables at a dingy all-night diner in downtown Nashville to buy her, and it's my sole possession in the world. I paid for it with carefully scraped together money from every tip I got, and I got plenty because I was the best waitress there, pasting a broad, welcoming smile on my face for every truck driver, blue-collar worker, and late-night drunk person. Sometimes if the waitstaff was full, I cleaned the kitchen, took out trash, or mopped the floor. Lou would text me any time one of his servers didn't show up or called in sick, and I'd drag myself up out of my bed at the group home and jog the two blocks to the diner, half-asleep but ready to put the time in for the dollars.

Louise isn't pretty, but she's mine.

Parked next to me is a sleek black Porsche, and on the other side is a red Maserati. I sigh. Almost a year since I've been a student here, yet nothing has changed.

I sweep my eyes over the grounds ahead of me. Welcome to Camden Prep, otherwise known as my own personal hell, a prestigious private school in the middle of Sugarwood, Tennessee, which happens to be one of the richest small towns in the US, home to senators, country music stars, and professional athletes.

Bah. Whatever. I hate this place.

Slinging my backpack over my arm, I sprint through the parking lot, carefully evading the cars, recalling a freshman guy who accidentally scratched another car once, and one of the Shark's, no less. Later, they cornered him in the bathroom and made him lick their shoes. The best advice for anyone who isn't a Shark is to stay away from them. Don't look. Don't touch. Pretend they don't exist. Those guidelines got me through my freshman and sophomore years. Junior year—well, we won't even go there, but now that it's my last year, I'll be living by those rules again.

Tension and apprehension make my heart race more and more the closer I get to the double doors of that ivy-covered main entrance bookended by two castle-style gray turrets. The final bell for classes hasn't rung yet, and I have exactly five minutes to get to my locker and get to class. Arriving late was my plan because *a girl like me has to have a fucking plan.*

As I jog, I tug at my new school uniform, a mid-thigh red and gold plaid skirt, something the administration instituted to blur the lines between the haves and the have-nots. As if. Everyone already knows who the rich kids are and who are the ones like me. Just look in the freaking parking lot. "I love you, Louise," I mutter. "All these jerks have is something their parents bought them."

I stop at the door, inhaling a deep breath. You'd expect a regular glass door for a school, but this isn't an ordinary place. The door here is made from heavy, beveled glass, the kind you see in old houses. Freshman year, I thought it was beautiful with the red dragon carefully etched into the upper section, but now—ha. Dread, thick and ugly, sucks at me, sliding over me like mud even though I gave myself a hundred pep talks on the twenty-minute drive in from the Sisters of Charity in downtown Nashville.

"Steel yourself," I whisper. "Beyond these doors lie hellhounds and vampires." I smirk. If only they really were. I'd pull out a stake and end them like Buffy.

Sadly, they are only human, and I cannot stab them.

I pat down my newly dyed dark hair, shoulder-length with the front sides longer than the back, a far cry from my long blonde locks from last year. Cutting and dying my hair was therapy. I did it for me, to show these assholes I'm not going to be that nice little scholarship girl anymore. Screw that. I gather my mental strength, pulling from my past. I've sat in homeless shelters. I've watched Mama shoot needles in her arms, in between her toes, wherever she could to get that high. I've watched her suck down a bottle of vodka for breakfast.

These rich kids are toddlers compared to me.

So why am I shaking all over?

No fear, a small voice says.

I swing the doors open to a rush of cool air and brightly lit hallways. The outside may look as if you've been tossed back a few centuries, but the inside is plush and luxurious, decorated like a millionaire's mansion.

Smells like money, I think as I stand for a second and take it all in. It's still gorgeous—can't deny that. Warm taupe walls. White wainscoting. Crown molding. Leather chairs. And that's just the entrance area. I walk in farther, my steps hesitant. Majestic portraits hang on the wall, former headmasters alongside framed photos of alumni, small smiling faces captured in senior photos. The guys have suits on, the girls in black dresses. By the end of this year, my picture will be encased in a collage and placed with *my* classmates. A small huff of laughter spills out of me, bordering on hysteria, and I push it back down.

Students milling around—girls in pleated skirts and white button-downs like mine, guys in khakis and white shirts with red and gold ties—swivel their heads to see who's coming in on the first day of classes.

Eyes flare at me.

Gasps are emitted.

Fighting nervousness, I inhale a cleansing breath, part of me already regretting this decision, urging me to turn around and run like hell, but I hang tough. I swallow down my emotions, carefully shuffling them away, locking them up in a chest. I picture a chain and padlock on those memories from last year. I take that horror and toss it into a stormy ocean. There, junior year. Go and die.

With a cold expression on my face, one I've been practicing for a week, my eyes rove over the students, not lingering too long on faces.

That's right, Ava Harris, the snitch/bitch who went to the police after the party, is back.

And I'm not going anywhere.

All I need is this final year, and I might be able to swing a full ride at a state school or even get a scholarship to Vanderbilt. *Vanderbilt.* My body quivers in yearning. Me at a prestigious university. Me going to class with people who don't know me. Me having something that is mine. Me making my own road, and it's shiny and flat and so damn smooth . . .

My legs work before my brain does, and as I start down the hall, the crowd parts, more students seeing me and pausing, eyes widening.

The air around me practically bristles with tension.

If I were a wicked witch, I'd cackle right now.

My fists clench, barely hanging on to my resolve.

Piper rushes up and throws her arms around me. "She's back! My main girl is back! OMG, I HAVE MISSED YOU SO MUCH!"

Seeing her exuberant, welcoming face is exactly what I needed. Pretty with long strawberry blonde hair pulled back with two butterfly clips, she's been my friend since we had a chorus class together freshman year. She can't carry a tune, but I love to sing. I had a solo at every single concert at Camden BTN. Before That Night.

She smiles as she squeezes my hand. "I'm so glad to see you. Also, my parents are insisting you come to dinner soon. It's been a while."

Indeed.

Before I can answer, someone jostles into us, moving away quickly, but not before I hear *snitch* from his lips.

My purse falls down with the force of his shoulder.

And so it begins.

Helping me get my bag, she turns her head and snaps at the retreating back of the person who bumped into me. "Watch it!" Then, "Jockass!"

Rising up, I crane my neck to see who it was. Red hair, football player: Brandon Wilkes. I barely know him.

She blows at the bangs in her face, schooling her features back into a sweet expression even though her eyes are darting around at everyone as if daring them to say one word against me. "Anyway, I'm glad you came back. We haven't gotten to talk much, and that is your fault, which is fine. I gave you space like you asked."

She never did pull punches.

I haven't called her like I should have, but I needed distance from this place and everyone here. I tried in the beginning, but when she'd bring up school and the football games and her classes and everyday things about the day-to-day at Camden, I felt that pit of emptiness tugging at me, a dark hole of memories and people I didn't want to think about. Her life went on—*as it should have*—while I was stuck wallowing in the past.

"But you're here now." She smiles, but there's a wobbly quality to it. She jumps when she hears her name over the intercom, talking fast as lightning. "Yikes! I need to run. My mom is here. Can you believe I forgot my laptop on the first day? I'm such a ditz! See you in class, 'kay? We have first period together, yes?" She gives me a quick hug. "You got this."

Do I?

Truly, I want to run and get back in my car and leave this place behind forever, but then I think about my little brother Tyler. Goals . . . must stick to them.

Before I can get a word out—typical—she's gone and bouncing down the hall like Tigger from *Winnie the Pooh*.

I miss her immediately, feeling the heat of everyone's eyes on me.

It's funny how no one really noticed me during my freshman and sophomore year here. Nope. I was the girl who kept her head down and blended in as well as I could, trying to keep my upbringing off the radar . . . until the summer before junior year when I ran into Chance at a bookstore and he showed interest. Then when school started, I got it in my head to be a cheerleader. Mostly, I told myself it would look good on my college applications, plus I assumed it would take less time than soccer or tennis—but the truth is I did it for *him*. I wanted Chance and Friday night football games and parties with the in crowd.

The lockers seem a million miles away as I push past all the onlookers, my hands clenched around the straps of my backpack. Whispers from the students rise and grow and spread like a wave in the ocean.

And of course . . .

The Grayson brothers are the first Sharks I see, holding court with several girls as they lean against the wall. Knox and Dane. Twins.

I flick my gaze in their direction, keeping my resting bitch face sharp and hard, taking in the two guys, their matching muscular builds, tall with broad shoulders. They may look almost identical, but they're like night and day. Knox is the cold one, never smiling, that scar slicing through his cheek and into his upper lip, disrupting the curve of his mouth and the perfection of his face. I swallow. Screw him.

I refuse to spend this year afraid.

His lips twitch as if he reads my mind, that slash on his mouth curling up in a twisted movement, and I glare at him.

You don't scare me, my face says.

He smirks.

Thick mahogany hair curls around his collar and his eyes are a piercing gray, like metal, sharp and intense, framed by a fringe of black lashes. His scrutiny doesn't miss much and makes me antsy—has since freshman year when I'd catch him looking at me, studying me as if I were a strange bug. When I'd get the guts to boldly look back—*Like what you see?*—he'd huff out a derisive laugh and keep walking. I'm beneath him. A speck. He as much as said so after our first game last year.

"What do you want?" he says with a sneer as I ease in the football locker room. Cold eyes flick over my cheer skirt then move up and land on the hollow of my throat. It's not cool enough at night for our sweater uniform so tonight my top is the red-and-white V-cut vest with CP embroidered on my chest.

"Where's Chance?"

He stiffens then huffs out a laugh and whips off his sweat-covered jersey along with the pads underneath.

His shoulders are broad and wide, his chest lightly dusted with sparse golden hair, tan from the sun, rippling with powerful muscles, leading down to a tapered and trim waist. He has a visible six-pack, and my gaze lingers briefly on a small tattoo on his hip, but I can't tell what it is. He isn't brawny or beefy-looking like one might expect from a guy blessed with his athletic prowess, but sculpted and molded and—

Dropping my gaze, I stare at the floor. I shouldn't be ogling him. Chance is my guy.

I hear male laughter from one of the rooms that branch off from the locker room, maybe the showers, and I deflate, guessing that's where Chance is.

Glancing up, I intend to ask him to tell Chance I came by to congratulate him on his two touchdowns, but my voice is frozen. Knox has unlaced his grass-stained pants and is shucking them off. His legs are heavily muscled and taut, unlike the leaner build of Chance. His slick underwear is black and tight, cupping his hard ass, the outline of his crotch—

"Like what you see, charity case? You can look, but you can't touch."

Anger soars, replacing my embarrassment. I know I'm just the scholarship girl at Camden, but why does he have to constantly remind me?

"Don't worry about me touching anything. I don't like ugly." The words tumble out before I can stop them. I meant his superior attitude, not his face, but I see the moment when he freezes and takes it the wrong way.

He touches his face, tracing his scar while his jaw pops. "Get out. Only players allowed in here."

"Asshole," I mutter as his laughter follows me.

Rumor is Knox doesn't kiss girls on the lips, but no matter how bad that scar screws up his face, he's still the head Shark nonetheless.

Today, he's wearing a fitted white button-up, his tie loose as if he's already annoyed with it. He spends a lot of time in the gym, I imagine, working on that muscular body, maintaining that quarterback status. He holds my gaze for several seconds before dropping his and looking down at his phone.

I hear him laugh under his breath.

Some things never change.

ABOUT THE AUTHOR

#1 Amazon Charts, *Wall Street Journal*, *New York Times*, and *USA Today* bestselling author Ilsa Madden-Mills pens angsty new-adult and contemporary romances. A former high school English teacher and librarian, she adores all things *Pride and Prejudice*, and, of course, Mr. Darcy is her ultimate hero. She's addicted to frothy coffee beverages, cheesy magnets, and any book featuring unicorns and sword-wielding females.

Feel free to stalk her online! You can join her Facebook readers group, Unicorn Girls, to get the latest scoop and talk about books, wine, and Netflix at https://www.facebook.com/groups/ilsasunicorngirls/. You can also find Madden-Mills on her website at http://www.ilsamaddenmills.com. And don't forget to subscribe to her newsletter: http://www.ilsamaddenmills.com/contact.